Glamourati

Irina Kova

Contents

Contents

1.   How to meet a prince

Monaco

As the four-decker yacht *Ocean Princess* sailed gracefully to its moorings in the port of Monte Carlo, so many onlookers gathered on the promenade that the flashes from their cameras made the air sparkle. *Maybe I'll get lucky this time and finally see some celebrities*, sighed the man with grey temples, squeezing through the crowd. *If only I were there*, was the thought that passed through the chubby woman's head as she elbowed her way closer to the yacht.

*****

The plane made a sharp turn and commenced its landing. Cannes, Antibes – the familiar profile of the coastline made Tash smile. She had missed it so much! Scotland had been so cold and boring. For a second, Tash was back on the set: long-haired fairies in translucent robes swirled barefoot in wild grass that was still wet from the rain; gnomes with thick ginger beards swept through them all like a herd of wild boar; and under the cliff, in the raging North Sea, naked sirens with silver, scaly tails awaited exhausted mariners. A week of movie magic had flown by so quickly. Now Tash was ready for a well-deserved holiday. Maybe the time for magic wasn't over?

The plane was still on its glide path when she impatiently turned her phone on. "Damn! The payment for the film work still hasn't come through." She took another look at her overdrawn bank account. "Not even enough for a taxi."

The car turned left off the A8 autoroute towards La Turbie. It was a while before Tash registered some slight disquiet at this unexpected detour, so relieved was she that Vivien had very kindly sent a car to pick her up from the airport. The driver, who was seemingly in tune with her thoughts, explained in French, "A lot of traffic, Madame. We would be stuck, otherwise. Grand Prix, you know, everywhere is blocked."

He was right. When the Formula One circus was in town, Monte Carlo turned into one huge traffic jam. Locals fled the chaos, and crowds of annoyingly noisy tourists filled the entire district. All this bustle disrupted the usual slow-paced village-like routine, overwhelming it like the Great Flood. The winding streets where the race took place were transformed into narrow tunnels by the addition of metal barriers along their sides. Around the port, multi-tiered stands grew like honeycombs in a hive. The city was paralysed, and getting from one part of it to another became mission impossible.

On Avenue Princesse Grace, Tash opened the window. A warm breeze burst into the car, filling it with morning humidity. With the rush of moist air came familiar smells and a huge black fly that made a complete circuit of Tash's head before landing expertly on her nose. "Just when I was thinking it would all be different this time …"

The heavy glass door was jammed. The concierge had to push hard to get the three-metre-high colossus to budge. He cursed as he checked the marble steps, which were wet from the recent rain, and reluctantly made his way down to the Mercedes parked at the entrance.

"Madame, my colleague will be along right away to help you with your suitcases." He could not carry them personally: his obvious sense of self-worth did not allow him to subordinate his rank to a task that was beneath it. Tash decided to hide from the scorching sun. She stood in the shade of the canopy while the driver unloaded the suitcases from the boot. Her phone tweeted incessantly, sending one after another of Anna's photos from yesterday's party in Cannes. "Is this Julien MacDonald?" Tash looked at Bella Hadid's transparent sequin-strewn outfit, which tomorrow every fashion magazine would shamelessly call a 'dress'. "And why on earth did I wear heels for the flight?" Still studying Bella Hadid's outfit on her phone, as she slowly placed her black lace-up boot on to the step, she suddenly felt that she was losing her balance …

Tash heard the clatter of her phone on the marble surface and, the next thing she knew, her backside had hit the wet floor.

"Are you okay?"

Tash raised her head. Here he was, the cause of her fall – young, strong, dirty-blond curls. He had been in such a rush to retrieve her suitcases that he'd somehow managed to knock her off her feet. She was suddenly aware of the …

"Pourriez-vous faire plus attention, s'il vous plaît?" she replied, rearranging her attire. The hem of her shirt-dress had treacherously swung open almost to the waist. "Please bring my suitcases to apartment twenty-seven."

"Of course, Madame."

As the young porter was helping her to her feet, Tash examined his well-built physique from head to toe. Oh, man! Would you believe it? Tod's brown loafers! He walked over to the car to fetch the suitcases, which the driver had left standing on the wet pavement. She grinned to herself. "Now I totally get why the concierge didn't want anything to do with my luggage. Even the porters here wear Tod's!"

Carolina was waiting for her in the hallway.

"My dear!" Tash sprang forward, throwing her arms around her. "The craziest thing just happened to me!"

Carolina froze in anticipation. *It was so Tash*, she thought, *to arouse her curiosity and then instantly forget what she was going to say*. Only after a long pause did the narrative continue.

"I managed to fall over right in front of your house!"

Carolina looked alarmed.

"But your porter saved me. A veritable Greek god!"

Her quiet, slightly husky voice didn't match her appearance. Beautiful young girls tended to radiate briskness and self-confidence; Tash's soft, low voice conveyed a note of timidity.

Carolina smiled. "I hope you remembered to lose a shoe so your young Adonis can find you?"

Tash burst out laughing. "Well, no, but I did tell him where to bring my luggage. And talking of shoes," she said, "I'd no idea that even the porters here wear Tod's!"

Tash moved closer to Carolina.

"I'm so sorry about you and Hugh." She squeezed Carolina's hand tightly. "But I must tell you" – she peered up through her long lashes – "I'm glad you're here with me and free at last of that unhealthy relationship."

"Unfortunately, this is only the beginning," Carolina replied calmly. "There's a long and tough battle ahead."

When Tash got out of the shower her suitcases were waiting for her in the bedroom.

"I do my own laundry now. The housekeeper comes just once a week." Carolina sat on the edge of the bed as she spoke. "In my present circumstances I have to save on everything." There was neither bitterness nor regret in her demeanour, just a look of straightforward candour.

Tash crouched down beside her and put an arm round her shoulders. "You know that you can rely on me for anything. Unfortunately, I've no money – you know what my earnings are nowadays. And as for Dad, well, he's losing it completely – only paints biblical scenes now. Who buys that sort of thing any more?" Tash lifted the edge of the towel she was wrapped in and playfully slapped her butt. "This is what people want – bare bums! Anyway, you won't find a better cleaner than me. So you can save on a housekeeper while I'm here." Her eyes alighted on the suitcases, which had been set down right next to the table. "When did the luggage arrive?"

"The porter called while you were in the shower." Carolina laughed. "I would have kept him, but he was as far from being a Greek god as his shoes were from being Tod's! Are hallucinations one of the symptoms of a fall?"

Tash paused for a moment, digesting Carolina's words. Then she started to laugh.

Carolina's face turned serious. "I've only been here a few weeks but I've already been put in my place. His friends and their wives have ostracised me. Hugh blocked all the accounts so I wouldn't be able to pay for a lawyer – he wants to leave me penniless." Not a single muscle in her beautiful face expressed either anger or resentment. "Even people I don't know particularly well withdrew my invitations to the race. He wants to hurt me, like he doesn't know that's the last thing I care about."

Tash nodded. "And there's no hope of a rapprochement?" she asked timidly.

"Not a prayer. But I will fight till the end!"

Tash sighed. "How could he change like that?" She remembered their fabulous wedding here in Monaco. Only four years ago they seemed to be headed for a long and happy life together, till death did them part.

"He's always been like that. I was just too young and too naïve to realise it."

8

Twenty minutes later they were getting into the car. Tash cast an appraising glance at her friend. Carolina's elegant style – white linen trousers, silk top and ballet flats – was more suited to English Oxfordshire than to flashy Monaco. Here women strove to emphasise their voluptuous forms with tight-fitting outfits. In just five minutes, the black Aston Martin, which Hugh had luckily forgotten all about, had dropped them at the Monte Carlo Beach Club. Spread across a tiny verdant promontory between Roquebrune and the sea, the Beach Club, in spite of its name, was actually located in France. Thanks to this technicality, it could boast a significantly larger footprint than clubs located in Monaco itself, where space is at such a premium that every square centimetre of real estate is worth its weight in gold. The club comprised a small hotel, tucked away at the rear of the site, and a strip of paved coastline called "the beach". On the beach, green striped cabanas were lined up in orderly ranks along the seafront. The older generation would seek shelter from the bright sunlight in the shade of these luxury tents, while the youngest guests frolicked in the pool. Everyone in between would stroll lazily up and down the club's famous pink paths.

Some light gusts of the mistral swept across the beach, playing with Tash's thick auburn hair as they swirled and eddied around her. Her long, toned legs in lace shorts had already begun to attract the attention of passers-by – admiring looks from the men and envious ones from the women. They saw someone who had it all. They marvelled at the flawless tanned skin and the tiny waist, and they followed every movement of the full bust as it rose and fell under a flimsy T-shirt in time to the beat of her steps. What they couldn't see was the timid, insecure girl that all this beauty hid from them, a girl who at that moment couldn't even afford the price of a taxi ride from the airport.

The restaurant was full. Each year at this time the beau monde puts its important affairs to one side and descends on Monaco for the Grand Prix. Since prehistoric times the race has claimed a place in every self-respecting jet-setter's social calendar – the season's logical next port of call following the film festival in neighbouring Cannes. The Eurotrash element would often honour the Grand Prix exclusively, London and Paris being just an hour away by air, and cities like Milan and Geneva no less easily accessible by road. American jet-setters, however, would land in Europe in mid-May, starting their tour in Cannes before moving on to Monaco. After the Grand Prix, they'd drift north, by way of Paris and Roland Garros, to the June season in London, filling their social diaries with contemporary art auctions, tennis tournaments, Formula One and much more. Those not burdened with work would cruise around the Mediterranean for the rest of the summer, while those with important business decisions to make would leave in August for the Hamptons.

Vivien, the angel who had spared Tash's blushes by sending a driver to meet her at the airport, was sitting with three middle-aged men. Always perfectly coiffured, she was the type of woman that not even Chanel or Valentino could make boring. Tash was sincerely happy to see her. Last year, at Vivien's forty-sixth birthday party – Tash wouldn't swear to the accuracy of the number – there wasn't a single empty seat to be found. Guests came from all over the world to pay their respects to this extraordinary woman. No questions were asked about her dark past. There were loads of rumours circulating, all hinting at the same shady story. It was asserted that Vivien Goldstein (née Lawrence) had realised at a very young age that youth and beauty were not eternal and that she could not rely on them to keep her head above water forever. Although she presented herself as a former model, the old-timers who'd known her back in New York claimed that she'd accumulated her money, influence and connections in a somewhat different way – namely, through blackmail. After all, it's common knowledge that in our quest for perfection it's a lack of persistence that thwarts us, not a lack of means. And Vivien was a great example of this.

At the age of twenty-one, Vivien Lawrence, an ambitious New York escort, was barely making ends meet. And so things stood – until the fateful day a well-known New York Madame introduced her to a well-known influential politician, obviously not young and obviously married. After a five-year love affair and numerous expensive gifts, Vivien demanded a more substantial investment in her life – specifically, one bound in real estate – which, to her chagrin, the politician refused. By this time, he had already found a younger, more accommodating replacement and he politely asked Vivien to vacate her rented apartment. She was furious, but giving up was never an option. She found a young lawyer who specialised in tenant evictions. Together they threatened the politician with a high-profile case, but he again said no. When the scandal broke, every tabloid was screaming about it, but for some unknown reason, it subsided as quickly as it had begun. Insiders claimed that the politician had paid a tidy sum to the young adventurers. The promising lawyer, Harvey Goldstein, set up his own practice, and Vivien Lawrence married him. There were rumours that the lawyer had a passion for men. Nevertheless, the couple was blessed with a daughter, Stella, whose slight resemblance to the old politician has never been noticed out loud. Over the past twenty years, the Goldstein fortune has grown exponentially, thanks to Harvey's successful deals secured by Vivien's connections. These deals were no models of transparency, but nobody wanted to go deeply into details. Vivien's influence grew to such an extent that no significant social event took place without her attendance. Her glamorous lifestyle, and the access it provided to the rich and powerful, allowed her – for a consideration – to bring together the 'right' people. Ah, if you only knew how many deals her artfulness had helped to close, how many beautiful couples it had brought together – and how many marriages it had destroyed!

Vivien rose from the table and rushed over to meet the girls.

"Here you are, my beauties!" She led Carolina and Tash back to the table. "OMG! You can't imagine how much I've missed normal people! Still haven't recovered from Cannes – I'm so tired of all the hassle and the wannabes. Everyone sucking up or on the make! No dignity! By the way" – Vivien turned to face the men – "please meet my friends from New York." The New Yorkers immediately got up to greet the ladies.

Vivien began the introductions in a well-modulated voice that had grown more cultivated with the years: "Mrs. Swensen-Young. Former Miss Sweden. You probably all know her sweet husband, the billionaire Hugh Young."

"Former husband," said Carolina, delicately correcting her.

Vivien looked at her inquiringly.

"We're getting divorced," the former Miss Sweden explained, forcing a smile.

Vivien was flustered for a split second, but immediately rallied. "Natasha or Tash," she said, looking expressively at Tash. "Our pretty doll who also has a master's degree, from where I don't remember." Vivien laughed. "A rare combination of beauty and brains."

Tash smiled thinly.

"Now we've all formally met, we can sit down," declared Vivien, not giving the guys even the smallest chance to introduce themselves. "Now I can carry on complaining about the nightmare I endured in Cannes. I remember the good old days when you still couldn't fly from New York to the South of France all that easily. There were no three-star shit-holes for fifty euros a night. The South of France was much more glamorous

11

then. Especially in May. Nowadays, just look who goes to Amfar!" She took a long look around the table – a sight that no doubt epitomised the moral decay of the French Riviera. "Trash! Every shifty stylist who has made his way into the fashion industry on the back of his orientation" – for some reason, Vivien cast a glance at Tash – "brings along his nouveau riche protégé who picks up the bill for both of them in exchange for a chance to rub shoulders with the elite. They're in a stakeout, waiting for the right moment to ambush some D-list celebrity they can introduce to a prominent 'socialite', or present to the glamorous wife of some government official or oligarch." She took a deep breath. "They are not called 'socialites' any more. Now they're fashion designers, Insta-bloggers and life coaches."

"But, Vivien, it has always been that way," said a tall dark man sitting to her right. "It's much easier to buy fame than to earn it. Anytime some new country emerges on the world map with a large enough economy to bankroll high-level corruption, the local elites, flush with all the poor people's money, rush to claim their place in high society."

"Yes, Richard, but at least they had manners back in the day. Today's wannabes spend most of their time sniffing in the toilets!" Vivien rolled her eyes.

Carolina and Tash looked at each other. They wondered what kind of manners Vivien had displayed twenty years previously when she was blackmailing her elderly lover.

"There is a big party on Alberto Visconti's boat tonight." Knowing Vivien's complaints wouldn't stop for another hour, Richard decided to change the subject. "We're all invited."

For a second, Carolina's grip tightened on the half of lemon she was squeezing onto her carpaccio. "I wouldn't be so sure about the *all*," she remarked nonchalantly, drying her hands with a napkin. "His secretary called me a week ago, cancelling my invitations to any Grand Prix parties."

"Alberto's secretary? But why?" Richard looked perplexed.

"Because of Hugh," said a low timid voice.

All eyes at the table turned towards a brown-haired man with a friendly round face, who'd been silent for most of the conversation. Mark – he of the timid voice – felt suddenly shy in the spotlight of this increased attention and meekly lowered his eyes.

Then, fearing that his comment might have been out of line, he looked at Carolina, trying to gauge her reaction.

"Exactly so," said Carolina, enthusiastically eating up the rest of her carpaccio.

Encouraged by her response, Mark continued, "Typical *Hugh*-style!" he said. Then, unnerved by his own courage, he quickly looked away.

Carolina was intrigued. This man seemed to know Hugh well. Mark suddenly realised that his last remark had caused a beautiful woman to take a genuine interest in him and he felt himself begin to blush. His statement needed some clarification but he didn't know where to start.

"I'll explain to you later," he whispered.

Carolina's presence was affecting him strangely: he was nervous and embarrassed. As if she were some complex equation he had to solve.

Her eyes flashed playful glances in his direction. Mark caught her mischievous looks and quickly turned away, anxious to conceal his embarrassment.

*****

Tash stared from her balcony at the turquoise sea. Alberto Visconti's yacht sailed slowly towards the port. Inhaling the warm, moist air, she closed her eyes and pictured herself on board. In just a few hours' time she would be dancing on the deck in her elegant dress with its silver streams made of rhinestones. How the guests will wonder at this magnificent stranger, their curious whispers drowned out by the music! How she'll waltz herself dizzy, barely able to make out her partner's face!

"What are you smiling at?" Her dreams were interrupted by Carolina, who had just finished dressing. She wore a long black dress with a deep slit, complemented only by red lipstick.

Tash glanced at the crystal-studded shoes standing next to her chaise longue. "Ah! You didn't let me finish my dream. I was examining my prince's face. I hope, at least" – she looked at her shoes – "I don't have to lose a shoe to help him find me. They're Louboutin. I spent all my savings on them."

13

"You're crazy! You should be thriftier. How can you spend your last penny on shoes?" Carolina raised her eyebrows. "I don't know how you can afford such a lifestyle on modelling fees."

*****

Out in the bay now, Alberto Visconti's yacht had all but slipped behind the bulge in the coastline where the Grimaldi Forum stood.

Only a week ago, Carolina Swensen-Young – tall and statuesque – had stood leaning against the wall of number twenty-seven, her tenth-floor apartment on Avenue Princesse Grace. "Thank you for the warning," she said into the phone and hung up. For a second her olive eyes betrayed a flash of despair that softened her chiselled features, but she immediately pulled herself together and whispered, "We'll see who has the last laugh." This was the fifth invitation she'd had withdrawn in the last few days. Hugh was keeping his promise. Three days previously, after receiving a letter from Andrea Pekleton – a lawyer well-known for her successes in high-profile divorce cases – he had immediately dialled his wife and shouted at the answering machine, "You're gonna regret it, you cheap bitch! You're nobody without me! And you're gonna feel it very soon!"

Carolina looked around the same apartment now. Rows of piled unpacked boxes, just delivered today from London, covered the entire surface of the floor. For a moment she closed her eyes … The face, frozen in fear, kept popping up again and again – the face of the boy a moment before he jumped out of their matrimonial bed and disappeared behind the bathroom door. Startled, she recoiled in disgust and rushed towards the balcony, drawn by the clean, fresh air. She stared at the snow-white sails of the *Ocean Princess*, proudly dropping anchor next to the Grimaldi Forum. Just five minutes before, the PA to Alberto Visconti, the yacht's owner, had informed her that, "To the great regret of Signor Visconti, the list of invitees to the Formula One race has been amended: the authorities have demanded that the number of guests on the boat be limited, and Signor Visconti is very upset that he cannot accommodate Mrs. Young at this event."

*****

Carolina had met her future husband, billionaire Hugh Young, four years ago. A skinny, brown-haired man with funny freckles on his face, he looked more like a naughty schoolboy. At the age of forty he dressed like a teenager, which only exacerbated the awkwardness of his body. The only offspring of a powerful clan, he was wasting his youth on Ibiza dance floors – until one fine day his life turned around.

One morning, at the age of twenty-eight, he woke up and decided that he would remain sober till his dying day. No one knew what made him take the righteous path. Some said he'd overdone it with drugs – and nearly died – others believed that he'd attacked his girlfriend with a knife and that his influential parents had had to hush it up with the police. Whatever it was, from that beautiful day onwards, neither a single drop of alcohol nor line of coke ever found its way into his body. Family connections and an innate business sense – a nose for the main chance – helped him to crank out several major deals, bringing together the nouveaux riches from developing countries with large political lobbies from the West. They established a fund that Hugh had continued to manage successfully ever since. He was an inveterate bachelor and known for his love of models, with a particular predilection for underage Eastern European virgins.

By the age of twenty-three Carolina had worked as a model, picked up the Miss Sweden crown, and secured a grant to continue her studies at London's King's College. Thanks to her short haircut, turned-up nose, and flat-chested, boyish body she didn't look a day over seventeen. Hugh was totally smitten. Tall, young, beautiful and playful, she rejected his advances unceasingly, preferring her peers from the uni. He invited her on dates and bombarded her with gifts, but Carolina, brought up in the best traditions of Swedish socialism, never put material considerations at the forefront of her priorities. His generosity did not impress her, which only inflamed his love all the more. For about six months he tried hopelessly to win her over until, finally, he was given an opportunity to fluff his tail.

Carolina's younger sister, Ingrid, lived in New York with her boyfriend, a young artist from Mexico. The sisters phoned each other frequently, and when Ingrid hadn't been in touch for a few days, Carolina got worried. The concierge said that he had not seen them for a week. Their parents didn't know what to do. They called the police, but the police refused to open a case before a certain amount of time had elapsed since the disappearance.

When Hugh called her on Friday afternoon, she was on the verge of despair. Sobbing, she told him what had happened.

"Do you have an American visa?" was the first thing he asked.

"Why do I need a visa? I'm a Swedish citizen, I don't need a visa." She was surprised at his naivety.

"Don't worry, no problem."

Four hours later they were crossing the Atlantic on their way to New York. Meanwhile, private detectives were already on the case. Police had been instructed to open a missing person case without delay.

"Sorry the plane's so ugly, it's not mine." Hugh apologised for the slightly worn seats of the private plane, the only one that had been available at Heathrow at that moment. "We couldn't use mine: it's not registered with an American company and you would need a visa."

The beauty of the plane was the last thing on Carolina's mind at that particular time. However, Hugh's responsiveness worked in his favour.

When they landed in New York, detectives reported that her sister was safe and sound on an ecotrip in Ecuador and was simply out of network reach. Carolina had no choice but to spend the weekend with Hugh. They came back to London as a couple. A month later, he proposed and they married in the summer.

*****

Hugh had long been accustomed to possessing everything he wanted and to disposing of everything he possessed as he saw fit. Two years after marrying Carolina, he had come to see her as just one more of his many acquisitions, bought and paid for and fully at his disposal. Every day he allowed himself greater and greater liberties, while demanding her unconditional submission. He stopped hiding his affairs, blaming her for her insufficient sexuality. Scandals were succeeded by reconciliations and Hugh's eventual remorse. Then the pattern would repeat itself, again and again. New humiliations, new insults, and new affairs. She would weep into her pillow at nights, too embarrassed to share her misery with anyone. After all, she had only herself to blame if he didn't want her. It took numerous sessions with a shrink to convince her that the reason for her husband's aggressiveness wasn't her but rather his bipolarity and narcissism. Her attempts to send Hugh to a psychotherapist made him even more aggressive. She couldn't take it any more, and after another ugly fight, flew to her parents in Sweden. A week later, moved by his countless calls begging for forgiveness, she decided to please him with a surprise: she came back.

She unlocked the door with her key and went straight into the dressing room, knowing that Hugh should be at work. She heard the sound of the TV coming from the bedroom. Hugh? Was he at home? She opened the door. The TV was on. She looked for the remote control. Suddenly she heard a slight rustling. Two frightened eyes, half hidden behind a long fringe, were staring at her from under a blue satin blanket. After a moment's confusion, a thin naked body slipped out of the bed. Carolina froze. A teenager of about sixteen quickly slipped into the bathroom, almost knocking her down in the process. She heard the sound of running water.

She snapped out of her consternation and, with trembling hands, searched for her phone in her bag. Police? But was he an intruder? After thinking for a couple of seconds, she decided to wait and see what would happen next. He must come out of the bathroom at some point. Carolina was frantically scrolling through every imaginable scenario that might make sense of what she had involuntarily witnessed. What had she just walked into? The boy seemed to have made himself very comfortable in bed prior to her arrival, so the idea of an illegal intrusion was rejected. He did not look like the housekeeper's son, living the life of the owners while they were at work. By all this rationalising, she was trying to drive away the last and most disgusting thought. But with every moment, the truth became more and more clear – and Carolina was amazed by her sudden calmness. *Well, if that's the way it is ...* And yet she decided to make one call. The low voice on the other end didn't take long to answer.

"I'm in our bedroom," she said in an icy voice. "Your juvenile lover has locked himself in the bathroom and isn't letting me take a shower." That was the first thing that came into her head. She hung up and sat on the edge of the bed, feeling neither hatred nor jealousy. There was only one feeling – a feeling of the most profound disgust, which gradually grew deeper and deeper. She felt a terrible fatigue in her shoulders. She got up, went to the bathroom door and knocked.

"Hey! I'm leaving. You can come out." She even felt sympathy for this boy. Well, he was probably imagining the most terrible consequences.

There was no time to waste and Carolina hurried straight to Mrs. Pekleton's office. She had heard the lawyer's name several times before in connection with multi-million-dollar divorce settlements. Fortunately, Mrs. Pekleton had a window in her busy schedule. Andrea Pekleton's face softened in a contented smile as soon as she heard the name 'Young'. A divorce? How wonderful! She instantly figured out the size of the bets and the likely margin for the house, then advised her new client to pack up her stuff immediately and move out of the marital home. After all, her continued presence under the same roof as her husband would only prolong her "deepest emotional suffering". She should choose one of the couple's other apartments and establish herself there, free of the "intolerable mental cruelty" that she, Mrs. Pekleton, would have plenty to say about in the months ahead. Carolina took the first flight to Monaco.

*****

A car picked up the girls at nine on the dot. The restaurant Hostellerie Jérôme in La Turbie was a small family business. Only ten tables, but the Michelin guide gave it two stars for producing some of the most delicious food in the world.

"Well done, you didn't wear high heels!" Richard had looked under the table to check Tash's shoes. "We've got a long night tonight. Good that it's not far, what with Alberto's boat moored right at the front," he said, trying to sound casual. That sort of berth during the Grand Prix, in such a prime spot for seeing the action, had cost Alberto a fortune. Tash was amused by Richard's naïve idea that his friend's obvious wealth added to his persona. This was a drop in the ocean for Alberto, when all was said and done, but for Richard it was wild extravagance.

"I'm not sure I'm ready for a long night." This was Tash's first day off after a gruelling, rainy week of filming in Scotland. She had a packed weekend ahead of her.

"*You've* arrived rejuvenated, but we're on our last legs. The festival was exhausting!" Richard, curious why Tash hadn't pitched up in Cannes, made sure to go through all the events she'd missed. She figured that, for Richard, describing ever more prestigious social functions heightened his sense of self-importance.

"I was working. In Scotland." Tash shyly adjusted her hair. Her genuine modesty only boosted his sense of superiority.

"What serious words from the mouth of such a young girl!" he said condescendingly. "When are you going to start enjoying life? Now's the time. You should be strolling till sunset and making the most of life, living like every day was your last. This is coming from someone twice your age. How old *are* you? Twenty? Twenty-three?"

"Twenty-seven in July."

Richard had already managed to pass on all essential information about himself and decided now to discover more about his companion. "Well, what did you film there in Scotland?"

"The first episode of a TV series. They needed models with naturally dark hair, white skin and light eyes. Turns out there aren't many around," Tash answered reluctantly. She didn't like Richard. She didn't like his bragging, his tone, his arrogance. She became more bored with every question.

"Yeah, that's a rare combination. Who did you play?"

"Sirena …" She reached for her phone, feigning the urgent need to reply to a message.

"Did you have to walk around naked?" Richard's voice turned low and hoarse. "Don't have any pictures, do you?"

"Richard, filming is strictly confidential. Even if I *had* pictures, I couldn't show them to you." Tash turned the other way.

She avoided Richard's gaze for the rest of dinner, despite his countless attempts to attract her attention. She knew his type all too well. They constantly hang around models, thinking that it would add zeros to their bank balance and centimetres to their manhood.

The music from the *Ocean Princess* spilled out across the port. Queues of people formed on the embankment, eagerly awaiting their turn to board. Chaos reigned at the entrance. Security guards, checking invitations, were unable to cope with the overwhelming stream of guests in tails and evening dresses. As usual at the Grand Prix, the numbers of those actually invited to a reception, combined with those hoping to slip in uninvited, vastly exceeded the reception's capacity.

As Alberto Visconti had struck Carolina off the guest list, Mark had stepped up, like a real gentleman, and offered to entertain her on his own boat, docked nearby. After waiting endlessly in line and finally getting on board, Tash deliberately lost the annoying Richard, who was following her around. The taste of freedom was intoxicating. She climbed onto the very top deck. It was not crowded. Armed only with a glass of champagne she settled into a sofa in a far corner, hoping Richard wouldn't find her there. The sea and the sky merged into one black space on the horizon, beyond the even rows of illuminated boats. Tash was enjoying the darkness. A soft breeze frolicked in her long hair, and trickles of rhinestones on her dress sparkled in the light like silver scales. A waiter poured champagne into her glass. She took a small sip and savoured the taste – she was surprised to discover woody notes, a hint of oak. *What else?* She thought she sensed the taste and even the smell of biscuit. The thought made her smile. And sandalwood, possibly … The smell reminded her of something. But of what exactly?

"Hello, Mermaid. Are you escaping the crowd too?" A pleasant baritone interrupted her tasting session. Tash turned around. She saw a dark silhouette in the bright beam of a searchlight. The owner of the baritone moved closer and Tash was able to make out blue jeans and a top – a pullover, worn directly against the skin with nothing on underneath. When the silhouette leaned forward to clink glasses and swap 'cheers' with her, Tash flinched. Her throat suddenly felt tight.

"Are the suitcases okay?" An ironic smile played on his tanned face. His bold gaze wandered from her rounded, gaping eyes to her deep cleavage. Tash was dying of shame. Her cheeks were ablaze! How could she have mistaken *him* for a porter? How dismissively she'd spoken to him! Oh god …

"I can watch the sea for hours," the stranger said quietly, seating himself next to her. "I've loved to ever since I was a child. I grew up in South Africa." He seemed not to expect any response from her. "I was raised by penguins. Lovely birds," he said and laughed. She thought she heard a longing for those careless times in his voice. "I've got a strange feeling," he said, looking at the horizon, "that you and I are on a desert island." He turned to her and examined her closely.

Her tanned face was covered with golden freckles, noticeable even in the dim light of a lantern. The almond-shaped eyes under her fluffy eyelashes were shining. She couldn't utter a word and just smiled shyly. The sound of the blues wafted from the speaker.

"Shall we dance, Mermaid?"

He took her hand and pulled her along to Barry White. Tash looked down at the stranger's feet and simpered. He was wearing the same loafers as that afternoon.

20

"Ah! There you are!" The intimacy was broken by Richard. "We're leaving."

Richard addressed himself to Tash, completely ignoring the presence of her partner. "You were right, there is nothing to do. Vivien and Zach are already waiting for us on the pier."

The stranger looked perplexedly at Richard. At first Richard had stood right next to them, as if he were claiming proprietorial rights to Tash. Then, noticing her confusion, he quickly grabbed her arm and led her to the stairs.

Tash obeyed meekly. As she approached the stairs, she suddenly felt that she was on the verge of missing something very important. At the last moment, she turned around and finally parted her lips. "Will we ... meet again?"

The stranger smiled. "Of course."

*****

Mark's boat was moored nearby. The men had already switched to whiskey, as Carolina and Vivien continued to savour the champagne. Calming sounds of jazz filled the deck from inside the lounge.

Carolina sat on a chaise longue next to Tash.

"Mark told me about Hugh." Carolina exhaled smoke from the smouldering cigarette she held in her hand. The ashtray was full of butts that bore the blood-red traces of her lipstick. "Years ago, when Mark set up his first fund, his main project was in Libya. And he was dealing with a senior official who provided support from Muammar Gaddafi." Carolina reached for her bag to get another pack of cigs. "Mark worked on this deal for several years. Hugh showed up only at the final stage to expand it to other African countries." Carolina lit her fifth cigarette of the last hour. "Hugh, using his connections, convinced Gaddafi that the official was an unnecessary link, likewise Mark – after all, everything was already set up now. Gaddafi put the official behind bars and broke the agreement with Mark's fund, replacing it with Hugh's. And then" – Carolina lowered her voice and looked at Mark – "Hugh framed Mark and accused him of financial fraud, but, thank god, the court acquitted him."

Mark and Zach moved into the cabin, away from the bustle of the noisy promenade. Richard was strolling back and forth on the upper deck, captive in the viewfinders of a thousand cameras, a prized snapshot for tourists who probably mistook him for the owner of the yacht. He looked so natural in the role. And Vivien could well have passed for his wife.

Carolina lit another ciggie and gazed sardonically at the couple prancing about in front of the tourists. She sighed. "Mark is so different."

All this time Tash was staring at the promenade. She was looking into the crowd for her stranger, imagining how he would come and take her away with him.

*****

A petite woman, in a hat whose brim was wider than she was tall, took a blatantly obvious glance at Tash's shiny golden sandals. Tash was walking along the pavement that stretched into the Monte Carlo Beach Club. Carolina's cabana was in the second tier at the farthest end of the club. The sea breeze inflated the striped umbrellas and tore wide-brimmed hats from the heads of elegant ladies. Tash spotted Anna and her husband Nick from a distance, two tall figures in matching turquoise polos and beige slacks. She recognised Anna's hand in this ensemble and it made her smile. As a native New Yorker, Anna considered the look she'd created to be the quintessence of Hamptons style, the Hamptons being her favourite social climbing venue. Anna had decided, nonetheless, to add little accents here and there, complementing the look with matching suede moccasins and Hermes belts. Tash grinned. That was exactly what usually gave the nouveaux riches away. Yes, they could easily copy a simple, elegant style from fashion magazines, but they could never resist highlighting their status.

Tash had met Anna in New York, through a common friend, years before Anna married. Tash immediately discerned the intelligence and perspicacity that, in Anna, often manifested as arrogance. Anna, in turn, was touched by the kindness and sincerity of the gorgeous Russian model. Both well-educated and well-read, they loved making fun of their common friend Katya: they would lure her to a philosophy lecture in French where, despite her excellent command of that language, Katya wouldn't understand a word; or they'd leave her to be torn to pieces by contemporary art connoisseurs at a charity dinner at the Metropolitan Museum of Art. These pranks brought the girls even closer together, and they realised that their friendship would last forever.

Although Mother Nature hadn't endowed Anna with ravishing beauty, it had been merciful to her when it came to allocating brains. Anna quickly realised that she would

22

only be able to obtain status – the index by which she measured success – if she chose to attend Princeton rather than fashion weeks. And so she devoted four years of her life to studying literature.

Anna sipped her fresh orange juice. "Ah! Finally a chance to put my feet up! Cannes was so exhausting! So much hassle!" Anna's yawn expressed the terminal fatigue that still hung over her in the wake of her busy schedule at the film festival. More accurately, perhaps, it was a reaction to the endless round of parties that she and her husband Nick – neither boasting any connection to the film industry – had happily attended of their own free will, even though their presence hadn't been required.

For the third time Tash reconstructed the events of the night before, regretful that she'd failed to seize her destiny.

"I'm such a loser!" She wrinkled her nose. "How did I let that awful Richard drag me away like I was a child?" She thought again of the stranger. "He doesn't even know my name. How on earth is he going to find me on Instagram?"

"Don't worry."

Anna was lying on a striped chaise longue, shielding her face from the burning sun under a copy of the *Financial Times*.

"You're going to meet your porter again. There's nothing to be upset about! You don't even know his name. For all you know, he could really be a porter or a steward on a boat; anyone can get into a party here." She looked disapprovingly at a beach boy who was passing by.

"I'm going for a swim." Tash looked offended. "And, by the way, he had a posh accent."

The bored owners of the neighbouring cabanas lazily turned their heads to watch the progress of the new sailor girl as she walked to the beach in a too-revealing white and blue striped swimsuit. Onlookers leered judgementally and gossiped. On the pier, bodies that resembled seals in a rookery added their silent disapproval. The sailor girl suddenly froze. She bent over as if she were checking something then hurriedly dived into the water. Effecting a beautiful crawl, she swam to the horizon, which was technically the edge of the paddock, an area enclosed by a net that protected bathers from Mediterranean jellyfish. *It would be great*, Tash thought, *if they had protective nets like these on the shore — to save tourists from the poisonous stares of all the gorgons!* Especially when it's that time of the month and you've just leaked into your white swimsuit! She made her way to the buoys.

Tash looked at the sea. A small sailing boat swayed in the waves. Tash thought she saw a girl on the deck. Her white dress fluttered in the wind. Her shoulders were covered by a luxurious silk shawl. A sudden gust of wind ripped the shawl off. But she was not alone. A blond guy had his arms around her frail shoulders, shielding her from the high wind. And there they just stood … She was drowning in his arms, feeling protected from all troubles. The buoy began to sway more appreciably and a swelling gust of wind forced Tash to open her eyes. She looked to the horizon once more and swam back.

When Tash returned, Anna was still digesting the speed with which her friend had managed to accord her porter a posh accent and a title.

"There are plenty of upper-class stewards, right, Nick?" Anna turned to her husband, who had belatedly found an appropriate use for the *Financial Times.*

"What, darling?" Nick finally looked up from his paper.

"Can stewards be posh?" she repeated.

"Dear, there is no such thing as class. Racial and social affiliations do not exist in the modern world. Your rhetoric just sounds vulgar." And he buried himself once more in the newspaper.

"Nick!" Anna grabbed his hand. "So *that's* why you belong to every possible members' club in the world? To talk to black workers from Stratford? And even now we're sitting in a private club, thanks to Carolina's membership!" Anna rode her hobby-horse over familiar ground, trampling her husband's political views under foot.

"My darling, it's purely a matter of comfort, nothing more. Please don't connect it to social stratification. All people are equal."

Anna was annoyed by his unrelenting political correctness. He had been born with a silver spoon in his mouth and yet he enjoyed holding forth on the subject of class equality. Anna detested his excessive respect for the staff; she found his calling the cook 'his good buddy' particularly ridiculous. Nick had practically been a slave to the housekeeper until Anna came into the picture and set everything to rights. She immediately introduced, if not class distinction, then at least worker subordination,

24

where the housekeeper had to perform the duties imposed on her by the employer, not vice versa.

"You over-fantasised as usual. You'll meet him again, if he's your destiny." Anna lay down and covered her face with a towel, thereby signifying that the conversation was closed.

Tash sighed audibly. "If he's my destiny …"

2. How to fix errors of pedigree

Sardinia

"Oi, you old perv!" The sound of a mighty slap drowned out the crash of metal against the hard terracotta tile. A silver ice bucket slowly tumbled towards the swimming pool, spilling its contents to melt in the searing Italian sun. Nearby, from beneath the Hotel Cala di Volpe's beach umbrellas, which were shaped like Vietnamese hats, lounging ladies poked out their heads.

A woman looking like a sack of potatoes interrupted her husband – a hairy hulk of a man – as he gazed at the wooden sunbed where a busty blonde was struggling unsuccessfully to find a comfortable position in which to put her exceedingly long legs.

Katya Volkova, or, as she called herself, Volkoff, placed her freshly pedicured foot on the smoothly mown grass. A blue thong, adorned with sequins, provoked the imagination of every member of the opposite sex that was looking on.

"Five more minutes and we'll go to lunch," she barked at Tash.

Not even an affront to her sanctum sanctorum, her shrine of piety and virtue on which she had blown thousands of dollars and years of training, could distract Katya from reading her *Daily Mail*.

She had spent the last hour clutching her favourite paper, avidly perusing the latest news from the world of the rich and famous. Tash didn't bother her friend, respecting her unalienable constitutional right to love the realm of show business. For summaries of important international events, like the trade war with China or the crisis in Venezuela, Katya relied on *Tatler* and the *New York Post*. Of course, she mused, Maduro's got no chance in Venezuela – just look at Juan Guaido's wife! Katya examined the First Lady's outfits, considering what she herself would wear were *she* to become a First Lady, an entirely possible development, after all. In New York she was a regular at raucous parties and fashion shows, and often cropped up in the society columns. And, best of all, her beloved tabloids routinely featured her on page six, treating their readers to accounts of her latest affairs with the rich and powerful.

"Have a look at this!" She waved the newspaper in front of Tash. "Hugh has ordered another article about Carolina."

Tash grudgingly took the *Daily Mail*. There was a shoddy picture of their friend Carolina staring at her phone outside a Chanel store, subtitled "Checking whether I have enough money in my account."

The article itself was a sordid hit piece, a cruel send-up of Carolina, whose affluence had recently been terminated by her husband.

"Why do you read this crap?" Tash chucked the newspaper disdainfully onto to the wooden table between them. Only a few days before, Carolina had told her that Mark, like a true gentleman, had stayed over in Monaco after the Grand Prix to help her sort some things out.

"Give it back, then!" Katya carefully uncreased the paper and re-immersed herself in its contents.

*****

The first time Tash saw Katya was at her grandmother's country house. That rainy morning, Grandmother Hannah had come to take Tash away with her because it had all got a bit too hectic and crowded at Tash's. Her mum lay on the bed – her face so white it seemed to have been sprinkled with chalk dust – and strangers were queueing to go up to her and kiss her, which, for some reason, was making them cry. Dad walked them to the train station and wouldn't let Tash out of his arms for a long time. On the train, a scruffy boy in chequered shorts, who was definitely older than her, was running around the carriage shouting, "Give up! You've been defeated!" and waving an imaginary sabre. She'd been taught that she should be quiet in public places and respect other people, so she spent the entire journey looking calmly out of the window and didn't cry even once. When they arrived in Moscow, they took a long ride in a yellow taxi from the station to Hannah's country house. The taxi driver braked sharply just as they were approaching the dacha. A tall blonde girl, who looked like a fairy, jumped out from under the wheels. She burst into laughter and flew on, chased by a horde of screaming gnomes.

Katya was the darling of the whole village. Tash watched with admiration how deftly she dealt with the boys. She attracted the ones she liked with a single glance and shooed away the others with a single word. Tash worshipped Katya's beauty. Katya was a real It Girl, worthy of the admiration of all the boys who flocked around her. Tash herself was so ordinary. By a stroke of good fortune she had ended up in what she then considered to be the epicentre of the universe – the small village of Peredelkino, near Moscow. When one of the local boys started paying attention to her, she couldn't believe that he could be interested in a short girl with thick pigtails, and she ran away blushing. More than anything, she was afraid that they would find out her secret: that she was not one of them; that her mother had died, and that she was living in a small town with her dad, "a tramp who started a family without figuring out how to provide for it," as Hannah used to say. A tramp who, furthermore, had saddled her with a stupid name – Tash. "After Natasha Rostova," as he explained.

Tash hated her stubborn curly hair and secretly cut it at the back so her braids wouldn't look so thick. She hated that she was short and too skinny. She envied Katya's straight golden hair, her posture and her grace. Katya reminded her of a beautiful princess from Hans Christian Andersen's fairy tales. Tash spent every summer holiday at her grandmother's, and each year she would find in Katya some new features to admire. But one fine day, that worship came to an end. She came to Peredelkino and found that Katya had cut her golden hair into a bob. And on that same day, Tash became aware that something else had changed too: in her reflection in the mirror, instead of ugly stubborn curls, she saw shiny brown hair. Now she had something better than Katya had. But she still couldn't figure out what to do about it. The solution, however, soon presented itself. Lesha was fourteen and the dream of every girl in Peredelkino. For the last two years, Katya and her friend Rita had fought for his attention, winning his favour successively. But this time Lesha chose Tash, who had got much prettier over the winter. She had grown taller and finally unwoven her ridiculous braids. Her skinny body was now curvier, and her eyes sparkled with the devilish twinkle you see in girls who have just crossed the threshold of puberty. Still unaware of her new 'beautiful' status, Tash refused from habit to go on a date. Lesha, however, was persistent, and by midsummer all Peredelkino knew that Lesha was in love with Tash. Now even Katya saw Tash in a new light. If Lesha had chosen her, it meant she was worthy. One sunny morning, Katya knocked on her door and offered friendship. To Tash's surprise, not only did her terrible secret not alienate Katya, it made their friendship even stronger. Katya decided to take care of her less fortunate friend. As for Lesha, this news plunged him into transports of delight – with a peacock's pride he paid for Tash at the local café and took her on excursions all round the city.

With her five foot ten inches, signature bob and highly sought-after androgynous look, Katya was a fixture on the runways of Paris and New York for ten years. However, her childhood dreams of real beauty wouldn't leave her in peace and Katya set herself the goal of achieving her ideal. She began to make adjustments to her appearance, got carried away a bit, and, by the time she was through, had chanced to modify almost every part of her body. Model agencies had patiently stood by her through her metamorphoses, but they couldn't forgive her final innovation – breast enlargement to double D. The catwalk was closed to her forever.

Such a dramatic turn of events didn't faze her at all, and the busty blonde with a fortune, a wealth of experience, top model status and a million Instagram followers returned to Moscow for the husband hunt.

*****

After half an hour Katya slowly got up from the sunbed and started pulling on a silk tunic embroidered with rhinestones.

"Get up, you lazy cow, let's go to lunch!" she commanded. Her strong deep voice was better suited to a truck driver than to a sexy model with the face of an angel.

They had been staying at the Stowes' villa in Costa Smeralda for nearly a week now. Nick was a first-class host and, so as not to cramp the independence of his wife's unmarried girlfriends, he'd provided them with a car upon arrival. To Katya, the vintage look of the miniature Fiat Panda 4x4 was a source of incredible delight. She insisted that Tash capture her from every possible angle posing with such a democratic car: in the driver's seat, on the bonnet – she even climbed into the boot. All to convince her Instagram followers that top models were no strangers to the simple pleasures.

White linen shorts and a T-shirt highlighted Tash's golden tan. The way her friend managed to get an even bronze tan sitting under an umbrella always amazed Katya. Incredible! Why does everything come so easily to her?

The girls sashayed gracefully to the table. Anna and Nick were sipping cocktails. Nick had thoughtfully chosen a place close to the pool so the girls could talk disparagingly about the other guests more freely. Over the years he'd got used to the amusing company of his wife's unmarried girlfriends. He listened patiently to their endless love stories and was particularly proud when, on occasion, he was called as an expert.

"Nick," said Tash, "what do you think, if we—"

"Oh no! Don't turn around." Katya's husky voice stopped Tash in her tracks.

Katya was facing the sea. Her admonition had left Tash no choice but to turn around regardless, whereupon she saw a tender heading to the shore. It took her a split second to make out Alex as one of the figures on board. Yes, it was him.

"Oh no!" she whispered softly. "Is this my fate? To be haunted everywhere I travel by ghosts from my past?"

The mood that had soared with the beautiful weather and the champagne fell immediately flat.

"What do you expect? By a certain age …" Nick paused tactfully, "… and given a certain lifestyle" – he winked and raised an eyebrow, implying that Tash's lifestyle didn't fit into a framework he would himself consider acceptable – "the number of ghosts is bound to significantly exceed the number of possible vacation spots, giving rise to situations such as this one."

He took a sip of chardonnay and held it in his mouth for a second, trying to tie down a new, elusive note. He smiled at his discovery, and at this demonstration of his own cleverness.

Tash's heated retort didn't let him savour the moment for long.

"There is no logic in what you say!" Her usually soft voice became forceful in only two cases. The first, simply enough, was when she drank too much. The second was more psychological, when she got started on the subject of what Katya called complex conclusions – a particular hobby-horse of hers. As it was still early in the day, Nick was dealing with a psychological episode. "Even if the number of ghosts exceeds the number of all holiday destinations, the probability of bumping into them in certain places does not depend on their number, but rather on their preferences."

Anna looked around the table. How this petty bickering bored her!

"It seems you both have big problems with logic," she concluded, moving the plates.

But she was wrong.

*****

The train slowed down. A black, faux leather suitcase propped open the compartment door from the vestibule side. A plastic tag depicting Edvard Munch's *Scream* – signed N. Romanov, in blue ballpoint pen – dangled rhythmically, swaying to and fro with the motion of the train. As the train arrived on platform four of Kazan railway station, Tash looked through the grimy carriage window, searching for her grandmother Hannah in the crowd.

Today, instead of the usual grunts and educational reproaches, her grandmother greeted her with unexpected warmth. For the first time in her life, Hannah Steiner was proud of her granddaughter. And there was a great deal for her to be proud about! Tash had stepped off the train as a winner – a winner of the National Mathematics Olympiad! And with the victory, she had secured a place at the university. No joke! For years Hannah had been planning to tear Tash free from the clutches of her worthless dad and take charge of her granddaughter's upbringing. Finally the opportunity had presented itself. "I'll have enough time to influence her while she's staying with me. She doesn't have any time to waste! Her loser dad couldn't support his family, he couldn't earn money, and he'd even dragged the poor girl into that charity nonsense – free courses for the poor, in their shit-hole! Why would she stay in 'the dump' among beggars when she could dazzle in the city? She's such a beauty! I hope she'll be smarter than her mother and not marry a loser."

Hannah patted Tash on the head. "Let your hair down," she said sternly. "I don't want to see that ponytail ever again. You are a beauty! Don't you dare go wasting it, young girl!"

From the first days of her granddaughter's stay, Hannah went on the offensive. "By the way, Katya got accepted by the modelling agency."

A manicurist with bleached hair filed her nails carefully, listening all the while to how Hannah Genrikhovna guided her granddaughter along the one true path.

"Why shouldn't you apply too? You are even prettier that Katya." She cast a critical eye over her granddaughter, who was dressed in a simple pyjama set. "Thank god you got your mother's face." Hannah looked sadly at a photograph of a beautiful young woman hanging in a brown frame above the table. "And I hope you've got my brains. Your parents would never win any Olympiad."

"Grandmother!" Tash sat at the table, right across from her. She swallowed, took a deep breath for courage and quickly blurted out, "Please stop going on about Daddy. You know he is trying hard."

"Have you forgotten? Stop calling me your grandmother." Hannah kept a close eye on every move of the new manicurist. "Call me Hannah. Practise at home and you won't mess up in public. How can I possibly have a seventeen-year-old granddaughter when I'm only forty-eight?"

The peroxided manicurist was about to smirk, but Hannah's icy gaze returned her immediately to her work. Hannah's age was the best-kept secret in the village. Indeed, she looked much younger than her sixty-five. The Hitchcock blonde had never been destined to meet "the one". Tash's father used to say that Hannah was doomed to loneliness because of her unbearable character.

Her personal life was a skeleton hidden very deep in the darkest family cupboard. Tash knew that Hannah had been born in Western Siberia, where Tash's great-grandmother and great-grandfather, ethnic Germans, had been exiled by Stalin in 1937. In the sixties, they were rehabilitated and returned to Moscow. Despite the hardships, her great-grandfather, a famous biologist, remained a supporter of communism and stayed in the Soviet Union until his dying day – even during "the thaw", when Soviet Germans emigrated en masse to West Germany. However, the young Hannah left for West Germany in the seventies, immediately after the Treaty of Moscow, between West Germany and the USSR, was signed. Nobody knew exactly what had happened in Germany, but two years later, Hannah returned to the USSR with a one-year-old daughter, a German passport and a bundle of German marks. She bought an apartment for her parents in the city, and moved to Peredelkino with little Maria in her arms. In the registry office, Tash's mother was recorded as Maria Genrikhovna Steiner, after her grandfather. Over the course of her long life, Hannah broke many hearts but didn't find the right man to share her life with. She gave all her love to her daughter. Maria inherited her mother's beautiful face and impeccable body, but, unlike Hannah, her beauty wasn't refined, but rather wild and free. Hannah dreamed of Maria becoming an actress, a shining star of the Moscow stage and Mosfilm's silver screens. She signed up her daughter to every imaginable art club, speech and acting class. But Maria applied instead to Stroganovka, got pregnant by a classmate – 'the tramp' – in the first year and moved with him to 'the dump' straight after graduation. Hannah couldn't get over her daughter's thoughtless behaviour and refused to accept the union. Only at her daughter's funeral did she finally come up to 'the tramp' and demand that Tash spend all her summer vacations with her. And she got her wish. When the school term finished, Tash moved in with her grandmother.

The agency informed her that she wasn't tall enough for the catwalks – just a couple of centimetres shy – but her face was perfect for magazine and TV advertising. Her German passport also came in handy, giving her a big advantage when it came to getting work in the EU. The prudent Hannah had made sure that all family members, with the exception of 'the tramp', obtained passports.

As Hannah had predicted, the temptations of city life fascinated Tash. She entered her first year at university with the firm intention of working hard, but by the second year she had given herself up completely to a life of partying. Morning lectures were a nightmare after sleepless nights on dance floors – she just slept through them. If she learned the secrets of marketing at all it was thanks to her natural intelligence. The uni, the shoots and the parties provided an inexhaustible source of new acquaintances. And indeed she had the numerous affairs that Nick had hinted at, tactfully alluding to them as 'a certain lifestyle'.

During those first two years she remained diligently under her grandmother's wing. Hannah had all the time she needed to knock her father's 'Samaritan crap' out of Tash's head and replace it with a healthy pragmatism. By the third year Tash was earning enough money to live on her own, skilfully juggling rich boyfriends who were ready to jump through hoops for her. Her beauty had blossomed like a spring flower.

*****

The first time he saw Tash, Alex immediately decided that this girl had to be his. And he put quite an effort into achieving that goal: regular calls, tons of flowers, planned chance encounters. Tash's girlfriends wasted no time in labelling him ideal: young, handsome and rich. Wasn't that the fairy tale?

She had no choice but to surrender. They messaged each other incessantly, spoke five times a day, made joint holiday plans – and he even introduced her to his mother.

But one cold December day, out of the blue, Alex ghosted her. She accepted his choice, convincing herself that there must have been a pretty good reason.

Nick watched how the poor things – his wife and her friends – tortured themselves with their typical female theories about the ghosting: he'd had an accident; some evil woman had got her claws into him. He finally took pity on the weaker, and therefore less intelligent, sex and decided to lift the veil on the mysterious disappearance.

"Well, he didn't see you as 'the one'!" Nick was trying unsuccessfully to cut an artichoke. "Would you like me to enlighten you? Give away the reasons men ghost?" Tash and Katya held their breath. "Feel free to take notes."

All eyes were on him.

"There are several reasons. Reason one is bad sex. Every man has his own fantasies – if you don't accommodate them, they'll be accommodated somewhere else. The second reason: sex again, but this time it's you who's not happy with the sex. You either complain or you don't express your enthusiasm strongly enough. The third reason: you are trying too hard, but he isn't ready for anything serious and doesn't want to lead you on. Number four: you are overcontrolling and not willing to adapt to his lifestyle. After all, guys want to lead and expect concessions. Reason number" – Nick looked at Katya – "five: you require too much effort. This is very tiring."

Katya smirked. "If they're not interested, there's plenty who will be. No one's forcing them."

"Reason six," Nick said calmly, continuing where he left off, "lack of respect. You tell him what to do, and that's emasculating. Reason seven" – Nick looked at Katya again – "you cadge presents. We love giving presents, but hate when you ask for them."

"You can't generalise." Katya seemed offended. "How else will they understand what they need to give if you don't hint?"

Nick smiled smugly, appreciating the effect of his speech.

"Reason eight: when you take everything for granted and do not express gratitude for his efforts. Reason nine …" Nick thought for a second.

"The list here is endless," Tash said. "Don't you think that you've just listed what's important to *you*?"

34

He ignored her remark. "Do you want to get married or not? Then, listen."

Anna looked at her husband. He was unique – such a sweetheart. He was as nice to the scaffolder as he was to the duke; he had an uncanny ability to defuse conflicts and he never got offended.

"Anna, would you kindly explain to your friends that a man – at least in the beginning – must be praised and cherished and indulged in all his whims." Nick was relishing his role of advice guru to inexperienced women. "Ask my wife how she behaved before we got married, how often she expressed her desires or dissatisfaction." Nick winked at Anna. "Now she's married and got me wrapped round her little finger."

"Getting a man to marry you is an art, but holding on to him is hard work." Anna was proud of her achievements. Nick sometimes joked that their marriage was a textbook example of how it's first after the wedding that a man finally opens his eyes – and a woman, her mouth.

"Also don't forget" – Nick smiled at the dark-haired waiter who was refreshing their glasses – "you are in a highly competitive environment. And if you don't do it, someone else will – someone with a strong determination to get married, like my precious wife had." Nick kissed Anna on the cheek. "These determined ones master everything so skilfully that a man doesn't know what's hit him till he's walking down the aisle."

Tash summarised the lecture. "Okay, I've got the idea: I will cherish and admire and smile like an idiot!" Everyone burst out laughing.

*****

Alex walked on the smoothly mown emerald-green grass. Captain Luca, an old Italian with a wrinkled face, had managed to find them a table for lunch at the Cala di Volpe. At the peak of the season, the usually tranquil Costa Smeralda turned into a *Who's Who* of the *Tatler* and *Vanity Fair* set; they checked in for a few days on the island before rushing on to other destinations. *Two days of this annoying fuss, and we'll be sailing to Corsica. The main thing is not to run into anyone I know* ... And it was while his mind was preoccupied with these thoughts that Alex noticed a familiar face – the face of his ex. Her friend Katya was unashamedly checking out his friends. Alex hesitated. It was the first time he had seen Tash since their de facto break-up. She was smiling. He smiled back, saving

35

himself and everyone else from the inevitable awkwardness that unresolved relationships inflict on subsequent encounters.

"Alex" – Katya grabbed his hand as soon as he got close enough to her chair – "introduce me to your friends immediately. What a waste that I've not been introduced to such handsome men before now!"

The handsome men occupied the table next to them. She knew about most of them from their love affairs with her friends. Well, so what! When after a turbulent and cosmopolitan New York, where the supply of eligible men comfortably exceeded demand, thanks to the constant influx of new recruits arriving from around the world to work or study or just live, Katya suddenly found herself in what she considered a provincial Moscow, where extremely high demand surpassed exceptionally limited supply, she had sadly concluded that the occasional encroachment on to romantic territory previously laid claim to by her friends would be inevitable. And it was not without great internal torment, it must be stressed, that she was ready to lay down friendship on the altar of great love.

An hour later, the hot Sardinian sun and three shared bottles of champagne had provided the necessary rapprochement between the tables. Nick was happy to find himself at last in male company. A week on the all-female team, providing boundless love to his wife and sympathy to her friends, had left him dead tired. Katya was already picturing herself as a coveted doe from *National Geographic* – waiting for the five young stags to start fighting over her.

*****

Alex admired the beauty of the rugged coastline from the stern of the tender. The wild beach sheltered a small lagoon in which a number of motorboats, for travel to nearby islands, lay tied to a wooden pier. At lunch, Nick had told the story of how his father had come to acquire this site in one of the most picturesque corners of the island – near the Hotel Romazzino – back in the days of the Aga Khan.

The house blended harmoniously into the landscape. So seamlessly was its architecture woven into the surrounding nature that, from afar, it resembled a hobbit house from Tolkien's novel nestling in the hills of the Shire. At seven o'clock a tender carrying the group of six young men tied up to the pier at the Stowes' house.

An old Italian man in uniform accompanied them to the upper terrace. Alex went to the railing and surveyed the site from above. Wow! Rectangular in shape, it comprised four levels. The coastline alongside the house stretched for much further than he could have imagined. On the seaward side, the house was bordered by a wild tropical garden. On the other side there were two tennis courts and a pool with a waterfall. But the architectural pièce de résistance was the upper terrace with its breathtaking sea views; this never failed to make an impression on even the most sophisticated of guests. He looked out at the massive scarlet disk hanging over the horizon, its reflection adding reds and sparkling shades of vermilion to the calm blue of the sea.

The host was sitting on a quilted brown leather ottoman. He flicked the ash from a half-smoked cigar into the crystal ashtray in front of him and got up to greet the guests. He was dressed in a white linen suit. Nick loved theme parties from his boarding school days and imposed a rule for his house guests: new day, new style. Today's theme was Hollywood chic. The air smelled of fresh lavender and rosemary, and Muddy Waters' velvety voice echoed across the terrace. Katya posed for Instagram in a long green dress against the spectacular backdrop provided by the sunset. Anna was in charge of the camera; no less glamorous herself, she searched for the most flattering angles to capture her friend's beauty. Tash reclined on a sofa explaining to the housekeeper in poor Italian that she needed salt to wash out the stain she had just got on her dress. A week under the gentle Sardinian sun had done its job – Tash looked great. Alex's gaze lingered on the deep cleavage of her chiffon dress before eventually dropping down to the stain. He took the housekeeper's arm and said in perfect Italian, "Puoi per piacere dare il sale alla bella signora?"

The housekeeper nodded and ran away smiling, happy to fulfil the request of such a gallant signor.

"Today is Ferragosto! People drink and have fun. Nick and I have a tradition: we watch the sun go down with a glass of wine in our hands and we make a wish."

Anna approached each of the guests, inviting them to come over to the wrought-iron railing and enjoy the sunset. "Make a wish!"

"Do they come true?" Katya perked up.

"Of course, silly girl! Everything that you really want comes true."

Tash got up from the sofa and went over to the railing.

Alex watched her. *I wonder what she is going to wish for?*

Katya looked impatiently at Alex's friends. *Oh Lord, how gorgeous they are! I wish that one of them will take me shopping tomorrow. No, wait! Why the hell am I wasting my wish on that when I'm quite beyond compare?* Katya thought deeply, searching for a worthy alternative. "I wish for … a bronze tan just like Tash's … and maybe a little brow lift on the outer ends."

While Nick was wistfully watching the sun go down, Anna's gaze inspected the terrace. *The house definitely needs renovating … But now's not the time. I need money for something else; I must, at all costs, lay my hands on Samantha Lewis's jewellery.* Samantha's husband, Eaton Lewis, had just been sentenced for money laundering, and for several days rumours had been circulating in well-informed circles that she was broke and needed to sell her diamonds. These diamonds were the real deal! Fifteen years with Eaton – fifteen years of constantly improving fortunes – had left Samantha the owner of one of the most desirable jewellery collections in London. *I need to hurry up and fix a necklace to wear for the marchioness's birthday party on the fourth of September.* Back in the day, when the marchioness was just a baroness, she had meant to marry Nick but Anna came along and stole him away. *She will be furious when she sees the diamonds around my neck!* This thought excited Anna immensely, and she gently patted her husband's head.

Nick looked at his wife. *How lucky I am with her! A caring wife, a wonderful hostess! The only thing we lack to complete the perfect picture is a child. We need a baby!*

Alex's gaze dipped into the warmth of the Mediterranean sunset, then returned to rest on Tash's shoulders, cool like sculpted marble … *She's so elegant and beautiful! If only she could have understood me back then! If she could only have seen my potential!* After all, he'd achieved everything himself! Not thanks to his uncle's connections, as she'd sarcastically claimed. He needed an understanding woman!

"What shall I wish for?" Tash's thoughts darted between a Loro Piana cashmere coat – it looked so pretty on the hanger in the boutique in Porto Cervo – and her desire to be approved for a Colgate ad. *But if I get the Colgate, I can buy the coat – and many others. So Colgate it is.* She glanced furtively at Alex. *Also, I'd really like him to finally understand what a huge mistake he made by ghosting me. So I'll wish for—* Her thoughts were interrupted by a familiar melody: "I Can't Get Enough of Your Love, Baby." Barry White's soft baritone wafted out over the terrace. When was the last time she'd heard that? Suddenly both

Alex and the Loro Piana coat turned into two tiny dots and disappeared into the humid Sardinian air. Tash's face lit up with a smile, and her shoulders no longer seemed cold but glowed instead with the warmth of orange terracotta in the last rays of the setting sun. She was dancing like no one was watching. After all, now she knew exactly what to wish for …

*****

Gianni, the grey-haired owner of the restaurant, had known Nick since the day Nick was born which, no matter how much Nick wanted to forget the fact, was almost fifty years ago. He remembered both Nick's grandfather – the Governor of the Bank of England – and Lord Stowe, Nick's father – one of the most influential industrialists in the UK. Gianni knew that Lord Stowe had left numerous trust funds to his only son, along with real estate in many parts of the globe. Lord Stowe had known his spoiled son well enough to hide his assets in trust funds and let Nick live off the dividends. But dividends from trusts, sometimes heavily mismanaged by greedy managers, weren't sufficient to maintain his lifestyle. After his father's death, Nick's extravagant ways didn't change. PJs, boats, models and entourage – all that required money. He had to sell houses, first in New York, then in St. Moritz and LA. The pragmatic Anna liked to jokingly call her husband "The Squanderer". After the wedding she put tight controls on the family budget, significantly reducing spending on entourage, which, without the regular infusions, evaporated with remarkable speed.

"Sardinian air agrees with you. You look stunning." Alex drew a chair back, helping Tash to sit down, and took a seat beside her. "I missed you …"

His father had walked out when he was three. Each day, the resemblance between Alex and his dad grew more apparent. Sometimes the pain of watching him was so strong that to release it his mother would take a belt and spank Alex for the smallest mischief. Over the years the pain subsided, giving way to a kind of awe at his phenomenal mind, looks and skills. Her brother, Alex's uncle, had made a meteoric rise over the past few years and headed a large state corporation. Every business in the industry was lining up to get his nephew on to its board of directors. Finally, Alex made up his mind.

39

Tash was a rare bird, given his track record with the opposite sex. She stood out from a series of mature girlfriends. Like a little tyrant, he longed for adoration and didn't tolerate the slightest disobedience.

On that morning, Alex stomped in front of the mirror, choosing a suit for his first working day.

"Which one is better?" He was holding two blue ties.

"What's the difference? You can turn up in sneakers and track suit and no one will bat an eye. As long as your uncle provides them with benefits, you are immune to criticism."

His eyes flashed with a fierce light. How could she suggest that they only hired him because of his uncle? What a stupid creature! With his new job he needed to find someone with more sense …

And he didn't call.

"You didn't call me either," he remarked.

She had a lot to say and wanted to explain in great detail, but she bit her tongue instead, remembering Nick's instructions. She was flattered by Alex's attention. Maybe she could get her revenge?

"I—" She began to speak, but a loud laugh rang out from behind.

She turned around.

Every time the subject turned to love she would recall a small reproduction of François Boucher's painting *Four Seasons: Spring*. The one that hung on the wall over her crib – the little sheep that spied on the young lovers taking refuge in the shade of a fairy tree. The pink-skinned girl holding a basket of flowers in her hands, and her beau gently straightening a flower pin in her hair. Later, when Daddy told her Boucher's story, Tash learned that the salons of the Marquise de Pompadour – the mistress of King Louis XV and the artist's chief patroness – were as far removed from sublime love and piety as was the marquise herself. Nevertheless, she still cherished that sweet pastoral as an everlasting image of true love. Young, carefree lovers, intoxicated with each other …

She'd heard about love at first sight, but grandmother used to say that love was an amusement for the rich – smart girls should choose money and status.

"Anna," she said softly. "It's him!" Tash nodded towards a table where there was much laughter. "The porter!" Her voice trembled, her cheeks turned pink.

The young group occupied the largest table in the restaurant. Their sleek tanned faces with defiant white-toothed smiles fit so organically into the restaurant's interior, with its white tablecloths and curtains, that one might think the maître d' had intentionally planted carefully selected models in strategic positions to recreate a dinner-in-paradise tableau. Anna looked at one of the guys. Tash was right: as it turned out, the chap was pretty darn hot. His curly dirty-blond hair framed a manly face with a strongly defined chin. His big blue eyes were set a bit too close, but this flaw made him somehow even more attractive. His posture, his bone structure – everything about him – showed breeding. Anna turned her attention to the woman sitting next to him. Her unremarkable face expressed absolutely no emotion. Her eyes just wandered nervously about the room searching for some object worthy of her consideration. She was dressed defiantly simply, in a white T-shirt. Her hair was pulled back in a bun. For such a glamorous establishment, where most of the guests tried to dress up, it looked a bit dismissive. Such incredible self-confidence, of course, revealed her background. The same background that poor little rich girls reveal when, gifted with neither beauty nor brains, they receive the attention and worship that their parents' money elicits and mistakenly attribute it to their own charm, talent and wit. Anna looked more closely at her ... she had seen that face before. It took her a minute to remember how she knew her ... Yes, that was her – that was the daughter of their neighbour, Alberto Visconti ...

"The girl next to him is our neighbour, her dad is some sort of Italian aristocrat. From that very aristocracy," she added with a grin, "that doesn't exist. I'll ask Nick to invite them to dinner."

Anna treated Tash like the younger sister she never had. She would support her in everything. Anna knew that, unfortunately, the poor thing had only herself to rely on. Her father had been leeching off her lately, barely able to make ends meet with his meagre salary. Anna had to agree with Tash's late grandmother Hannah – Tash simply couldn't afford the luxury called love. That was an indulgence that poor little rich girls

41

like the daughter of Alberto Visconti could count on – and, yes, damn it, even Katya, who'd made a fortune on the catwalks. Tash would have to content herself with the fate her grandmother had worked so hard to prepare her for: she must monetise her beauty in the best way possible – namely, by marrying some millionaire.

Anna was a typical natty American blonde with flawless skin. Born into the family of a wealthy American banker, from early childhood she dreamed of status and recognition. Her parents gave her everything they could – love, care, money, and a diploma from Princeton. But Anna wasn't satisfied. She didn't find a single worthy titled candidate at Princeton, so she went on a tour of Europe hoping to secure some posh Euro trash. This ended in failure and she had to return to the States. When she reached her thirties it suddenly hit her that the quality of guys around her wasn't improving. So she finally decided to lower her standards. Nick Stowe was forty-five at the time. She met him at one of those parties in the Hamptons, where young and not-so-young women go to meet their future husbands. When she found out he was a lord, she used all her charm to bewitch him. Anna adored the social life, and Nick, with his tons of useful acquaintances, was ideally suited to the role of Anna's husband. She, in turn, proved to be a major find for Nick: the perfect hostess, educated and sensible, she knew how to make a subtle compliment, choose the right gift and write a courteous thank-you note. Anna's wedding caused unbearable envy among her ambitious university girlfriends. Lacking Anna's visionary zeal, they had jumped into marriage with classmates who had excellent pedigrees and family money – classmates who seemed to them, at the time, to be at the top of the social ladder. Who would have thought that Anna Bailey, with her undistinguished features, would get a real English lord? If she had married a guy her own age and from a similar background, had three little munchkins with him and lived happily ever after, it would never have occurred to them to envy her – but marrying an English aristocrat was a completely different matter.

For many years Anna witnessed how tough life in New York could sometimes be for Katya. Anna was too pragmatic to fool herself that she'd had anything but the greatest good luck to have been born into a wealthy American family. She knew what Katya, an immigrant from Russia, had had to endure at the beginning of her career – fierce competition, lack of money, lack of sleep, visa problems, constant suspicions of being a gold digger (she wasn't one back then) – before she became a seasoned and successful model. What about Tash? Tash always blamed her height for preventing a brilliant career on the runway. But she was wrong. Even if she'd been a head taller than Katya, she had neither Katya's resilience nor her ambition. In the world of fashion only the strongest survived.

Nick said, "Stop deciding for her." It was a familiar refrain. "If Tash had just a particle of Katya's determination and your confidence, she would have surpassed you both in every respect. But she's set herself different goals. She doesn't need billions and titles, she just wants to be happy."

Nevertheless, in her capacity as elder sister, Anna did everything to guide Tash in the right – in her "absolutely objective" view – direction.

*****

Alex was confused. They say "if you want to know what a woman really thinks, look at her, but don't listen." Tash's attention had suddenly shifted to Anna. Then Tash got up abruptly and slowly walked to the ladies', wiggling her hips in a such a seductive way that male visitors risked severe neck injury to keep their eyes glued to her back, all sexy and tanned in a revealing dress.

Anna observed Tash's manoeuvre from her seat. She appreciated the virtuosity with which Tash had performed it – the mastery that had come with years of practice. The goal was achieved: 'the porter' had stolen a few glances in her direction.

Finally Alex grasped what had just happened under his nose. He was filled with jealousy and rage but he wasn't about to throw in the towel. He called on Nick as an ally and pressed him to move on from the restaurant to the boat as quickly as possible.

While Alex and Nick were discussing their next move, Anna and Katya described to Tash what was happening out on centre stage.

"He's looking over here."

"He is, but he's not showing any signs of making a move," Katya said. She genuinely believed that it was a man's obligation to conquer a woman, and a woman's obligation to respond with complete surrender.

Her words made sense. After all, if it was a case of love at first sight, everything ought to have worked out all by itself. He should have carried her out of the restaurant in his arms – or fought with Alex for her honour, like a knight in shining armour, and then carried her off in his arms. At the very least, he should have treated her like an impregnable fortress, just *taken* her – and then carried her off in his arms! But there was definitely no place in Katya's fairy tale for a scenario like this one – where the heroine provocatively saunters past the hero, successfully attracting his attention, only for him to respond by not even trying to get to know her.

Suddenly Tash felt tense. Her exposed back was too naked. Her evening dress was inappropriate, her hairstyle, pretentious. She hated Nick for his stupid idea about Hollywood chic. She was sure the table behind them were laughing at their ridiculous outfits. Why on earth was she in this stupid dress when all his friends were wearing jeans?

"Am I mistaken or would I be completely out of place in their crowd?" she whispered into Anna's ear. "It seems we've been sent invites to different parties. We're black tie and they're casual."

"Don't you worry." Once again Anna looked carefully round the room. "If anyone here isn't following the dress code, it's clearly not us. Look, everyone's overdressed."

Tash looked around. Anna was right.

"Well, why does it feel like there's a deep chasm between us, not just a couple of metres?"

Katya intervened. "That, my dear, is because that is how it is. There is not only a chasm, but an entire universe separating you from their parents' deep pockets. The guy, Anna's neighbour, the one from the non-existent aristocracy, he can buy this restaurant – lock, stock and barrel – and you, my dear, can't even pay for your own dinner."

Anna looked at Tash, whose eyes were beginning to well with tears. She was biting her lip nervously.

"Besides," Katya added, "don't forget about their pedigree. They don't need people like us. Our great-grandfathers polished their shoes and, if our grandmothers were young and beautiful, they'd roll with them in the hay. There's no way I'd ever date an aristocrat with all their boring traditions. Give me 'new money' every time!"

"Shut up, Katya. Nick married me—"

"Oh, come on." Katya didn't stop to listen to Anna. She turned to face Tash. "A bird in the hand is worth two in the bush." And she pointed to Alex with her eyes.

"Is that all I am too? A bird in the hand?" said Tash, loud enough for the entire table to hear. A pin-drop silence fell.

Nick was the first to break it. "A bird? You're a peacock! Look at your dress."

A waiter put a glass of whiskey in front of the clueless Nick.

Alex realised that his moment had come. Now or never! He had to eliminate his rival. "You are the most beautiful bird I have ever seen." It was the exact line the conqueror in Katya's fairy tale would use – the one before which, according to Katya's theory, the heroine would have no choice but to surrender. "I don't understand why I didn't tell you this before."

His words became all the more flattering; his attentiveness, all the more intent; his thoughtfulness, all the more touching. He worshipped her. He repented, and confessed that only after losing her did he realise how dear she was to him.

*****

Tash was dancing to Sinatra's "My Way" in the first rays of the morning sun, a bottle of champagne in her hands. Her dress fluttered in the breeze with the sway of her movements.

"You know what I just realised?" Anna, staring at Tash, leaned back on a white couch. "This song should be your motto. Your Way … The way you want it. Right, Nick?" She turned to Nick, who was snoring softly next to her.

"Don't wake him, I'll ask for him to be taken to the cabin." A hunky steward threw Nick over his shoulder and carried him away. Anna, who had got pretty mellow, couldn't resist the temptation to hurry after them.

"Look, what a beautiful view," Alex said softly.

The boat was anchored opposite Cala di Volpe. The apricot-coloured disk rose swiftly from beyond the horizon, reflecting a red strip on the turquoise water. The sea was calm, almost flat, and only Frank Sinatra's voice disturbed the silence.

"Let's go to the cabin …"

*****

Tash ran her hand over the crumpled sheet. Silky Egyptian cotton gently caressed her naked body. It was dark in the cabin. She opened the blinds with the button and let the golden sunlight stream inside. Tash stretched, got up and walked to the bathroom. The soft-pile carpet tickled her bare feet.

The bathroom walls were covered with light marble slabs alternating with dark wood panels. The room looked like a giant chessboard from a padishah's palace. Right in the middle of the room stood a bath made of black stone on bronze baroque legs. "Wow! This room is twice as large as my living room!" Tash turned on the tap to fill the bath with water. She wanted to sit on the edge but the stone had yet to warm up – the shock of the cold against her buttocks caused her to recoil. She jumped up, and her gaze settled on a large oval mirror in a massive gilded frame. A beautiful young woman looked back at her. She was strong, determined and self-confident. The murmur of the water grew less insistent, gradually subsiding. Tash raised her leg over the granite edge and plunged into the water, letting her head sink below the surface. There, under the water, she opened her eyes. She saw a bathroom wall covered with pale grey tiles with pink flowers on them. There were tin towel racks and a yellow rubber duck that quacked hysterically given just the slightest squeeze. Mum was dressed in her chintz robe, which she always wore when bathing little Tash. For a moment, she thought she heard Daddy's whisper: "You must be honest with yourself! Never betray yourself!" And then, the death rattle of Grandmother Hannah – "Promise me that you won't repeat your mum's mistakes." And only Mum didn't say a word …

Tash got out of the bath, casually shaking off her wet hair. She looked at her reflection again, but there was a slightly different look in its eyes.

Breakfast was served on the lower deck. Was she the last to come down? All the players from last night were in their places. She noticed a pile of paper shopping bags tied with ribbons on the floor.

"Have a good night's sleep?" Alex looked remarkably fresh; his shirt was dazzling white, not a single crease on his shorts. Tash glanced sheepishly at her crumpled dress and straightened her hair.

Nick, as was his habit at breakfast, browsed through the latest issue of *La Stampa*, simultaneously enlightening Katya, on this occasion, about how much clout the Agnelli family, who owned the newspaper, had in Italy.

"They are marvellous people" – Nick took a gulp of 'Vintage Tunina' and held it in his mouth – "but you can't escape their tentacles in the north of Italy. Somehow they are all over the place." Nick wiggled his fingers, miming the tentacles of an octopus.

"That doesn't stop you from hanging out with the octopuses," Anna said, stirring sugar into her coffee. She glanced at Tash. "Tell us, instead, some more about our neighbour Alberto."

"Oh, Alberto." Nick finally put the newspaper down. "He ... he is an extraordinary man!" The epithets beautiful, extraordinary, outstanding came most readily to his tongue. "His father was an Italian prince and a friend of my father, and, although Alberto was older, on summer holidays we would terrorise the local kids together. He married early, and we parted ways. As far as I remember, his wife wasn't a stunner, but she came from some noble European family, besides being filthy rich. At first he was after her sister, but she had chosen another guy, so he switched to the youngest. She was only seventeen and a bit on the bulky side ... But he was determined to pin her down before someone else did. Alberto managed to make a decent fortune thanks to her family ties."

The abundance of royal blood in the hood couldn't leave Anna unmoved, and she immediately reminded her husband about the promised dinner invitation. It turned out that Nick, with his inherent sense of duty, had already called Alberto's house and been informed by the manager that the owners had left early that morning.

Anna watched Tash, trying to guess how she'd taken the news. Tash was relieved. There was no longer any need to make a choice between the bird in the hand and the two in the bush. There was no such a thing as destiny, after all. She had to admit that she was rather pleased about Alex's persistence.

Meanwhile, Alex realised there would be no more talk of mysterious royals and he asked what time Tash would like to go for lunch.

"But I'm still wearing the dress from last night ..."

"Nick and I went to the hotel and bought everything while you were asleep."

"Ah, so that's where the big bags with the ribbons came from!" She laughed and kissed Alex on the cheek. He pulled her closer.

"We are leaving for Corsica tomorrow. Would you like to join us?"

"Of course she would," Katya answered for her. "And me too." Sardinia bored her to tears, and the prospect of a week on the high seas with some young stallions around stirred her imagination. To Katya's delight, and Anna's discontent, Tash agreed.

3. How to play against the rules and win

Moscow

"You're damn late!" Alex looked pointedly at his Patek to make sure she was ten minutes late, then rolled his eyes. He had been waiting for her at the entrance of the restaurant on Malaya Bronnaya street. "Okay, let's go." He straightened the silk handkerchief in his breast pocket and walked inside.

Tash was late because Katya had insisted on showing her every single item that she'd brought back with her from Paris Fashion Week. It was hours before Tash could get away. When Katya moved back to Moscow from New York she bought a lovely pad in Patriarch's Ponds, in the historical centre of the city. The convenient location made it the perfect spot for their get-togethers. "Don't be silly, I'm not that late." She smiled guiltily, stroking the sleeve of his jacket, which was made of the finest wool.

She was dressed in blue jeans and black T-shirt and fit perfectly into the laid-back interior of the restaurant with its wooden chairs, cast-iron radiators and huge closet at the entrance. An Indian summer was in full swing, and guests tried to get as close as they could to the wide-open windows. The working day was drawing to a close and the streets began to fill with 'strap-hangers', as Katya jokingly called people who travelled in from the suburbs to enjoy the city. The hostess escorted them to their table. Alex, who loved to observe the people around him, sat facing the room.

"Katya will be joining us in a bit, she's just putting her face on. Where are your friends?"

"Parking." Alex was in a bad mood. She had kept him waiting.

"Can imagine how long that will take …"

Parking in the city centre wasn't an easy task and without a driver it turned into an endless tour of the local streets and alleys, driving round in circles in the hope that the owner of some stationary vehicle would eventually deign to leave the area.

Alex watched as a tall figure in a turquoise trench coat pushed through the crush of guests waiting at the entrance to be seated. Men turned their heads, watching the spectacular blonde with the big boobs. Katya was not alone. A small, elegant woman of about thirty-five, dressed in a bright-blue Chanel tweed suit, followed her.

"Hi, Alex!" Katya kissed Alex on the cheek. "Here I am. I met Ella at the entrance. Have you met her?" She turned to Tash.

Tash smiled. "Not yet. Pleasure to meet you."

"And this is her boyfriend, Alex." Katya sat down next to him. Ella had no choice but to sit in the empty seat opposite.

Tash examined the newcomer with curiosity. Thick brown hair, nice face with flawless skin. Nothing remarkable – apart from, perhaps, her pearly white teeth. Ella looked like she was doing a PhD in the philosophy department. All that was lacking to complete the look was a pair of horn-rimmed spectacles. Her behaviour was impeccable – she pronounced all her words correctly, never swore, and when the waiter poured wine she could have easily won an Oscar for the look of horror in her eyes. Ella was especially enthusiastic about her career. She had written several books "at a very young age". This led her to the realisation that being a scribbler wasn't her calling, but directing was; it was here that she "finally found her way to express herself". She prattled on about the challenges of directing, about her constant wandering between the continents, about the script of her latest film and about the "empty vessel of her soul …". Her monologue was as enthusiastic as it was long, and Alex's friends, who'd joined them at the table, began exchanging glances, hoping that someone would dare to interrupt her and change the topic.

But Ella wasn't bothered about them. She'd found a grateful listener and dedicated her lecture on Hollywood exclusively to Alex. He couldn't take his eyes off her. Wise, mature … She agreed with his every comment. Her clever grey eyes radiated admiration. He knew that look – young inexperienced provincials and his mother looked at him that way.

Tash pinched Katya discreetly, showing with her eyes that a trip to the loo to analyse the situation was way overdue.

"Will you excuse us?" she said with a smile. "Ella, do you want to come with us to the loo?"

"To the restroom?" Ella asked indifferently, obviously considering 'restroom' to be a much more appropriate choice of word in a restaurant. "No thanks, I'll stay with the guys."

Tash was furious. She was shouting at Katya. "Who the hell does she think she is? What just happened?"

"Tash, I'm so sorry. I had no idea it would turn out that way." Katya bit her lip, and looked guiltily at Tash. "I met her a few times in Paris, with her then husband, and ran into her just now at the entrance. So I invited her to have dinner with us ... Sorry."

"To have dinner, you say? She just pounced on Alex like a hungry dog! He's such an idiot!"

Katya was happy that the fit of rage had passed and her friend's face had become Confucian calm.

Tash looked in the mirror. A playful tomboy smiled back at her. She pictured a dapper narcissist and a thrilled PhD student who had just shamelessly flirted with each other at the table, and she grinned at her new find.

"I don't even know what annoys me more – the arrogance of the post-grad in her grandmother's Chanel suit or the rudeness of the dandy? Or maybe it's all for the best? I swear they deserve each other!" After Sardinia, Tash and Alex, still hot from the Italian sun, went in at the deep end, but the smouldering embers of their Mediterranean passion didn't last long. The stock of adoration and praise was exhausted, and Tash couldn't follow Nick's strategic advice any more. The capricious child in Alex turned into a despot and suppressed any attempts to challenge his right to rule as he saw fit.

She turned to Katya. "You know, I just realised: I haven't loved him even for a second. It's all Nick with his moralising! The only thing Alex needs is adoration, it feeds him! But now it's the post-grad's turn! Let's not go back to the table ... Let's just run away and have some fun ... That would be a great way to end a relationship!"

Alex watched from his seat as Katya and Tash walked towards the exit. Right in front of the door, Tash turned around, reviewed the mise en scène one final time, and, to enhance the dramatic effect, blew Alex a kiss.

"I want to get drunk," Tash shouted, as the door slammed shut behind them. People passing by nodded approvingly, supporting the plan. She couldn't stop smiling. "Let's go to a bar!"

The bar was just starting to fill up. Behind a neon-lit counter with multicoloured bottles stood two bored bartenders.

"Four tequilas!"

Katya looked at Tash in horror.

"I just broke up with my boyfriend." She tried to look sad.

"OK, I don't mind. Tequila it is! I only live next door anyway."

The bartender masterfully poured four shots of tequila as guys on both sides applauded and cheered. Six shots later, the girls were discussing the characteristic features of Russian architecture with some Turkish builders who were standing to their right. The bar was packed by now and Tash had to scream in the builder's ear to make herself heard over the loud music. Thoughts of Alex and Ella had vanished entirely from her mind. As she danced with one of the builders, it was a bright and happy future that she saw ahead of her. While Tash was considering a move to Turkey with the builder, Katya set about networking on the other side of the bar. The number of tequila shots, in consequence, was increasing exponentially. "Two more tequilas."

"Make it four instead," said a voice from behind. The bartender poured the tequila into shot glasses. Tash took two glasses from the bar and turned to hand one to Katya.

"Is that one for me?"

She looked up. His mischievous gaze worked its way slowly down her face, settling boldly on her mouth. She felt a chill in her upper lip and ran her tongue over it …

For all the innocence of what she was doing, he knew that he had never seen anything sexier in all his life than those lips. This time she didn't look like a mermaid, but rather like an inexperienced freshman who had hit the alcohol a bit too hard. Her luscious lips were so tempting. They aroused his basest desires. He pulled himself together, adjusted a strand of his dark blond curls and smiled.

Tash had an urge to pinch herself, to make sure he wasn't a figment of her imagination brought on by a sudden tequila-induced delirium tremens.

"Nice to see you, Mermaid!" He drained his glass.

Tash had no choice but to follow his example. "What are you doing here?" she stammered. All the while her mind was working feverishly: *Why the hell did I have to bump into him after ten shots of tequila?* She wanted to dematerialise so he wouldn't see her in such an indecorous state. She lowered her eyes and tried to slip unnoticed, as it seemed to her, through the crowd. But her manoeuvre failed.

He blocked her way, laughing. "Think you're going to run away from me again? Forget it." He put his arm round her shoulders and held her close.

But she no longer wanted to run. She had calmed down now and looked up obediently.

"Come, I'll introduce you to my friends." He took the remaining glasses from the bar. "Where is your friend?"

Tash was pleasantly surprised that the only feminine presence at the table was an untouched Veuve Clicquot. As the turquoise trench coat swung open with each introduction of its owner to these new friends, Tash managed to pinch herself in every available part of her body to finally make herself believe that this wasn't all a dream.

"Nice to meet you, Katya. I'm Ben." He turned to Tash. "I think it's finally time for us to meet?"

"Natasha," Tash whispered.

"Like Natasha Rostova." Ben put a glass of whiskey on the table. "So we finally meet."

Meanwhile, Katya was enlightening Ben's friend about her outstanding modelling career in New York.

"And so-o, I became a to-o-p mo-o-del" – after ten tequilas Katya was stretching her vowels somewhat – "and then I moved to Moscow. And now I live a sto-o-o-ne's throw from here." To keep her balance, she was holding on to the back of a chair. "I suggest we go-o back to my place."

That's what Tash most wanted to hear.

"You want to go?" she asked, in a low voice.

"Anywhere with you," he said, just as softly, and put his hand on her waist.

*****

The marble worktop was crammed with a variety of delicacies from which Katya and Tash had to quickly make snacks that were at least on a par with anything the best chefs in the land could create. After all, the way to a man's heart was through his stomach. And there were as many as five of them in Katya's living room.

"Did you twig who it is? Who Ben is?"

Yes, Katya remembered Ben perfectly well from Sardinia. Despite occasional lapses in her random access memory brought on by tequila consumption, her long-term memory worked flawlessly. Tash hastily laid out cheese on a plate. She wanted to finish the appetisers quickly and rush back into the living room, so that this time she wouldn't miss out on her sudden good luck.

The snacks were devoured instantly and Tash went out to prepare some more.

"Let me help you." Ben stood up, like this was the cue he'd been waiting for.

As soon as she crossed the threshold of the kitchen, Tash felt his hands on her shoulders. He kicked the door shut and eagerly pulled her towards him. She picked up the familiar delicate scent of sandalwood. She could feel every beat of his heart. His fingers played with strands of her hair, delicately, like a musician teasing the strings of a precious violin. Her arms wrapped themselves around his neck, and her hips pressed snugly against him. Only a few millimetres separated them from the kiss.

"Fate keeps pushing us together." Ben's lips edged closer to hers. She always knew what his lips would taste like. A new, unfamiliar feeling swept through her body. He held her tighter. She was overwhelmed, blown away by this new emotion. Heat from somewhere deeply visceral flowed like volcanic lava throughout her body.

"Well, well, well, we are hungry!" A loud voice from the doorway brought Tash back to earth.

"C'mon. D-o-o-n't be shy. Everyone twigged what you're up to here. Ha! Your friend James is taking bets on how lo-o-ong you'll be cutting the salami," Katya said and opened the refrigerator. "You'd better help me ..."

Like two somnambulists they took the plates and followed her. Ben's friends were playing backgammon. James was chit-chatting near the window, holding a glass of wine.

"I caught them. Ja-a-mes, you wo-o-on!" Katya put the plates on the table. Everyone except Tash and Ben burst out laughing.

"Ben, I had a bet with Katya that you'd kiss. Katya argued it would never happen – Tash would never do it with a stranger." James stepped away from the window and sat on the sofa next to Katya. "Now Katya owes me a kiss."

Katya took James's face in both hands and pulled it closer. The kiss lasted exactly five seconds, after which she went back to eating her salami as if nothing had happened.

They talked forever. Ben told her everything – about his work, and his family, and that he was leaving the next morning. For a month.

"I didn't want to go out, but James persuaded me. Didn't want to drink before tomorrow's …" – he looked at his watch – "… today's flight."

Tash lay across his knees on a big green sofa. He ran his fingers through the soft locks of her hair.

"I thought about you …"

Tash looked up at him as he held her hand tightly in both of his own.

"Why didn't you find me before? I told you which apartment to bring my suitcases to." Her face flushed with embarrassment. "And then, in Sardinia?"

"You want the truth?" He ran an index finger across her face, stopping at the corner of her lips. "I asked the concierge who owned apartment twenty-seven." Ben lightly pressed a finger on the hollow on her lower lip. "He told me that Mr. Hugh Young and his wife lived there." Tash trembled at his every touch. "There was a man with you on the boat, and in Sardinia you were also sitting with a guy."

It was her first memory of Alex tonight. Bless Katya for bringing Ella!

*****

She was awakened – at 1 p.m. – by the sound of laughter coming from the living room. Her head was pounding, her throat was dry. "I wonder how much I had to drink?" Under the weight of dusty sacks stuffed with bricks, and through the din of rusty rails screeching in her head, she could make out two opposing feelings. One was unpleasant. It made her chest constrict, her temples throb and her hands clench. *Is it from the tequila?* The other feeling was a pleasant one; it relaxed her facial muscles so that her mouth spread itself into a silly grin. *So, the unpleasant one is because Alex dumped me. Or did I dump him? Rather, he dumped me, and I left him straight afterwards. And the pleasant one …?* She thought for a second and a grin formed and lingered on her face, which was still puffy from the night before. *Oh yes, I met Ben!*

Tash opened the door of the guest bedroom and pootled along in the direction of the voices. From the kitchen came the clatter of dishes, and in the living room, which was bathed in autumn sunlight, a brunette was reclining on a green quilted couch. Faina Rozman was years older than Tash. Her weekend attire of simple grey trousers and a turtleneck immediately marked her out as a white-collar professional.

"Seems it was hot in here last night!" Faina stared at Tash, who was standing barefoot on the oak herringbone parquet floor, her hair still dishevelled from her unscheduled lie-in. Warm rays of September sun caressed her white body through a translucent pink nightgown. Always with her lawyer's instincts, Tash thought, returning Faina's stare.

Faina had had to miss their eventful dinner last night. An hour-long meeting had dragged on until midnight and, exhausted, she'd gone straight home. A newly made partner of a big international law firm, she oversaw the IPO of one of the largest metallurgical companies. She had been waiting on the promotion for the past three years, but only secured her place at the top of the legal Olympus when a friend of her father, a famous Israeli billionaire, agreed to do an offering through them. Faina had it all: natural intelligence and business acumen. Her ability to bring deals and wealthy clients to the company made her an indispensable asset of the firm. She could lead an idle life, jetting around the world on her own plane. But ambitious by nature, Faina had chosen for herself a different path: she'd prefer victories in the boardroom to any in the bedroom. At the same time she couldn't stand women like herself, finding them extremely boring. She preferred the company of stunning models, who brought fun and excitement into her life. She wasn't beautiful herself, a heavy jaw made her face somewhat masculine. But Faina enjoyed extraordinary success with men, nevertheless – there were many who appreciated her sharp mind, her insight and her connections. In her youth she had leapt into marriage with a fortune hunter who started cheating on her from the very day of their wedding. After a few years he realised there was no way he was going to get close to her father's cash so he ditched her for some second-rate singer. Following that, the scales fell from Faina's eyes for good. From the bitter experience of her ill-fated marriage she learned to understand and see through people – a skill which had served her well many times thereafter.

"You can't imagine, Mummy. Don't even know where to start …" Tash sank into a chair and stifled a yawn as she tried to gather her thoughts. Her nipples looked even pinker through the pink fabric of the peignoir. "First, I broke up with Alex. Katya, please bring us some coffee," she shouted through to the kitchen. "I'm falling asleep …"

"I'm all ears." Faina spoke with a strong accent. Her father had emigrated from the USSR to Israel during the second wave of emigration and met her mother there. Faina was born in Haifa and only learned Russian at school.

"It all started when our mutual friend, who is now innocently preparing the coffee, brought a certain Ella to dinner." Tash chuckled. "She dressed like my grandmother and had the look of a post-grad who seduced high school boys—"

"Not Ella Becker?" Faina grinned.

"Yes, yes, it was her," shouted a voice from the kitchen.

Faina listened carefully to Tash's chronicle of the previous night's events.

"Mummy, you know Ella?" Tash asked.

"I met her a while ago. She wasn't a director then. I'll tell you sometime."

Katya came in carrying a tray, and the aroma of fresh coffee filled the room. Tash jumped out of the chair and grabbed a cup.

"I love you girls so much! I haven't been in such a great mood for a long while! Katyusha, thank you for bringing her! In the end, Alex will have his post-grad and I'll get my Ben!"

Holding a saucer in one hand and a cup in the other, Tash performed a pirouette.

Just like a Renoir ballerina, Faina thought. Then she asked, "Wait a minute … And who is this Ben? Looks like I've missed something."

Tash put her cup on the table, flopped down on the couch next to Faina, put both arms round her so that Faina felt the warmth of her body, and said with a laugh, "What a silly girl you are, Mummy. My Ben …"

And Tash again told her everything about Ben, making sure she didn't miss out a single detail.

"If Ella hadn't joined us," she added with a sigh, "I wouldn't have broken up with Alex and I'd never have met Ben again. Just imagine!"

Faina imagined. She knew very well that if Tash hadn't met Ben, they would have been sitting here now discussing how to get Alex back.

4. Sex education

Moscow

She read the invitation again: *Dinner is served at 20:30.* The taxi was late, but she still had another hour and a half to stop by Katya's.

The door was unlocked, and she walked in to find Katya at her favourite activity: admiring herself in one of the mirrors tactically placed throughout the apartment, reminding the owner how beautiful she was. Katya greeted Tash and then glanced at the TV screen on the opposite wall and sighed. "Why can't we ever meet such men?" She was referring to the smiling face of Tom Brady, who talked to a reporter after the game.

"Well, you have to be a Gisele to meet a Tom." Tash had to admit the handsome quarterback looked as if he'd just stepped off the cover of the magazine.

"Ouch. I'm a much better model than Gisele, and I'm younger too."

Tash's phone chirped. A silly smile lit up her face, her eyes sparkled, then blinked nervously. She always blinked when she was excited. She read the text out in a trembling voice: "Hi, hope you're well. I'm back. What are you up to? Ben."

"Isn't that the first message he's sent in a month?" Katya's voice brought Tash back to reality.

"Yep." Tash sighed as she re-read the note in anticipation of responding. "Now Ben is a Tom Brady, just as smart and just as handsome."

During Ben's absence, Tash had managed to endow him with all earthly and heavenly virtues, a kind of knight in shining armour.

Katya finished her makeup and moved to the dressing room.

"I agree with the second point," she shouted from there, "but remind me what exactly makes him smart? You barely talked."

"He graduated from Harvard." Tash emphasised the word Harvard. The storied school completed the perfect image she had created of him. The myth that intelligence depended on university rank was firmly embedded in her head. "He studied literature."

Katya appeared in the doorway with three outfits on padded hangers: a black silk trouser suit, a short gold brocade dress and a blue jumpsuit.

"And?" she said indifferently. She shook her head, dropped two outfits on the couch and squeezed into the golden mini.

Katya would never put too much value into a person's education. In her humble experience, most rich men – she didn't notice the rest – had either mediocre education or no education at all, which did not bother her. She started working at seventeen and always regarded university as a waste of four years.

By her twenty-eighth birthday, she had achieved incomparably more than many of her peers who graduated from the best universities. The fame she achieved in fashion and a luxury apartment acquired with her own money only confirmed her theory. Even after a decade in New York, she still got confused between Columbia (University) and Colombia (the country), but most of the men around her were captivated by her blonde hair and big boobs and didn't care about anything else. As one suitor once said, "Beauty is above genius, because it does not require understanding."

"Remind me what he does?"

That, along with "how much does he earn?" was Katya's favourite question.

"He's investing in renewable energy," Tash answered breathlessly. "He has such an interesting story."

She made herself comfortable to tell her friend everything she knew about Ben, but there was very little information to share. His last post on Facebook was from 2010, and Instagram had only a few picturesque landscapes published once a year. She studied all his followings, most of which were private, under a magnifying glass, but didn't find anything particularly negative. He didn't like whores' pictures and didn't follow porn accounts. The scant information that she managed to get from social media in no way compromised him.

"He was born in Botswana. His parents were there with the Red Cross; they taught local kids art and English. When it was time for him to attend school, the entire family returned to England. He told me what a mischief he was and the hard times he gave his tutors at Eton."

Katya couldn't resist a smile when Tash unintentionally emphasised the name of the elite boarding school, like it held some kind of magic spell.

"He went from Windsor to Boston, and then after Harvard, he returned home to England. He's worked on various renewable energy projects around the world, and now he's involved in some kind of a solar panel venture here in Moscow." She pronounced every word about Ben with an exceptional pride, putting special significance in his achievements. "But his dream is to return to Africa and, like his parents, help the poor."

Katya looked at Tash and shrugged. "He must be incredibly rich to afford such a luxury. It's like the poor little rich girls who say: 'All I want is to drink wine, save animals and have a nap.'"

Katya envisioned a bored man in a khaki Ralph Lauren safari ensemble, sipping a glass of chilled chardonnay while watching elephants wander around a large white tent in the middle of the desert.

"Okay. Enough about Ben," Katya said as she modelled the form-fitting dress and waited for feedback from her friend. "I have to decide what to wear. I still can't fully get Moscow style."

Years in the industry made Katya a connoisseur of the world's fashion styles and trends. She knew that you could spot bold cuts and flashy colours in London or Milan, but never in New York and Paris, which had showcased a rather bohemian look like no one cared. On her return from New York she couldn't comprehend how Moscow with Red Square and the cake-like St. Basil's Cathedral remained in the simple non-flashy camp.

The only legit explanation of this phenomenon was given by the judicious Faina, who today celebrated her fortieth birthday. "The glamour of the primary capital accumulation in the late nineties and the unprecedented economic growth of the early and mid-2000s were replaced by anti-glamour trends after the financial crisis of 2008. Restraint was due to oversaturation and fatigue, orientation towards a more democratic European culture, as well as the general deterioration of the economic situation and the welfare of citizens."

Out of all the words Faina said, Katya recognised only two, "glamour" and "anti-glamour". But the explanation sounded so convincing that she took notes, memorised it and put it here and there into convos about fashion with men who seemed to be intellectuals to her.

*****

The space so familiar from Tash's childhood looked so different today, more elegant. How many times had Daddy brought her here on tours, and Grandmother forced her to attend lectures, saying that "every decent girl must understand art". The solemn colonnade of the Corinthian order dazzled with splendour. The hem of her dress, made of the finest flesh-coloured tulle and covered with Swarovski crystals, dragged along the pink marble of the main staircase of the Pushkin Museum of Fine Arts.

Men following Tash could not take their eyes off her chiselled silhouette, like she just descended from the ancient Greek frescoes that framed the friezes on the ceiling. Women whispered enviously, discussing the frivolity of her diaphanous design.

Faina was greeting her guests on the upper flight. She looked like a giant firebird sitting on the top of a mountain in her shiny blue dress. "You look adorable!" she said, before kissing Tash on the lips.

A dinner for two hundred was served in the museum's White Hall. Daddy had once told her that it was entirely copied from the inside of the Parthenon. Tash floated through the hall imagining herself a guest at a feast in Ancient Greece. Like a hetaira in a transparent toga crowned with a golden tiara, Tash's long hair fell in curls around her shoulders.

Long tables with white tablecloths were set along the marble colonnade. Tash found her name on the card and glanced at the cards on either side. As expected, she didn't recognise the other names. Faina was an over-achiever. Her frantic energy splattered like a fountain and sometimes it worried Tash. It seemed she was just running away from something she was too scared to admit. Even for her own birthday, the pragmatic birthday girl had seated the guests in a way that everyone would leave the venue with a feeling of no time wasted, whether it was a useful contact, new love or just a pleasant impression from an entertaining conversation.

Tash's neighbour on the right happened to be a handsome man who introduced himself as Sasha. Half an hour later, Tash knew the story of his life. Sasha was from the Far Eastern part of Russia and served as vice-governor of the region. He didn't aspire to big politics, but his proximity to the governor made him the right person to manage government contracts for the development of the region, with a huge budget. He also had shares in a crab-catching company founded with the governor's son, which, by a happy coincidence, received the largest catching quotas from the state. He was in his late thirties, flashed a Breguet on his wrist and a wedding ring on his ring finger, which didn't stop him from flirting with Tash.

After dinner, the party moved to the atrium, where less-privileged guests invited only to the drinks were greeted by the hostess. Bryan Ferry, a long-time family friend and a favourite of Faina's dad, sang "Slave to Love" seductively to the beautiful crowd. Tash was swaying near the bar, entertaining Faina's colleagues with the story of how the two had become friends years earlier when Faina walked right into Tash at a bar, spilling a full glass of red wine all over her snow-white blouse. "That's why I'll only drink champagne in her presence," Tash joked. "Well, unless I'm wearing red!" And with that she cheered the others and downed her fifth glass of bubbly. The liquid courage was what she needed to finally message Ben.

When the crooner finished his performance, a DJ took over and his hip-hop mix encouraged the guests to pack the dance floor. Tash squeezed through dancing couples before she could look for her friends at the tables, which were set along the perimeter of the atrium. Faina saw Tash first and waved her over to where she was sitting with Katya.

"I hope you don't mind, but I invited Ben." Tash landed on a chair next to her friend.

Faina's cheeks were flushed from alcohol. She moved closer and, trying to be heard above the music, screamed in her ear, "Of course! Now I'll be able to see what it is that you find in him! Let's have fun! It's my birthday! Yay!" Faina slapped Tash's bum and then her hand squeezed her buttocks and slowly slid down. Tash looked at the tipsy birthday girl, who seemed oblivious to her actions, and then to Katya, who sat distractedly beside her.

Katya had chosen a blue jumpsuit revealing her gorgeous back to the respectable men sitting at the table next to them. With one contemptuous glance, Katya dismissed the young guys crowded around her on the dance floor hoping to get her attention. Tash looked sympathetically at the unfortunate ones, desperately trying to win Katya's favour, when suddenly her gaze stopped on one of the faces. The curls had grown since she saw him last, and now they covered his forehead completely. His blue eyes tenaciously followed her movements. "You look stunning." He pulled her closer and kissed her. "Let's get out of here," he whispered in her ear.

Against her principles and all reasonable arguments that came to mind, Tash wanted to just give in and follow him. He didn't try to win her over or to please her, and Tash found his relaxed manner disarming. He was so confident in what he wanted that she grinned and thought, *at least I know he just wants to sleep with me.*

The sparse apartment smelled of sandalwood. High stucco ceilings, minimal furniture and a few posters from the Soviet era. There was nothing personal here, except, perhaps, the PlayStation and a small selection of toiletries.

Tash grabbed a cashmere blanket from the chair in the living room and walked out onto the balcony. She looked down. A thin layer of snow covered the frozen ground, and a yellow stripe of the Garden Ring shone bright in the darkness. It looked like a postcard. Cars moving in opposite directions in an orderly fashion added dynamics to the otherwise static view of Moscow at night. The noise of the street drowned out the music.

"Friends brought the freshest burrata from Italy, and I also have bread and red wine," Ben shouted from the living room.

The cold, almost wintery, wind cut her to the bone. She looked through the window inside the room and watched Ben pour the red into the glasses, carefully comparing the amount of wine in each. He cut the bread and neatly arranged slices in a basket and the cheese on a plate. He brought it all to the living room, adjusted pillows on the sofa and lit candles. Frozen and touched, Tash returned to warmth. She took off the blanket and sank deeply into the brown tufted chair. The light was playing with the crystals on her dress.

"You look like a real fairy from a fairy tale." Ben put his drink down on the coffee table.

I'd rather be a princess," Tash smirked to herself. But this thought, barely conceived, immediately disappeared under the rush of warmth spreading throughout her body from the touch of his wet lips. Her heart was pounding.

He cupped her face in his hands and kissed her passionately. Then he pulled her hair back and ran his tongue along the nape of her neck. Tash felt how his other hand was softly sliding up her thighs.

He knelt in front of her and squeezed her tight buttocks with both hands.

"From the first meeting I knew you had an excellent ass!"

Tash grabbed the arm of the chair in anticipation as he lifted the dress with an abrupt movement so it gathered in folds and pushed aside her nude silky shorts. She felt the moisture of his tongue as he explored her inner lips, now wet and hot from his kisses. She suddenly felt dizzy. Unable to cope with overwhelming feelings, she moaned with pleasure.

"We won't need this piece of clothing any more." He quickly pulled off her shorts and returned to pleasing her.

Each time when she felt herself on the verge of orgasm, he slowed down, switching to innocent kisses down her thighs. He sometimes bowed before her as if she was his queen, obeying her royal orders, before he started teasing her, like an obstinate subject who had suddenly usurped power.

"Take off your clothes!" Ben got up. Only now did she realise that he was still fully dressed.

Tash complied. She unzipped the dress and pulled it over her head. Naked and drunk, she looked up at him, awaiting further instructions. Ben picked her up and carried her to the sofa. With a quick movement, Tash unbuckled his belt and was about to move on, but he stopped her.

He caught her hand. "Not so fast, I'm not done with you yet." And he knelt down in front of her again.

"Baby, you're so good. I know that it will only get better." That's how Ben summed up an hour and a half of continuous passion. Tash tried to get up off the sofa to get her shorts.

"Please don't. Don't put them on. I can't stop looking at you." Ben pulled her hand and deftly laid her back on the sofa. She didn't resist. She liked being in his arms, she liked feeling his breath on her neck, she liked feeling him inside her.

"I've been waiting for burrata for two hours, and still no sign of it. Let me go to the shower." She made a second attempt to get up.

"No," he said firmly. "You are going to lie here with me, wet and sweaty, until we fall asleep exhausted." Hugging her shoulders, he entered her again.

After another hour, he dozed off. Tash took a shower, quietly picked up her clothes scattered all over the floor without waking him and slipped out onto the stairwell.

*****

Tash zipped up her trousers and looked in the mirror. Her silver dress from yesterday was dangling on a hanger suspended from the handle of a wooden wardrobe. Flashbacks from last night were twinkling in her head. But whichever fragment she tried to focus on led her back to the exhilarating memory of making love with Ben. She bent over to tie the laces on her boots, and her panties got wet remembering how he took her from behind. His touch was enough to bring her to orgasm. She ran her hand over the rough surface of her jacket, imagining his barely grown stubble. The cold key in her hands reminded her of how he'd kissed her frozen fingers. Tash smiled. She was late for Faina's lunch, but because of the surging memories, she could not leave the house for a good hour.

The first person she saw was Katya. Instead of greeting Tash, she shot her a cold glance. Katya's straightforwardness was intimidating.

"Look who's here." Katya looked at her from under her long bangs. "Could you kindly explain to us where you disappeared to last night?"

"You know the answer." Tash sat at the table, choosing which of the snacks would work best with her current state.

"And how about the rule of the fifth date?"

One of their girlfriends, who had just received an honours degree in the online course "How to marry the guy of your dreams" had revealed to them the biggest secrets of the universe that led to a walk down the aisle. Rule number one claimed that sex before a fifth proper date was a recipe for failure. Tash hadn't even made it to the first.

"Did he even bring you breakfast in bed?" The condemnation in Katya's eyes was replaced by curiosity.

"I didn't stay the night," Tash admitted.

Rule number two of the same course forbade all ladies from staying the night with their future husbands in order to create an illusion of independence.

"Smart move. The less passion you express, the more passion you excite," Katya said between bites of beet and herring salad.

Tash wasn't so sure she had done the right thing leaving Ben to sleep alone. She re-checked her phone. *Why hasn't he messaged yet?*

*****

"You tore me inside!" She looked in horror at the puddle of blood on the sheets, which was gradually seeping into the mattress. "Grandmother will kill me!"

Tash jumped off the bed and ran into the bathroom roaring. "Katya promised it would be cool!" The pain subsided, but blood was still running down her legs.

Tash had met Alyosha at the end of June. He was nineteen and handsome, and had quickly passed Katya's inspection. However, Tash knew her grandmother had strict ideas about a worthy boyfriend and her approval would be much harder to gain, so she kept him away from their home and kept their relationship a secret. She set up meetings with her new beau only outside Peredelkino. While Grandmother Hannah thought her granddaughter was attending lectures at the Pushkin Museum of Art, Tash rushed to meet Alyosha at his uni to wander around Moscow together. Had Hannah shown a little more vigilance, she could easily have caught them kissing on a bench in Gorky Park or smoking weed on Arbat. But naïve Hannah could not get enough of her granddaughter's passion for art history. A month passed and kissing alone was clearly not enough. By this time, they had studied each other's bodies so well that the question of when hung in the air. Tash knew Alyosha was an experienced lover because he often boasted of his sexual conquests.

Naum lived two houses away and studied at MGIMO at the Faculty of International Relations. Everyone knew he fancied Tash. His black hair, stiff as springs, reminded her of a bird's nest, and his skin was always shiny. Naum was pleasantly surprised to see Tash on the doorstep of his dacha. She asked him to help set up her computer, and he hurried back to her home with her.

Naum could not take his eyes off her long legs, barely covered by a defiantly short chequered skirt, as they sat on her bed. A fat fly was flying around the computer.

Naum never understood how it happened, but Tash's hand miraculously ended up on his penis. The erection was so strong that his jeans were swollen and squeezed his crotch painfully. He unzipped his fly, and Tash's head slid down …

When he opened his eyes, Tash was sitting next to him, watching the fly flying over the blood stain on the sheet. He tried to hug her, but she pushed him away and rushed into the bathroom screaming and blaming him. Naum didn't know what exactly he'd done to upset her. He knocked timidly on the door, but heard only sobs in response. Before leaving, he tried his luck once again and asked what was wrong with her computer, but since there was no answer, he walked home confused.

Tash felt like a dirty whore and cried all night. But by the morning the thought that she was now ready for Alyosha overcame the shame. She called Alyosha and they hurried up to his small apartment in the suburbs. As soon as he realised that she was not a virgin and all this time she had just been playing him, he coldly informed her that he was leaving on vacation for a month. The next Saturday she saw him at the club with a striking blonde of about twenty-five.

Naum called several times inquiring about computer, but Tash refused to leave her room, claiming poor health.

*****

"The only thing he mentioned," Tash tried to remember his precise wording, "was that he really liked it."

"That's brief. Although, of course, he should have called as soon as he woke up and did not find you nearby."

Keeping up with Katya's courtship expectations wasn't an easy task.

"By the way, Faina and I had an amazing time without you. Your dinner neighbour Sasha entertained us all night."

For some reason Katya and Sasha's union didn't surprise Tash at all. He ticked all the boxes of Katya's ideal man – relatively young, relatively rich, apparently generous and very married. Katya had always been a real courtesan of the modern days. She belonged to the type that, regardless of their love of money, was awfully afraid of losing their independence. And if you dared to enquire why on earth they needed independence so much, you'd hear something like how good it was to rely on yourself, to have no one to be accountable to, etc., when in fact it all could be boiled down to a simple truth: "What if I miss someone better because of my current relationship?"

Faina's birthday lunch was held in her father's estate outside of Moscow. It was a much more casual affair than last night's event. Lev Rozman resided in Tel Aviv with his wife and usually only visited the Russian capital alone. Most of his business assets were there, along with his twenty-year-old mistress, Angelica.

Children were scurrying around the long, food-laden table. Married matrons, keeping an eye on their riotous offspring, gossiped about their acquaintances, discussed their latest interior design lectures and their absolute need to redo their homes, shared experiences about their unfailing dedication to yoga and the latest low-calorie diets, while simultaneously stuffing their faces with the most fattening dishes from the table.

At the opposite end of the table, their husbands were sampling fine wines from Lev's cellar, discussing business projects and joking about their affairs. Each of them had at least one mistress, of which their wives were very well aware. The men managed to skilfully manoeuvre between family and extra-curricular activities, juggling their schedule masterfully. Evenings, weekends, holidays and long family trips belonged to the family. Mistresses settled for lunches and hour-long trysts in a fully paid-for or, if lucky, purchased apartment. The men popped in looking for consolation after a gruelling day at work, to watch football or just to hang out while their child was kicking the ball at an after-school lesson. The mistresses also got to go on business trips.

For holidays and vacations, mistresses often got together and drove, flew or sailed away to exotic resorts in cars, planes and boats rented or bought for them by their generous lovers. There, the women endlessly searched for "normal relationships", but for some reason, they had never been found.

The delicate balance suited each side of the triangle. Wives had stability, family and status; mistresses had independence, fun and money; and husbands had love, support and sex.

"I just can't stand this facade!" Katya said as she looked sceptically at the women, talentedly performing the roles of diligent wives assigned to them. "They probably go shopping together on weekends and walk around as exemplary couples. And afterwards he" – Katya pointed at a man about forty-five years old with greying hair – "drops his son off at theatre class and then rushes to bang Dusya from Lipetsk while his wife is cooking dinner for her *happy* family."

Faina appeared at the doorway in a black trouser suit. She landed next to Tash and hugged her shoulders. "You left without saying goodbye, but I did manage to grasp that he looked like a real thoroughbred stallion." Faina's arm stayed on Tash's shoulders. "How did it go?"

Tash chuckled at her friend's precision. Memories of his muscular body lightened up her face: her eyes sparkled, her cheeks flushed and her lips spread into a dreamy smile. The phone chirped on the table.

"I bet it's him," Katya said affirmatively. "Let me read it!"

Tash obeyed and passed Katya the phone.

Katya read out loud: "I'm at a very important business dinner and am knackered. By the way, you were amazing." Katya passed the phone to Faina. "Uh, 'by the way'?"

"Maybe he's just shy," Tash suggested timidly, trying to hide her disappointment.

"Of course, that's it. He is shy!" Katya was indignant. "Read between the lines: 'By the way, you were awesome, but actually, I'm really tired, and how I feel is the most important thing. I didn't write to you all day because I had no time for you, and now I am sitting at an unusually important dinner with a friend, since no self-respecting business associate would never spend their precious weekends with me.'"

"Oh, stop scaring her. It's not that bad." Faina defended Ben with a laugh. "It can easily mean something else: 'I'm just home watching TV, but I want to look in demand, so I'm pretending to be at dinner. I have to message after sex because I'm a gentleman. Moreover, regular sex is essential. And since I'm not in great demand, but sex is in demand, I'd like to message you, so you can supply my demands.' I'm just surprised he didn't message you earlier."

Faina and Katya were choking with laughter.

"We are so cynical. Imagine if everyone said what they really think? Instead of 'I love you so much, baby,' they'd say, 'I'm dying to sleep with you.'"

Katya made a funny face. "'Darling, you are so sexy' really means 'I think that by inflating your ego, you will buy me this ring.'"

"Or here's another one." Faina lowered her voice, trying to sound like a man, and said, "'I'm not ready for a serious relationship. I'm overwhelmed with work and there is simply no time to think about something other than work at the moment' means 'I like sleeping with you, but in a couple of years I'm planning to marry the boss's twenty-year-old daughter.'"

"I came up with a better one," Katya almost shouted. "She says, 'Darling, it was the best sex of my life,' but really she means, 'By extolling your cock, I will always win against your wife because she tells you the truth that in bed you are zero.'"

There was a dead silence at the table. Only now did Katya realise that while they were generating examples, the husbands had rejoined their wives and all had been quietly and attentively listening to their conversation.

"Well, we would all choose ignorance if it meant we could live in happiness instead of knowing the painful truth," Tash concluded with a smile.

*****

Tash turned the handle of the front door. The pungent scent of lilies burst into the tiny hallway of her flat. Faina's driver had handed her a bouquet and a small silver package. Tash tossed the gifts on the mirrored table and glanced at the clock. She wasn't even close to being ready. She couldn't shake off the strange aftertaste from the conversation with her friends and replayed it in her head.

"Why did Western women start all this?" Katya was admiring her magnificent cleavage. "As a result, men have gone unforgivably lazy and truly believe that we women owe them something!"

"In modern society, views on gender identity have changed radically," Faina intervened. "If back in the days, the majority were cisgender, now more and more people are becoming transgender."

Katya rolled her eyes.

"It has even become fashionable. In Israel, the gender system is not binary," Faina continued.

Tash immediately noticed Katya's confusion and hastened to translate Faina's speech into more accessible language. "Faina means that more and more men do not identify themselves with the male sex and, accordingly, women with the female."

Tash's explanation made Katya even more confused.

"You mean homosexuals and lesbians?"

Tash laughed. "Not exactly. Everything is much more complicated. Sexuality has nothing to do with gender identity. You can be born a woman, feel like a man, and be sexually attracted to men. Or to women. Or to both." Tash looked at Katya. "Here you are, for example. You were born a woman. You identify yourself as a woman and you love men."

Katya nodded happily, stroking her chest. "Yes, thank god, we are all normal here."

"I would not be so categorical about normality," Faina said calmly.

Tash glanced at Faina. In all the years she'd known her, Tash had never once heard stories about Faina's love life. Most of the time they would be discussing Katya and Tash. Was Faina's busy schedule to blame?

"Is there something you want to tell us?" Tash inquired innocently.

"Not yet." Faina gently smiled at Tash and then turned to Katya. "So what were you saying about emancipation?"

Katya continued, "Yes. Women have been striving for this equality for so long. And now we ended up carrying everything on our shoulders: work and family. From beautiful and vulnerable, we became …" she paused, "… well, you know. And the worst thing is, along the way we confiscated a man's desire to conquer, to protect and to pamper. Everything that makes a man feel like a man!"

Katya would always stop at a door, hoping that some passer-by would open it for her, and only after proving the contrary, would she open it herself.

"Some women put up with a lot out of fear of being alone," Tash interrupted her. "A woman can work to be interesting to her man, to motivate him, so that he respects her and considers her opinion. But I agree, a man should remain a man."

"Exactly! And load his woman with gifts!" Katya chimed in.

Tash laughed.

"Would you be able to sacrifice your career for the sake of a man?" Faina asked unexpectedly.

"You mean to become a trophy wife?" Katya got up from the sofa and slowly sashayed into the kitchen, demonstrating with each step the curves of her perfect body. "And what a trophy!" Her slender figure disappeared through the door.

Faina looked questioningly at Tash.

"I would be able to sacrifice a lot for the sake of the man I loved. A worthy man!" Tash answered, but the question continued to nag at her – was Ben such a man?

*****

It took twenty minutes to choose the jeans. Tash arranged six pairs of blue denim trousers on the bed and wondered which ones she should wear tonight to meet Ben. An ordinary heterosexual man might consider it ridiculous, but every modern woman would sympathise with Tash's torment. High waist or medium rise? Skinny or straight? Dark rinse or indigo? Perhaps invisible to the ordinary eye, but striking to the experienced gaze of a true fashionista.

Next, she set her sights on choosing the perfect fitted white T-shirt, of which Tash had countless.

Finally, she threw a fur coat over her shoulders and ran out of the house. Despite being late evening, everything sparkled around her, as if a stray wizard had wrapped the earth in a silvery veil. Her lacquered boots sunk into loose snowdrifts. Tash walked to her car, which was parked in the neighbouring courtyard. In the hour and half of her "creative" changing, the snow had covered the car with a thick white glaze. Ben must be mad. She should have picked him up an hour ago.

For nearly thirty minutes, she had been watching his face. How he frowned when France scored, how his eyes lit up when England went ahead. In a month of dating Ben, Tash had become so enthralled with rugby that she was happy with every point England scored. They regularly saw each other two or three times a week, which seemed to be the schedule for most modern sexually mature humans in big cities. Lots of sex and little emotion provided the illusion of a relationship.

Tash never stopped admiring his gorgeous body – he was physically perfect and incredibly attentive in bed. However, his excellent physical treats came with a price: a total lack of emotions. He was unwilling or unable to express his feelings. Sometimes she wondered whether he could even express them to himself.

England had earned the fame of the forge of cold hearts for a reason. As soon as Ben had turned seven, his parents had sent him to boarding school, relinquishing their obligation to raise him, while they continued enjoying their life. Eton instilled good manners in the young man and tempered his body and spirit, but it did not teach him emotional literacy.

Ben hugged her. "Mermaid, you're so beautiful. You know ..." he hesitated, "... your jeans are real Etonian blue."

Tash was delighted. She hadn't wasted all that time choosing her outfit after all.

"And what a stunning bracelet. Is it gold?"

"Yes! Imagine, a friend gave it to me today. Delivered by a driver. Strange, isn't it?"

Tash had been caught off guard when she unwrapped Faina's present. When she called her, Faina said that the gold Cartier "Love bracelet" was one of the unwanted birthday gifts she'd received and decided to give away.

"You have wonderful friends!" Ben chuckled, but suddenly his face grew serious. "Uh-huh ... I have to tell you something."

Really? Had she really managed to melt the ice of the northern seas and reach the depths of his insular consciousness?

Ben got up and stepped over to the coffee table. He took a shiny booklet from a pile of papers and returned to his seat.

Tash held her breath. She wondered if this could be a brochure for an upcoming trip he wanted to take her on … or maybe it was for their honeymoon … Tash's heart pounded with anticipation as she fluttered her eyelashes and held her breath.

"Look," he said as he handed her a glossy booklet.

There was a beautiful Victorian house on the cover. Tash was confused. She turned the pages in her hands, waiting for clarification.

"My parents put our house up for sale," Ben said resignedly. "The other day my father called me and asked if I had a job. Imagine!" He tucked a strand of hair behind his ear with a sharp move. "They want to sell the house where I was born, where I grew up, where I spent all my childhood … and he has the nerve to ask if I have a job! They don't even know what work is!"

His eyes were as cold as steel. Tash noticed how new shades of grey sparkled in them. Ben had never let himself go. Tash admired and, to some extent, even envied the notorious English restraint. Now something vaguely resembling despair flashed in the depths of his eyes.

"They spent their whole lives between the Côte d'Azur and our country estate, receiving guests and doing whatever they pleased. And guess what, they spent everything and now I have to work!"

Tash glanced at the booklet again. The price tag underneath the picture was fifteen million pounds.

Ben sat closer and looked at the photos. "This is my room. Here's the room where I kissed a girl for the first time. And we had so many parties there in the garden." One by one, he showed her photographs of the impressive house. "How will I live?"

Tash was perplexed. He reminded her of Ranevskaya from Chekhov's *Cherry Orchard* when she received the news about the sale of her family's garden combined with the crying main character from a third-rate play lamenting that his parents ruined his life and left him broke. The melodrama of the situation amused her so much that she could not help laughing. "Are you kidding?!" She tried to sound as serious as possible. "Baby, you are not even thirty! I guess you better think how to make enough money if you need to buy your parents a new house."

She knew what poverty was. She'd seen it in its ugliest manifestations on Mondays and Thursdays in the art class that Dad organised for children from deprived families. She saw second-hand clothes, exhausted mothers working at three jobs to afford enough food and criminal fathers no one wanted to hire. Tash had started as her father's assistant, but over time she took the place of the teacher by cutting and sewing. She remembered their happy faces when a new item was ready and they could put it on and look no worse than their peers.

After Africa, Ben's father began writing books about his vision for the development of poor areas in Botswana, which nobody read. Ben's mother painted pictures in the Chinese style of chinoiserie, which no one bought. They spent winters in Antibes in the exclusive French Riviera and summers in the picturesque Cotswolds, in central England. In fact, they never spent time at the expensive Victorian house Ben was pining for in London.

"Mermaid, you're right." Ben was smiling again.

5.   Chic overdose

London

What beautiful scenery! Tash admired shimmering tall trees from the car window. Snow covered the ground with a white downy blanket. Golden rays broke through the branches of trees and splintered in the green paws of the pines. She slowed down to enjoy this fabulous view. She couldn't stop smiling. They met almost every day, and every morning, even if they did not spend the night together, he would call to wish her a lovely day.

She jumped the steps and stopped near the long-legged hostess. The hostess checked her out with a bored glance and immediately gave a playful smile to the eligible man standing behind her. Tash chuckled. She searched the room for Ben. He always chose a place in the farthest corner. Wooden planks creaked under her boots. Ben and James got up to let her sit next to the window.

"Let's eat quickly so we can go skating!" Tash looked out on the frozen water of the beautiful Moscow River where women in sable furs practised axels in the middle, while couples glided in long loops around them and men with kids played pick-up hockey at the far end. She couldn't wait to join them, to feel the hardness of fresh ice and breathe in the crisp air as she recaptured the pleasure of her youth.

But instead Tash found herself in a surprising new role, that of mother to a fledgling toddler. Ben was beyond helpless on the ice and held Tash's hand tightly. His legs would slide apart clumsily and he struggled to remain upright. After a few laps of struggling, but miraculously still standing, Ben gave up.

"Mermaid, I'm not sure skating is my thing. Besides, I'd rather admire you from the bar."

After sending her ungraceful partner to the side, she decided to demonstrate her own grace. She had spent years of hardship at ice skating school, while her friends had fun wandering around, but it was about to pay off. Tash accelerated. Her cheeks flushed from the cold as she glided gracefully on the solid surface, attracting rapturous glances.

She pushed off with the tooth of the left skate, turned around its axis and gently landed on the edge of the right. From there, she quickly went into a layback spin. The goal was achieved. The toe loop jump showed her athleticism and the spin her feminine artistry. She glanced at Ben, who had been staring in awe the whole time. She wanted to skate longer, practising all the elements she had learned in her childhood, but a glance at her clumsy partner, wrapped in a wool blanket, made her change her mind.

"Mermaid, that was incredible! You continue to amaze me." Ben gently wrapped her hands with his, warming them after her skating. The smell of cinnamon from the mulled wine filled the air. "I have to fly back to London for Christmas and then to Gstaad on New Year's. I will miss you a lot." He hugged her and then added, "I'll miss these fingers." Ben kissed her hands. "And these delicate hands and this beautiful body." He looked at her slyly. "Will you miss me?"

"Ahh! There you are! Cooing doves," James called out. He looked like a Mexican peasant in a red plaid blanket. The only thing missing was a sombrero. "When is the wedding?"

Tash made a grunting sound and blushed.

"Only after we've raised a glass at *your* wedding," Ben joked in response.

"That means 'never,' knowing what an inveterate bachelor you are, James," Tash added, laughing.

He sat down next to Ben and said, "Ben, I bet you will be married sooner than me."

"And what are you betting?" The mulled wine was having an effect on Ben.

James thought for a moment. "You'll buy me a bottle of Petrus; the year I was born."

"And if I win?" Ben took off his blanket, his face was flushing.

Tash laughed at the two tipsy men who were quickly trying to one up each other.

"I'll do the same."

"Agreed. Tash, you are our witness."

She smiled and nodded. She was glad she had made the right choice in choosing Ben over skating.

"Now you have to be friends with me, at least until the first wedding. There is no escaping him," James joked.

"Escape? Where are you planning to go? It's not that easy to get rid of me, Mermaid!"

Ben hugged her, pulled her closer and then kissed her on the lips.

James was observing the scene playing in front of his eyes. He suddenly got up. "I'm raising the stakes. You will marry sooner than me. And you will marry Tash."

The cunning smile wouldn't leave James's face. Ben was taken aback, but reacted immediately. "What do you bet?"

James blew on his hands, red from the cold. "I will pay for the honeymoon of your choice."

He walked closer to Ben and patted him on the shoulder. Ben couldn't stop laughing.

"Tash, I suggest we get married just to make this idiot pay for our trip."

*****

"I don't want you to leave."

They were watching *Fatal Attraction* on TV.

"If I don't see you for a while, I'll start chasing you like Glenn Close." She raised her head from his knees and looked at him. "Do you have pets?"

"Yes. We have a spaniel, Rocky, in the Cotswolds."

"Well, if you ever leave me or, God forbid, cheat on me, think about your spaniel. Do you want him to end up in the pot?"

"Mermaid, Rocky has nothing to worry about. With your love of animals, I imagine I'd end up in the soup rather than him."

The next morning after dropping Ben at the airport, Tash went straight to Katya.

"He'll be landing soon. I won't see him until next year," she murmured plaintively. She was tracking his flight in real time.

79

"I have a meeting in an hour. Let's take a break from Ben and let him have a pleasant flight." As usual, Faina brought some common sense into their conversation. "Are you coming to Courchevel for New Year's? The house will be empty; my parents are going to Lapland instead."

The Rozmans had built a house in the French Alps fifteen years ago, had spent five consecutive Christmas holidays there and then found this pastime rather monotonous. And since Lev loved variety in everything, he and his wife now celebrated each New Year in a new place.

"We've already promised to stay at the Stowes'—" Katya was interrupted by the sound of Tash's phone. By the smile on her face, everyone knew who was calling.

Like a bullet, Tash burst out to the corridor to answer in private. "Have you landed?" she asked in a soft, low voice.

"Yes, Mermaid. I have an idea." He paused. "Why don't you come here for a couple of days? The weather is wonderful; the sun is shining. You can fly in today and we'll go to your favourite restaurant tonight."

Tash had to lean against the wall to keep her balance. A slight shiver ran through her body and a silly smile froze on her face.

"I'll look at the flights and call you back."

She then returned to her friends and uttered breathlessly, "He invited me to London. Now."

*****

The landing at Heathrow was smooth. Tash got up as soon as the "fasten your seat belts" sign went off. She texted Ben as she was leaving the plane, but it didn't go through.

It was 8:45 pm and she arrived dressed for dinner. If all went according to plan, she would be at the restaurant by 10:15.

She had only brought a carry-on for three days. "Worst case, I'll buy new clothes," Tash said to her friends after Ben's invitation, but then she immediately added with a laugh, "Well, that's not *exactly* the worst case."

She passed passport control and rushed towards the exit to join the taxi queue. Limo drivers lined up with signs trying to locate their passengers, and the heads of relatives peeped out from behind them. A beige woollen dress, high-heeled boots and a blue faux fur jacket made her stand out from the crowd. The drivers exchanged glances, hoping she was their ride.

"Madame, may I give you a ride?"

Tash turned her head and caught her breath. Ben stood before her smiling. "How was your flight?" He gave her a quick kiss on the cheek and took her bag.

"OMG! You came to pick me up."

"Yes. I had a spare hour, so here I am."

Tash was ready to throw herself on his neck and kiss him from head to toe, but she decided to show some restraint in the crowded area. She was in England after all.

They took the elevator to the car park.

"Well done, Mermaid. Didn't expect you'd arrive with just one bag. I thought you would have a lot of luggage, like most girls. I even took a bigger car to be safe." Ben slammed the boot of the Range Rover and opened the front door for her.

"Which other girls?" Tash frowned, showing that there should be no girls with any amount of baggage in his life.

"And now" – Ben started the engine – "I want to greet you properly." He grabbed her shoulders and pulled her sharply towards him. She felt his lips brush against hers, gently at first, then more imperiously. She was drawn to him like to a magnet. She didn't want to open her eyes to find out that this was a dream.

As quickly as he'd drawn closer, he pushed her away.

"We must go. We'll be late for dinner." He pressed the accelerator pedal.

"How can you be so handsome!" With her index finger, she delineated his profile, sliding down to his neck, down along the buttons of his shirt. She hesitated when she reached the buckle, but Ben confidently put her hand right on the swollen fly.

"I missed you." With one hand on the steering, he tried to pull up her tight dress with the other one. She guessed his intention and did it herself. Ben glanced quickly at her hips, then switched to the road, but his gaze kept on returning back. Slender legs in nude nylon stockings with a thin elastic band wouldn't allow him to concentrate.

"How can you be so sexy!" He touched her inner thigh with the back of his hand. She jerked as if she had been shocked. Her legs clenched as his hand snaked upward, now touching her skin, now stroking the thin fabric of her stockings. She stared straight ahead, not daring to look down. Now, only his movement could bring her to ecstasy.

His fingers slid inside her fold. Tash closed her eyes. Her body tensed and she released a soft throaty moan. She leaned back. She stared at the road again. When she felt Ben remove his hand from her legs, she finally decided to look at him. He raised his hand to his lips.

Tash leaned over the armrest to kiss him. The kiss was short but electric. She raised one eyebrow and said, "You need to keep your eyes on the road." She smiled and lowered her head.

The Range Rover sped down the M3 towards London. He held the steering wheel with one hand and Tash's head with the other. They entered the city.

"I have to stop, wait." Ben turned sharply off the main road into the first courtyard they came across.

Her caresses increased in crescendo and slowed down in diminuendo. The gentle touch of her lips was like a chaste, submissive violin. The lyric flute accompanied the biting. Tash's loose hair swayed with the movement of her head as a tense trombone suddenly played. Ben let out a loud groan. Drumroll. He then held her in his arms.

"You are the best girl in my life! Whatever happens, remember that." For a second, a shade of sadness slipped across his face before his usual smile returned.

"Nothing is going to happen, silly. You are mine! And I won't give you to anyone."

"Let's stop by home. It's on the way."

Ben made a turn towards Holland Park. After a few bends, he stopped in front of a three-storey house. It looked even more beautiful than in a glossy booklet.

The house was right on the edge of Holland Park in a row of white stucco buildings, luxuriating in fresh greenery despite being mid-December.

"What's the name of the street?" Even in the dark, Tash could see the splendour of the nearby houses.

"Phillimore Gardens."

Ben turned the key in the lock and opened the door for Tash. She walked into the spacious foyer from the picture.

"Wow, it looks much smaller from the outside." Tash was studying the boiserie on the walls.

"That's because it was built in depth." Ben proudly filled her in the history of the house.

"There is also a beautiful garden. Come on, I'll show you your room."

"My room?" She was sure they were sharing a room.

"Since my parents are away, we can easily afford several rooms."

Ben took pride in playing the host. This house suited him so well that she slowly began to understand the bitter disappointment he felt knowing it was for sale. His family's history and traditions were wrapped up in this house, and losing it would mean losing part of his identity.

"Let me show you the house."

Tash happily nodded.

Ben escorted her through five bedrooms, each decorated in a different style. After the tour, they returned to the foyer.

"So which room do you prefer?" He took her luggage.

"My favourite porter!" She kissed him on the cheek. "I liked the bedroom overlooking the garden. With the painting that looks like a Gainsborough."

"Not a bad choice. That's my parents' bedroom. And yes, indeed it is a Gainsborough. A portrait of my great-great-grandfather."

Tash's eyes widened. "I thought you said your parents wanted to sell the house because they ran out of money?"

"They'd rather sell the house than the paintings." Ben shrugged his shoulders and sighed. "Why don't you freshen up and I'll wait for you in the living room."

Ten minutes later, she was descending the marble staircase into the dark hallway.

"Ben, where are you?"

"In here."

She walked towards his voice and the dim light glinting in the distance. She crossed the threshold and froze.

A long dining table was impressively set for two with a pair of Rocaille candelabras at opposite ends and a bottle of champagne on ice. Silver domes covered delicious-smelling dishes.

"Welcome to London, Mermaid!" Ben took her hand and walked her to one of the Chippendale-style chairs with a red velvet seat. "What would you like to start with?"

Tash was biting her lip. "Do you always have dinners like this with girls?" Her eyes filled with tears in a flash, and before he could answer, she burst into tears.

"What's wrong? Did I offend you?" He squatted down in front of her and took her hand. "We can go to the restaurant if you want. We don't have to eat here."

She opened her mouth to answer, but the tears continued.

"Ben … Ben … I'm just so … so …"

Ben hugged her shoulders and looked into her eyes. "I really want to make you happy. I mean it."

She sobbed one last time. "You did … you do!" Her tear-stained face shone in the candlelight; she was smiling. "I'm crying out of happiness. I wish this day would never end! It's the happiest day of my life!"

Tash opened her eyes. She heard Ben's baritone voice singing Coldplay in the shower and smiled as a ray of sunlight sneaked into the room through heavy tapestry curtains.

She walked to the window and opened the shutters. December sun shone into the room, and its cold light bounced off the silvery silk monogrammed wallpaper.

Tash had to stand on her tiptoes to open the latch on the big French windows. The bolt did not budge, but after a short struggle, it slid down with a clunk. She went out onto the balcony where a magnificent garden opened out in front of her eyes. The manicured lawn was covered with light frost; large drops of water gathered on the roses below. If there was heaven on earth, this was it. She leaned over the wrought-iron rail to admire the flowers.

"What have you found there?" She felt his wet body envelop her from behind.

"What a beautiful garden! I want to go down to see the flowers."

His fingers were already tugging at her nipples. The wet body burned her with cold, but everything inside her was on fire. Her buttocks contracted. She grabbed the rail with her palms, arching her back. Ben grabbed her waist with one hand, pressing lightly on her neck with the other one. She obeyed, enjoying his push, and groaned in pleasure. Ben kissed her back, picked her up and carried her back into the bedroom.

They spent the entire morning in bed listening to music and playing PlayStation.

"Let's have lunch at the Ledbury. I'm starving."

A light breeze blew into the room through the open balcony door. Ben got out of bed lazily and slowly donned a silk robe. Tash was fascinated with his lordly movements. She straightened her posture to mimic his magnificence and affected a posh accent. "Darling, you look so privileged getting out of bed at 1 pm for lunch at the Ledbury. Work does not suit you. What a pity that your parents squandered everything your ancestors had acquired for centuries and now you have to get up in the morning and go to work like an ordinary person. You need to find a rich heiress to help you carry on this lavish lifestyle!" Tash laughed at her own joke, but there wasn't a hint of a smile on Ben's face.

That evening they were lying on the burgundy Persian rug in the living room playing backgammon. Ben stared at the wooden board, pondering his next move, while Tash admired the red flames dancing the Argentinian tango in the fireplace.

"Would you like to go to the ballet tomorrow?" he asked, his eyes still glued to the board.

"The ballet?" Tash clapped her hands and smiled at the pure chic overdose.

Ben finally made his move and then started humming "The Waltz of the Flowers" from *The Nutcracker*.

"Wait a second." He picked up his phone and soon the murmur of the harp spread throughout the room, followed by French horns, flutes, a clarinet and strings.

"Would you honour me with a dance?"

Tash coquettishly gave him her hand, and they began to waltz around the living room.

"We will have a beautiful day tomorrow!"

The Royal Opera House was sold out. Although the whole city was imbued with the Christmas spirit, the festive atmosphere at the opera felt extra special. Maybe it was the beautiful architecture or the anticipation of the ballet, or maybe Tash just felt incredibly happy being dressed up at the special event with Ben. Nothing in the world could spoil her bliss. She was with Him. At *The Nutcracker*. At Christmas. They made a beautiful couple and she felt the admiration of those around them. Tash was proud of her prince. Proud of his elegance, his looks, his love of the arts and his dedication to her. Maybe he was her man from the Boucher pastoral after all?

Earlier, once she realised she was going to the opera, Tash had called Lulu. Lulu, her modelling agent in London and Vivien's long-time friend, adored Tash and had been trying to persuade her to move to the UK. Lulu squealed with joy when she heard Tash's voice and swore to do the impossible – get her a size eight designer gown for the next day's performance.

In a couple of hours, Lulu sent her the address of Alexander McQueen's showroom, where a red silk dress was already waiting for her. This was a common practice in the fashion industry. Showrooms and shops willingly provided sample pieces for fashion shoots and red carpets. It was a win-win; the brand got promoted, while the stock remained intact. During the season, one sample usually got passed around models, celebrities and lucky girls working in fashion. In fact, that green Alexandre Vauthier dress that hugged every hot starlet's curves this season could have easily been the same sample dress.

In less than five minutes, Tash walked out of the showroom with a big paper bag and a bigger smile.

"That was it?" Ben looked astonished. "You don't have to go to the store and buy things like normal people do?"

"No. Brands want their dresses to get PR, so they supply them to celebs and models."

"But it will be on you at the ballet and not in a magazine." Ben wouldn't give up.

"Stylists always get plenty of options, and there's a good chance that some of the dresses will never be worn."

"Cheaters!" Ben laughed.

"Me? Never! I'll be the best ad for McQueen tonight. And you should be happy. Lulu saved us three grand."

Ben's eyes widened. "Three thousand pounds? Let's go."

They were in bed when Ben hugged her and whispered, "I want to fly away with you somewhere far, far away … to Africa."

"I'd love to go to your Africa," Tash answered quietly and tapped her nose on his neck.

The morning came, and it was time for her to leave. She got back to her apartment late in the evening. She got into a bath to warm up from the cold outside. She was staring at the yellow candle smouldering slowly when her phone rang. With wet hands, she reached for it.

It was Carolina and she sounded excited. "What are your plans for Christmas?" She got straight to the point. "Mark has rented a huge house in Gstaad for the holidays. I said that I would only go if he invited you too. Please come!"

Tash couldn't believe her ears. Now destiny was leading her to Ben. She wanted to kiss Carolina. "I'm coming!" She almost dropped the phone in the tub. "I have so much to tell you!"

6. How to survive in a vanity fair

Gstaad

In the middle of the Swiss Alps, the picturesque village of Gstaad came to life during the Christmas holidays. Starting in mid-December, guests from all over the world flocked there to compare the size of their wallets, the degree of their power or the length of their pedigrees. By a lucky chance this year, the slopes were already covered with snow in December. Mark, an avid skier, had chosen a chalet closer to the ski lift to devote his vacation to skiing. The house was located away from the centre of the village, in Wispile. Carolina, who had been in an antisocial mood in recent months, was glad to spend time with close friends away from Hugh's nasty acquaintances and the secular bustle that gripped the village. Vivien came to Gstaad with the exact opposite goal. Every day in her diary was pencilled in with dinners, social events and charity dinners.

The local vanity fair had been in full swing for nearly a hundred years. European, Arab and Latin Americans flaunted their titles, inheritances, connections, power and influence. And, of course, snobbery. If someone were to complain that elitism was inherently English, they only needed to visit Gstaad to stand corrected. Nestled nearby, Le Rosey, the infamous boarding school, had produced more snobs over the two centuries of its existence than all the English boarding schools had in a millennium.

And unlike entry into the English upper class, where lineage mattered most, in the Swiss Alps money talked. If one were lucky enough to have millions, but upbringing and titles had somehow sidestepped one, there was no reason to lose hope. One could buy one's way in to high society by purchasing a chalet in Gstaad or enrolling ones' underperforming kids at Le Rosey. Either way, schmoozing with celebs and creating new intercontinental multi-mega-million-franc strong connections would result in entry into the world's elite. The Latsis and Bertarelli, Eccleston and Garavani would become one's neighbours, and their offspring would become one's children's best friends. While in the Land of the Rose, excessive extravagance immediately revealed an inept and gauche social climber, in the Land of Rosey, dashing extravagance was admired and met with an additional bonus in the form of "let's be friends forever, well at least until your money runs out."

The doorbell wouldn't stop ringing. Mark glanced out of the window and saw the yoga teacher bouncing in the freezing cold. He let her in and led her through the living room, which was upholstered in wooden clapboard and had panoramic views on three sides. In the distance, on a hillock, the Palace Hotel towered over a small village like a fairy-tale castle.

"Nice view!" the teacher remarked on her way to the basement, where the students were waiting for her in the studio.

"I didn't tell Ben that I'm here," Tash whispered as she crossed her legs in the lotus position. "I'd rather bump into him."

"As you wish." Vivien was holding a glass of red in her hand.

"Wine and yoga – what a wonderful combo. Do you ever take a break?"

Tash was always amazed by Vivien's astonishing health and her ability to keep her face persistently fresh despite her daily libations. Tash herself was gradually turning into an evangelist of a healthy lifestyle. Constant dieting, litres of water, probiotics and exercise had become her closest allies. Lately she allowed herself alcohol only on vacation, weekends or on occasions of exceptional importance.

"Well, I do spend a fortune on spas." Vivien settled on the floor, putting the glass of wine next to her. "What about your Ben – does he like surprises?"

"Let's start, girls." The teacher knelt in front of them on the rug. "We'll begin with shavasana."

Every minute in Gstaad was filling Tash with happiness, because every minute was bringing her closer to a reunion with Ben. The dim, flickering light in the spa was so relaxing after intense skiing that Harvey was snoring on the chaise longue, wrapped in a terry towel. Tash and Carolina had spent about half an hour in the hammam and joined the others lounging around the oval pool. Tash looked at Mark, then at Harvey, and smiled, imagining how well Ben would fit in.

After a cosy supper at home and under enormous pressure from Vivien, they headed to the epicentre of the local social life – the lobby of the Palace Hotel.

Carolina insisted on a table at the far end of the foyer. While Tash was examining the fancy coats of arms on the vaulted ceilings, Vivien fluttered from table to table like a swallow, greeting her numerous acquaintances.

The grand fireplace, decorated with hunting trophies, provided intimacy and chic warmth to the atmosphere. In the middle of the room, a cumbersome floral arrangement towered over the hall, blocking visitors from prying eyes.

"Hypocrites," Tash shouted, slumping into a comfortable chequered armchair. "I remember how they were running after you just to say hello when you were here with Hugh two years ago, and now they turn their heads away like you are a leper."

"Don't worry about them. As soon as they find out how much money Mark has, they will get back to their race." She laughed. "They don't care who they suck up to." She glanced around the foyer again.

After the "circle of honour" was finished, Vivien returned to the table with her long-time friend Stavros Lefteris. He looked good for his sixties and was the son of a famous Greek shipping magnate. Gstaad could boast a full collection of shipping kings of all sorts who had chosen the tax-haven village over St. Moritz back in the 1960s.

Despite his rather advanced age, Stavros was still enjoying his status as an eligible bachelor living off one-twelfth of his later father's enormous fortune. And according to Vivien, he was still hoping to merge his fortune with that of some young and beautiful heiress to solidify his decreasing assets. Every year he organised a charity dinner at the hotel, inviting only the *crème de la crème* of the world elite. This year, Vivien had kindly agreed to co-host it and brought few fancy American names to an already remarkable guest list.

Vivien knew that Carolina and Mark, who happily avoided most social events, wouldn't be able to refuse Stavros's personal invitation.

*****

"What's wrong with me? Do I have a big stain somewhere?" Tash checked whether everything was in order with her ivory dress. The distasteful look that Julia, a seventeen-year-old with an Audemars Piguet Tourbillon larger than her own hand, gave her spoke volumes. Julia's companion hesitated, dropped his eyes and nervously wrinkling the napkin in his hands. The rest of the guests spoke to each other, defiantly ignoring the presence of Tash and Carolina. Only Gregory, whom she'd happened to meet once before, greeted her with a smile, for which he was immediately subjected to harsh condemnation from Julia.

To avoid unnecessary gossip, Mark, Vivien and Harvey were waiting for Carolina and Tash at the table.

The women whispered and turned their heads away. Like a trail of foul-smelling cheese, a chill spread through the hall as Carolina approached.

Tash was furious that they all, even a spoiled teen, would feign such contempt. Julia's mother was a typical tuft hunter who had made her way into high society with her husband's wallet. The easiest ways to get really rich in Russia, as in most developing countries, were as old as the universe – theft and robbery. The names of the crimes might have undergone some changes into the more acceptable "corruption" and "hostile takeover", but the intent remained the same. In the nineties, Julia's father went through several shady incarnations from a romantic kingpin to a more prosaic MP to a self-proclaimed "Spanish businessman", who occupied a beachfront villa in Marbella. His name flashed in high-profile investigations like the Panama Papers for money laundering. Reputable banks closed his accounts, and a Spanish court opened an investigation, which he hoped the motherland would be able to squash. But there was no such scandal that could have shaken the status of Julia's family in Gstaad, because who would snub even a suspected murderer if their daughter wore a watch worth one hundred and fifty thousand francs?

Tash walked the hall, watching how the offspring of the richest families in Europe, who usually annoyed her with their obnoxious courtship, obviously ignored her. If their gazes accidentally met, they merely nodded tensely and immediately returned to their companions.

But for now, the show was over. Landing on a chair, Tash closed her eyes and took a deep breath and slowly exhaled. The brief meditation was enough to get rid of her sudden rage.

Tash was examining her neighbours at the table. Mark, Carolina, Harvey, Vivien and three of Vivien's friends from the States, whom she'd heard about at breakfast. Perhaps the brightest one was a full-figured brunette who looked like an opera singer batting dramatically long false eyelashes. Next to her sat a bald man in round glasses, who was clearly her husband. And finally, Oliver, an androgynous blond of about twenty-five.

The woman, Veronica, was indeed a singer, although not of opera. She had gained fame in Mexico after she bore a son to the elderly married head of the state bank. She had moved to LA as his official mistress, bought a clothing brand and made friends with one of the Kardashians. This friendship put her brand on the map and added millions of subscribers to her Instagram. Luckily for American fans, the focus on her clothing line and an overly hectic social schedule ended her singing career.

"Dear guests," Stavros began his speech, "today is a very important day. Today we must make a choice between the Greek word 'xenia,' meaning hospitality, and the word 'xenophobia' that has recently become so familiar in our lives. And I'm happy to confirm that at our charity dinner we choose xenia – so welcome to all of you. I would also like to thank you all in advance for your generous donations towards the benefit of the suffering Syrian refugees."

As soon as he finished his speech, his place on the impromptu stage was taken by Antoine de Valon, the lead auctioneer from Sotheby's. He made a few jokes about Greeks being famous for their generosity and added that he understood why Stavros was so zealous about this issue. After all, he knew first-hand about the bleeding wound of Europe. The refugees flooded the lands of his native Greece, namely the island of Lesvos, which served a staging post on their journey to Europe. And now their dirty tents, which occupied the entire coastline, prevented him from enjoying the scenery during his boat trips. Tash, appalled, looked around. Julia and her friends roared with laughter. Antoine enjoyed a round of applause for his wit and immediately announced the start of the auction, all proceeds from which would be directed to the Syrian refugees.

"Again, why on earth are we helping them? Are they having a bad life in Syria?" Veronica wondered, after her husband bought a postcard signed by Madonna for fifty thousand francs.

"Honey, there is a war there. Of course life is bad in Syria."

"You'd rather help me. Or Oliver. We need to get Oliver a new fur coat, don't we?" She patted his hair the way a good owner pats their dog.

Oliver blushed.

"Oliver takes care of my style, and we should take care of him."

"Of course, Veronica!"

Antoine de Valon took the mic. "We now present the lot that was kindly provided by Mr. ..." he paused to read a note, "... Mr. Hugh Young, who unfortunately has not honoured us with his presence today."

Carolina shuddered. From how her biceps tensed, Tash knew how tightly she was squeezing Mark's arm under the table.

"The lot is an evening trip on his eighty-metre yacht in the company of his charming wife." Looking directly into Carolina's eyes, Antoine faked a smile. "On our behalf, we would like to thank Mrs. Young for the honour of her company to anyone who pays for the suffering refugees. What a generous gesture from the Young family!"

Hugh was notorious for buying the best works by contemporary artists, which made him the darling of all auction houses.

Antoine continued, "Mr. Young has also agreed to cover all the buyer's travel expenses, getting them from anywhere in the world to Monaco. The starting bid is ten thousand francs."

All eyes were on Carolina.

"Who is this Hugh Young, and why the hell are they all staring at me?" Clueless Veronica batted her false eyelashes.

"I met him once," Oliver's timid voice broke the silence.

All this time Tash was watching Carolina. For a moment, when the auctioneer uttered Hugh's name, a flash of anger crossed her face, immediately replaced by her usual calmness. Oliver's confession, however, puzzled her.

Mark raised his card and said loudly, "Twenty thousand!"

"Twenty-five," echoed a voice across the hall.

Tash turned around and saw a handsome brunette with vacant eyes.

"Thirty." Mark didn't give up.

"How do you know Hugh?" Carolina asked Oliver quietly.

Oliver hesitated, assessing whether he should confide in this gorgeous stranger. After a quick internal struggle, the fascination of belonging to the life of the powerful won out. "He had the best pool parties in LA," he whispered, rolling his eyes. "Believe it or not, at one of them, I met my Jose."

Oliver suddenly felt himself extremely important. The young rich chick seemed to be interested in him. She was perhaps a little jealous of his acquaintance with people like Hugh Young. He explained that a few years earlier, Hugh used to throw parties at his California house. Aspiring actors from all sorts of sexual backgrounds were dying to get on the invitation list, hoping to catch the attention of some famous film producer. Wait staff served limitless drinks and drugs to all, while top DJs mixed hits for all the high guests to fornicate to. Hugh and his producer friends loved to peek into the bedrooms where drugged young couples had sex. Sometimes they just watched, sometimes they joined in. A few times Oliver saw with his own eyes how Hugh took young male or female companions for the night. In fact, Jose, Oliver's current boyfriend, had been selected one evening a couple of years ago and received a tidy sum from Hugh for his silence. He initially used the money for random acting courses, but after he met Oliver and wised up, he decided to use it for tuition and went to university to study his craft.

Carolina held her breath.

"And how old is your wise boyfriend now?"

"Nineteen."

Carolina grabbed her phone from the table and searched the age of consent in California: eighteen. She barely registered that Mark had paid seventy-five thousand francs to dine with her on her estranged husband's boat, but that didn't matter any more. She now knew that she'd get whatever she was entitled to. She was about to bleed him dry. He must be punished. After all, two years ago, Jose was only seventeen.

"Oliver, thank you for sharing that. I've got a feeling that Jose has a great future as an actor."

The next day, Tash received a surprising phone call from Gregory. He sincerely apologised for his friends' behaviour the night before and invited her for dinner. She accepted and then silently thanked his father for squandering their family fortune and not letting Gregory become a typical product of French aristocracy with an inflated sense of self-importance. Fate had forced him to get a job, learn compassion and treat others with a kindness not often shown in their circles.

Tash entered the lobby of the Palace Hotel. A huge Christmas tree was strewn with sparkling baubles and lights, and golden garlands adorned the wall porticos. The guests were dazzling too; ladies in gowns and men in suits. Everything screamed the holidays. She couldn't find Gregory and went to say hello to a Brazilian acquaintance.

"What are your plans for New Year's?"

Tiago tried to look at Tash while asking the question, but his jet-black eyes were glued to the curvaceous backside of the passing blonde. Tash smiled. Her plans were the last thing on his mind at the moment. For men like him, a woman he couldn't have sex with wasn't worth his time.

"Wait a second. I'll be right there ..." He sprang like a lion after its prey when he noticed the blonde entering the smoking room.

Tash turned and recognised a man nearby. He was the same one who had been matching Mark's bids at yesterday's charity auction. He sat imposingly on an armchair with his outstretched legs crossed. She smiled. He was under thirty, Latino, tall, handsome and seemed terribly confident.

"I suppose we've never met," he said smoothly. "I'm suggesting a game. Each of us must guess as much as possible about the other."

"You have exactly five minutes before my dinner starts." Tash smiled.

His gaze slid across her face, lingering a little longer than usual on her lips, and then scanned her down to her heels. After a moment's silence, he said, "You must be Italian. Around twenty-six. And you work in fashion."

"Interesting." Tash tried to sound as Italian as possible. "Could you justify that?"

"Dark auburn hair, stunning, judging by the accent not Latin American, otherwise I could assume you were Brazilian. Very stylish – so most likely Italian. Young, but I see maturity in your eyes. As for fashion, it is clear. You put quite an effort into this outfit, even to the smallest detail, although it looks casual. You have time to put things together. So you are either a loafer or working in fashion. But you don't strike me as a lazybones!"

She smiled and blushed slightly. So her Ralph Lauren black leather leggings with high flat boots, white T-shirt and Balmain jacket did the trick. Her thoughts were interrupted by the beep of her phone. Gregory was waiting at the entrance.

"Let's keep up the mystery until our next meeting. I'm running late!" And with that, she headed to the exit.

The porter opened the door and she climbed into the front seat of a black Porsche Cayenne. Gregory kissed her on each cheek.

"You look fantastic. I really like your style."

Five minutes later, they were walking up the wooden stairs of the Alpina. Hotel Alpina's tremendously high ceilings and open space, stylishly consolidating several halls into one, showcased a huge technological advance in comparison to the early-20th-century Palace Hotel with its thick support columns and low vaulted ceiling. The refined finishing of Alpina didn't flaunt its status but casually evoked exclusiveness by its sky-high prices.

Tash looked around anxiously. It was her third day here, but still no sign of Ben.

A group of Gregory's friends were waiting for them at the table. Julia frowned, but smiled tightly at Tash while Gregory was introducing her to the others, who didn't make an effort to hide their disdain.

"Never mind," Gregory whispered. "They're just jealous. You are hot, smart and with me. People are always jealous of someone better than they are."

Julia whispered to her neighbour. "Look who's here. And alone."

All gazes turned to the entrance. Tash also turned her head to see who was responsible for such a stir. Her dark-haired friend whom she had just parted ways with was walking towards two women in their sixties.

"Oh, he's having dinner with his mother. I wonder where Sofia is?" Julia fidgeted. "Philip," she said in a loud and squeaky voice. "How are you?"

He looked really handsome. Long hair and a stubble gave him a rather relaxed look despite his impeccable suit. Philip walked over and greeted everyone. When Tash's turn came, his dark eyes sparkled with pleasure and his mouth stretched in a broad white-toothed smile. "Oh, the mystery didn't last long." He winked at Tash.

A slight shiver ran through her body, and for a moment, she even forgot about Ben. She smiled at being the centre of attention in the frosty group. Everyone at the table was now looking at the two of them.

"I see. You know Tash?" Gregory interjected.

"Tash?" Philip paused. "Yes, she is my new girlfriend."

It became so quiet at the table that Tash could hear her own heartbeat. She felt like the main character in a soap opera who hadn't read her lines. "Why are you telling everyone? We agreed to keep it a secret!"

The sight gag. The curtain. Philip smiled. He leaned over to kiss her and whispered, "I knew right away that you were my girl. Now I have to join my mum. Don't kill the joke." And with these words, he left.

"Tash," Julia's ginger friend immediately remembered her name. "Are you dating Philip? For how long?"

Tash was amused by their unexpected attention. She also wanted revenge for Carolina. After all, she was Philip's girlfriend. "It's very recent," she replied.

*****

"Gregory, it was a joke, Philip and I just met," Tash had to confess, when he drove her to the entrance of the Palace.

"Well, I have to admit you are a great actress! Can I ask you something?"

"Of course—" But he didn't let her finish. He pressed his lips against hers. She was about to push him away when she heard a persistent knocking on the window. There was a woman with a big smile on her face indicating that they should open the window.

Gregory blushed. He took a deep breath and then he pressed the window button. The woman put her head into the car. She had a grey bob and was about sixty years old.

"Hi, Mum. Where are you going?"

97

"Gregory, where are your manners? You have to introduce me to your companion first. What did I teach you? Hello, I am the mother of this womaniser. Dory." She held out her hand through the window.

"Mum, this is Tash, my friend. We just had dinner and I am dropping her off."

"I saw how passionately you were dropping her off."

"Now that everyone has met, can I ask you what you are doing here?"

"First, get out of the car when you talk to your mum. Second, I am not obliged to report to you!" Dory wrapped herself in her sable coat and headed towards the hotel entrance.

"Mum, wait." Gregory jumped out of the car. "Where are you going?"

"I'm going to Gringo. Do you want to come with me?"

"I'm leaving tomorrow. I have to get up early."

"Then maybe Tash wants to join me?"

"No, Mum. She does not want that. She wants to sleep."

"Not at all," Tash intervened, "I'd be delighted to join you." She jumped out of the car and followed Dory.

Tash judged that this would be the best way out.

Gregory, taken aback, was freezing by the car. "As you wish. I could have dealt with you separately, but together … I give up."

"I won't see you again year. Happy New Year! And see you next year." Tash kissed him quickly and ran after his mother.

*****

"I liked you right away, when I saw you at Stavros's dinner. What are you doing with that womaniser, my son? He needs to get up early? At his age, I did not sleep at all, and he couldn't go to the club with two young ladies." Dory rattled like a machine gun. She didn't wait for an answer and continued, "What brought you to this village? Wouldn't you rather be in Saint Barth or Punta? There are either retired people here or children.

Literally no one to catch. Would you like to join me in the bathroom?" Dory winked. "To powder our noses."

Tash finally realised why she was so talkative. Dory quickly handed her a sachet full of white powder and pushed her towards the stall.

She felt lightness in her forearms and had a sudden clarity in her head while unrolling the fifty-franc bill. She was now reassured what a brilliant idea it had been to go with Dory to Gringo.

They entered a small rectangular room with tables on both sides and a dance floor in the middle. A dark corridor with a bar led to the second hall with a pool, a popular stomping ground for local youngsters.

"My friends are here." Tash led Dory to Vivien's table.

"Oh, Vivien, it's been ages." Dory threw her fur coat to the manager and landed next to Vivien. "We've known each other for thirty years, at least, right?"

Vivien grinned. "Officially" she was forty-six, and thirty years of friendship with sixty-year-old Dory made her own story look quite suspect. Tash noticed how after a couple of minutes of whispering, a white powder sachet moved to Vivien's hand.

"A bottle of Dom Pérignon, please. Now, honey, tell me about yourself." Dory switched back to Tash.

Before Tash had even opened her mouth, Dory was already telling her the story of her life. Gregory's parents turned out to be local legends. His father, Fred, a notorious playboy, once threw a mega-party in Las Vegas in 1966 in honour of his friend Gunter Sachs's wedding. He was also one of the first to build a house in Costa Smeralda in Sardinia thanks to his friendship with Karim Aga Khan. He was married six times and had had affairs with every second female of childbearing age in the European upper class.

It didn't come as a surprise that Fred, who had not worked a single day of his life and blew through almost all of his inheritance, spent his ninetieth birthday alone with his memories of the good old days at the Eagle Club, a storied private club in Gstaad where he had lifetime membership as one of the few surviving founders.

Dory's name used to ring out in the eighties. Since then, her fame had faded, but her passion for parties did not. She reaped the benefits of the luxurious and carefree life of her extended family and friends by renting out the real estate that she had inherited during her lucrative divorce from Fred. That barely managed to cover her extravagant lifestyle. She also relied on the generosity of her friends welcoming her to their boats and villas. Had she ever decided to write her memoirs, there would have been enough material for many juicy volumes. Even in her sixties, her vivacity was off the chart.

"You have no idea what my twenty-seven-year-old lover is up to. I visit him in New York every two months. The sex is out of control! He is Colombian, unbridled and passionate."

Tash almost choked on her champagne. The idea of Dory having wild sex with a young South American was a bit much.

"And your ex-husband?" Tash couldn't wait to turn the conversation to another topic.

"What about him? He was always a womaniser, but we're still friends. He also has a twenty-year-old girlfriend in Milan. I doubt he still gets hard, but fresh meat is better than aged. He's never been a stud, though. It's a true blessing we are not obsessed with our penis working all the time. I believe impotency is God's punishment to men for all their sins during their potency. Hallelujah!" She laughed. "I was Fred's last wife out of six. Besides Gregory, he has three sons and a daughter. So, if you're counting on his inheritance, forget it. The poor boy will have to work all his life, because his mum and dad squandered almost everything."

"Dory, I'm not counting on anything. We're just friends," Tash answered shyly.

"I know, honey. I was joking. In any case, you are too beautiful for him. He needs a simpler bride, but one with money. And we'll find a decent husband for you. What are you doing for New Year's? Don't tell me you already have plans. You have to go with me to Valentino's, and then to my young friend's chalet. And I don't take no for an answer!"

Tash laughed in disbelief at her crazy new friend. Resisting Dory was indeed pointless.

*****

The guests were showcasing their expensive outfits. Celebrities, tycoons, royalty, and designers were all catching up on the latest village gossip. The majority were over forty. Tash noticed only a couple of young women – an heiress to a famous Italian designer and another to the throne of a European principality, whom she recognised from the tabloids.

Gourmet dishes on china, champagne in crystal and starched tablecloths set the stage for the predictable dinner. Dory was enjoying her status of patroness, taking her inexperienced protégé – a stunning tall auburn-haired woman in a slinky black gown – out. The protégé, however, could not wait to escape the numbing dullness of the event and move to the chalet of Dory's younger friend, where Ben was most likely celebrating New Year's. There was still no news of him.

"Dory, when are we leaving? I'd like to celebrate New Year's there."

Dory was reclining on the sofa in a pink lace dress with a pink fur boa and flirting with a white-haired Italian.

"Honey, may I introduce you to Jean Carlo, my long-time friend. Jean Carlo is the king of fashion in our little village."

Jean Carlo cast an avid glance at Tash's cleavage. "*Bellisima!*" He brought Tash's hand to his lips, holding it longer than he should.

"Nice to meet you." Tash pulled her hand back and smiled tightly. "I'm leaving."

Dory quickly reasoned that her beautiful protégé was her entry ticket to the party and followed her. On the way, while Dory was filling her in with titbits about strangers from Valentino's party, Tash was picturing herself waking up in Ben's arms the following morning.

*****

Tash was admiring the design of the chalet. High ceilings, spacious rooms, wenge walls decorated with neon works by Dan Flavin looked more like a New York loft than a ski chalet. The architect, however, had managed to keep the cosiness of the mountain house despite the modern touches.

Dory grabbed Tash's hand and led her around. "It's still half an hour before midnight. I'll introduce you to the daughter of my friend Alberto Visconti. She is a wonderful girl; you'll become good friends."

The name Visconti rang a bell, but Tash couldn't remember where she had heard it.

"Flo … Flo …" Dory pushed the guests, making her way to the blonde wearing ripped blue jeans and a white sweater. She was standing next to the bar, leaning on it with both hands.

"Flo." Dory touched the girl on the shoulder. The girl turned around.

Tash smiled at the funny koala appliqué on her sweater. Then she looked up and saw those eyes. Icy blue, showing through heavy eyelids. Flo stared at Dory with her back against the counter and forced the semblance of a smile.

"Happy New Year!" Crazy Dory reached out to kiss her on both cheeks. "Please meet my good friend Tash."

Flo turned to the tall auburn-haired woman and took a step towards her. But her legs no longer listened to her. Her mind was wandering in the open space, defying gravity. She was slowly sliding down. She felt Dory grabbing her arm, but gravity pulled her body down, and in the next moment, she felt solid floor under her buttocks. She was weightless. She no longer felt her body, as if she was floating above it in another dimension. She laughed at how old Dory was trying to lift her up. "Why are you spoiling my vibe? It feels so good down here," she slurred incomprehensibly to herself.

Flo finally seemed happy in a horizontal position. Friends gathered around and whispered merrily about something. The only thing she could distinguish in their speech was the word "ketamine". Dory disappeared. The tall auburn-haired woman in the black dress tried to help her up, but then she squatted down next to her. "Are you all right?" she asked.

"I'm damn fucking good! I'm better now than all of you put together!" Flo smiled at her thoughts.

"There she is." Flo heard Dory's voice. The auburn-haired woman turned her head. Flo saw her shudder and put her hands on the floor to keep from falling. And then Flo saw Ben. Her Ben. Handsome. In a white shirt and a blue club jacket. He gave the woman his hand to help her up, and then he bent down.

"Flo, Flo." Ben took her head in his hands and looked into her pupils. "Can you hear me?"

She nodded. Ben sat down next to her and put his arm around her shoulders.

"Is everything okay? Ben?"

Ben finally looked up. He looked at Tash, who was standing right next to Dory. He looked at her beautiful face staring at him blankly. He looked at her slender body wrapped in a slinky black dress. The very body he fantasised about on long nights. *She's so beautiful*, he thought, and his heart ached at the reality of the situation.

Tash averted her eyes. Thank god she looked away because he had never seen them so perplexed. He saw how she squeezed her hands together, as if everything inside her was twisted into a stiff spring. He knew it because he felt the same. Ben just stared at her. A guy came up to her and gave her a glass of champagne. Ben made a motion to get up. Tash looked over him into the distance. And then he shuddered in pain as she looked disconcertingly directly into his eyes.

Tash felt like an imposter in this big gorgeous house. A lost little country girl – lonely and twitchy. Dan Flavin's neon pipe artwork blinked on the walls, bright flames danced in the fireplace. Strangers laughed. Her chest contracted so much it was hard to breathe. She clenched her fists in order to somehow endure the pain. No, she was not hungry. No, she would not come out today or tomorrow or the next day. She would never leave Grandmother's house again. She couldn't chance bumping into Alyosha with his blonde.

Frozen in place, Tash scanned the room. Happy faces everywhere. Screaming numbers, a countdown. Music thundered. Laughter and cheering spread throughout the hall.

A guy jumped up to Tash, handed her a glass of champagne and kissed her on the cheek. "Happy New Year!"

Tash's legs trembled and she silently gasped. Alberto Visconti. She finally remembered that name. It was on his boat where she had met Ben. The yacht of his girlfriend's dad. His girlfriend. Then she knew where she had seen Flo's face before. She had been sitting next to him in the restaurant in Sardinia.

"Where's Phil? I want to introduce you to him. He's such a darling." Dory's voice interrupted her stunning revelations. "Sorry about Flo," Dory continued. "I've known her since she was a child. Her parents are my close friends, one of the most powerful families in Italy, actually. They are related to royals. Fabulously rich, but charming people. And Ben ..." she paused, "... they've been together for as long as I can remember. I don't find anything remarkable about him." Dory shrugged her shoulders, meaning that his family was neither royal nor fabulously rich. "He's always very friendly, but I think Flo could find someone more *fitting*. Oh, here's Phil!"

"Tash? Dory? Happy New Year!" Philip greeted them both with his gleaming white smile.

"You know Tash?" Dory looked confused.

"What a pleasant surprise," Philip said, smiling. "You appear and then disappear." He was examining Tash carefully.

"It never occurred to me that Phil and Philip ..." Tash didn't finish. She just answered him with a small smile. This was the first pleasant experience of the new year. "Dory kept telling me that we were going to see some Phil, who is a real darling."

"Dory, you did me a huge favour by bringing Tash here, and now, if possible, can I steal her from you? I'd like to introduce her to some other guests. As far as I understand, you have already met one of my dearest friends, Florence." He nodded towards Flo and Ben, sitting together on the floor. "Now let's get acquainted further."

Philip took her arm and led her away from the bar. They stopped at each guest, clinked glasses, congratulated each other and drank champagne. The waiters barely had time to refill their glasses. By the end of the honorary circle, Tash was leaning on Philip's arm, afraid of losing balance in her high heels. All the time, she could feel Ben's gaze piercing her back. She glanced furtively in his direction. He didn't take his eyes off her. Tash was glad that the champagne had confused her thoughts and numbed her pain. She didn't want to sober up. Her greatest desire was to wake up on the first of January of the previous year, before she even knew Ben existed.

Lost in thought, she paused by a counter.

"Mermaid, I would like to wish you a Happy New Year!"

She heard Ben's voice beside her and felt a stab in her chest. She raised her hand up and said firmly, "No, you don't get to call me that. Not now, not ever again."

Ben turned to the bartender. "Vodka soda and a champagne."

The bartender topped up their glasses. Ben took hers from the counter and handed it to her. "I don't even know where to start." He drank his vodka in one gulp and fell silent. She followed his example. They looked at each other, unable to say anything.

"It was all fake. All a lie, which I probably would never have discovered if I hadn't come here." Tash shook her head in disbelief at this farce. She was ashamed of her own stupidity.

He spoke first. "If I were you, I would want to kill me!" He looked up at her with his ice-cold, indifferent eyes. "Is there any way I can make it up to you?" He turned to the bartender. "Double vodka with soda and a champagne, please."

They drank another round. Her head was spinning. It became unbearable to even look at Ben.

"You are despicable! And I hate you!" She grabbed her bag from the counter and headed for the exit. Philip intercepted her before she left.

"Running away again?" He hugged her limp body and she didn't push him away. She looked up and saw the warmth emanating from his guileless brown eyes. Not cold like Ben's, but hot and passionate. She felt safe. With eyes like that, he would never reject or betray her. He led her upstairs.

*****

Anna's voice on the phone was interrupted by loud music.

"Anna, Ben has a girlfriend." Tash got all misty as she began to sober up. "I'm such a fool!" Tears ran down her cheeks. The driver turned around and asked, "Are you all right, miss?"

Tash nodded.

"Can you get to Geneva? My driver will pick you up there. Oh, Tash, we love you, and we'll take care of you. Forget about him. He's a bastard! We'll find someone a hundred times better."

7. Full house, or How to play a card correctly

Courchevel

It felt like someone was squeezing her temples with pincers. Fireworks flashed outside the window, illuminating a black-and-white photograph of Brigitte Bardot on the wall of the sombre living room. "What have I done? Everything happened so quickly."

Tash remembered the wide-open window, the icy touch of the starched sheets. Philip was disappointed. Yes, she remembered when they finished, his last kiss blew cold. She looked at Bardot's perfect face. What a noble chin! She tried to close her eyes, but it didn't work. A poker face with a defined jawline appeared in front of her again and again. The same frosty stare as Flo's.

The rustle in the hallway brought her back to reality.

"Goth nit or! Is it really so hard to remember? Goth nit or!" Carolina repeated loudly.

Mark laughed.

The bright light of the chandelier blinded her. She couldn't help but smile when she saw the bewildered faces of Carolina and Mark, taken by surprise by her presence. Her heart warmed for a second. She briefly reconstructed the events of the night to a tiddly Carolina, who only caught that Tash urgently needed a car.

"Mark, ask your driver to take Tash wherever she wants!"

"Of course, dear! He can take her right now."

Packing didn't take long. She grabbed clothing from the closet and threw everything into the suitcase. Carolina would send the rest. She kissed her friend, thanked Mark for his hospitality and jumped into the waiting car.

"Why do men cause so much pain?" Tash asked the driver.

He smiled. "I always thought the same way about women."

*****

The car was climbing reluctantly up the serpentine road, leaving two grooves in the crispy white snow behind. The snow had piled up after the night blizzard and forced the driver to stop to put chains on the snow tyres. The bright mountain sun blinded her eyes through the windows covered with morning frost. Tash stared indifferently out the window at the line of mountain peaks drawn across the blue sky.

The village was quiet. The tourists hadn't yet woken up from the roaring festivities of last night. There were remains of firecrackers scattered all over the crisp snow. The car turned left and began to climb narrow winding streets. Soon the driver pulled up at a dark wooden gate decorated with silvery garlands.

The first person Tash saw was Katya. She was lying on the carpet in a short green dress, lifting her legs to the music playing from the phone beside her.

"Wanna have some?" Katya handed Tash a rolled-up bill and nodded at a plate that held some white powder.

Tash shook her head.

"Go directly to bed!" Tash heard Anna's voice behind her.

Anna kissed Tash and carefully brushed the hair back from Tash's sad face. "And then pull yourself together, guests are arriving soon for lunch."

Tash glanced briefly around her room and went straight to the bathroom. She wanted to wash off all the dirt that she had got herself into the night before: Flo's overdose, Ben's betrayal and then casual sex with Philip.

"Take a rest and get ready for a new day with new people. You need to take your mind off that Ben." Anna turned the tap to draw her a bath in a tub the size of a pool.

"No." Tash took off her dress. "All men are dirty, disgusting liars. How clever it was of the nineteenth-century women like Kitty from *Anna Karenina* to go to the spa to recover from unrequited love. Thankfully, we have our own spa to wash away that grime and heartbreak." Tash plunged into the bath.

"Let me call our Kitty then. She will heal you faster than any water."

108

"Why would she waste her time with us if guys will start arriving soon?" Tash smiled. It was her first cheerful thought this year.

"Oh, you are so hopelessly behind. You don't know? Katya's been seeing Sasha."

Tash sat up, but quickly sank back.

"Remind me, who is Sasha?"

"That married guy from Russia's Far East."

Tash chuckled. "Okay, get her in here!"

A minute later, a blonde bob appeared in the doorway. "You're not upset with me?" Katya asked as she sat down on the edge of the tub.

"Of course not, silly. Why?"

"Well, you met Sasha first. And also I didn't tell you right away."

"First of all, I was too occupied with my own life. And second, you know me, I don't date taken men. It's against my rules."

Katya coughed. Tash was amazed at the speed at which the cough spread to Anna. The malicious smirks on their faces made her realise the profoundness of her latest statement in the light of recent events. Katya and Anna couldn't hold their laughter any more. Katya scooped up the lather and slathered her friend's snub nose. Tash hesitated for a minute and splashed water all over her. When Anna came to break them up, Katya's dress was wet through. She judged that the damage had already been done and pushed Katya into the water.

"Tell me, is your thoroughbred stallion and his druggie blonde filly capable of such fun?" Katya emerged from under the water choking with laughter. "They are far beneath us, mongrels!" And she grabbed Anna along with her.

"Indeed, water is a cure," Tash concluded catching her breath. "They knew it more than a century ago."

It turned out, that after Faina's birthday, Sasha had driven Katya home and was awarded an invitation to tea, at which he was grilled about the seriousness of his intentions.

109

"I told him straight away, 'I like you, but you are married. What can you offer?' He saw my apartment, so he knew how much money I put into it."

Any guest who had barely crossed the threshold of Katya's "nest" found themselves in the virtual kingdom of the mistress of the house. Katya's face looked at him from every wall from the covers of different framed fashion magazines. He was able to examine the tiniest details of her perfect body in works by the best photographers. She didn't hesitate to educate the uninformed about her million-dollar advertising campaigns and her Instagram page with a million followers.

The truth was that over the years she had managed to build up a small fortune. Although the peak of her modelling career was far in the past, Katya still garnered plenty of adoration at the vanity fair. She might have been moved from the main window, but she still attracted plenty of frivolous admirers from her perch in the side window where she exhibited with a gilded tag with a lot of zeros.

"*Tout de suite* he realised that I'm not going to waste my time with married old him just for his beautiful eyes. They weren't that beautiful anyway. He thought for a bit and then said that he would be happy to provide for all my needs in exchange for our *friendship*." Katya snapped her fingers and continued, "The following day, he offered to stop by Graff. I told him directly that diamonds would make a nice addition for special events. And to seal the deal, I sent him my US account details."

Tash had known Katya from childhood, but she never ceased to be amazed by her captivating candidness. "Whenever a woman *gives* herself to a man, he always gets the bill later," Katya loved to repeat.

Tash wrapped a towel around her body and they moved to the bedroom.

"We flew to Zurich the following day. Since then, he's seen me every day."

Tash crawled under the duvet. Her hot body instantly warmed the silky sheets. The dim light of the chandelier scattered in soft waves, tinting the furniture with a yellow shade. She was warm; at last, she was warm. She was floating on a white fluffy cloud. Katya's voice brought her back to earth.

"His wife is okay, but not a top model!" Katya smiled. "She looks after the children, goes to yoga classes and lunches with her girlfriends while he entertains me. He's funny and handsome and rich. He chats a lot and tells all sorts of stories."

"Yes," Anna intervened with sarcasm. "So funny that he came here with his wife and children. They are staying in the hotel, and he comes to our chalet every day with his *stories*."

"What?" Tash looked astonished. "His wife and children are here? And he's not afraid?"

"Afraid of what?" Katya dropped indifferently. "He is coming soon. Came at four in the morning, when they went to bed. He brought me this." Katya held out her hand to showcase a gleaming emerald ring. "He said it matches the colour of my eyes."

"He gives a ring to another woman when his wife and children are literally next door." Tash shook her head, but Katya waved her hand and smiled at her ring.

"The more beautiful a woman is, the faster time and money fly with her. If a man cheats, his woman either married a player or made him a skirt-chaser herself. It's not my problem if he wants to tell his stories to me, not to her."

"The poor dear must have heard them a million times." Anna suddenly decided to express her support to all married women of the universe. "Believe me, over time, spouses get bored with each other and may not even talk for weeks. Then, out of boredom, they start making friends, then children and grandchildren. Look at me and Nick. Why do you think we always have guests? We need buffers and a new audience for our stories. Nick, by the way, has a group of female friends he lovingly calls his 'old bags' who are absolutely charmed by his boring stories. When I refuse to listen any more, he simply reels off the rubbish to them. It all works out – but if I ever found out that he spent so much as a penny on some slut, I would kick him out broke." Anna seemed to be feeling inspired by her new feminist role.

"I'm falling asleep. We'll have plenty of time later to dig deeper into this dung in search of pearls or an emerald, as in your case."

And Tash, elegantly restraining a yawn, fell asleep.

When Tash opened her eyes, mountain profiles were barely visible against the black sky. She glanced at the phone: 7:43 pm. WhatsApp exploded from missed messages: Carolina, Vivien, Dory – but not a word from either Ben or Philip.

She ran her hand over her wet forehead. Her face was covered by a thick layer of sweat. The inside of her chest clenched with pain. "Katya was right about Flo; she is a thoroughbred filly. They're both thoroughbreds. Of course, he would choose her. They're like brother and sister. I bet they've been going to Mustique and hunting since childhood. And I don't even know where damn Mustique is." Tash grabbed her phone from the bedside table and searched. "Well, okay, now at least I know where it is."

*****

Tash jumped off the ski lift. It was indeed a perfect day for skiing. The sun was playing on her cheeks, warming them from the morning chill, and the snow was creaking under the weight of her skis. She was happy to be alone on the slopes so she could fully enjoy her new mindset for the new year. She planned on conquering new mountains and forging her own path.

That morning she had been woken by a call from London.

"Miss Romanov," she heard a hoarse voice. Lulu, her agent, always called her by her last name. Tash suspected that by doing so Lulu was hinting to clients that Tash was one of the miraculously surviving descendants of the Russian royal family.

"I booked a fucking good job for you! No need to thank me. Just bring your pretty puss here next week. And don't drink too much! You need to look *caliente*, not puffy. They want you, Miss Romanov. You! And they're paying big bucks. You're gonna need to stay here for a month or two, so get your tight ass ready for some hot shoots!"

Tash smiled. It had taken her a while to get used to Lulu's rather rude manners, but after getting to know her, she now couldn't imagine her agent without toilet humour and extravagant antics.

Tash decided to use yoga mindfulness techniques to make her skiing meaningful. "I dedicate my first descent of the year to my new happiness, new life and new love!" She solemnly proclaimed her intentions before starting to move.

Most of the skiers were only coming alive at this hour, so she was gliding down an almost empty slope. As her speed increased, so too was her faith in herself and in her prosperous future. As soon as the main lift loomed ahead, she decided to go faster on the last run, stopping to carve turns, going into a downhill. She was racing towards a new happy life, and nothing could thwart her trajectory.

"Mama!"

112

Tash heard the heart-rending squeal and then she hit something very furry and very fluffy and rolled head over heels down the hill.

She opened her eyes in a snowdrift. "How symbolic, starting my new life with a somersault." Tash moved her arms, then her legs; everything seemed to be intact. She looked around. The creature which had so inconveniently interrupted her greater plans for a bright future sat a metre away wrapped in a sable coat. To her left, a child of about four was crying desperately.

"Mama, I promise, I will never do that again!" He knelt down, got up again, then sat down again, shaking his mother with his little hands.

Tash didn't know where to start: scold this brainless tot for jumping out into her path all of a sudden or ask the woman if she was all right. In the end, Tash turned to her neighbour in the snowdrift. "Are you okay?"

"Oh my god, I'm so sorry. He can be such a brat at times. I told him to slow down and hold my hand!"

"Please don't scold him, he's already crying." Tash got up.

The child was quietly whingeing, "Mamaneverwilldoitagain …"

"Are you sure everything is all right?" She reached out to help the woman up.

"Yes, thank you very much!" The woman rose to her feet. She was pretty, about Tash's height, slightly older, about thirty, maybe thirty-two, with gorgeous blonde hair. "Give me your address, I should at least send you flowers."

"Please don't, it's all fine. But you can come and visit us. I'm Natasha."

"Lisa." She shook the snow off her fur. "You must come to our hotel, so I can buy you dinner. I insist. We're staying at the Cheval Blanc."

The sun terrace was crowded. Drake's cool tunes blared from the stereo, enticing overheated skiers and snowboarders to dance. Anna headed the table. In a white ski suit with its metallic sheen reflecting the sun's rays, she looked like a real star, one who had either fallen from the bright-blue sky or popped out from a fashion show. Next to her sat Faina, who had landed in Chambery just an hour ago. It took her only two days to realise that New Year's with her parents and their friends in Lapland was rather a hasty idea. On the first, Faina was on board her father's Gulfstream infinitely pleased with her decision to leave her parents in Santa Claus's homeland.

On Anna's other side, Katya sat, stylishly wrapped in a sable with perfect makeup and a fresh blow-dry. She was a top model, after all, not just a regular skier, and wanted to stand out from the crowd. Nick, in his red ski suit, looked like a ski instructor who was honoured to get invited by his rich clients to lunch with them.

Tash was on the phone with her new friend, and after ten minutes of persuasion, she agreed to dine with Lisa at her hotel.

"It's good that you're meeting her tonight. There is literally nothing to do with us. Faina is tired after her flight" – Anna nodded towards Katya – "and Katya is in a relationship now. You need to go out more because—"

"Look who's here," Katya interrupted the conversation, glancing at the entrance.

Faina giggled at seeing the odd couple. Alex was wearing black and Ella was in head-to-toe cobalt.

"Oh, blue again. It looks like it's her favourite colour," Tash quipped. The last time she had seen them at that insidious dinner, Ella had been in a tweed suit of the same shade.

The couple stopped indecisively, looking for a place to sit. Tash's inviting gesture solved the problem.

There was a slight confusion at the table, and only clueless Nick was genuinely happy to see them. "It's been a while. From Sardinia, right?" Nick stood up to greet Alex. "Would you like sit with us?"

Alex crumpled his hat and shuffled the snow with his ski boots. He looked around nervously, hoping to find support in this awkward situation. Unexpectedly for him, it came from Tash.

"Have a seat!" Tash said confidently. There was no hint of embarrassment in her voice as she sincerely wanted to break the ice.

Katya looked at Tash with admiration, amazed at her composure.

Alex helped Ella to sit, and then settled down next to Nick, who immediately captured him with a discussion of the slopes. Ella kept quiet, and Faina decided to make a small talk.

"So, what are you working on now, Ella? I heard you became a *director*?"

Tash grasped a touch of sarcasm in Faina's question.

"Yes, it's been a while. We just got back from LA. I've started filming a documentary about Grace Kelly."

Tash bit her lip to stop from sharing her thoughts: "Oh that explains it all. That's what she is aiming for and what her ridiculous suits are for!" Everything was slowly falling into place in Tash's head. "Princess Ella." Tash chuckled at her discovery.

"Tomorrow I'm having a little dinner in my chalet. Why don't you both come?" Faina pronounced the invitation loudly for Alex to hear.

"Brilliant idea," said Nick.

"I'm not too sure; we go to bed early." Ella tried to evade the invitation, but Alex piped up. "It's okay, we'll go to bed later." Alex turned to Faina. "We're certainly coming."

*****

By nine o'clock, Tash was ready. The driver was waiting for her, and in five minutes she walked through revolving glass doors into the dark foyer of the hotel. She passed around the high divider made of wood and saw Lisa on a soft velvet sofa. The culprit of the morning incident wouldn't take his eyes off the iPad. As soon as she saw Tash, Lisa picked up the phone. "We are downstairs, come down and ask the nanny to pick up Vanya." Lisa called the bartender: "Double whiskey, please. Natasha, what would you like?"

"Sparkling water, please."

She noticed approval in Lisa's eyes.

"I don't drink either. Don't find it pleasant any more. But my husband does it for both of us. And here he is."

A man was approaching them, lovingly holding the hands of a little girl of about three and a boy of about eight. Tash's eyes widened, but Sasha kept his poker face.

"Apparently we know each other." Sasha brought his kids closer to Tash. "Meet Tash." Sasha gave Tash a friendly kiss on the cheek. "I didn't make the connection that Tash and Natasha are the same person. Lisa told me everything. You're just an ace! Thanks for not letting my wife get hurt." Sasha looked at the perplexed Lisa and explained, "Tash stays with my friends, the ones I went to yesterday."

As soon as the nanny came down, Sasha ordered, "Kids, bedtime!"

Straight after hearing his dad's order, Vanya turned his iPad off and walked up to him, waiting for new instructions. The nanny took the children to their rooms, no tantrums and no whining, and the adults moved to the restaurant.

"Well, girls, how did you manage to meet on the slopes? Who would have thought?" Sasha sipped his second double.

"Where else can I meet people? I am either in this hotel or walking with the children. So who else lives in this chalet?" It was the second time over dinner that Lisa had mentioned the mysterious chalet.

"It's four of us – a couple, me and my girlfriend," Tash replied.

Lisa looked at Sasha furiously. "I'm wondering who exactly you know there?"

Sasha calmly continued sipping his whiskey. "Nick, my old friend. We are going to do a joint venture in Mongolia. I'm providing government support, and he's going to invest." Not a single nerve trembled on Sasha's face while he was making up this rubbish. "Everything is for you, my sweet. You love the glamourous life and diamonds, so I have to work hard."

"I don't need your crazy high life. I wanted to spend New Year's at home." She turned to Tash. "I don't need much. I pray for my kids to be healthy and have food on the table. I'm a very simple woman."

Sasha burst out laughing. "Oh yeah, simple woman! Look at yourself – there is a minimum of six grand's worth of stuff on you, not to mention your jewellery."

Tash examined Lisa carefully. Indeed, her long-sleeved Valentino dress would have cost that amount alone. Tash glanced at her diamond earrings, which were at least two carats each.

"Stop washing our dirty linen in public. You're drunk," Lisa raised her voice. "You'd better go check on the kids."

Sasha, like the children earlier, obediently got up and walked away.

"Do not pay him any attention." Lisa turned to Tash. "He's been pissing me off lately. I'm tired of his numerous business trips and booze. Even on family holidays, he's always absent. But the bastard is such a good dad! The children adore him; they don't listen to me at all. I've thought about divorce, but decided that we should stay together for the sake of the children. So, I turn a blind eye to his affairs as long as there is no one serious. Oh, fuck him! He's been cheating for our entire marriage. Sorry, I just had to get these feelings out," Lisa said, obviously looking for support. "It boils up."

"No worries." Tash was torn between sympathy for Lisa for his cheating and sympathy for Sasha for her constant nagging.

Lisa continued, "In the end, I've opted for reimbursement. For each affair, I treat myself to something special, and I have to say, I've got a lot of furs. I just don't have anywhere to wear them, so I brought them all here."

She laughed nervously.

Ten minutes later, Sasha came back.

"The kids are asleep, boss. How about a nightcap?"

"A nightcap? You're already drunk." Lisa paused and then suggested slyly, "Or maybe a nightcap in your chalet, Natasha? I'm sure you have drinks there."

It was only just past eleven, so it would have been suspicious for Tash to flake out on the grounds of the late hour. Sasha was slowly sipping his whiskey, as if the thought of his wife sharing a drink with his mistress didn't bother him at all. It probably didn't.

Tash went outside to call Katya. After a snap analysis, Katya commanded, "Bring them here. We'll figure it out." So Tash returned to the spouses with an invitation.

For the first time that evening, a shadow of confusion crossed Sasha's face. "Holy shit!" he said aloud. He asked for another bottle of wine and the bill, and then he tipped the waiter three hundred euros.

"Why do you always splash money? Was our dinner really three thousand?" Her comment in the car remained unanswered.

"Right here." Sasha showed the driver where to stop.

Tash pushed the front door. Miles Davis and John Coltrane provided the soundtrack for the night. The setting of the sitting room reminded Tash of the opening scene in an Agatha Christie play. The characters took the places assigned to them by the director – Miss Katya Volkoff.

Nick was bent down by the wine cabinet door, choosing a bottle. Anna and Faina sat at the table, feigning a card game, and Katya, in a short red sweater dress, sat demurely on the white sofa with a magazine.

"Good evening. How was your dinner?" The hostess got up to meet the guests. She introduced herself and took Lisa's coat. Lisa hesitated a little and handed Anna a bottle of wine.

Nick joined them. "Oh, Sasha, Château Lafite! Marvellous. I'll bring the opener."

He hugged Sasha's shoulders, demonstrating their "intimate friendship", and forcibly sat him on the sofa opposite Katya.

"Katya, hello." Sasha tried to break free from Nick's tenacious grip, but he didn't let him go.

"Hello," Katya said indifferently, while looking at her magazine. Anna and Lisa moved towards her.

Sensing danger, Tash dodged them, and with a cat-like jump, managed to take an empty seat beside her. Lisa and Anna were left to sit on a free sofa.

Katya continued her "reading", although she hadn't turned a page since the guests' arrival.

"Katya," Anna called to her, "please meet Lisa."

Katya reluctantly raised her eyes and turned her head. "Nice to meet you."

Finally, Katya was able to examine her rival. It took her only five seconds to make sure there was only one top model present. She feigned boredom and returned to reading.

The audience was watching the scene in silence. Nick and Sasha from the couch, and Faina from the table where she began to set up the backgammon board. Anna and Tash looked at Lisa, then at Katya, then at each other.

"I'm very pleased too," Lisa answered the back of Katya's head.

Nick poured wine, and uncomfortable silence gave way to the heated discussion about New Year's Eve. Lisa apprised them of how fabulous their family celebration was, and how fantastic it was when the whole family was together. Her parents were also here, but unfortunately, there was no room for them at the Cheval Blanc, and they had to huddle in the neighbouring "terrible" Les Airelles.

Fearing that there would be no second time, she quickly listed all the resorts they visited, all the hotels they stayed in and all the brands they wore, so that no one, god forbid, would suspect them of ignorance.

"Enough," Sasha said ironically. He imagined the forthcoming discussion as soon as they left the threshold of this house.

"No, I'm really interested in hearing about your trips, especially about New York." Katya peeked up from the magazine and stared at Lisa with genuine attention. It looked like she had decided to drive the last nail into her rival's coffin.

For the next fifteen minutes, Lisa "educated" Katya about where to go and where not to go in New York.

At a quarter to three, the guests departed. After a short silence, Katya looked at the others. "Who wants to start?"

They encouraged her with a friendly laugh.

The tension that had hovered over them for the previous three hours quickly evaporated. The spirit of friendship, joy and fun returned.

"I'm glad we met." Katya again took up a horizontal position. "Now I've seen the enemy. How *terrible* Les Airelles is!" Katya emphasised letter "r" imitating Lisa's strong Russian accent.

"I'm not sure it was entirely ethical on your part," Tash said, still feeling a little guilty for bringing Lisa around.

"What fascinates me is how Sasha acted completely nonchalantly. Poor chap, he must have been stressed between the two—"

"So he is a poor chap now?" Anna interrupted her husband. "He brought his wife to his mistress! And now he is a poor chap because of your spiritual generosity." Anna splashed her indignation out and smiled snidely. "Don't you ever think about pulling that stunt with me! I'll forgive your infidelity only if your mistress pays you for sex and you contribute it towards our household income."

Tash weren't sure whether Anna was joking or serious.

"To sum up," Katya said, changing the subject back to herself. "I have no competition. And … Sasha just messaged me. I wouldn't want him as a husband anyway. He'd rather stay with Lisa and cheat on her with me."

*****

Ella glanced at her watch, then at Alex and then rolled her eyes. It was eight, and he still wasn't ready. "Punctuality is the politeness of kings," she said.

In the few months they'd been together, Alex learned what mattered to Ella the most. She was well-mannered, talented and, unlike Tash, ambitious. She knew what she wanted for herself – and for him. Her new documentary about Grace Kelly was due out this summer, and California had become their second home for the time being. Art advisors from the Los Angeles County Museum of Art, carefully handpicked by Ella, became his best friends while she was working on set. Her friend, a fancy art dealer, helped him with the purchase of a couple of conceptual paintings, and now Alex was seriously considering starting his own art collection.

Ella's exquisite manners would be the envy of any duchess. She knew how to sit, which fork to use and even how to hold her teacup with a slightly raised little finger. Alex knew little about her background, but he was certain that she for sure had some blue blood in her veins. How deeply she was offended by the choice of Princess Diana's sons! She couldn't forgive Prince William for marrying "doors to manual"'s daughter, and Prince Harry and Meghan Markle's wedding caused her a lingering migraine.

Ella tapped her heels on the hardwood floor, following the butler into the living room. Alex was scrutinising the pictures, paintings and figurines that filled almost all the walls of the hallway and corridor of Lev Rozman's chalet. He recognised some details borrowed from Marc Chagall's works. The paintings were hung in a chaotic manner. Outlandish mermaids, exotic roosters and fantastic fish looked at him from everywhere. His time with the art critics in LA wasn't wasted; he'd learned to see what he needed to see.

As promised, Faina kept her dinner intimate. She sat Mr. Galvin, her boss and a senior partner at the law firm, at one end, next to Nick, reasoning that two passionate whiskey aficionados were also doomed to joint business success. She didn't find anything reprehensible in putting Tash and Alex across from them, and Ella beside Jacques, a bachelor millionaire who was a next door neighbour, opposite them. Faina, Oren, an old friend of her father's, Katya and Anna sat at the other side. The hostess was enjoying watching Alex give judgemental looks to his flame, who was openly flirting with Jacques.

"I think Donald Trump is a shame for America," Ella said confidently in broken English in response to Mr. Galvin's remark about the supremacy of populism in the modern world. "He doesn't understand anything in politics."

"But he was very successful running his companies," Katya intervened, suddenly remembering hearing how Fox News was praising Trump when she was flipping through the TV channels. "It's not easier than running a country."

"I don't agree." Ella didn't give up. "Business and country management skills are not compatible. Politics should be left to the politicians. And all his ideas about globalism … I am an ardent opponent of globalism."

"Trump is against globalism," Alex corrected her irritably.

"Ella, you can ask our dear Jacques," Faina said quietly, "about the difference in the management in business and politics. He left his brother running the company when he took over as Minister of Foreign Trade. Jacques, do you believe that you can apply your successful business experience in another area, for example, in government?"

All eyes were on Ella's neighbour. "Of course, my humble position in no way can be compared to the position of Monsieur Trump." Jacques smiled apologetically and added, "But, *oui, bien sûr* both experience of *diregent de la* company and my life experience are simply necessary for me to work in the ministry."

Ella, embarrassed, looked at Alex for support, but he deliberately ignored her.

"Trump's opponent looks awfully familiar. How could I know her?"

From the start of the dinner Oren had kept studying Ella's face.

"You don't remember her? She was married to Dad's friend," Faina whispered. She wanted to continue, but the doorbell rang.

"Sasha," suggested Katya and Nick in unison.

The arrival of a new guest defused the atmosphere, and the guests slowly started moving into the adjacent room where a roaring fire and desserts and digestifs from Lev Rozman's wine cellar were waiting.

Alex continued ignoring Ella, bursting into laughter at every joke Tash made. After the fiasco with the minister, who quickly lost all interest in her after her ridiculous statement, Ella frantically sought a new ally in the territory that had become hostile. The new guest, Sasha, presented as Nick's partner in a Mongolian project, gave the impression of a pleasant and well-to-do man. She noticed a wedding ring on his hand, but Ella didn't attach particular importance to this trifle, and within five minutes, she was excitedly enlightening him with details of her documentary.

Katya cooed merrily with Jacques, while not missing Sasha's behaviour in her peripheral vision. She saw how his eyes sparkled from the attention with which Ella so deftly was wrapping him. He was clearly fond of Ella's blatant assertiveness. Katya had no illusions about men. Yes, Sasha was a playboy who wanted the attention of all the women around him, except he wanted some more than others. But Katya wasn't about to be jealous of someone like Ella. She was used to having the upper hand in her relationships, and knew that whenever she was involved in a break-up, it was because she was the one doing the dumping.

She rose suggestively and walked gracefully into the living room. Apologising to clueless Ella, Sasha jumped up and rushed after Katya. Slowly all the guests followed them, leaving only Ella and Oren by the fireplace.

Ella smirked modestly. "It seems we were left alone," she said before displaying her perfect white teeth.

Oren was studying her round face, barely touched by fillers. She had changed a lot over the years, and if Faina hadn't told him, he probably would never have remembered on his own. "I didn't recognise you right away," he said quietly.

From the beginning of the evening Ella had had a vague feeling that she knew him from somewhere, but couldn't remember where.

"Yes, I think we've met somewhere. At some reception in Paris, perhaps? I lived there for a long time." Ella raised her cup close to her lips, slightly protruding her little finger, which Alex liked so much.

"No, my dear," Oren chuckled. "It was much earlier. In Herzliya. When you didn't yet know where Paris was."

Her fingers gripped the handle tighter and her smile froze.

"I still remember that party. So much fun. I remember how Vladimir, our stingy Vladimir, who died recently, poor fellow, invited the cheapest strippers imaginable, but there were plenty of you. At least three of you for each one of us. I'm sure I don't need to remind you further, Christina."

A man coughed behind her. Stunned, Ella slowly turned her head. Sasha had accidentally overheard their conversation from the doorway.

"Uh, I've left … uh … my phone on the table." He quickly slipped into the room, grabbed something from the coffee table and rushed back into the living room.

*****

Meanwhile, in the living room, Faina was filling the girls in on the details of Ella's story.

"I didn't tell you straight away because I wanted to double-check all the facts with my mum. Ella is …" Faina twisted her hand expressively in the air and, not finding the right word, continued, "… the first time I saw her at our house in Herzliya, my dad's friend introduced her as Olga. She was younger then and had a nice body. But my mum, who should have worked for Mossad, recognised her immediately. Once when she was going through Dad's phone, she found their correspondence. This Olga, under the name of Christina, had sent him her naked photos. They slept together a couple of times and he paid her. That was pretty much it."

123

Ageing and balding Lev Rozman was a legend with the ladies, but the thought of leaving his long-suffering wife, who had gained an extra thirty kilos, never crossed the millionaire's mind.

"This Olga-Christina managed to catch my dad's friend. The next time I saw her, she was the new Ella, a conservatively dressed respectable lady with manners. She bought a fake degree, converted to Judaism and wrote a book. Unfortunately for her and fortunately for the arts, her literary career was a flop. But instead of giving up easily, Ella decided to retrain as a director because her husband had connections in the movies. She produced a film, and her husband ran away with another stripper, leaving Ella an apartment and a modest allowance."

Katya opened her mouth, but closed it again and sat in silence.

Tash got up and went out onto the balcony. She wanted to be alone and put the thoughts that were raised by this story in order. "To unmask falsehood and bring truth to light" from an old school essay, which her father had helped her write, came to mind. Tash wept quietly. What was going on in her life? Where was Daddy's "to be, not to seem"? Where was her happiness?

Large flakes of snow swirled in the darkness of the night and landed leisurely on the wooden planks of the balcony. Was there love? Or was it an illusion? Or was it just an invention to achieve goals?

Tash closed her eyes and focused on her breathing and the small triangle between her upper lip and nose. Inhale … exhale … inhale … exhale … inhale … exhale.

She looked around. The hillock was covered with a thick layer of silvery snow. Frost tingled her flushed cheeks, but she was warm. She was sitting on a sled. Her mother wrapped her in a warm blanket and gently pushed her down the hill. Tash was sliding down; the wind was whistling in her ears. Bang! She was rolling without a sled. She couldn't tear her short fur coat, Grandmother's gift, which made all her friends jealous. Everyone knew that her parents were the youngest and most beautiful couple in the neighbourhood. Tash quickly climbed the hill. Now Mum and Dad would push her again, and she would slide down like an arrow. Instead, they were standing under a tree, not paying the slightest attention. How could they forget about her? Tash pounded Mum on the leg. "Why are you kissing him? You don't love me any more?" she cried. Mum smiled. She bent down, adjusted Tash's hat that had slipped over her eyes, and quietly whispered in her ear, "When you grow up, you will also have children and you will love them very much. Just as I love you." Mum kissed Tash on the forehead. "But your husband will also be dear to you. And you will kiss him so he doesn't think you love him less."

Something soft fell on her shoulders. She opened her eyes and saw the tall figure of Faina wrapping a blanket around her. Faina grabbed Tash's frozen hands and rubbed them thoroughly. When they warmed up a bit, instead of releasing them, Faina timidly raised them to her lips. Tash laughed nervously and tried to pull her hands away, but Faina didn't let them go. She ran her fingertips along the edge of the bracelet, the gold Cartier bracelet that she gave Tash after her birthday, and finally dared to look up. Tash was cowed. In this gaze she spotted what she had long feared to see.

The snowflakes continued their slow dance around the two figures on the balcony, frozen in dead silence. Tash knew that something had to change. She couldn't go with the flow any more.

Tash freed her hands, hugged her friend tightly and quickly disappeared behind the glass door.

The phone chirped, and a message from Lulu popped up on the screen: "Miss Romanov, are you ready for the shoot? London is waiting for you, doll." Here was the answer.

"I've got some news," she said to her friends. "I'm moving to London."

8.   How to climb the social Olympus

London

Tash needed a change, but on the way to the airport, she realised that this time it was for real. The last few days were kind of a blur. She was lucky to find a tenant for her grandmother's house given the current economic situation in the country. Her only concern was her dad and how he would survive without her. Tash sent him some money, enough to help in the short term. Anna was in London, Katya promised to visit at least once a month, and Carolina agreed to stop in on her way between Monaco and New York. So Tash knew she'd be entertained in her new home.

*****

Lourdes Lucetta – everyone called her Lulu – was Vivien's long-time friend. The forty-five-year-old Italian smoked like a chimney, swore like a bargee, brawled with clients, often slept through appointments and was many times dragged into dodgy deals. But her allure was captivating. After nearly thirty years in the modelling business – first as a model, then as an agent – she knew everyone in the world of fashion and beauty. A tall platinum blonde with a face wrinkled from sun and cigarettes, she still had the enviable body of a twenty-year-old.

"Come over after the casting. I have some business for you," Lulu's hoarse voice crackled in the receiver.

At precisely 2:30 pm, Tash pressed the brass bell button for Lulu's office in Covent Garden. She heard a loud crash out of the speaker, followed by the clang of the opening door. Tash glanced around the old, shabby hallway. A greasy carpet covering a cracked marble staircase indicated that Lulu's business was not doing well. On the second floor, wooden steps, which replaced the marble ones, moaned plaintively under Tash's feet.

"Miss Romanov, let me look at you. Haven't seen you in ages." Lulu made Tash turn around. "You look stunning, doll. Where are the jeans from?"

"Current Elliot, boyfriend cut. I can't get enough of them. They are just perfect."

"Your ass looks perfect! I'm only wearing black nowadays." Lulu's loud voice made the crystal pendants on the old wall lamps vibrate. "I'm in a black phase."

Lulu struck a pose to show off her black high-waisted leggings, short cashmere sweater and beaded vintage vest.

"Come in." She let Tash pass through the front of her. "How did the casting go?"

"I guess it was okay. They'll call next week. I've just moved, and there is so much work in London. I didn't expect it."

"Don't get used to that. It's because you're the new kid on the block. And of course, because you have the best agent!" Lulu smiled. "Ask other girls, they've been sitting without work for ages, making ends meet. Trust me, not everyone who moves to London lands a great flat in Knightsbridge and as many jobs as you."

Lulu led Tash into her office.

"But it's not work that I wanted to talk to you about. A friend of mine has a nice house in Ibiza, and I'd like to introduce you guys. If you stay there in the summer, you can work there; I'll arrange shoots for you. But first he wants to invite you to dinner."

And there it was. She had heard rumours that Lulu was engaged in some sort of pimping. Over the years in modelling, Tash had studied the market from the inside out and knew that the fashion industry was not only about shoots and shows, but also about providing arm candy and entertainment for powerful men. In the books for internal use, there was a figure next to each model's photos: the introduction fee.

Introductions, dinner parties and fun trips were routine in a model's life. Some acquaintanceships remained innocent, others went further. And as long as men continued dreaming of the beautiful and famous, the demand for models would not decline. And demand determines supply. What man hasn't dreamed of showing off to his friends in a Bugatti with a supermodel by his side?

Beauty and fame bought a woman a lot. Dinners at the fanciest restaurants, invitations to exclusive events, outfits from the best designers, trips to the most fashionable resorts, expensive gifts and interesting friends. Even though the latter often turned out to be as boring as mushrooms, eager for recognition through the objects of their possession, this nevertheless did not diminish the joy of the other advantages. The answer to why it was *de rigueur* for models was quite obvious. The question was why it was quintessential for these unfortunate toadstools.

Enlightenment came a few years ago, during Paris Fashion Week, when Tash and Carolina jokingly divided the guests at glamorous events into three categories.

A-listers consisted of actors, singers, top models, fashion designers and artists. They were the bait who enticed the other (paying) guests to attend. A-listers were paid all their expenses, plus an impressive attendance fee.

The invitees of the committees represented the second tier: big spenders, B-list celebrities, intermediaries (buyers, art consultants, journalists) and sponsors.

Everyone else belonged to the third and most extensive category: those who wanted to be amongst the beautiful crowd and who could afford it, those who came to hang out and could hardly afford it and, finally, those who wanted to hobnob with all the above and scammed their way in. They were Atlases of the entire fashion industry and, in fact, of the entire consumer industry.

Tash agreed to dinner on the condition that she could bring along a friend, Charlotte Bouvier. She knew Charlotte loved the company of rich men.

"Bring as many as you want," Lulu agreed. "The more the merrier."

*****

"Natasha, this is Francesco Ferrero," the deep Italian voice said. "Lulu gave me your phone number and said that you would honour me with dinner tonight. The driver will pick you up at nine."

Francesco chose Gordon Ramsay's eponymous restaurant on Royal Hospital Road, one of the fanciest spots in town. According to Lulu, Francesco was born into money and came from the wealthiest Italian stock. He turned out to be a tall brown-haired man with a smile that never left his face. The range of his interests was so broad that it included seemingly incompatible things. Finding something that he didn't excel at was nearly impossible. He played tennis professionally, skydived, did Ironmans and had even learned how to fly his father's Gulfstream between his family's houses scattered around the world. He was involved in high-tech investments and resided in New York.

His life was filled with adventures as full as his wine glasses with Sassicaia. At the end of the dinner, he sang "Santa Lucia" in a velvet baritone, which was greeted by a standing ovation, offered Tash his house in Ibiza to stay at, and then went to Farnborough, where his jet was waiting for him to return to the States.

*****

The alarm clock rang and rang. Tash glanced at her watch: 6:40 am. She wanted to linger in bed, but the shoot was in an hour.

At seven, she was in the back seat of an Uber reporting to Lulu about the dinner last night. "Francesco is lovely. I'm going to the filming now. Will keep you posted. And … good morning!" Tash knew Lulu would not hear this message until eleven, when the shoot would be in full swing and she could not answer.

Lulu hadn't lied when she said Tash would have a busy schedule in London. Each day began with an early rise and ended late at night. She was usually wiped with exhaustion and didn't have time to see Anna.

When she left the set, occasional snowflakes swirled in the evening air, melting before reaching the ground. All day, the film crew discussed the impending massive snowfall. This was her first English snow. More precisely, its pathetic likeness. She remembered February blizzards in her hometown. Sometimes they had to dig out the cars buried beneath the packed snow.

"I wish them happiness and prosperity!" Tash twirled the menu in her hands. She loved Cipriani's evening atmosphere. She liked its hum, the tables with white tablecloths arranged so close to each other that it made it impossible to pass without disturbing the neighbours. She liked hearing scraps of conversations at the neighbouring tables. It was the real show. A cabaret where people came for entertainment. Where women shone in the most revealing outfits from the latest collections, and men felt like spectators at a fashion show. She loved Cipriani for its theatricality, in which she preferred to stay in the audience.

"I can't even describe the expression on his face! Now that I'm over it, I even feel a little bit sorry for him. Did he really expect that I'd listen to him?" Tash twisted her face into a disdainful grimace and waved her hand to call the waiter.

129

"I would have listened. Everyone should be given a second chance," answered Anna.

It was their first conversation about Ben after returning from their Christmas holiday.

"Oh, give me a break! What could he tell me? 'Yes, I have a girlfriend and I can't leave her because she is terminally ill' or 'I promised to marry her at my parents' grave.' Well, she's not dying and his parents are very much alive and well. The only truth would be something like: 'I am an ordinary man who doesn't recognise monogamous relationships. And I want to fuck everything that moves,'" Tash sneered.

The waiter who had come to take their order stepped back.

"She's not talking about herself, she's talking about an acquaintance," Anna explained to the waiter, fearing she'd be branded as a whore in the eyes of the restaurant staff, where her husband was a regular. "Octopus carpaccio, cucumber salad, sea bass, dorado and spinach on the side."

The festive season had added centimetres to her waist, so Anna was now on the strict keto.

"I will be more vigilant," Tash said as she straightened curls left after filming. "For some strange reason the absence of another girlfriend of my boyfriend seemed to me rather obvious."

Not to put things on the back burner, she took her phone out of her bag to clear her social media from all unknown guys.

"Hallelujah." Anna served them each some carpaccio. "You deserve a good guy. Who is on the list? Francesco? He sounds decent."

And Anna delved into the merits of Francesco, whom she had never met. She could do this delightfully for hours. "And most importantly, he is madly in love with you," she summed up her presentation.

"Do you ever consider one tiny factor, whether I'm in love with him or not," Tash said with a smile. "We were filming in Shoreditch today. I absolutely love it there!"

"I can see. Your hats, vests and shirts, they don't do well in Mayfair."

Tash looked around. Anna was right. They were surrounded by men in club jackets and women in flashy dresses. Tash glanced down at her boots and wide plaid shirt and smiled apologetically at the elegant couple at the next table.

"I'm sure Francesco would have influenced you in the right way, made you a lady. Okay," Anna said as she took out her phone and started tapping, "the next candidate. Point two."

"Are you seriously writing a list of my suitors on your phone?" Tash cackled, trying to take the gadget from her.

"Philip." Anna looked up from the screen. "What about him?"

At the mention of Philip, Tash's face changed. Her attempts to erase the humiliating act from her memory were in vain. Each reminder made her hate Ben even more.

"I haven't heard from him since New Year's. He messaged me the following day and nothing since." Tash was engrossed in the plate with the fish.

"Well, who else?" Anna did not know which name to put under number three.

"Gregory." He was the first to come to Tash's mind. "It's quite possible to put his name on the list of applicants. And by the way, it's his birthday party this week. If you want, you should come with me."

"The same Gregory who tried to kiss you?"

Tash nodded affirmatively.

"Yes, let's go! Anyway, Nick's away on a business trip."

Anna asked for the bill. When it arrived, she reached for her wallet, but Tash got it first. Lulu was the source of an endless supply of new jobs, and the fees this month exceeded expectations. For the first time in her life, money was no concern. The rent from her grandmother's house covered her London rent, and her current income was enough to cover the rest, including a small allowance for her dad. This new independence opened up new, hitherto unknown, emotions and a thirst to move forward, ignoring the obstacles. At last, she thought, she had developed that notorious self-reliance that shrinks usually spend countless sessions trying to help their patients find.

*****

The private club, 5 Hertford Street, occupied five floors of an old Mayfair mansion. Tash was walking down the steep stairs in six inch heels, holding onto the burgundy velvet railings with both hands. Anna followed her, staring at her slinky black vintage L'Wren Scott dress, bought today at a second-hand shop on the occasion of Gregory's birthday.

"I'm six foot three in these heels! But you're still taller! I hope everything in your life is as grand as your height! Happy birthday!" Tash hugged Gregory and introduced him to Anna.

Gregory smiled at her and, turning his attention back to Tash, added, "Thanks for your kind wishes, beautiful. Come with me, I'll introduce you to the other guests."

Tash was seated next to the ginger Camilla from Gstaad, who bombarded her with questions about Philip and bored her senseless with titbits about her lavish lifestyle. Tash tried to remain pleasant and catch the host's eye, but despite her tight dress and high heels, Gregory was not paying any attention to her. Instead he was mingling with the other guests. Sometimes, when passing by her, he stealthily stroked her back or quickly kissed her neck. Anna, meanwhile, seemed completely engrossed in a conversation with some guy at the other end of the table.

As soon as the dinner was over, Anna ran up to Tash to share the news.

"Tash, I have to tell you about Karl. He's fabulous! We were talking about art all evening." She sounded excited and a little taken by him. "He owns an art gallery in San Francisco. Can you imagine anything cooler? And we have so much in common. We were actually in the same group at Art Basel. Isn't that something?"

"Anna, you're married. Remember Nick?" Tash smiled nervously.

"Oh, Tash. He's in New York. You know, he's there, I'm here, and there's an ocean of lust between us. Enough about me. Where's Gregory? What's your news?"

"I wonder why, when they stop paying attention to us, we fancy them more?" Tash nodded at Gregory, who was entertaining a curvy brunette in a red dress.

"Oh please, don't be a child. Everyone knows the best way to get someone's attention is to stop giving them yours."

Tash needed to say her goodbyes because of an early-morning shoot. As she was leaving, Gregory saw her out. The valet whistled for a cab and Gregory opened the door for her. Tash's dress was so tight that instead of fluttering into the taxi like a butterfly, she flopped down on the seat like a clumsy caterpillar. Gregory stuck his head inside the window, pulled her face close and gave her a passionate kiss.

"Thank you for coming. I'll call you next week." He slammed the door and waved.

The phone was ringing stubbornly. Tash knew that if she didn't answer, Anna would come to her house.

"He is incredibly interesting and such a great company." Anna was going through the details of their night out, mixing them with all the merits of her new acquaintance Karl. Anna did not stop. "And he's very down to earth, which is something special considering his background and his circle. We're having dinner next week. Also, he has an art show preview next weekend, and we're invited. It's utterly invigorating to connect with creative people."

"Who was Gregory with when I left?" Tash asked, after a long-awaited turn.

"No one at all. He was just being a good host. But we left before the party was over."

"We?" Tash exclaimed in amazement.

"It's not what you think. He just dropped me, wanted to see where I live. It was all very innocent."

"Um-hmm, it doesn't sound so innocent. And to what extent did he satisfy his interest?"

"He came in for a nightcap." The Stowes lived in a sizeable terraced house in Eaton Square.

"Anna!"

"Oh, Tash, he knows I'm married," Anna continued. "It was just a friendly, harmless drink. He *adored* our art collection and immediately invited me to his exhibition." Anna purred with satisfaction.

"Exactly! He adored that you, succumbing to his charms, will persuade your rich art-loving husband to buy his paintings. What a smart ass!"

"You, my dear, are a cynic! Karl's not like that."

*****

The following Monday, Gregory asked Tash to dine with him at Harry's Bar. From her cursory experience of living in London, she knew that when a man took a woman to Harry's Bar, he had serious intentions.

London life revolved around belonging to the club. The centuries-old tradition played into the hands of enterprising restaurateurs who received additional income from membership fees together with free advertising of an institution cutting out "unclubbable" mortals. Harry's Bar was one of them. After a bottle of fine wine, Tash relaxed that her fears were in vain. Gregory was more courteous and considerate than ever, and they had a lovely dinner. While their Uber parked outside Tash's building, Gregory said, "Since our last meeting, I was dreaming of continuing what we started in Gstaad. I live only two minutes away. Would you like to come over for a cup of tea?"

"I have an early shoot tomorrow morning. Let's put it off until better times. Maybe this weekend?" Tash suggested.

"I have something this weekend, but I'll try." Gregory looked upset.

*****

All week Anna had been busy with preparations for her dinner at Karl's gallery on Friday. She wanted to look stunning, so she decided to try all kinds of treatments that promised eternal youth, instant lifting and extraordinary hydration. Friday morning took her by surprise. Her face was peppered with dark brown crusts from a laser treatment she had a few days earlier. She couldn't cover them up, no matter how hard she tried, and the only solution which came to her mind was to get hair extensions to divert attention from her face.

Anna's driver picked Tash up at six and drove to Daniel Galvin, where Anna had been prepping for four hours.

Anna's long blonde curls not only distracted attention from the scaly marks, but also made her look younger. It was clear from her smiling face that she was happy with the result.

Between the beautiful guests and the expensive paintings, the paparazzi were busy clicking away. Karl had a full house, but it was a bit of a motley crew. Hipsters with green hair and businessmen in tailored suits, grey-haired men and pretty undergrads, aspiring artists and established collectors all lined up at the bar.

Karl was entertaining a group of businessmen who all wore penguin-like black suits.

"Look how cute he is!" Anna breathed with admiration.

Tash looked up. Karl was indeed handsome. Dishevelled dirty-blond hair and huge, saucer-like eyes gave him a boyish look. A long plaid shirt with tight pants immediately gave away his arty background. Karl looked like a kid entertaining his parents' friends while his parents were away on business. Tash wondered how much longer he'd be able to sell this look. At forty, he might look more pitiful than cute. She didn't say this out loud to avoid offending the feelings of her friend, who was clearly intoxicated by his spell.

Charlotte Bouvier's presence did not surprise Tash in the least. This preview, as Charlotte truly believed, was her natural habitat – the environment of the rich and famous. She grabbed an exhibition catalogue at the door and rushed straight to the bar. With a glass in her hands, she browsed back and forth a few times, hoping to find someone she knew, but upon not succeeding, she decided to have a look at the paintings. She opened the catalogue in front of one of them to check the price. By the third painting, she was joined by Karl's gallery assistant, who started blathering about the artists presented in the exhibition. This was the last thing Charlotte needed now. She had already hired a man in a black jacket in the role of her guide and was annoyed with the gallery assistant, who encroached on her matrimonial plans.

Tash was watching the interaction from afar. No wonder the naïve assistant did not recognise Charlotte's true intentions. Charlotte tried so hard to be like *la petite bourgeoisie* that she actually managed to look like one. Each time she faced a choice between imitating a poor little rich girl or *une femme fatale*, she chose the former. And since the two personas were contradictory, it was impossible to combine them.

Tash chuckled. Poor, poor little Charlotte! She was not pretty enough to wear the baggy shirts and long skirts often donned by ultra-rich chicks. Their clothes were stylish and expensive, yes, but never sexy. Why would they dress sexy when their "incredible magnetism" was their inheritance. Poor little, but *not* rich Charlotte had such anxiety over fitting in that she glaringly stood out. Her careless style did not buy her a place in the cherished *beau monde*, but money would have. Instead of chasing high society, she should have chased money. After all, money buys everything, including status. But Charlotte wasn't the only one chasing that dream.

Countless nouveau riche were willing to squander their millions for the right to rub shoulders with some third-rate baron at a dinner party or some hotshot rapper in the VIP section at Coachella. The new aristocracy favoured by those with new money was Celebrity with a big shiny C, who in turn have been parasitising envious upstarts for decades. If you thought the Oscars and the Grammys were the top coveted awards in the industry, you'd be woefully mistaken. The real prizes were sought long before the ceremonies. Who was going to win the right to fly Leo on their private plane or invite Adrien on board their yacht or Kim to their summer house? Status seduced so many into believing that it was imbued with their exclusive enjoyment, all while appearing to be absolutely free. A delusional perk for the desperately deserving.

"Charlotte!" Tash hadn't seen her since that dinner with Francesco Ferrero.

"Tash, what are you doing here?"

Charlotte was surprised to see Tash, with her plebeian background, at an exclusive event of this kind. She glanced up and down at Tash. She thought Tash's pretentious business style – a crisp white shirt and high-waisted wide-leg black trousers – was in bad taste for an art event. In the distance, Charlotte noticed a classmate who could introduce her to Karl. She was about to say goodbye to Tash and move on to a more useful acquaintance when she heard that Karl himself had invited Tash, or rather her friend Anna, to the event and to dinner afterward.

Charlotte despised Anna. She considered her an upstart who had successfully married status. But since Nick belonged to the right social circles, where Charlotte was so eager to fit, she had to restrain herself and play nice.

"Oh, are you going to dinner as well?" Charlotte could not hide her dismay that after going to the best schools and usually being aware of all those present, she was not on the list, but the plebeian and the upstart were.

"Yes. It looks like Karl is hoping that Nick will buy all of his paintings. If you want, I'll ask Anna to put in a good word for you."

Charlotte, a young brown-haired woman with deep-set hazel eyes and a typical French profile, was born in Paris. After her parents died in a car accident, she was sent to her grandparents in Geneva. Her dad had taken care of her education by setting up a trust fund and paying for her studies at Le Rosey.

From the first days at school, Charlotte suffered from imposter syndrome. She was inferior to her classmates in absolutely everything. In her brains, communication skills, and most importantly, in money. Her stainless-steel Rolex, which she inherited from her mother, could not compare with gold Hublots. Her grandmother could not afford to buy her the latest Prada collections. But the biggest distress she suffered was over summer holidays.

All her classmates went to their houses, scattered all over the world, and often invited friends. Charlotte had nowhere to invite her friends to apart from her Parisian apartment, which her grandmother decided to rent out to replenish the budget. So Charlotte started making up stories.

At first, they were intended to convince her classmates that she was worthy of their friendship. Gradually, she started to believe them herself, and by university, she had a whole arsenal of tales that ranged from her secret inheritance to her noble roots.

After graduation, her girlfriends landed jobs in fashion PR, set up jewellery or swimwear brands, or became art advisors. The smarter boys focused on family ventures; the rest saw their calling in creative industries. Some found vocation in photography and directing, others became DJs, artists or art dealers like Karl. But their penchant for idle joys still served as their distinctive feature.

To truly belong became Charlotte's sole motivation for life. She copied her friends and set up a T-shirt business, which predictably did not result in success given her lack of style and ingenuity. But unlike most of her friends who lost their investments along with their focus, she at least didn't lose her grandmother's modest income in the process. Instead of looking for a job, she focused all her might on leading an idle life with enviable persistence, cherishing a dream that one day she would climb higher than any of her classmates with all their riches and ultimately land where she longed to be – in high society.

Karl was explaining something about one of the paintings to Anna when Tash joined them.

"You must remember Tash," Anna said to Karl. "You met at Gregory's birthday."

"Of course, how could I forget Tash."

From the expression on Karl's face, Tash knew he had no idea who she was.

"I believe we've met before," he said before giving her an air kiss and half hug. Tash thought this was probably his standard response when meeting a new person.

"Saint Barth, last New Year?" The name dropping began.

"No, I've never been to Saint Barth." Tash smiled inwardly knowing that she had just failed Karl's test to evaluate her importance and wealth.

Karl quickly turned back to Anna, instantly losing interest in a person who was so clearly beneath him. Tash discreetly asked Anna to ask him about Charlotte.

"Do I know her? Who is she?" Karl hesitated to answer.

"I think you know her. There she is." Anna pointed to Charlotte, browsing between the pictures.

"Oh! Unfortunately, the dinner is full."

The message was clear. Despite her best efforts, Charlotte did not pass muster.

The black and gold design of Isabel's gave an exquisite event even more polish. In February, artists, art dealers and collectors from all over the world traditionally flocked to London for auctions, exhibitions, openings, dinners and parties. After dinner, music played louder and guests moved to the bar. Anna was glued to Karl, so Tash decided to leave.

She was looking for a cab on Albemarle Street when someone called her name.

"I'll take you home." Gregory took her hand, kissed her palm and led her to his car.

He didn't drop her hand during the drive, regularly bringing it to his lips and kissing it. He stopped just before her building.

"Actually, why don't you come to mine? I'll bring you back as soon as you want. Please?"

Tash hesitated.

"I promise." He hit the gas before she changed her mind.

His house was indeed not far.

"Do you live here alone?" Tash was studying the paintings in the living room. They were magnificent. "Are they what I think?"

"All originals. My grandfather collected art. And yes, I live alone ... well, sometimes my mum will come and stay with me. It's *technically* her house." He gave her his most sincere smile. "What would you like to drink?"

She sat on the large settee upholstered in antique tapestry while Gregory opened the doors of the carved, gilded wooden wine cabinet and chose a bottle. He grabbed two crystal goblets from the sideboard on the way.

"To us," he said, as he passed her a glass. As she took a sip, he looked into her eyes, gradually lowering his gaze to her lips, then to her chest. He took the glass from her hand and put it on the table.

The soft touch of his lips got her curious about what would follow. His arms wrapped around her waist, his fingers struggled against the buttons of her blouse. She executed the presumed script, which expected her to put her hand on his fly. She did but was surprised not to feel any significant elevation. She continued her search suggesting he needed more time.

Gregory dropped to his knees. His tongue penetrated her mouth like a hungry raptor. He lifted the hem of her blouse, she raised her arms, and as soon as the blouse was on the floor, his lips went straight to her breasts. She felt his awkward kisses sink lower and lower.

Gregory pulled her trousers off and quickly spread her legs. He started with her inner thighs, then moved to her lower abdomen, leaving the surface of her skin moist from sloppy kisses.

"How wet you are! Do you like the way I tease you?" He had managed to slobber over the entire inner surface of her thighs.

Tash didn't know what to answer. She felt nothing but pity for him – his movements were so inept.

He finally got up and unbuttoned his fly, but the miracle did not happen. Not in the least embarrassed that he was still soft, he moved towards her. Tash shifted a little and he was forced to land in an empty seat. As if nothing had happened, Gregory continued the conversation about wines. Half an hour later, when decorum was observed, Tash got ready to bounce. He begged her to stay and sleep beside him, and feeling guilty that it had all ended so stupidly, she agreed. The ridiculous farce had exhausted her so much that she instantly fell asleep.

"Gregory, Gregory."

Someone was ringing the doorbell persistently. A few minutes later, a knock was added.

"Gregory, there is someone at the door." Tash pushed Gregory, snoring peacefully next to her.

"What? Who?" He was half-asleep and didn't understand what was happening.

"Someone is knocking on the door!" Tash screamed.

Gregory jumped up like a scared jackrabbit.

"Oh, no! What should I do?" He grabbed his head. "It's my girlfriend."

Tash didn't know whether to cry or laugh.

"Girlfriend ... what? How long have you had a girlfriend?"

"About two years. She is going to kill me if she sees you. What should I do?" Gregory ran to the balcony, seriously considering it as a good escape for Tash.

"Don't even think about it." Tash giggled, trying not to show disrespect for Gregory's tragedy. "Take the fall for this yourself."

As they whispered, the knocking and screaming did not stop.

"Gregory, who are you with? Open the door!" Now Tash could hear a cry added to the screams. "Open it now! I'll kill her!"

"How pathetic would it be to be killed by someone's angry girlfriend when you didn't even manage to sleep with her boyfriend," Tash thought behind a visible smile as she dressed quickly.

About ten minutes later, the angry lioness gave up and the pounding and screaming subsided.

"She's probably going to try the back door now," Gregory said quietly as he leaned against the front door and, making sure the passage was clear, pulled Tluckash towards the door.

They heard the footsteps and the creak of the door from the side of the kitchen. Gregory pushed Tash through the front door and quickly slammed it shut.

"I'm going to kill her!" Tash heard the noise of a struggle inside as she ran faster away from the house. Being killed by an unknown raging girl was not part her life plan.

At the end of the street when she finally felt safe, she took a deep breath and laughed. "It could only happen to me. Twice in the new year! What luck!"

9. World Laundry or How to cleanse a tarnished reputation

London

Tash got pulled into London life with shoots, gym, yoga, walks and fun get-togethers. But what she loved most were the trips to the Stowes' country estate.

She adored the English rural landscape so much that she never wanted to return to the city.

Meadow Hill was spread over five acres of a picturesque hillside in Oxfordshire. From the large Victorian house at the very top, one could see the entire estate. When Anna first arrived at Meadow Hill, she had been overwhelmed by the sheer scale of "mouldy old" that had accumulated in the house over a century. Inspired by the French Riviera, she completely redesigned the interior in Provence style, which she viewed as the quintessential example of European chic. Anna also made sure to up the indulgent factor by adding tennis courts and an indoor pool with a spa. Everything was shiny and new. Nick, however, miraculously managed to save the old stables from demolition, so a bit of his treasured "mouldy old" remained, albeit far from Anna's scrutinising sight.

"I would happily sit here forever, with sheep and cows grazing around outside and a couple of kids running around inside, and just invite my friends over to dispel the boredom," Tash said dreamily as she sat on a floral chair in the main sitting room.

"There is a pretty good chance that could be arranged. I'll ask Nick to call around. Perhaps you'll like one of the country bores, and we'll become neighbours." Anna placed a deep bowl of mixed berries in front of Tash. "Eat these to improve your complexion," she said. "It would be great to throw a party here."

"Or we can just go out to one of the cute country inns in the area."

By cute country inns Tash meant the five-star hotels that had been converted by owners from properties like Meadow Hill into business ventures.

"In a restaurant? Here in the village?" Anna displayed as much contempt on her face as she could. "Are you crazy? No self-respecting local would ever go to a restaurant like that. We only visit each other. These hotels are for foreigners and the nouveau riche."

Tash bit her tongue rather than point out to Anna that as an American who'd married into money, she was both.

"By the way, Karl messaged me," Anna said casually. "He said he has a wonderful Rothko."

"Rothko?" Tash tensed. "Mark Rothko?"

Anna did not dare to look up at her. "I mentioned to him once that Nick has long dreamed of having one."

Tash tried to catch her eye. "And what did you reply?" Tash put a blackberry in her mouth.

"I told Nick, and he asked me to find out more." Anna was looking intently at something on the phone.

"So, you kind of got Nick's blessing to go out with Karl?"

Anna finally looked up and smiled. "Tash," she said calmly as she closed the door to the living room so that none of the staff could hear their conversation, "Karl is my friend and he is an art dealer. He's merely going to help Nick find the painting he wants," she said in a chaste manner.

"Do as you wish. But you know my opinion – you're playing with fire." Tash looked out the window and shook her head at the dreary view. "Will the rain ever stop?"

*****

Karl was pacing back and forth under the overhang of the Claridge's Hotel. Tall glass with metal art deco patterns reflected the rain while he waited. Anna said she was around the corner. He saw the blue Bentley turning from Davis Street.

The porter hurried to open the door. A long grey cashmere coat softly hugged Anna's slender silhouette over a striking black knit jumpsuit. Despite her height, Anna preferred wearing heels even during the day. Karl grabbed her hand and took her inside the hotel.

143

"Do you remember the plan? I'm the one negotiating, you are just sitting and smiling," Karl instructed Anna about the upcoming deal.

"Don't worry, I remember." Smiling, Anna stroked Karl's back, trying to relieve his concern.

She was about five centimetres taller than him in heels, and she looked at Karl as if that difference gave her superiority in wisdom.

A week earlier, Karl had mentioned that his good acquaintance, an art dealer from Hong Kong who specialised in abstract expressionists, including Jackson Pollock and Mark Rothko, so dearly loved by Nick, was coming to London.

The art dealer was buying a Rothko from one of his American clients, who wanted to make a transaction in Europe for tax reasons. Anna immediately called Nick, who had always coveted the abstract artist's creations. An hour later, Karl sent Anna a photograph of the painting and said that the provenance was impeccable.

"Nick asks how much he wants for it." Anna sat at her mahogany desk writing out a long list of errands for her driver.

"I just spoke to him," Karl said with a gasp, adding significance to his voice. "Andy, the dealer, wants eleven and a half million pounds. I assume that he added at least five percent to the seller's price for himself. But it's still a trifle for Rothko."

"Or he just named the price in dollars, not in pounds," Anna joked. "But in any case, it's not our business to get into his pocket. The only thing we're interested in is whether your commission is included."

"No, that's just Andy's price. I can't lie to you," Karl said sweetly, despite having just negotiated with Andy for the price of eleven million, even.

"Hmmm, honest and cute." Anna was drawing hearts on a piece of paper intended for the driver. "I'll speak to Nick and call you back later." She hung up.

Nick's venture capital office in New York was the only profitable branch, so he tried to spend most of his time there. The Barcelona subsidiary had to close a few months earlier under pressure from the trustees of the late Mr. Stowe's trust. They had the London office at gunpoint, so it was most likely destined for the same fate. Nick's objective was to demonstrate thriving activity resulting in a profit to the trustees, so that they, in return, would finance the travel, purchases and other attributes of his luxury life with his wife.

After Nick hung up with Anna, he asked his PA to connect him with one of the trustees.

"John is on the line," the secretary said into the speaker.

"Good afternoon, John. How is your father doing?" Nick sympathetically attended to the health of the senior Mr. Hawke, who had recently undergone heart surgery. "Getting better?"

"Yes, thank you, Nick. With your prayers," John answered. "How are you? How is Anna?"

"I am very pleased to hear about your father. Please send him my regards. All is well here, thank you. Listen, John, I have some business to discuss. We are offered an excellent Rothko for eleven and a half million. The sale is private, not through the Auction House, therefore it's so cheap. It's really peanuts for a Rothko. I think now is a good time to invest in art when the financial markets are so volatile." Nick had to convince John to allocate the money from the trust to buy the painting. Over the years after his father's death, Nick had learned how to convincingly redirect trust money to cover his extravagant life.

"Why do you need a Rothko? You already have a lot of art work."

"This is just such a bargain! In a year's time, we can double the price at Sotheby's." Nick was sure that he knew as much about art as Charles Saatchi.

"Nick, the trust has no spare money right now. Why don't you sell something from your collection to buy the Rothko? You bought a Hirst and a Hockney some time ago. Maybe they've increased in price, and it makes sense to sell them."

John was right. Nick had become interested in British artists immediately after the financial crisis and convinced the trustees to invest in them. He would ask Anna to check with Karl about how much their Damien Hirst would go for.

As always, the five o'clock at Claridge's was noisy. Sharply dressed guests were welcomed into the luxurious lobby by bright green armchairs with geometric patterns set against yellow walls. A giant green-and-white floral arrangement towering in the centre of the room evoked a playful air, directly below a spectacular pale-green Chihuly chandelier, which Karl said consisted of over eight hundred separate pieces of glass. Art deco peculiarity perfectly matched the eclectic crowd.

Foreign speech and alluring accents could be heard throughout the treasured hotel. One could see Arab women in burqas, tanned Brazilian industrialists, elegant Belgian art dealers and American financiers. The Claridge's Foyer was the epitome of London's cosmopolitanism, a crossroads of cultures, nationalities, languages and religions, as well as a global money laundering hub, where everyone gathered to partake in the English tradition of afternoon tea.

Andy took a table at the far end of the room by the mirror. From the Christie's and Sotheby's brochures laid out in front of him, one could easily guess his *métier*.

Karl patted Andy on the shoulder.

"Hi, buddy, here is your potential buyer, Anna."

Andy stood up. Anna, smiling, turned her cheek amiably for a kiss. Andy, a short, skinny Chinese man of about thirty-five, wore a gold brocade jacket and high-waisted skinny black trousers.

"I wish all my buyers were as beautiful." He pushed the chair closer. "Anna, sit next to me."

Karl scowled at Andy. Was this rascal intending to take Karl's commission? Karl had been in the art world long enough to learn the rules: everyone had a right to cheat, swindle, steal a client, underpay a commission or even slip in a fake.

"I'll sit next to you, buddy, and Anna can sit opposite," he suggested.

After an hour of negotiations, including calls to Nick, Nick's calls to trustees, and Andy's calls to his client, they all finally agreed: Nick would give his Hirst for three million towards the eleven million for the Rothko. The trust would transfer the remaining seven to an escrow account until the transaction was closed. Andy and Karl were delighted with the opportunity to earn commissions on both paintings in one trade. Nick was happy because he finally became the owner of a long-desired Rothko. Anna

146

was happy for Nick and Karl, and the trust was happy to get rid of the illiquid Hirst, which had grown in value by only a hundred thousand, unlike the Hockney, which had skyrocketed since 2009.

*****

London proved to be the perfect place for a young woman. Over the past few months, the number of Tash's acquaintances had grown exponentially. With her tight schedule, Tash barely got together with a tenth of those whom she managed to meet. Sometimes she arranged several dates in one day: lunch with one, after-work drinks with another, and dinner with a third. Only a few lingered until the fourth date, and there was no question of the fateful fifth.

Thanks to Lulu's efforts, her work was booming, and so was her social life. Plays, balls, concerts, exhibitions, sporting events … something was always happening in the city.

Tash turned the key in the lock, pushed the door and entered her dark apartment. Her body ached and her head felt like cast iron. She went directly to the living room and collapsed onto the sofa.

She woke up from the sunlight hitting her eyes. Her muscles throbbed and her head felt like it was about to split in two. She took her temperature: thirty-eight point five.

"I've got fever. We have to cancel the shoot," she said to Lulu's answering machine before crawling to her bed.

She was in pain, and the shivers and nausea were killing her. She couldn't eat and could barely sleep. By evening, she was envisioning bizarre thoughts for her future.

She saw herself in a nursing home as an old, sick, godforsaken woman. Then she saw a cosy living room where an old couple sat holding hands in front of the fireplace surrounded by adoring grandchildren. It was Ben and Flo.

Lulu's call distracted her from her dark thoughts.

"Are you sick?" Lulu coughed into the phone.

"Yes, and I can imagine how I will snuff it alone. It's freaky."

147

"It's too early to think about death, Miss Romanov. You have enough time to find someone to spend your retirement with. Even I haven't lost hope yet." Lulu's hoarse voice, as usual, sounded optimistic. "I'm the one getting old. And I'm getting so out of shape, the stairs in this building are killing me." She laughed and then coughed. "Anyway, you'll be fine. Get better soon. I rescheduled the shoot, so not to worry—"

"Lulu," Tash cut her off in mid-sentence, "you've been coughing a lot lately. You should check it out."

"Okay, doll, you convinced me." Lulu hung up.

While Tash was on the phone with Lulu, messages from Katya popped up, one after another: "They pressed criminal charges against Sasha." "He's in London." "He wants me to come over."

A minute later, Katya's calm voice was reporting the case. "He left Russia three days ago. He was warned beforehand that charges would be pressed the following day, so he left with just one bag."

Tash heard the sound of a hairdryer in the background and could picture Katya gossiping at the salon. "He's staying at the Four Seasons and wants me to join him," Katya yelled into the phone, shouting down the hairdryer, "to help him with an apartment and to get settled."

"What about his wife? Shouldn't she be accompanying her husband in exile?"

"The children are at school. You can't pull them out like that, so she's staying in Russia."

*****

The porter opened the door and helped Tash out of the car. She walked through the glass doors of the Four Seasons Hotel and turned left into the bar.

She recognised Katya's blonde bob behind a wide man's back and her long legs in bright-blue trousers barely squeezed under the low bar table. There were other guests in the bar: two businessmen at one table, checking some important data on their laptops, and two bored prostitutes, nursing one glass of wine for an hour to save money while waiting for potential clients.

Katya waved happily.

148

"Finally. We've been waiting for you."

"Well, you have to update me." Tash hugged her friend and then her lover.

Sasha hesitated. "Nothing to tell, really. A common scenario: they pressed charges to do a smooth hostile takeover. They want to squeeze me out." Sasha looked more confused than upset.

"And what are the prospects?"

"Not bright. Either prison in Russia," Sasha said between sips of wine, "or life here, but without the business."

Alex had told her last summer that a massive redistribution of assets was happening in Russia. His uncle, the head of the state company, complained about the increased influence of the military forces. The treasury was running out of money, so it was much harder to steal. All spheres of influence had long been divided between the clans, and it was almost impossible to snatch a titbit without disturbing one of them. The number of silovikis (Russian strongmen who held political power) was growing, and the corrupt system which had been built over decades had to somehow feed itself. So they looked to successful businesses, opened criminal cases and began their blackmail. Everyone knew how initial fortunes were made; there were simply no companies that could not be tapped into. And even if, miraculously, the businessman turned out to be crystal clear before the law, a criminal case was simply fabricated. They were offered either a voluntarily waiver of their assets and a ticket abroad or jail time at home.

"Thank god you have something to live on! Business is only a headache." Katya truly believed that if her beloved had not had a business, they would have been able to travel more often. "We saw several apartments today," she continued. "But I think it's much better if he and his family rent a house, and I'll have an apartment nearby."

The plan of renting a house for Sasha's family in the immediate vicinity of an apartment for his mistress sounded amazingly natural coming from Katya's mouth.

After dinner, Katya and Sasha went to Harrods and then to the spa. It was not for nothing that Katya came to London. She would not fall behind her usual maintenance schedule, even in exile.

Katya looked at Sasha as a long-term project and invested her precious time accordingly. To avoid sidelong glances from those who would view him as a corrupt official who made a fortune out of the suffering of the common folk, she would enrol Sasha for polo and golf lessons. He absolutely must learn to play polo! In the meantime, she would look at possible charity ventures or some kind of intellectual club for herself. She was keenly aware that to create something charitable and intellectual, one did not need to *be* charitable or, God forbid, an intellectual. Katya knew that nothing whitewashed corruption money better than polo, golf and charity.

*****

Tash hadn't spoken to Lulu for five days, and her last message sounded somewhat cryptic. She invited Tash to her office, slipping that this was not a telephone conversation.

At two o'clock, Tash was at Covent Garden and was greeted by Lulu at the door with her usual cigarette in her mouth.

"Come in, Miss Romanov!" Lulu led her into the office. She had barely finished her cig before lighting up another one.

"Remember last time we spoke, I promised you I'd go see a doctor?" Lulu puffed greedily, as if it were her last cigarette ever. "So, I went." Lulu paused. "Immediately after talking to you." She took another drag, closed her eyes and slowly exhaled. "I have lung cancer. Stage three. I don't have much time left."

Tash couldn't get a word out. Her ears were blocked. Something clenched in her chest and her legs suddenly became like lead. She looked at Lulu, who was smiling cheerfully as if she merely had a cough.

"Why did you get so quiet? It's okay."

"I ... I don't understand." Tash was in shock. "How? How could they identify it so quickly? Didn't you feel anything? Stage three? Surely there's medicine, a treatment. We live in the twenty-first century. People do not die in their forties. This is impossible."

"They very often do die. And you know" – Lulu watched the cigarette smouldering in her hands – "I'm actually not at all afraid of death. I realised that I am much more afraid of being old and lonely. It's better to burn out quickly, like this cig, than to suffer from diseases, wrinkles, the indifference of men and so on. There's nothing keeping me here. I have no family, no children, nothing to make me live for. My friends will survive without me. You girls, too, you'll all get settled. And that's what I wanted to talk to you about."

Lulu sat at the table and started going through the papers. "You are a smart cookie; you won't be a model all your life. You have another five years, maximum, and then what? I thought about it and decided," Lulu said as she got all the paperwork together and pushed the stack to Tash, "that I want to give you all my contracts so when I die, you will continue my work. It's not rocket science, and you'll have some additional income. We don't have much time. I have to teach you everything before they send me to a hospice."

Tash was crying. "But Lulu," she babbled, "you won't die! I will help you in everything until you recover."

"Miss Romanov, I already talked to the lawyers to re-register everything for you. You just need to sign some paperwork." Lulu spoke more firmly than ever. "I'm proud of you and I know that you will do everything better than anyone."

"No, I disagree." Tash fiddled with the papers lying in front of her. "If you want, we can be partners." Her eyes lit up. "In fact, I have several ideas to develop your business." Tash rose from her chair. "I don't want to go into details now. Let's wait until you sort your illness out, but I want us to be partners." Tash walked around the table and hugged Lulu. "Everything will be fine." She squeezed her tightly. "Our business venture will be a blast, I know that," she said as she wiped her tears away. "But I need a business partner, a healthy business partner. You have to think about your health and take care of yourself." Tash took the pack of cigarettes from the table and threw them into the bin. "And this is not part of our business development plan."

Lulu smiled. "I know." She looked at Tash gratefully. "I have the best business partner in the world!" She kissed Tash on the cheek. "Don't forget to sign the papers tomorrow."

*****

After the formalities were settled, Lulu introduced her to all the intricacies of the business, paying particular attention to possible pitfalls. As Lulu suspected, Tash turned out to be a diligent student, and her fresh outlook on the business had already begun to pay off in the form of new clients.

Lulu had chemo once a month; the rest of the time she sacredly devoted to work. She seemed to find new meaning in life. She surrendered herself completely to their new project, which seemed to overshadow the disease. Thanks to their joint efforts, the number of contracts doubled, and soon, Tash had no time for her own shoots, choosing only jobs that either fed her ego or greatly fed her bank account.

10. How to get high in high society

Ibiza

"Hola guapa, que tal?"

A swarthy guy with an obvious fake Off-White backpack whistled loudly and blew Tash a kiss. She bristled at his blatant come-on and ignored him as she lifted her suitcase off the luggage carousel and rejoined her friends. A couple of minutes later, Anna's brown Louis Vuitton popped out from behind the curtain, but Charlotte, still empty handed, paced amongst the now dwindling number of passengers from the London flight. She walked around nervously, not taking her eyes off the cherished curtain, waiting for it to unveil her bag. The carousel stopped.

"No! Oh, the bloody Spaniards! How can they lose luggage on a direct flight?" Charlotte was indignant. The three women looked at each other and shook their heads.

"Not really the most auspicious start to our trip, is it?" Anna said as Charlotte stormed off to complain.

At the lost baggage counter, a bored woman in her fifties with pink hair lazily handed Charlotte the forms.

"Precisely how can you lose luggage on a direct flight? It was either not loaded onto the plane before we took off or it was lost here. It didn't just disappear. It must be here somewhere. Will you please ask someone to look for it? Maybe it was diverted to another carousel."

The blank expression of the tired woman spoke volumes. "Fill out the form. We will look for your luggage, and if we find it, we will send it to your address." The woman glanced at the old clock on the dirty wall and sighed.

"Are you seriously saying that no one is going to search for my luggage? Now, while I'm actually here?"

"Look, just fill out the form. There's a queue behind you. Next …" And she turned her absent gaze to the next passenger in line.

While Charlotte was filling out the papers and cursing under her breath, Tash and Anna walked back to the carousel. Tash looked around and then walked right up to the opening in the wall, bent over the conveyor belt and opened the curtain. The missing suitcase was right behind it.

Charlotte was over the moon when she saw her suitcase was safe and sound. She returned to the counter and, pushing aside the passengers, shouted, "Ha, we found it! It was right behind the curtain. Because of your laziness, the airport would have suffered financial losses delivering the suitcase to me, and I would have suffered undue stress and a spoiled vacation." She then turned to the passengers in line and added, "I advise you all to look carefully for your suitcases before you leave."

The woman rolled her eyes and sighed once more. "Congratulations. Next …"

*****

Francesco's villa was located on the north coast of the island. Spread over the gorgeous hills of San Miguel with an enviable 360-degree view, it occupied several hectares. The sunnier side boasted lazy fan palms and gnarly olive trees, while the shady slope was covered with majestic cypress and cedars.

Tash walked leisurely along a winding gravel path admiring the scarlet rhododendrons planted along the way. With each step, she felt her muscles relax as a light breeze kissed her neck and hidden cicadas greeted her with their tropical song.

The expansive villa consisted of nine private homes built in traditional Thai style, each set around an individual pool. The interiors were unique, with no repetitions in colour or decor. After inspecting the homes, Tash headed to the main pool, where Anna and Charlotte were already waiting for her. It took her several minutes to get there, but once she arrived, she admired the masterpiece. It was an incredibly long deep blue infinity pool, no less than twenty-five metres, that seemed to merge into the distant azure sea between the hills. Heaven! She saw a male figure in tennis whites approaching from the side with the courts.

"Welcome! Please look around and take whatever bedroom you desire. I want you to be my happy and relaxed guests," Francesco said as he wiped sweat from his forehead. "Feel free to make yourself at home. I have to finish the match, but I'll join you all later."

"You understand what we're doing here, right?" Anna whispered in Tash's ear. "He's crazy about you and invited us just to make you comfortable."

Tash smiled shyly because Anna was so right. Tash knew the rules of this game too well. How many times had she hoped that everything would be different, that she wasn't just eliciting primary sexual feelings from men who merely viewed her as a prize – but every time it was a disappointment. Some gave up quickly, not receiving anything in return. Others didn't lose hope and patiently continued their courtship. The players understood throughout the game that the end was inevitable, and someone would eventually have to surrender. She was tired of it and wanted to play a different game. A game not built upon lust but one with a stronger and more honourable foundation. A game where both participants would win in the end.

"I don't know who Francesco is crazy about, but he's definitely not for me." This was her final verdict. She glanced at Charlotte.

She was eager to enjoy her position at Francesco's house. She liked that she was in Ibiza, she liked that it cost her absolutely nothing, she liked that she would flood Instagram with photos from the fabulous villa, and her friends would finally understand that she meant something in this life.

"Maybe you should pin him down. What do you think, Charlotte. Do you like him?"

"I wouldn't mind …" Charlotte looked thoughtfully towards the court. "But it's pretty obvious that he fancies you."

"Nonsense. Besides, men rarely know what they actually want! A couple of stories about my love for an imaginary man and Francesco will stop thinking of me as a victim. Believe me, I know how to make a friend out of a fan." Tash pushed her towards the court. "Go, cheer for him, men *love* to be admired."

Charlotte obediently got up and went to support Francesco.

"She has no chance!" Anna said after the retreating figure of Charlotte.

"There is always a chance. It all depends how you play your cards. She has *carte blanche*. They live in the same villa and will see each other every day. She will have a million opportunities to prove herself. Physical appearance has nothing to do with the quality of the person, and she's a very *motivated* woman."

Anna laughed. "Yes, but unfortunately her motivation can't compete with your beauty."

*****

"Is this better now?" Anna's long leg in a black ankle boot with metal details on the toe kicked into view from the doorway. Then the rest of her appeared in black micro shorts and a tight grey T-shirt with chains.

Tash had to admit that Anna had finally succeeded in understanding what to wear to the DC10, a famous club in Ibiza which had been converted from an old airplane hangar. But twenty minutes earlier, Anna had appeared before her dressed in a white silk fringed robe and slippers with Swarovski crystals.

"No, no and NO!" Tash had screamed. "You will cut your feet, lose the stones from the mules, and that white silk will turn into a grey rags in an instant. Put on your sneakers and shorts!"

Anna, disappointed, left to change. This time Tash was more supportive.

"You're still too chic for the club. Chanel boots? They are destined to inevitable death."

"I could not care less. Karl will be there, and I don't want to look like a bum." Anna couldn't comprehend that looking like a bum was the very essence of DC10 style.

Charlotte was waiting for them on the terrace.

"Well, what do you think? Am I looking good?" She spun around for inspection. Her sexy denim jumpsuit accentuated her round tight butt and hugged her in all the right places. A sliver of pink lace was visible beneath the plunging neckline, and platform sneakers added an extra ten centimetres to her height. "Do you think he'll *finally* notice me?"

Despite the intensified efforts of the three participants in their plot for the love match, weeks of staying at the villa hadn't brought Charlotte any closer to Francesco. Both Tash and Anna contributed to this union in every possible way, often leaving them alone together or suggesting scenarios that they thought might attract them to one another, but to no avail. Lulu organised jobs for her protégé-turned-business partner as promised, and Tash was mostly away either producing the shoots or participating in them as a model. The timing could not be more fortuitous for the inevitable convergence of two lonely hearts.

"You look drop-dead gorgeous!" Tash, enjoying her role as a cunning pimp, cheered up the bewildered Charlotte.

"Sexy as hell!" Anna agreed. She turned to Tash and gave her a thumbs-up.

Francesco showed up from his bedroom.

"Well, are my beauties ready to go?"

The trio nodded their pretty little heads in unison. While Francesco, satisfied with the look of his brood, was taking his sunglasses out of their case, Tash pinched Charlotte's tight butt imperceptibly, giving her a signal for action.

"Ah, I will remember this night forever!" Charlotte cooed so sexily that she almost choked.

Anna could hardly restrain her laughter, and Francesco smiled broadly in response.

The driver was waiting in the car.

"DC10." Francesco turned Jamie Jones on. "This is for the mood," he said, handing them each a small bottle of juice. "Decide for yourself how much you need. I'm drinking it all."

"Hmmm, how much do I need?" Anna looked at the contents in horror. "I don't know!" She opened then closed the cap in confusion.

"Drink half a bottle, wait for half an hour. If you don't feel it, have another go." Charlotte was giving professional instructions on how to take MDMA.

The queue at the entrance was enormous. It would be a real nightmare to be stuck at the back. While still in the car, Tash felt slightly dizzy. The vibrations from the rumble coming from the club reached her eardrums, and the signal was immediately sent to her brain, which carried it throughout her body in the form of multiple reactions, sometimes contradictory. Her legs were pacing rhythmically, her hands were making imaginary circles, while her body was gradually losing gravity. A giant bodyguard pushed their way through the crowd. In just a couple of minutes they were already at the terrace. Anna and Charlotte were agog, like kids at Disneyland. Their heads were constantly turning to check out all the smiling people in weird outfits.

"Now I understand why it's called *circoloco*," said Anna, pointing at a man with a green Mohawk in only leather shorts. His girlfriend wore nothing but a micro-bikini on her tattooed body.

The dance floor was crawling with ravers. Ripped guys and lean women held bottles of water and paced to the beats echoing from the powerful speakers across the terrace. All eyes were on the DJ. The multicoloured beams of LED lights pierced the dance floor and immediately dissolved in the air, stale with sweat. Tash felt a sense of lightness, like her whole being had been gradually merging with the surrounding atmosphere. Nothing mattered anymore, only the music and the neon lights. A source of infinite bliss.

"It's not working on me," Anna complained as she marched in place, greedily downing the rest of the juice. Her pupils dilated completely and her jaw clenched tightly.

"Don't overdo it, you're already high!"

The last thing Tash wanted was to deal with other people's problems at the moment of her sacred union with the music, when only she, the dance floor, the DJ and the universe existed. Nothing else mattered. Tash put her sunglasses on and continued to move, smiling. People danced up to her, said something and smiled. She smiled back and kept dancing. She was happy. She loved this crazy environment, loved her friends, loved the music.

She felt someone's hands wrap around her waist. She continued to dance, because the universal love that embraced her expanded to everyone, including the owner of the hands. Still under the spell of the all-encompassing feeling, she turned around. He held her waist while she studied him closely. He was wearing a burgundy Moroccan robe. A strand of dirty-blond hair peeked out from under a Turkish turban on his head. His eyes were hidden behind blue sunglasses, but she knew those eyes too well. She smiled in silence and turned around. Ben hugged her from behind and they continued their dance.

"Take some more." Ben handed her a little packet with grey crystals.

Time seemed to have stopped. She didn't see what was happening around her. Only Ben was added to her perfect universe in his blue sunglasses and Moroccan robe. She lost track of time, but as soon as the contents of the packet were emptied, the ghost of harsh reality loomed in the distance. Her mouth was dry. Ben pulled her hand and she obediently followed.

Gregory's annoying ginger friend rushed up to them. She examined Tash's neon sneakers, fishnet leggings and pink tutu with genuine curiosity. She finally asked, "And where is Philip? Where is Flo?" The decibels of her high-pitched voice rattled in Tash's ears.

Tash wasn't ready to answer questions and smiled stupidly. Ben muttered something in response and, grabbing Tash's arm, walked towards the bar.

"I don't want to see or hear anyone except you!" He took his glasses off and Tash saw his eyes. A thin blue border gleamed timidly around his huge black pupils. "I missed you so much!"

"Me too!" She didn't want to go back to reality. "Let's run away from here."

On the way to the exit, they bumped into Anna and Karl.

"Where are you going?" Karl spoke to Ben. Anna in black sunglasses, greedily gulped water from the neck of the bottle. The fact that Tash was with Ben didn't surprise her at all.

"Charlotte's gone home with Francesco," Anna reported happily.

"We'll discuss everything tomorrow." Tash blew Anna a kiss goodbye and followed Ben to the exit.

"Cala Jondal, por favor," Ben said to the taxi driver and, without hesitation, squeezed her closer.

Either from the ecstasy or from something else, she saw tears in his eyes. All the way to Cala Jondal, Ben caressed her face and her neck, not daring to sink lower. In response to those light touches, Tash slowly ran her fingertips over his chest.

As soon as the gate closed, Ben picked her up and carried her towards the house. She tilted her head back to admire the spotted disk of the moon glowing in the blackness of the starry sky, then she stretched up to kiss Ben on the cheek. They heard loud voices and music playing at the back of the house. For a second Ben hesitated, deciding where to go, but glancing at her smiling face, he took her straight to the bedroom.

A glass table lamp illuminated the spacious room. Ben laid Tash gently on the bed and hesitantly pulled her closer. There was nothing erotic about this hug, just an endless feeling of closeness. So they lay for several minutes in silence, hugging like close relatives.

The smell of a joint filled the room. Puff after puff, her eyelids became heavier. Strange visions flickered over her head. She felt something warm and soft crawl under her pink tutu. She reached out to the source of warmth and felt Ben's thick hair. She could only distinguish temperature fluctuations in her body. She rose when a burning stream of energy penetrated her body, then fell back when it left. Her body was floating in the air. Together with the source of energy, they rushed, crossing space, as a whole. She didn't want to return to earth.

The sun had almost reached its zenith and was as hot as burning coals. Warm air broke into the room through the open window. The wide blades of the ceiling fan moved slowly, pumping the air choked with sweat and marijuana in circles. She didn't find Ben next to her. She reached for her phone – it was dead.

She heard voices outside the door. Tash remembered that Ben was staying at a friend's house. She got out of bed and wandered into the bathroom. On the table by the bed there was rolling paper, a lighter, stems and seeds, and a small piece of note paper: "Mermaid, I have an early flight. I decided not to wake you up. I told my friends that you and I came here after the party and fell asleep while waiting for everyone. They will drop you at home. It was nice to see you! See you soon!"

She read the note several times. Her mouth was so dry that she couldn't swallow and her head was cracking with pain. But it was nothing to the pain burning inside her. She lay down again, tried to get up, but being unable to cope with her body trembling with anger and resentment, she crashed back onto the bed. She closed her eyes. Music was ringing in her head, multicoloured beams of light were flashing before her eyes, and above the DJ booth, the inscription in neon light was lighting up with the beat: it read "It was nice to see you! See you soon!" Ugh!

She woke up with a burning sensation inside. The sheet under her was soaked through, and her body, dehydrated during the night, was covered with drops of thick salty sweat. She must have been lying like that for more than an hour. The air conditioner didn't work and the hot air from outside filled the entire space. She felt the remnants from her dinner moving up her stomach to her oesophagus and approaching her throat. Tash tried to contain herself, but it was too late.

She was sitting on a grey sandstone floor, her auburn hair messed up in a tight knot. She saw bits of last night's dinner stuck on the inside of the toilet bowl. She felt neither the temperature of the hot floor, the sickening smell of her own vomit nor the dryness of her eyes from continuous sobs. The only thing she could recognise was a piercing pain in her chest, in the very place that her favourite heroines called "the heart."

She got up slowly. A cold shower gradually brought her back to life. When the voices outside faded into the depths of the corridor, she left the room and tiptoed to the exit.

She took a few steps towards freedom and sighed with relief, closing the heavy front door behind her. She straightened out the crumpled pink tutu, looked up and caught sight of the house guests, all watching her closely from the long dining table.

The silent scene was broken by a young man with a bun, who seemed to be leading this feast. "Good morning!"

Tash looked in vain for familiar faces. Instead she heard a bitter laugh from the far end of the table. The round face grimaced and the thin mouth changed into a malicious grin. Camilla had her answer to last night's question.

"Good morning!" Tash said shyly. She nervously straightened the thick braid which she had managed to hastily make from her tangled hair.

"Please have a seat, we just started our lunch." The young man with the bun got up to take her to the table.

"I'm so sorry for interrupting your lunch. Thank you, but I'm not hungry. I'd rather go."

Her cheeks were flushed, either from the midday heat or from sudden shame. Or from a bit of each. Tash felt naked under the piercing gaze of the curious onlookers.

"We would be honoured if you joined us, but if you want to go, the driver will take you right away."

"Thank you. You are very kind, but I really have to go."

The young man escorted her to the car.

"Alan, please take this lady wherever she needs." He turned to Tash. "It was nice to meet you. I'm Charles."

The car was passing smoothly around the corners of the winding roads of Cala Jondal. On any other day, Tash would admire the rugged rocky coast, enjoy the smell of blooming bougainvillea and the chirping of cicadas, but now she hated this beauty. The brightness of the sun, the crystal blue of the sea and the clearness of the sky irritated her eyes. As soon as they passed Sa Caletta, Tash closed her lids.

"Left or right here?" The driver's question woke her up. They passed San Miguel and stopped at a fork.

"How long did I sleep?" Tash rubbed her eyes. "To the left, thank you." She smiled at the driver.

"Half an hour, maximum." He turned left. "I tried to drive carefully, miss, to not wake you up." He spoke with a strong Spanish accent. "Mr. Charles called and asked to take your phone number to invite you to dinner tonight. He also left his number." The driver handed her a piece of paper with the number. "And said you have to ask him if you need something."

"How gracious of Mr. Charles. Do you know how long he is going to be in Ibiza?"

"He spends his summers here. I've been working for him for several years now, he's a very good client and friend."

The car drove up to the massive gate of the villa. Tash peered out the window for the guards to let them inside.

"Thank you very much! And kindly thank Mr. Charles."

There was a muffled sound of a tennis ball coming from the court. Francesco waved as soon as he saw Tash, said something to his partner and rushed towards her.

"Well, hello. And where have you been?" The usual white-toothed smile never left his face. Only now did Tash admit the existence of other people in the universe and thought that Francesco could well be upset at her behaviour.

"Let's go to the terrace." He took her arm and led her there. Tash followed every small movement of his face, trying to guess his mood. Why was he dragging her to the terrace? She was so rude to spend the night away without even warning the owner of the villa. For the second time that day, she felt ashamed. Bloody Ben! She lowered her gaze to her filthy sneakers and followed Francesco.

On the terrace, a dessert table was set apparently from the lunch that had just ended. Anna and Charlotte were playing backgammon in the shade. As soon as Francesco came into view, Charlotte jumped up and greeted him affectionately.

"My love, how I missed you!"

Tash, taken aback, watched the two embrace dramatically. Tash wasn't the only one who seemed to have had an eventful night. She looked to Anna, who was lost in a daydream. Tash smiled. She was at home surrounded by friends. Rather odd friends, who were more preoccupied with their own business than where she'd been all night, but still her friends. For a second, she even pouted, but looking at the newly formed happy couple, she immediately forgot about her grudge.

"I think we all have something to share." Tash winked at Francesco, who was gently stroking Charlotte's hair. They looked like a match made in heaven.

Charlotte was eager to give Tash the details.

"It was like lightning flashed between us in the club. We realised that we really liked each other." She gave Francesco an affectionate look. "And we decided to spend the night together."

"Of course, the lightning was nothing but G-induced," Anna remarked sarcastically, awakened from her dreams. "G" or Roach was famous for its powers to induce sexual attraction to a nearby person and was often used by despicable men to seduce inexperienced girls.

"That's not true," Charlotte said, looking at Francesco for support. "It just made us realise that we are not indifferent to each other." She got up from the chaise longue and flopped down on Francesco's knees.

"How did it go with Ben?" Anna lowered her voice, unsure if she should raise the topic.

"Yes, we are very interested in the details!" Francesco was stroking Charlotte's round bottom, wrapped in navy shorts.

"Not much to report." But her tear-stained eyes said otherwise.

"And where is he now?" Anna's gaze penetrated Tash's soul like an X-ray, and her moralising tone returned Tash to the idea of what kind of an idiot one had to be to trust Ben again. Large drops of tears ran down her cheeks.

Francesco gently lifted Charlotte from his lap and walked over to Tash.

"Is this how many tears fit into women's eyes? No man in the world, you hear me, no man is worth being so upset about. Especially for a beauty like you. Tell me now what happened?" He sat down next to her and put his arm around her shoulders.

After calming down a little, she briefly told Francesco her story with Ben. Anna corrected her periodically, adding comments.

Francesco thought for a moment then said, "I'm sure he loves you. It's just that for us, it's always hard to break an already established relationship. We rarely leave. Only when women kick us out. Ben ran away because he was afraid of the consequences of falling in love with you again, and he has nothing to offer you. Until the situation with his girlfriend is resolved, there is nothing you can do. You have to live your life, otherwise you will always remain the other woman."

Tash said nothing. She just nodded.

"Thank you." She stroked his arm gently. "Now I need to change and charge my phone."

Tash closed the door. She lay down on her untouched bed and stared at the ceiling. Then she remembered how she had woken up that morning and started crying. The pink-cheeked face of her mum showed up within a few seconds. Sometimes her mother's long dark hair fell into her crib and tickled her cheeks. Tash laughed, trying to catch a strand. Her mum took her in her arms and gently lulled her. In those moments, little Tash wasn't afraid of anything in the world.

Twenty minutes later, she got up. Her phone had charged. She pulled the piece of paper the driver had given her out of her bag and wrote a message to Charles.

Then she returned to the terrace, fresh and smiling.

164

"The house in which I had the honour to spend the night belongs to Ben's friend Charles. He turned out to be a very nice chap, and to smooth the awkwardness of this morning, he's invited me to dine with them tonight."

"What about me?" Anna looked piteously at Tash. "These doves are a couple now." She nodded towards Francesco and Charlotte. "I don't want to be the third wheel!"

"Of course, you're going with me."

*****

Anna looked at her friend and thought, "Damn, that girl has excellent taste – Tash knows how to mix and match better than any stylist!" Khaki shorts and bronze sandals accentuated Tash's golden tan. She'd inherited an innate taste and basic harmony skills from her parents. She enjoyed creating things and had mastered sewing in home economics at school. From the sixth grade, she sewed for herself and for her friends, and from the eighth grade, she starting selling some of her items. Anna was aware that her own taste wasn't so impeccable, and she faithfully followed Tash's advice. She wore high-waisted wide-leg trousers to make her legs look longer; nude shoes with a pointed toe to make the shape of her calf irresistible; high collars to visually enlarge her breasts. Anna loved shopping with Tash, knowing that she wouldn't let her buy something unless it made her look utterly fantastic. It was on Tash's advice that Anna bought the dress she was wearing, which looked like a fishing net over a nude bodysuit.

"Very sexy! You look like the Queen of the Sea." Tash touched Anna's skin through one of the holes in the dress. "I adore Ibiza because you can wear anything here. No one cares, even if you go to a restaurant in your underwear."

"Is that a dare?" Anna jokingly lifted the hem of her dress to climb into the Range Rover. She settled comfortably in the passenger seat.

La Paloma was Tash's favourite restaurant on the island. Produce from its own organic farm was served in a simple family atmosphere where chilled guests could relax far from the touristy hotspots. It was only fifteen minutes from their villa. They passed the turn to Balafia, one of the few places in which the spirit of hipparion Ibiza was still flickering, and drove up to the parking lot.

Charles was waiting for them at the entrance.

"Nice to see you again." Charles smiled and brought Tash's hand to his lips. "I hope you had a rest?"

"I did, thank you. Charles, this is Anna."

"So nice to meet you. Let's go, everyone is already waiting for us at the table."

There were at least thirty people at the table, most of whom she recognised from that morning. The ratio of men to women, as usual in Ibiza, was about one to three.

"Do you want to meet everyone?" He was ready to introduce her to each of those present. "Here are my friends from LA, they've been here for a month. Dan runs a gallery, there is his girlfriend next to him and her friend. Next to them is my friend Andrew, whom I have known since birth."

"And who are the three girls at the end of the table?" Tash turned her head to the left.

"It's a long story." Charles poured Tash wine. "Three Brazilian Instamodels. One of them is dying to hook up with Andrew so they can move into our house. Her friends don't mind spending time with me."

"What do you mean to move into your house?" Tash looked perplexed.

"You don't know how it works in Ibiza?" Charles paused. "They come here and either stay at someone's house or rent an apartment. As soon as this someone leaves or the money for an apartment runs out, a frantic search for a new victim begins – with a place they can move to. As long as these ladies have a roof over their heads, they are all prudes," he added. "But the closer it gets to the fateful moment that they might need to leave, they magically change to libertarians just to stay in someone's house. And they bring their girlfriends." He winced. "Andrew seemed to like one of them. The one over there with the big silicone boobs, and he doesn't mind spending a week with her." Charles glanced at Tash. Her almond-shaped eyes became round, and her plump lips parted and folded into a heart.

"I don't get it." There was genuine surprise in her voice. "Why wouldn't they just leave?"

"First of all, they love parties, drugs and fun. Second, they love rich guys. Another chance for them to climb the ladder. For guys, this is a perfect no-strings-attached fling. They are stunning, hungry and ready to please. No brainer."

Charles was right. In fact, there was nothing in their actions that other women wouldn't do, just the conditions for these girls were more extreme.

"You're so cynical!"

"Please, my last girlfriend was a famous model, or rather, she became a famous model while going out with me." He looked slyly at Tash. "We met in Ibiza." He became serious. "I felt really sorry for you this morning and sent Ben a flaming message. He acted like a coward, not a gentleman. I don't know what exactly happened between you, but leaving you in stranger's house was a bit over the top. If I were you, I would never talk to him again."

"You messaged him?" Her heart started pounding. "What did he reply?"

"He answered in his usual style that he was the one to blame. That he feels very bad, but there was nothing he could do."

Charles and Tash looked at each other sympathetically.

"How long have you known him, Tash?"

Tash smiled – it was the second time that day she had to tell her story, but this time, to her surprise, she didn't feel like crying.

Charles listened attentively, admiring her, but trying not to get distracted throughout.

"Let's get back to this topic at lunch, the day after tomorrow? This is a long conversation, and I now need to entertain my guests."

"Imagine, Anna is the wife of Nick Stowe." Andrew was very pleased with his discovery and rushed up to share it with Charles.

"How wonderful! Nick and I are neighbours in Oxfordshire. We'll have to arrange a neighbours' dinner when we all get back." Charles then addressed the group. "My dear friends, I would like to raise this glass to friendship. Thank you for honouring our modest dinner with your presence. I really hope that this is not our last meeting, and please know that the doors of my house are always open for you."

Tash looked at the Instamodels at the opposite end of the table. Would they take it as a signal for them to board?

"Are you now thinking the same?" He nodded towards the girls. "Let's bet one of them ends up in Andrew's bed tonight, followed by the morning story of having nowhere to stay."

"I don't want to lose the bet."

"So, Anna is married to Nick." Charles whistled. "Our fathers were very close. But then the tragedy happened." The story of how Nick's father's partner had diluted his stake while he was having fun on the Côte d'Azur and Nick's father couldn't handle the mess and committed suicide had long been recycled in the tabloids. "We always had a lot in common with Nick, but, unfortunately, we lost touch. I heard he married an American, but I never once had the pleasure, until tonight." He nodded towards Anna.

As soon as the car door slammed shut, Anna turned to Tash. "Do you know who that was?" She nervously squeezed a pack of gum. "Charles Montague, heir to one of biggest families in the UK. Their estate is at least fifty bedrooms, but that is not the problem. Andrew and the LA guy are. They are close friends of Karl's. What should I do now?" Anna was getting hysterical.

"The fact that someone is friends with someone doesn't mean that someone is going to tell this someone something. I don't think Karl talks a lot about you. But the more people know about your affair, the more likely Nick will find out eventually." Tash paused. "The sooner you stop, the better." Tash looked into Anna's eyes. "I'm your friend, but you know my attitude to infidelity. Lying is a sin. I will never cheat."

"Never say never! All situations are different. A reasonable woman, which I definitely am, shouldn't marry without the consent of her mind and take on lovers without the consent of her heart. There are always happy days at first: new acquaintances, new houses, new trips … and then you get bored. Nick is good man, but, Tash, he bores me. Karl is my passion." Anna sighed. "Are there any normal men on this planet?"

Tash couldn't help laughing. She grabbed her phone and started looking for something. After a few seconds, Tash handed it to Anna. There was a photograph opened on her screen. "There he is. A normal man. This one is rich, smart and kind, and funnily enough, he happens to be your husband, in case you've forgotten."

*****

She opened her eyes. Charlotte and Francesco, passing by her window, were debating whether the model seen with Leo yesterday at Cipriani was a Victoria Secret model.

Tash didn't want to get up. She lingered a little more, then got up. She stopped at the sight of her own reflection in the mirror. No, she wasn't a thoroughbred English filly, auctioning for millions, but at least she was a tight African gazelle. Long shins with a pronounced relief turned smoothly into curvy hips, a tiny waist and firm breasts – her special pride. Everything was proportional and harmonious. Two round pink-brown buttons looked directly into the mirror and a small bean protruded invitingly from under the fine silk. She was horny. Lightly touching the plump breast, she slightly pressed on the nipple and quietly ran her finger along her body, finding herself at the very bottom. She felt the moisture of silk when she touched her love button. Tash closed her eyes …

… The room was dark, someone had drawn the curtains, and only the wrought-iron bed in the middle was illuminated by the floor lamp. A blonde with a boyish figure lay on it. The door opened and the girl smiled at her guest. Tash got up and leaned forward. His dirty-blond curls fell down over the girl's flat chest and his strong hands slid down her thighs. Tash wanted to move, but she couldn't take a step. She silently watched as he caressed the fluttering flesh of his mistress. Tash turned away in rage, but some invisible force brought her gaze back. Finally, she managed to step forward and touch his shoulder to announce her presence. Without stopping, he turned his head and, grinning, pushed Tash away with all his might. She was lying on the floor, choking with tears, and they were laughing at her …

Tash thought that from the reality of her dream she had lost consciousness for a moment. She was sitting on the floor in front of the mirror. Tears ran down her cheeks. She threw herself on the bed and buried her head in the pillow so that no one could hear her scream.

Tash opened the wooden blinds, letting the morning rays into the room.

"Are you up?" Charlotte heard the creak of the shutter. "Everyone's up already, waiting for you," she said, smiling. "Today is our sea day. But we have to leave right now. Do you mind having breakfast on the boat?"

It took her exactly five minutes to get ready. Two bikinis and a knitted beige dress she'd wear for lunch. That was enough. She jumped into denim shorts and walked over to the closet. Three tall stacks of T-shirts were waiting for her on the shelf. After fiddling with them for a few seconds, Tash pulled out a blue cotton one that read MY GIRL in Cyrillic. She pressed the T-shirt gently to her cheek. It was Daddy's birthday present. Damn, she forgot to transfer money to him this month. He must be dying of hunger there.

She had worried that lately her father had abandoned painting completely and devoted his time to helping the homeless. Tash's late grandmother Hannah liked to grumble, "That *clochard* is a typical proletarian. A 'leftist' at its worst. Penniless himself, but he still runs to help the poor. And the state should support these parasites? I pray," she said to Tash, "that he doesn't leech off you!"

Tash picked up the phone from the table and opened her banking app. She studied her accounts carefully. Her financial affairs had definitely improved. The joint venture with Lulu was paying off.

A few weeks on the island and the ambience of decadence started sucking Tash into its nets. Homo sapiens flocked to Ibiza to metamorphose into creatures, get loose and sink into their carnal desires. And Tash reasonably feared that, should she spend a month or two on the island, the alluring aroma of escapism might begin to suit her tastes.

Every day she inquired about Lulu's health, and she, in turn, reported to her the latest news. Lulu was happy that in her current state some of her work had been taken off her shoulders. She never tired of repeating that Tash had turned out to be not just a prudent student but also an initiative partner who immediately found ways for further development. Even on vacation, she managed to work and make necessary calls.

"Daddy, I sent you money. I love you and miss you. Your pumpkin."

Formentera, or the Mediterranean Maldives, was only half an hour away by boat. The small island in the vicinity of Ibiza boasted relaxing white sand beaches, often compared

170

to coral islands, throughout the year, except in August, when they were filled with noisy Italian tourists. Caves, turquoise water and fabulous landscapes attracted Instagrammers, and restaurants with the freshest seafood, the rest of the tourists.

Tash went aft. The captain slowed down. Music was blasting from everywhere, drowning out the sound of the dropping anchor.

The season was in full swing: the boats were so close to each other that the tenders had to slow down, squeezing between them. Formentera's impeccable setting didn't change from year to year, other than getting busier. The whitest sand and shallow waters gave the sea a dazzling azure colour, in which the blue sky was reflected even more intensely.

"The water is phenomenal," Charlotte gushed, making circles in the clear sea with her graceful foot.

Tash stood at the edge of the stern and gazed into the blue abyss. In fact, she was checking for jellyfish. Satisfied with her search, she dived below the captivating surface. It was pure bliss – floating on the waves, looking into an infinity of heavenly blue sky and not caring where the current took you.

At exactly two, the restaurant's tender moored to the boat. Nevertheless, two o'clock was considered kids' time in Ibiza, but it was already busy at the entrance. Only a handful opened their eyes before noon; some were just back from the after-parties. Tanned lean men in light linen shirts and shorts, muscular women in swimsuits and pareos. Although most of the guests were a long time over forty, the ambience was spry. Guests were cheerful, smart, carefree, which is exactly how Tash described them to herself.

Tash noticed how the stout man sitting with three couples was following them with his gaze while the hostess escorted them to the table.

"Luisito, querido!" he shouted.

Francesco glanced at him and immediately turned away.

Over paella, Tash casually enquired about the plump gentleman. Francesco said he and his group were all rogues. With a strong Italian accent, he described each one of them with such accuracy that the girls immediately knew who he meant.

"He's been long awaited in a Mexican prison," he spoke of a youngish man with curly hair. "The other one fled Italy." Francesco was talking about the stout man's neighbour. "He doesn't go to Sardinia any more. As soon as his boat enters Italian territorial waters, he will be immediately grabbed by the scruff by tax authorities. That woman," he referred to a woman in a golden sarong with rocks in her ears, "was a Colombian model. She arrived in Italy as a minor and slept with a top politician at one of his famous parties. That's how the star of that Italian TV anchor rose. Her friend next to her pinned this sucker down here, in Ibiza, when he was fresh out of Venezuela with several plundered millions." Francesco was talking about the stout man. "He was mashed and stoned most of the time." He grinned as he recounted the story. "They took him to Vegas and got married. This is how the poor thing got into the web of debauchery and decadence!" Francesco looked pointedly at Charlotte, seeking approval for his moral principles.

"I don't wanna hear about their sins, they look like they're having fun! C'mon, Francesco, saints are just sinners who haven't been caught."

*****

Brakes squeaked and gravel flew from under the wheels as a dusty black Wrangler parked outside. The door flew open and a golden goddess stepped onto the sinful earth. A real Generation Z angel who communicated with God via Instagram.

"So lunch at Es Xarcu looks very promising," she said to the camera. After reviewing the story, the angel decided that the angle was unflattering. The girl climbed back into the Jeep and repeated her speech with a perfect smile: "So, lunch at Es Xarcu looks very promising." She jumped out of the car again. "I'm meeting my bitch!" she announced to her followers.

Story number two came out better. Now was time to show her followers the venue. She looked around the room, but saw only forty-year-old FOPs with their biddies all bloated from fillers. The group on the right seemed younger, but then she remembered that she wanted to film the view. Concentrating on one object at a time for more than fifteen seconds was agony.

"What a dope view!" She filmed all 360 degrees for Insta.

The view really was "dope". The restaurant was hidden in a small picturesque bay. It could be reached either by a steep descent from the top of the hill or by tender.

"And here she is!" She pointed the camera towards the small passageway from which Tash emerged. "Ta-aash, Ta-aaa-ash." She was already rushing through the restaurant towards her attractive "bitch," not paying the slightest attention to the condemning glances of the guests.

The day before, Tash had accidentally bumped into Vivien's nineteen-year-old daughter, Stella, in Formentera. It turned out that Vivien, succumbing to fashion trends and the persuasions of her daughter, had rented a villa in Ibiza for the whole summer, but after only a few days, she was revolted and took off to her beloved South of France, leaving an empty house at Stella's disposal. Tash invited Stella for lunch out of politeness, and she unexpectedly agreed. Francesco and Charlotte were busy grovelling over some important Latin American politician, so it was just her and Anna.

Thanks to her mother's connections and her biological father's cash, Stella became part of the most desirable social circles from an early age. Boyfriends looked at her with adoration, friends accompanied her with dedication, and fashion designers who knew her from the cradle called her simply *l'etoile* (star). Nothing made a woman more desirable than the news that her billionaire father, who reluctantly recognised her as his daughter, had put her in his will. Neither her frivolous nature, constant flaking, nor weekly shopping spree could dissuade them of her complete irresistibility. Where a mere mortal would have been called "ill-mannered," Stella was only "slightly eccentric".

"So this is the girl who shoved us off for her story?" When Charles smiled, the dimples appeared on his pinkish cheeks. "I wanted to offer her a glass of wine, but she was glued to her phone," he said about Stella. "Please sit down next to me," he said. Tash and Anna sat down on his other side.

"What a gorgeous friend you have, Tash!" Charles, like all other males at the table, was mesmerised by Stella's youth.

"She is such a catch!" confirmed Tash. "An Instagram star."

After hearing the familiar word, Stella finally deigned to distract herself from the phone. "What a dope tee!" She rushed to examine the Celtic designs on Charles's T-shirt, spreading it out with her hands and stroking his chest. "Let's drink! We're in Ibiza." She guffawed and guzzled her glass of rosé.

173

While Stella was impressing Charles with her deepest knowledge in different fields, from culture (how TikTok changed social networks) to family (which showbiz stars were not yet married) to geography (which countries Billie Eilish was going to tour in) to finance (who were the highest paid Instabloggers), Anna was once again checking whether Karl had messaged her and Tash was studying the Instamodels who took places by Andrew's side.

They looked like triplets: medium height, high cheekbones, plump lips, silicone breasts, a giant-sized ass — straight from the pages of an X-rated magazine. Anna loved to repeat that a man's intelligence was determined by his preference in women. The taller and thinner the woman was, the more intelligent, according to Anna, who was both tall and thin. On Anna's scale, Nick stood at the top of the pyramid of men's intelligence, while Andrew slid to its very bottom. As expected, all three of his fans moved into Charles's house. However, there was a slight confusion during the relocation. While Brazilian number one — Charles allocated numbers to them rather than bother with names — the one Andrew had initially liked, went to the loo, her friend, number two, jumped on top of him and kissed him. When number one returned, she lunged at number two with her fists. Andrew, ever the gentleman, stopped the cat fight by offering to console all three at once.

"Maybe Karl hasn't called because he's also spending his nights with some bimbo," whispered Anna, suspecting that Karl could actually be that dumb.

"Well, so did Ben when he was here."

Charles had had enough of admiring Stella and turned to Tash. "I swear to God, since he's been with Flo, I've never seen him with anyone. And I see him quite often." He took a sip of wine, and this time, finally breaking away from Stella, he moved to Tash.

"There's nothing to discuss," Tash snapped.

"I agree." Anna had to give her two cents. "His behaviour can't be justified."

Over the years with Nick, Anna had perfected the skill of peremptory statements. Her hitherto dormant leadership qualities had grown in the fertile soil of her spouse's softness.

Charles cleared his throat. "I wouldn't be so unambiguous," he began. "Ben and Flo have been dating since the dawn of time. During that period, his family managed to lose almost everything. And she comes from one of the most famous, wealthy and influential families around. Flo is young, beautiful and … crazy about him. I've known Ben since our days at Eton. From day one, he tried to get into our circle, even though he's from a perfectly decent background. But who needs an aristocrat without money nowadays? Perhaps some divorced American actress," he answered himself.

Anna stifled a laugh.

"Little bullies. We were ignoring him because his title was as not flashy as ours, and his parents didn't keep horses." Charles shook his head at his past behaviour. "But everything changed as soon as he started dating Flo. Now no one thinks about how Ben got into our group, but believe me, it was Flo who was his ticket to the magic world of his childhood dreams. It's a pairing of convenience," he continued. "Besides, they have a lot in common: the same values, the same circle of friends. His financial status is a disappointment, though. Trust me, Ben has a soft spot for you, otherwise he would never have brought you to my house. But …" Charles paused while looking for the right word, "… he'd be an idiot if he doesn't marry Flo. And I'd be the first to tell him that."

Tash already knew that without Charles stating it, but his bluntness only confirmed Ben's choice. But one question was still up in the air.

"And what about love?" she asked timidly.

"He will get love later. From someone else," Charles replied cynically. "Most of my acquaintances, my parents included, married for convenience, and then they either found love on the side or simply sublimated this useless feeling. Tash, to marry for love, you need to be either filthy rich or plain crazy."

"Are you going to marry for convenience?" Anna asked.

Charles's mouth gradually broke into a smug smile. "My mother added her American millions to my father's title. Fortunately, thanks to the prudence of my parents, I can afford love." And with these words, he kissed Stella on the cheek.

Stella was distracted from her phone and gave Charles one of her seductive looks. "I'm dying to dance today." Her eyes flashed with adoration.

"As you wish, my princess."

"Just look who's here." Anna pulled Tash's hand and pointed to the entrance with her eyes.

"Who is it?" Stella was intrigued by the newcomer with spiky hair and tight jeans who was causing such a stir with his arrival.

Karl sauntered towards them and put his hand out to shake Charles's hand. "Hi, I'm Karl." His eyes narrowed in on Stella and her impressive cleavage.

Stella smiled and jumped up to kiss him hello. She'd already had a few drinks, and she hugged his neck in a way that directed his head onto her chest.

Anna coughed loudly and immediately turned away. The blonde was provoking Karl with an inviting insolent look. Her youthful directness was disarming. Charles wasn't the only one getting upset by her sudden attention to Karl. Anna's eyes sparkled with anger. She was whispering something into her friend's ear.

"What are you gossiping about?" Karl didn't want any plotting against him.

"We're just discussing Charles's generosity and hospitality."

After Anna's statement propping Charles up, Karl pondered which tactic to choose next. His animal instinct prompted him to seduce such easy prey, but at the same time he viewed Charles as a macho equal. His mind urged him to return to Anna and leave the blonde to his rich friend, who might be useful to him in the future. Without saying a word, he moved his chair next to Anna and turned his attention to her. Anna immediately forgave him all his sins. Stella had no choice but to return her attention to Charles.

Karl was delighted that Anna and her friend had gone back to their villa to change. Anna's jealousy stifled his freedom-loving spirit. The rest of the guests moved to Charles's. Stella didn't mind flirting with him and Anna had finally left the scene. Charles turned on the music and the guests shifted to the pool. Stella frolicked in the water with the owner of the house. "The fancy pants got lucky with such a house," Karl thought as he settled himself on a chaise longue and watched the red-hot disk of the sun roll over the horizon. He was hoping Charles would soon leave Stella's side.

In a white Moroccan gazebo, Andrew, like a padishah, was attended to by his three concubines. Karl chuckled. They must have drained more than one bottle of G. He wondered why Andrew wasted his precious time on such useless creatures when there was a bigger fish swimming around. Stella was the whole package. Karl raised his head to the heavens and thanked the Lord for creating such fools!

Charles never left Stella alone for a minute, and Karl was getting bored with this game. The sun had gone down, and it was time to move to the summer lodge that Charles had rebuilt specifically for receiving guests. Stella finally came out of the pool and ran into the house to change. Karl followed her discreetly. She sneaked into Charles's bedroom and came out in his T-shirt, tied at the waist with a belt. This outfit made her even more seductive. He pranced towards her, then heard someone calling his name. "Damn!" He saw Anna approaching.

Half an hour later, the chef announced that dinner was ready. Charles installed himself at the head of the table, and number one and number three immediately took up position on the flanks. Stella settled near Tash, and Karl had to plonk himself next to Anna, who wouldn't stop talking about the falling morals of modern youth. Karl chewed his beet and goat cheese salad carefully in an effort to avoid such polemics.

Anna was proving how immature the younger generation was when her monologue was interrupted by a heart-rending cry that came from somewhere in the depths of the site.

"Help! Help!" a man yelled.

Karl saw Charles's face darken. He leapt up and disappeared to the opposite lawn, behind the cypress tree trunks.

"I think they were shouting from the pool," Stella said quietly.

Several guys ran after Charles. There was a deathly silence at the table. The guests looked at each other in silent confusion. The only talking was in Portuguese from number one and three. Charles had been gone for several minutes and the wait was getting unbearable. Karl went to check if everything was okay.

As he approached the pool, the voices became louder. The bright spotlight blinded him and he had to cover his eyes with his hand. On the deck, he saw a bunch of people gathered in a tight circle. Karl went closer. In the centre of the circle, Andrew knelt with his bare knees on the stone tiles. He was moaning. His body was convulsing and his trembling hands gripped the lifeless body of number two.

"Andrew went to get more G, and she decided to take a dip and drowned. When he returned, her body was floating on the surface. We tried to give her mouth-to-mouth, but it was too late."

11. How to feel like a businesswoman

London

"Mrs. Anna, Miss Tash is getting up," the housekeeper said and quietly closed the door behind her.

An Indian summer blanketed London with warmth. A light September breeze tickled Anna's skin, and she could not resist the temptation to walk onto the balcony.

Tash opened the massive oak door.

"Anna, are you here?"

The spacious living room with high ceilings and stucco mouldings was flooded with sunlight through large French windows. An oval dining table in the middle of the room, covered with a handmade lace tablecloth, was set for two.

"I'm on the balcony, come out here," a voice said from behind the heavy curtains.

Tash hadn't been to Anna's since June, before Ibiza. The large room looked different somehow, but it wasn't until she looked to the far end that she spotted it. A bright pumpkin-coloured canvas above the blue antique Chesterfield sofa caught her eye. It was the Rothko, the orange Rothko, with its traditional transition of tones from dark poppy to pale amber. The work was magnificent – no wonder Nick was so eager to get it.

"Did you get lost?" Without waiting for Tash, Anna returned to the living room. "Oh … do you like it?" She stood next to Tash in front of the painting. "I will never stop enjoying it. Thanks to Karl!"

She was dying to share the latest gossip from Paris Fashion Week with Tash. For all of her adult life, Anna had striven to become an It Girl, and now, when she'd finally reached certain heights, she was scared to miss important social events, fearing that she would be replaced by some starlet, eager to take her place in the front row. Anna had begun travelling exclusively with Karl because after the Rothko transaction, his presence in her life was legitimised in Nick's eyes, as well as those around them. They served each other's networking goals. Their circle of "useful" people was constantly growing, and Anna joked that soon there would be no room left in their notebooks.

"Imagine … we're sitting at Valentino and Bella Bakhtiar flopped down next to us. I don't know how she manages to still get in. Thank god her place was in the second row, and she had to change seats." Anna's face showed the disdain she felt for the second row at fashion shows.

London, New York, Vienna, all knew crazy Bella. Together with her husband, and another two million Iranians, they had fled to London from the horrors of the Islamic revolution. They didn't run light – taking with them the corruption money accumulated over the country's oil boom, during which black gold revenues of the state of Iran settled in the pockets of the Shahinshah Pahlavi's family and friends. The tabloids were recycling their names thanks to their friendship with Prince Andrew. Their weekly expenses numbered in the hundreds of thousands of pounds. Bella's husband was caught in a financial fraud and was banned from doing business in the UK, so the family had moved to New York. However, the American prosecutors turned out to be more perspicacious than the Brits, and Bella's man was thrown behind bars. Bella, who'd shone in the light a mere ten years ago, was finally deposed from the podium. Her house next to the Stowes' in Eaton Square had to be sold, and it became impossible for her to live on the same grand scale as before. The situation was aggravated by a drunken brawl in a private member's club, which ended with a suspended sentence. As a result of these troubles, Bella's former glory had finally faded, but the habits of a luxurious life remained. The dark-haired beauty decided to lead the same lifestyle as before, with only one difference – without spending a penny. She went to fashion shows, put aside the most expensive jewellery and outfits, but never bought anything. Either out of habit or out of pity, the designers continued to send her invitations, and she willingly accepted them. True, the front row was replaced by the second row, but a Valentino show was still a Valentino show.

"Ah," Anna interrupted herself. "Here's another thing. I saw Vivien there; Stella walked for Gaultier. Can you imagine? People went crazy. Seriously, they'll invite anyone onto that stage." Anna could not forgive Stella's flirting with Karl.

"Jealousy doesn't suit you. Why would you elevate her by paying attention?" Tash's voice and intonation were enough to calm Anna down. Tash's words had always worked on her better than any meditation. "Vivien is a godsend for brands, so they want to keep her happy. And it didn't cost them anything to include her daughter on the catwalk. Besides, Stella has hundreds of thousands of followers on Instagram. She is an influencer, after all, and everyone wants a piece of that action."

Anna made a condescending grimace. "Oh please … she's a bratty opinion leader." Dressed in an expensive linen trouser suit, she proudly settled on a mahogany chair with silk upholstery. "But I wanted to talk about something else," she continued capriciously. "My birthday is coming up and we have a party to plan. Nothing extravagant, probably seventy people, more or less. I have to call all Nick's acquaintances who always invite us." Anna rolled her eyes. "I would like to invite Charles; he took such sweet care of us in Ibiza. Even when you freaked out and left, we still saw him several more times. Here's my concern: do you think he has any clue about me and Karl?" Anna clearly expected a negative answer.

"Charles is far from being a fool. And you didn't exactly hide much. Fashion shows are one thing, but sharing a bedroom … is a bit different. But Charles won't tell Nick. He's too cynical about the institution of marriage and he's not a gossip."

"Great, so I'm inviting him." Anna liked living on the edge. "I still can't believe that we survived that horrid ordeal. When you ran away after that girl's death, Charles was just great. He dealt with the police, organised everything with her relatives. She was from the middle of nowhere in Brazil, thank god, and she had a bunch of brothers and sisters. Charles transferred money to her parents and managed to keep it out of the press. But Andrew, in my opinion, kind of fell apart and never really came to his senses. Karl said Andrew has vowed to never touch drugs again."

"It's for the best. How have we not spoken for so long?" Tash had really missed her friend over the summer.

The death of the Instamodel, no matter how much they'd mocked her, left a deep imprint on every participant at that ill-fated dinner. Innocent partying had turned instantly into universal tragedy. They were laughing one minute and overcome with shock and sadness the next. The grim reality of a life lost quickly sobered everyone up by the time the police arrived for questioning. It was all too much for Tash, and she escaped the island's idle decadence the next day.

She was happy to get back to her life in London and had wandered empty city streets, enjoying the silence. For the first time in her entire life, she was getting high from creation, proud of her own usefulness. She had purpose. After all, it wasn't only Dad who needed her, but so did Lulu and her models. She needed to work. She needed to move forward.

"Let's get Katya involved in organising your birthday," Tash suddenly blurted out. "She needs to take a break from idleness from time to time." Tash remembered how last week Katya had complained that she was languishing with boredom while Sasha was tied up with his wife.

*****

Preparations for Anna's birthday were in full swing for more than a month. The list of invitees was increasing every day, and as they approached the landmark date, it had reached two hundred and fifty people.

Katya seemed to find her calling in organisational work. Without any experience of life in London, without acquaintances, she managed to find a great venue and gather a team of professionals through her New York connections. At first, Anna was worried that she hadn't hired professionals, but she realised along the way that if Katya was passionate about something, she would give it her all.

Anna Stowe's birthday fell on a Thursday. Cars queued up outside the entrance to One Embankment. The passers-by were wondering what ladies in oriental outfits and men in harem pants were doing in central London. The guests followed a path covered with Moroccan carpets to the entrance of the makeshift tent. The hostesses checked guests' names against their lists. After one more cordon of guards, the invitees found themselves at the famous Eastern Bazaar. The air, as in a real bazaar, was saturated with fragrant incense. Katya had spent all day at the Southall Market, searching for the right ones. On one side, she had placed rows of oriental outfits for guests who had neglected the dress code. For the ladies, she prepared Indian saris, scarves of the finest silk and handmade jewellery from the Kuchi tribes. The men were provided with Uzbek ikat robes, harem pants and Persian turbans. On the other side, there were rows with appetisers – oriental canapés. Waiters, dressed as street vendors, invited guests to taste their delicacies.

After the bazaar, the guests shifted to the recreation area, where they could perch on Turkish divans placed around the perimeter or settle on the carpets that covered the floor. Young men in turbans put pillows with tassels and oriental ornaments under the backs and elbows of the guests and fanned them with peacock feathers, and masseuses dressed as concubines massaged their shoulders. Fortune tellers spread cards in small cabins. Katya had to go through at least twenty sessions herself to hire the best, although she knew her destiny without tarot cards. The belly dancers shook their hips in front of the guests; some ladies followed suit, and even Nick couldn't resist and succumbed to the revelry.

When most of the guests were ready, the dancers dragged them along to the main hall. The path lay through a dark corridor, lit only by the light of torches juggled by fakirs standing along the walls. From the darkness, the guests entered a spacious refectory.

"Wow!" Anna, not privy to the details, was shocked by Katya's work. "This is extraordinary!"

Judging by the smiles on guests' faces, she wasn't the only one who thought so. Katya rejoiced at her triumph. Everyone admired the level of organisation, attention to detail and thoughtful interior.

"The food is delicious. Where did you find the catering?" Anna didn't know a single contractor. The only thing she knew was the final estimate, which, according to Anna, turned out to be much lower than she expected.

"Happy birthday, my dear! You shouldn't bother about such things!" Katya kissed the birthday girl and went to her seat.

"I can't believe that you met Anna's budget." Tash smiled slyly. She was thrilled that a fortune teller had just predicted her wedding the following year.

"I didn't match it," Katya answered playfully, stirring vegetable tagine on her plate. "At some point, I exceeded it, and Sasha and I decided not to upset Anna, so we just paid all the additional expenses." Katya smiled as she took a forkful of couscous.

Tash leaned forward to see Sasha's face, sitting on the other side of Katya.

"It wasn't much. Don't worry." Sasha winked at Tash. "This girl," he said, nodding to Katya, "knows how to work with contractors. She should have managed the workers in the Far East with me. She would have immediately put things in order there," he said with admiration.

After dinner, magicians and dancers filled the room entertaining the guests with elaborate tricks and impromptu dances. Then the lights went out and the music started. Multicoloured neon lights cut through the darkness and aerial acrobats started their dangerous routine on ropes that dropped down from the ceiling in a flash. Rope-walkers moved along invisible ropes, and fakirs juggled with coloured torches on specially constructed platforms. Their actions were accompanied by a striking and swirling light show.

"I can't believe it! Is this really what I think it is?" Anna was glowing with happiness.

"Guy is an old friend of mine since modelling times. He helped me a little bit." Katya was enjoying the results of her work. She had known Guy Laliberté since her arrival in New York, and he had helped her by connecting her with artists from Cirque du Soleil, which he had only recently sold.

"So here is the beauty who organised that *petite fête de la famille*." Katya looked up to see Nick with a tall handsome stranger with his hair in a bun.

"Brilliant work!"

Tash stood and smiled, turning her cheek to the new guy for a kiss.

"Charles, have you met Katya?"

"Sadly, no, and I can't find any worthy excuse for this! May I sit down with you?" He locked onto the place between her and Sasha.

Katya patted the pillow next to her. As soon as Charles took a seat, Sasha peeped over his shoulder, demonstrating displeasure with his eyes.

Katya bristled and wrote Sasha a short message on her phone: "You have a wife!" She didn't look in his direction again.

Charles tried to engage Sasha in the conversation too, but his limited knowledge of English excluded him. Katya, on the other hand, was getting more and more engaged with every minute. Charles's keen mind and cynicism, his awareness of fashion and his understanding that Katya wasn't just a model, but a *top* model, with a brain no less, stirred her up.

Nick was away for several minutes, and Anna sneaked off to chat with Karl. He was telling her about his gift when Nick came up to them.

"Can I steal her from you?" Nick asked menacingly. He took Anna's hand and led her away. Anna followed him, sparkling in a turquoise lamé dress, massive gold earrings and a headband of antique gold coins.

At the exit to the bazaar, four young men lifted Anna and put her on a palanquin. The guests gathered on the street applauding her appearance. As soon as the birthday girl was in the centre of the improvised platform, a fountain of fireworks lit up the firmament. Fireworks exploded on the opposite bank of the Thames, and the lights flying into the sky reflected in the river in colourful sparks. The music increased and decreased to match the mesmerising bursts.

Anna was overwhelmed and there were tears in her eyes. She wanted to share her happiness with her loved ones. She looked at Karl, at Nick, and then noticed that guests were turning their heads to a bright spot approaching from the side of the embankment. Wrapped in garlands, like a Christmas tree, and tied with a ribbon with a big bow, a black Bentley Bentayga with a giant card inscribed with "Happy Birthday, Anna!" stopped in front of her.

*****

At ten o'clock in the morning, three posh ladies in unitards and trainers were leaving a meditation studio in Belgravia. They had failed to completely clear their chakras in the half-hour session, and there were plenty of topics to discuss. They went to the nearby Baker & Spice café.

"I'm in love with Charles! He is the perfect man for me!" It was the fifth time Katya had mentioned that she'd spent the best time of her life with Charles after Sasha left. "I just realised that even if it doesn't work out with Charles, I won't stay with Sasha. I don't want to ruin his family." Sasha's shares had plummeted since Katya met Charles. "I'll tell him about it today."

"Hallelujah!" Anna encouraged her. "Tash and I have been thinking that for such a long time. And, Katya, you have to seriously consider taking your organising skills to a professional level."

"I've already thought about it." Katya was beaming with happiness. "Charles was stunned to learn that I'd done everything in a month, and he asked me to take care of a reception at his house next fall. We're having dinner today."

"Wow! Smart cookie! You know he has one of the largest estates in England," Anna casually mentioned as she sipped fresh cucumber and celery juice. "By the way, Karl gave me an antique edition of *Alice in Wonderland*. How sweet of him." Anna looked tenderly at the juice.

"And Nick gave you a car with a bow for two hundred grand. Isn't *that* sweet?" Katya pointed out.

*****

On the way to Lulu's, Tash deliberately decided to take a walk along Portobello Road. Street vendors were already folding their tents, but due to the good weather, the street was still filled with tourists and locals. A guitar-playing busker was singing Dire Straits, and the barkers called out to pedestrians to try their products. Tash passed the stalls and turned left onto a small street. The noise of the market immediately died down, and she was able to walk for several minutes in dead silence. She wanted to gather her thoughts before the meeting.

Each of their recent meetings had been a challenge for Tash, reminding her of the finiteness of life. Lulu's fight with cancer had been going on for six months, and every time Tash had a free minute, she tried to stop by her.

She took out a key from under the rug and opened the front door. "Lulu, it's me," she called as she walked down the dark corridor to the bedroom.

"I'm here," came a hoarse voice from the living room, "watching *Game of Thrones*."

Tash found Lulu sitting staring at her computer. From the TV, screams just announced the Lannisters' victory.

"You're working again? You have to rest," Tash said reproachfully. After unloading the contents of the bags onto the dining table, she walked over to Lulu.

"I'm in a great mood. Look what I've found," Lulu said, pointing to the computer screen. "It's a study here in England. They're testing a new lung cancer vaccine on people under fifty in advanced stages. It's made from embryos and boosts the immune system to make cancer-fighting antibodies – and they accepted me! They wrote to me that I'm the perfect candidate. I will be given an injection every six weeks for several years instead

186

of chemotherapy. I can't handle chemo any more." She sighed as she took off the headscarf that covered her thinning hair.

"Great news! Is it in London?"

"Yes, I'll go to the hospital for two days for vaccinations and all the studies and then I'll be free for six weeks. And then it happens all over again. I am so happy! I want to live more than ever! But enough about me. I wanted to praise you for your latest work. Our clients at Vodafone are very happy with the models. And your idea to hire ordinary women for the tights advert was smashing! We earned ten times more on this, since we didn't have to pay huge fees to models. You have a head for ideas. When I get better, we will make an agency with you—"

"Lulu, that's exactly what I wanted to talk about. I think there are too many models now and agencies are somewhat outdated. I've got a few ideas! The first one: we create a curated platform so models and clients can communicate directly, and the latter will pay a percentage of the fee. We will still be selecting new models for our platform based on their photos, and clients will be finding them, but we wouldn't be involved in organising shoots and the fees any more. Let them agree on their own, and we can take a commission from each booking. In the meantime, we continue to work with our existing models as agents. The second idea is to start a talent management business to promote upcoming artists and influencers. We can start with Stella, Vivien's daughter. She's already made her debut in the Gaultier show at Paris Fashion Week, and she has nine hundred thousand followers."

"Can I kiss you, Miss Romanov? What would I do without you? It's time for you to stop your shoots, keep only covers and big-brand ads. And get to grips with our agency. And yet ... we need to find investors."

"I took care of that too. I already spoke to Francesco, and he's ready to invest in us."

"Today is the best day I've had in several years. I got into a promising new trial for cancer, and you figured out how to make us rich." Lulu danced around the table. "Are you up for a whiskey?"

"Lulu, stop it! You're still on chemo." Tash got up to stop her, but it was too late. Lulu had already poured a glass of whiskey and wasn't going to stop halfway.

"To our agency ... and ... my life!" she added.

12. How to sell yourself

New York

It was only a few weeks away from the most depressing time for single people – Christmas. From the twenty-third of December, big cities become extinct, and remaining in their captivity is tantamount to social suicide.

Nick left it to the last moment, hoping to persuade Anna to celebrate Christmas at Meadow Hill, but Anna insisted that they, as usual, go to her parents in New York. Full stop. There were no other options.

"Tash, do you know who is going where for New Year's?" Tash was strolling down Knightsbridge when Anna rang.

"Hmmm … wait a second." She lifted the collar of her coat so the icy December wind wouldn't blow into her neck. "Charles is taking Katya to his parents."

Katya and Charles's dinner date after Anna's birthday had lasted till Sunday, and only on the condition that Katya would return to his house the following day. Charles nobly gave her all of Monday so that she could end her relationship with Sasha, but he wouldn't give her enough time to change her mind about the relationship with him that had developed so quickly.

The break-up with Sasha was short. Katya sent him a message saying that she also wanted a family and wishing him and his family all the best. She said that from the next month on, she would be paying for the apartment herself. That evening Sasha showed up with an expensive Audemars Piguet watch, hoping to settle everything, to which he received a tough rebuff. His last argument was a vow to leave his wife and marry her. Katya retorted that a cheating husband wasn't part of her life plan. Because Katya didn't accept the watch, he realised that her decision was very serious, and in return, he demanded that all the gifts presented to her over the time of their affair be given back. With great sadness, Katya parted with the jewels accumulated over the past year, but her feelings for Charles overrode all others, including greed.

"And Carolina?" There was hope in Anna's voice that at least someone had already planned the New Year's and she wouldn't have to come up with an option herself.

"She and Mark are going to Saint Barth."

"Excellent." Anna interrupted her. "I'll look at the hotels now. Are you coming with us?"

The option to stay in London for the New Year scared Tash no less than a death by hunger after lavish holidays. "I'm in New York next week for work, so I can fly directly from there. By the way, I think Francesco also mentioned something about Saint Barth."

"Okay. I'll leave it with you, then. You're in charge of organising our trip." And with that, Anna hung up.

Francesco confirmed he was going to Saint Barth. After a brief correspondence with hotels, it became clear that a few weeks before Christmas there were only presidential suites left on the island – at eight thousand a night.

"Why don't we rent a house?" Tash suggested to Anna by phone.

"If you find one, we're up for it."

"Rodrigo, we need a villa on Saint Barth. Urgently! I know you can do it."

Rodrigo Valero ran a few trendy spots in London and New York. He was a well-known fixer and an old-time Saint Barther, and his connections ranged from famous film producers to Saudi princes.

"Kid, you know it's impossible," a voice croaked on the other side. Rodrigo had just woken up after a stormy night. "All the good villas have been bagged since summer, and now it's December."

"I know you can! That's why I love you," Tash chirped.

"Okay, I'll try. But I can't promise anything." Tash knew if Rodrigo got down to business, the result was guaranteed.

Two days later, she smiled when she saw his name on the phone screen.

"You owe me, big time! Nutsy Bella Bakhtiar booked the villa but can't pay for it – as usual. The owner would lose a tonne of money if it sat empty during the holidays. That's why he offered such a good deal. You are one lucky lady."

Tash couldn't agree more. It was one of the coolest villas on the island. She was already dreaming how she would frolic in the waves of the Caribbean at sunset.

The countdown had begun. Two more weeks until all worries would be forgotten under the bright Caribbean sun.

*****

Transatlantic flights became routine for Tash. Three films and she was in New York. She had several meetings scheduled while she was there, and her business development was starting to pay off.

But first, she had a photo shoot. She dropped her stuff off at the hotel and went straight to the studio. Today was the rehearsal. She knew how fortunate she was with this job. She had been at one of Karl's art dinners when he happened to seat her next to the photographer who was shooting this ad. He immediately saw her as the face of the perfume and convinced the creative director that there couldn't be a better model than Tash in the ad, thereby ensuring her a considerable fee and her face in every fashion magazine throughout the year. She immediately imagined how her face, seen by Ben accidentally in Flo's magazine, would stir up his memories. This feeling gave her much more pleasure than the thought of the fee.

On the way to the studio, she called Katya.

"I can't believe I'm living in New York again."

Tash heard a sonorous laugh. "I'm having a feeling of déjà vu."

"Me too," Tash agreed. "We only need Anna here to make it like our younger days. And now Carolina is here with Mark. I think they'll get married."

Tash felt that their relationship was destined to succeed. The timid introvert melted in front of Carolina's beauty and confidence. After the abuser Hugh, she'd dreamed of an honest and trusting man, and Mark seemed to be perfect for this role.

"It would be nice for her to get a divorce to start with …" Katya laughed. "You can discuss it with her over dinner tomorrow night. Nine o'clock at ours."

The taxi passed Chelsea art galleries and turned off 20th Street onto 11th Avenue. The December sky was reflected in the Hudson in all shades of blue. Tash looked out the window. They had driven only thirty streets from the hotel, but the view had changed dramatically. On the Upper East Side, ladies in mink coats were rushing to shop after leaving their hairdressers, while in bohemian Chelsea, students in sneakers and oversized coats wandered between galleries and coffee shops.

The first person Tash saw as she stepped over the threshold of the studio was the creative director.

"I've heard you and Lulu are making a platform."

Tash was routinely amazed at how fast rumours spread in the fashion world. "It's in R&D, still early days."

It was true. Only a month ago, with the promised seed investment from Francesco, Tash was able to hire some genius developers to start building the software. As CEO, she was planning to hold several fundraising meetings in New York. She was determined to see it through to completion and succeed. She had to win the game and make Ben regret his choice in the end.

Tash went out onto the terrace, watching the grey doves hovering over the buildings. They landed on rooftops in search of food and then, frozen without motion, flew high into the sky. She remembered how right after graduation, she had come here for the summer. Katya was already an established model and she'd helped Tash out with work. The look of the pigeons covered in slush reminded her of how she'd run from one casting to another, knee-deep in the snow, and queued frozen in the cold corridors with a hundred other models, to finally hear "no, we're looking someone taller" or "no, we're looking for a different type."

Now Tash was standing in Pier59 Studios set to star in an ad for one of the world's top brands, she was the head of a successful modelling agency and was developing her cutting-edge platform for models who reminded her of herself when she was first starting out. It was a full-circle moment.

*****

Carolina was coming in an hour, so Tash had plenty of time to freshen up before dinner.

There was a knock on the door. Tash took the delivery and happily unpacked the package. The leather dress ordered on Net-a-Porter in New York, where sales were in full swing, cost half the price here as in London. How amazing it was to live in the twenty-first century!

"Why do you always stay in uptown?" Carolina asked as soon as Tash got into her limousine. "You still go downtown all the time. Mercer Street, please," she said to the driver. "Mark takes the subway straight from work. And he's bringing his friend Zach. You must remember him from Monaco, he went to dinner with us when I met Mark. He's a hedge fund manager and just got divorced."

"Any news about Hugh?"

"Remember that kid Oliver from the charity dinner? Mark arranged for Jose, his boyfriend, to have a meeting with the best agent in Hollywood. Mark invests in movies a lot. Anyway, Jose agreed to testify against Hugh. Now he's on the hook."

"Are you going to sue him?" For sex with a minor, Hugh could easily be thrown behind bars.

"Only in the worst case scenario. I want to get what I'm entitled to, but I think Hugh will become much more agreeable under the threat of a lawsuit."

*****

Charles's New York apartment occupied the top two floors of a red-brick building on Mercer Street. Tash was jealous of the huge panoramic windows and high ceilings that immediately plunged her into the urban vibe after old-fashioned Victorian London. In his apartment, as elsewhere in New York, there was a grand sense of scale. A massive table made of solid wood was set right in the middle of the four-hundred-square-foot living room. It was decorated with floral arrangements and bronze candlesticks and was set for six people. It was already dark outside and candlelight provided some intimacy to the otherwise soulless loft.

"Have you seen the city's Christmas decorations? New York does them better than London!" said Katya, who had never actually spent a Christmas in England.

"I think the best festive spirit is in Paris. The way they decorate the Champs-Élysées and Avenue Montaigne, and oh, that lovely Christmas market!" Carolina sighed dreamily.

193

"I prefer London. Nothing compares to Winter Wonderland and, of course, *The Nutcracker* at the opera." Tash remembered her magical pre-Christmas trip last year.

"London after Brexit! No amount of decorations will beautify the country's economy."

Tash looked at Katya in surprise. Perhaps for the first time in her life, she heard a sober judgement about politics coming from her lips.

Charles looked proudly at his new love and added, "What happened to our country – the stupid referendum – is a shame for the Tories, a shame for our entire system. With all due respect to Mr. Cameron, and I've known him since childhood, his bluff didn't work. He put Britain's welfare at stake and blew it out in disgrace. Such selfishness and conceit are unforgivable for a politician. Throughout my life, my father was preparing me for the House of Lords, but after Brexit, I refuse to belong to a party of narcissists who cannot see beyond their noses. The chaos and endless arguments with the EU have become simply unbearable."

"That's not the only reason." Katya straightened the sleeve of her white blouse. She looked like a real New Yorker in a shirt and blue jeans. "I absolutely don't share the English passion for country life. We went shooting a couple of times, and I almost died of boredom. You sit in a huge house with five friends, like in a Jane Austen novel, without a soul around for several miles. That's why we moved to New York."

"Closer to Trump." Mark's joke caused a burst of laughter at the table.

"Sorry, Charles, but for me personally, as an EU citizen, thanks to Grandmother Hannah," Tash said firmly, "Brexit brings a lot of unnecessary trouble. But I value democracy above all. Democracy is government of the people, by the people and for the people. The victory of the majority, however slim, in the referendum is unshakeable. And democracy is certainly not forcing people to vote again and again until they vote the way the elites would like."

Zach was watching Tash in fascination. Every minute opened up a new side to her, the presence of which he had not suspected five minutes earlier. Her arguments sounded convincing, and the enthusiasm with which she spoke was infectious. Here was a woman who clearly knew what she wanted. But Zach wasn't the only one watching Tash closely. Katya looked at her friend and wondered where the timid girl who she met twenty years ago in Peredelkino had gone. There was no trace of her shyness, and her perpetual

194

indecisiveness had evaporated. Something had changed in her. Tash had matured more in the past year than in the past ten.

"I don't really like talking about politics," Mark intervened in the discussion. "But if we're talking about democracy and referendums … don't you think it's not correct to equate the voice of an eighteen-year-old guy from Liverpool, who barely made it to graduation, to the voice of, say, the Governor of the Bank of England, who has worked in his post for the last twenty years and knows the UK economy like the back of his hand? Don't you think that their votes should be spaced on the electoral scale as polarities in order to weight the vote depending on the competence of the voter?"

All eyes were on Tash.

"Mark, we all want to arrive at common ground, but that is obviously not democracy at all. It's very Orwellian: everyone is created equal, but some are more equal than others. Please! Your system allows you to juggle it as you wish, where all decisions would be made in favour of the elites, due to the fact of their greater knowledge, excellent education and better positions. This means that they would always get more points and have more power. But if we take the time factor and the potential of the new generation into account, then we have to ask who does the future really belong to?"

Zach was smitten. In one go she had killed all his stereotypical beliefs about the shallowness of the world of fashion. He cleared his throat and said conciliatorily, "Returning to the theme of Christmas. It's beautiful everywhere. Tash, how long are you in New York for?"

He admired the colour of her skin in the candlelight.

"Till Christmas. And then Saint Barth with this lovely couple." She nodded at Carolina and Mark.

"So I have plenty of time to prove to you that New York is no worse than London at Christmas." Zach smiled. "Would you like to see *The Nutcracker*?"

Carolina winked and nodded at the same time, indicating that she must certainly accept Zach's offer.

Zach wasn't Tash's type, but she didn't want to say no to his offer. She was free from any obligations and nothing prevented her from agreeing. She smiled and looked around the room. In her head, she calculated the total fortune of the guests at the table was over half a billion. She couldn't have dreamed of a better moment for fundraising.

"With great pleasure," Tash replied. "In the meantime, I would like to consult with everyone about my company. There are a few things I don't really understand," she said innocently as she took one long look at the men.

The Montagues, whose lineage dated back to the time of the Crusades, were permanent members of the *Sunday Times* "Rich List", and Charles, as the eldest son, was to inherit the title, the money and the estate. His personal fortune, thanks to his shares in the family business and his own successful investments, was on the same list, but in a much more modest position.

Mark Greenberg and Zach Cohen met while studying at the Massachusetts Institute of Technology. After MIT, they both moved to Silicon Valley to gain experience in the burgeoning tech market. In this field, Mark succeeded considerably better, while Zach, disillusioned with the process, returned to New York to start metal trading. Over the course of several years, his business took off so much that he founded his own hedge fund. Zach had won the title of "Fund Manager of the Year" a few times for the monumental return on investment he secured for his clients.

Mark made his fortune by successfully gambling on and investing early in ventures that turned out to be unicorns, growing his assets exponentially with their capitalisation.

"Our company is building a platform which connects models with customers. A beta version is currently being developed, and we have seed investment in place, but we will need more cash for promotion."

Carolina clapped her hands. "Mark," she said sweetly as she stroked the lapel of his jacket, "let's give Tash some money for her platform. I think it's a brilliant idea for you all to chip in so Tash will have the best platform in the world."

"You're also an entrepreneur?" Zach couldn't hide his admiration for her merits. "Come to my office with your business plan. I'll see what I can do."

Tash was pleased with how cleverly she'd played her cards to attract the investment, and Zach was pleased with how cleverly he'd played his – to attract Tash.

The shoot went like clockwork. Instead of the planned two days, they fitted it all into one. She was entirely free until Saint Barth, so she could devote all her time to her brainchild.

Zach wasn't long in calling. "Which evening do you have free for the ballet? And which day are you able to come to my office with your business plan?"

At twelve o'clock in the afternoon, Tash, dressed in a fitted black suit, was admiring the view of Manhattan from Zach's fifty-third-floor office in the financial district. He introduced Tash to two red-cheeked guys who specialised in tech, and she began her pitch for the three of them. Partway through her presentation, Zach left for a conference call and the two men began their interrogation of her business model.

After an hour of agony, Zach knocked on the door of the conference room. "Are you all done in here? Can I steal her for lunch?"

"Yes, we've reached a common understanding. Now we just need to wait for the beta version to be released, test it and get the investment committee's approval. There are no objections from our side."

Tash rejoiced with restraint.

"That means she can't refuse to lunch with me now," Zach said happily.

Zach was spending Christmas with his kids, but he had no plans for the New Year and decided to join the crew in Saint Barth.

Despite all his efforts, his attempt to prove to her that New York was better than London failed. He courted Tash and took her to the Lincoln Center for *The Nutcracker*. Instead of enjoying the ballet, she stifled tears, recalling how happy she had been a year ago with Ben at the Royal Opera House.

After the ballet, they stopped by the Gramercy Hotel for a drink. Tash relaxed in a low velour chair sipping a cocktail, while he went to the bathroom.

When he returned, she was staring absently into the distance holding the phone in her hand. "You have no idea what just happened. Hugh's plane crashed on take-off in Hong Kong."

13. All that glitters is not gold

Saint Barth

The helicopter hovered briefly in the air before descending to Gustavia airport. Tash was glued to the window, admiring the turquoise waters of Colombier Bay, dotted with boats like cupcakes with sprinkles. "Welcome to Saint Barthélemy," the pilot's voice announced over the headphones. Tash couldn't contain her smile.

As soon as the luggage was unloaded, Tash got into the convertible white Mini Cooper that was waiting for her at the airport entrance.

"I'll follow you." She let Francesco and Charlotte's white Jeep lead the way.

The car climbed several hundred metres uphill and slowed down at a roundabout. Tash read the signs for directions: Gustavia, Flamands, Gouverneur. She wondered what all these new places looked like, but her thoughts were loudly interrupted by the roar overhead. The motor plane flew just a few metres above her head, almost snatching her straw hat off in the process.

The white Jeep turned onto Flamands. They swept up a narrow, winding road sandwiched between green hills. Tash wanted to see the houses built on both sides of the road, but most of them were hidden behind lush vegetation.

Ten minutes later, Francesco stopped at high metal gates. They swung reluctantly, and Tash saw a garden with a narrow asphalt driveway leading upward. As soon as the gates closed behind her, she felt like an exotic bird locked in a giant golden cage. The humid air was filled with the sweet scent of tropical flowers, the patchwork inflorescences of which were barely distinguishable between hibiscus bushes and tall cacti. Tash whistled – dozens of birds responded. She had to slow down to give way to a lanky turtle that was leisurely crossing the path. The house stood impressively at the top of the hill, looking exactly how she'd imagined. From the sea side, two figures in white were approaching. Nick in white linen slacks and white shirt and his wife in a white knitted dress looked like an ad for a vacation in paradise.

Nick introduced himself to Francesco.

"Thank you so much for looking after my girls in Ibiza. What would I do without you?"

Tash greeted them warmly. "Thank you, guys, for this wonderful vacation. I absolutely adore you all." And she ran to hug Anna.

"Thank you for finding the house," Francesco shouted after her.

"We should really be thanking Bella for always booking but never paying," Tash replied, laughing.

A wide terrace with a swimming pool was bounded on one side by the house itself and by a cliff from which the island was visible at a glance on the other. Tash stood at the edge of the pool, admiring the views of Flamands. "Breathtaking!"

Anna sat down on the side of the pool and dangled her legs into the water. Tash kicked off her sandals and joined her.

"We went swimming today!" Anna announced loudly, then added in a whisper, "Karl arrives on the thirtieth."

"Anna! Why do you continue to tempt fate? This is supposed to be a relaxing vacation."

"Oh, don't be so dramatic. Like everyone else, he comes here for the New Year and then moves on to Tulum."

"Who's coming?" Nick stood behind them with two glasses of wine.

"Some of our acquaintances … from the party crowd." Tash hoped her voice sounded convincing enough. "Nick, what do you think about them?"

Nick squatted down.

"You know, when I was young, I was out of hand. At first, I wanted to prove to my father that I was worth something, then, after his death, I couldn't overcome the pain of loss and was out of control. I partied as if there was no tomorrow, craving fun, searching for a happiness that eluded me. That reckless behaviour continued until I met this wonderful lady." He hugged Anna's shoulders. "She saved my life by turning my world upside down. She helped me realise that I was living in a dangerous dream state and not in reality. That I had to be able to live life in this very moment, in a sober mind." He glanced sideways at his glass of rosé. "Well, *almost* sober."

Tash's eyes sparkled. She was about to offer a witty response, but Anna's abrupt retort changed the mood. "That's one way to find out who your true friends are – get poor and sober!" She was applying sunscreen over her long legs and shaking her head. "We're on vacation, not at a ghastly AA meeting." Too much philosophising made her sick to death. Despite her Princeton degree, Anna was a true philistine and rarely went beyond carnal desires and simple values. Anything that didn't clearly focus on achieving financial success or raising one's social status was strictly out of her range of interests.

Tash had been watching the men for several minutes and it looked like they were likely to become good pals. It took them exactly five minutes to discuss plans for the week, so the agenda was instantly exhausted. Francesco entertained Nick with stories that made Nick laugh incessantly.

"Francesco is a gem. Why did you hide him from me?" Nick poured more wine into the near-empty glasses.

"Well, Nick, you should have come to Ibiza," Charlotte said from the other end of the pool. "You would not have regretted it."

Tash glanced at Anna, who nearly choked on her rosé. Anna jumped into the pool and motioned for Tash to do the same so they could speak privately.

"I have to neutralise Francesco. Their friendship does not serve my interests in the least," she whispered before diving under the water.

*****

Anna was putting the final touches to her makeup in front of the mirror. She wondered what Karl was doing now and wanted to message him. She was startled by Nick's arms curling around her hips. Her silk robe slid down to the marble floor, revealing her white body, still untouched by the sun.

Nick turned her around and knelt down. Pressing his lips to her belly, he whispered, "I wish there was a little girl like you in this tummy." Anna tried to push him away, but he was persistent, so she surrendered. While Nick was panting like a dog, she gazed at the empty bed, dreaming of how she and Karl could enjoy each other on it if only Nick was away. She thought that they might be able to sneak away from the New Year's party for a little while Nick was chatting with Francesco. Oh yes, she remembered, she must squash that friendship.

"What do you think of Francesco? I have a nagging feeling there's something off with him. He seems a little too perfect, don't you find?" Anna raised his head with her hands. "What do you think?"

He recoiled and got up rapidly. "How can you think of Francesco at a moment like this? Why are you so cold?"

"I'm not cold at all, silly. I just thought to ask you about it."

She was worried she'd gone too far. She took a deep breath and submitted herself to fulfilling her marital duty. She heard her own groan. It originated in the depths of her abdomen, rose up her throat with light vibrations and broke out from her lips with soft heat. She didn't understand what had caused this reaction. Was it disgust from Nick's touch, or was it a moan of delight from some hitherto unfamiliar feeling? Or maybe both sensations merged into one and didn't let her go.

"Ah, that's how you like it – dirty and rough." He lifted her up. She felt his whole body go on the rampage as he dragged her onto the bed. He threw her on the mattress. Her thoughts were confused. For a moment she thought she was with Karl. She even thought she saw his reflection in the window. But then she realised she was with Nick and that thought pierced her heart.

When he'd finished, Anna tried to get up, but he didn't let her go. "You know I want a child. Just relax and let the magic happen." Nick laughed. He looked at his serene wife. Her long blonde hair was spread haphazardly over the pillow, and her usual eagle eyes seemed out of focus. "Now, what were you saying before about Francesco?"

His question snapped her back to reality. "I'm just curious that he's too good to be true. Perhaps we should make more inquiries." The last trace of Anna's confusion was gone. She was the same arrogant person with whom he had fallen in love five years ago.

She glanced at the clock and jumped up. "Oh, look at the time. We need to hurry; we're late for dinner."

She escaped from his embrace with the reassuring thought that all would be fine; she had just finished her period.

The journey to the other end of the island took twenty-five minutes. The hostess, who introduced herself as Maria, accompanied them to a large round table. Nick couldn't stop looking at his blushing wife. He could still feel the warmth of her body on his skin. Each time he made love to her, he fell in love with her all over again.

There was not a single empty seat in the restaurant. Dramatic red drapes with gold fringes, gilded chandeliers and ornate chairs almost screamed luxury and set an expectation for its customers to splash money. Cold champagne encouraged guests to hot dances, unbridled fun and, most importantly, further spending.

Tash recognised her friend's chiselled figure from afar. Mark, like a slave guarding his queen, followed Carolina, protecting her from intrusive glances. They had landed just an hour ago, but Carolina had already managed to check in to the hotel and change into an evening dress.

"This is Mark," Carolina introduced her companion to those who didn't know him.

He shyly showed up from behind her and smiled timidly.

"Mark, have a seat with us," Nick said. This time tenderness warmed Anna's heart. Nick's innate kindness evoked affection in his wife.

Katya's meeting with Charles's parents was the main gossip at the table. Even Hugh's plane crash faded into the background. According to omniscient Anna, who knew all the gossip, Charles's father, the Marquess Montague, a member of the House of Lords and chairman of the foreign policy committee, was impressed by Katya's perfect English and her cosmopolitan views. Apparently, she didn't at all resemble a Russian spy with a bottle of novichok in her hands, an image so well drawn in his mind by English propaganda. To the marchioness, Charles had astutely sent a selection of fashion magazines with Katya on the covers, knowing they would make the right impression on his American mother. Having looked at the magazines, it wasn't Katya's beauty that impressed her but that she wasn't some penniless environmental activist, like the daughter-in-law of their neighbour, the Marquess of Volderry. Katya immediately found a common language with Charles's father. He was first and foremost a Marquess, but such boring pursuits as study and self-development were never part of his range of interests. Having read no more than a dozen books in his entire life, he entertained Katya with stories about horse breeding, which she enjoyed with extraordinary enthusiasm and even noted how wonderful it would be to make special harnesses from eco-leather for them.

Charlotte listened eagerly to the conversation about individuals of such high status. She held her breath each time she heard the word "marquess" and vividly imagined how she would behave in this highest society when her time came at last.

Nick took over from Anna and told everyone the story of how the Marquess got his title. During World War II, the Montague estate was heavily bombed by the German Luftwaffe. When a shell hit the house, his father and his older brother died on the spot, making him the sole heir. However, his luck ended there. The notorious inheritance tax, which in England amounted to no less than forty percent, was waiting for him. But cunning English law played a cruel joke with the Marquess by declaring that the death of the father and the elder brother didn't occur simultaneously but with a difference of several seconds. They concluded the father who died first left everything to the eldest son, and the eldest son, in turn, having died, left an inheritance to his brother. Thus, the tax had to be paid twice. He inherited pennies from the entire estate, and if Charles's mother, a wealthy American from Texas, hadn't turned up, no one knew what poor Charles would be up to now.

Nick's story amused everyone, especially Tash, who had burst into tears from laughter.

"We're all here, except for our newest happy couple who foolishly traded sunny Saint Barth for the chilly English countryside. Let's send them a photo to remind them of what they're missing."

Everyone smiled at the camera, except Francesco who hid behind Charlotte's head.

Nick could talk to anyone, about anything and as long as they were keen on conversing. There wasn't an area he wasn't well versed in. The men immediately found mutual ground with Mark on investments.

"You must know Francesco's company."

Mark looked with interest at the charming Italian, who was cracking jokes for the ladies.

"What's your company's name?" he asked Francesco.

Francesco smiled dazzlingly and said, "Forgive me, my ladies, but I have to attend to the male part of this lovely soiree." Turning to Mark, he replied, "Glen Capital. And yours?"

Mark took advantage of the opportunity to prove himself. Before Carolina came into his life, work had been his main passion. Now, with the other businessmen, Mark happily delved back into the world of numbers. Carolina looked at him with love. She felt so lucky to have found someone with the qualities that her late husband had lacked.

"Look, here is Carolina," a couple said as they approached their table.

Carolina forced a smile, holding Mark's hand.

"We would like to express our condolences to you," the lady said ingratiatingly, but as soon as she realised that Carolina wasn't radiating friendliness, she immediately added, "Aren't you in mourning?"

The woman glanced down at the low cut of Carolina's white dress, and slowly turned her gaze to Mark. "I heard you were at the coffin with Lady Young."

"I don't think it's appropriate casual conversation to discuss the funeral of my late husband. Victoria, you should really have better manners." Carolina turned away, showing that the conversation was over.

The woman snorted loudly, grabbed her companion's hand and left.

Carolina was indignant. "After our separation, they shunned me and ignored my calls, but when Hugh died, they suddenly became *so* concerned with my health and well-being. All the two-faced vultures flew back around as soon as they heard how much I got."

Once the news circulated that Hugh hadn't changed his will and Carolina had inherited a huge jackpot, a string of suckers, hangers-on and social butterflies had descended on her from everywhere.

Immediately after learning of the tragedy, Carolina took the first flight to London. She hadn't crossed the threshold of their house since she'd caught that guy in their bedroom. She ran her hand along the wooden railing and looked around. She half-expected to see Hugh walk by in his short pants complaining that she was a worthless housewife, and that he was going to eat out. She went into the dining room. Her mother-in-law, Lady Young, was sitting at the table staring at the newspaper in front of her.

"They write that a famous financier died tragically in a plane crash," she said quietly. "His wife and family grieve over his untimely death." She looked up at Carolina. "Are you grieving?"

Carolina took a few steps towards Lady Young and stopped. She wanted to cry, but for some reason she had no tears. Lady Young shrugged and motioned for Carolina to sit down on a chair next to her.

"My child, I know how much suffering he caused you, but I am sure that he loved you in his own way. Forgive me for not being able to raise him to be a good husband." For a moment, Carolina thought a shadow of regret flickered over the stoic woman's usually inscrutable face.

"I have no one else left." She turned to Carolina. "Now that he's gone, I have to tell you something. I hope this will help you to forgive him."

Carolina took her hand in hers and squeezed it tight.

"When Hugh was eleven, we all stayed with a dear friend of Lord Young's in Cannes. Abdullah, a member of the Saudi royal family, was his largest investor. There were parties every day, the fun never stopped. Hugh was the only child in the house and was always on his own. But Abdullah turned out to be a warm and welcoming host. He entertained him, found topics for conversation, played tennis with him, they even had their inside jokes. However, by the end of our stay, something had changed with Hugh. He became very private and stopped communicating with everyone, including Abdullah.

"Lord Young was awaiting a large tranche from the Saudi royal family, and we had to return to London to prepare the papers. But even once we were back at home, Hugh never did return to his earlier self. We merely chalked it up to adolescence. Then one morning, he didn't come down for breakfast. I went to his door, but he wouldn't answer me, and the door was locked. Together with the gardener, we broke down the door. Hugh was in bed. His eyes were closed … I thought he was dead. The gardener felt his pulse, but his heart was still beating. He was barely conscious, but while we were waiting for an ambulance, he muttered something about being betrayed. The doctors said he'd taken a pack of my sleeping pills.

205

"When he regained consciousness, I made him tell me the truth. He said that when we were in Cannes, Abdullah visited him every night, but after his wife's return, he never came back. Hugh thought Abdullah had fallen out of love with him. When I filled Lord Young in on all the ugly details, he declared that Hugh had a good imagination and had made up the entire story. We never mentioned the subject again. Until today, I've kept this secret, not admitting its veracity, even to myself. But now, when neither Lord Young nor Abdullah … nor even Hugh is alive" – she raised her eyes full of tears – "I hope the truth will help you treat your memories of him differently."

Carolina looked out the window. Bare trees towered starkly against a grey-pink sunset. It got dark so early! She turned her gaze to Lady Young and squeezed her hand. Gone was the haughty high-society lady the whole world feared and in her place sat a pitiful, shrivelled grieving mother sobbing softly and wiping her tears with an embroidered handkerchief.

*****

Tash only had time for a quick bite of breakfast on her way out. The shoot would begin in half an hour.

The wind ruffled her hair as the car sped up the serpentine roads on route to the picturesque Gouverneur Beach on the other side of the island. At six in the morning, there wasn't a single soul on the beach except for the crew. Photographers were setting up the lights and stylists were pulling outfits from suitcases. Tash was the first of four models to arrive for the Mango beachwear shoot. She looked out to the inviting sea where hypnotic white-tipped waves crested across the bay. She could swim until they were ready for her.

Tash took off her dress and plunged into the cool water. The salty spray felt like a thousand needles and instantly woke her up. She swam about two hundred metres, turned over onto her back and stretched out on the surface, staring at the cloudless sky. The waves soon made it uncomfortable; the current carried her farther out to sea. She had to fight hard to finally get close enough to shore to feel the sandy bottom under her feet. The photographers on the shore were still testing equipment. She sighed with relief, stood and waved to them. Just then, a powerful wave, strengthening in the shallow waters, knocked her down and dragged into a whirlpool. The sand crunched on her teeth and her eyes stung from the salt. Somehow she got up, but a strange feeling that something was missing made her freeze. While she was struggling with the force of nature, the bottom of her bathing suit had become untied and disappeared in the current. She didn't know whether to laugh or cry from the absurdity of the situation, but the photographers knew what to do. They seized the opportunity and immediately snapped the scene away. Remembering that she was a model above all, Tash threw off her top and walked ashore like she was on the runway. They all laughed at the awkward accident.

"What a crazy way to start the working day! Please delete those," Tash said with a laugh.

"No worries, love. We will."

Once the other models arrived, they started the shoot.

*****

Tash was awakened by a knock on the door and then Anna's voice. "Can we come in?"

Anna and Nick entered with big smiles and a bottle of bubbly. While Anna was pouring the champagne, Nick opened the blinds.

"The celebrations will last twenty-four hours and there is no way to escape!" Anna handed Nick and Tash each a glass. "Happy New Year, my beloveds!"

In the Hotel Taiwana foreign speech was heard everywhere. Egyptian billionaires and Mexican drug lords, New York developers and African gold miners all flew in to the island to celebrate New Year's before leaving for other resorts. Saint Barth, located in the heart of the Caribbean, combined European polish, French hospitality and Latin American fun. It was a Mecca for the rich and powerful over the holidays.

Anna, Francesco and Charlotte went to the beach to pal around with high-net whuffies, while Nick and Tash decided to wait for Carolina and Mark in the restaurant. Zach had just landed and they picked him up at the airport.

"Do you remember the name of Francesco's company?" Mark asked Nick, once they'd settled themselves at the table. "We discussed it with Zach and neither of us had heard anything about him."

"Oh, I never bother about such details. He'll be back soon. Just ask him."

Tash smiled. Not to go into details and trust everyone was typical of Nick.

"Maybe you know, Tash?" Zach looked a little worried. "He invested money in your company, after all, and if we're going to invest, we need to know our co-investors."

"Glen Capital, I think." Tash shrugged. "I can ask the lawyers after the New Year. It'll be midnight soon in London."

She smiled, imagining a lawyer frantically going through work files with champagne in one hand during the countdown.

*****

It was already jammed at the entrance to Villa Rockstar in Eden Rock. Men urged the security guards to let them through faster, holding the arms of their glamorous companions in sparkly outfits. Everyone in the crowd was *someone* and considered themselves much more important than the *someone* next to them. Despite the hoopla of the event, Tash soon realised that the first hour of the new year was no different from the final hour of the year gone by. The revellers were different, but they were still as inebriated and only slightly more amiable. Tash passed the security and found herself in a spacious foyer leading to the pool. On her way to meet Carolina and Anna at the bar, she heard someone call her name, and a miniature figure appeared in front. Stella wanted to hug Tash but ended up hanging over her shoulders.

"Happy New Year!" she slurred. It looked like Stella had begun celebrating a while ago. "Come with me, I'll introduce you to my friends." She dragged Tash towards the pool. "My friends are so funny, we don't even leave the villa." They passed the pool and were walking between tables to one of the gazebos.

The party was bustling, and even more people were entering. Smartly dressed tanned people with glasses in their hands gossiped about their friends and gave each other New Year kisses. She soon saw a group of models and few lucky guys. That was Stella's New York crew.

Tash was sipping champagne when someone touched her shoulder.

"Happy New Year!"

Anna had mentioned that Karl was already on the island, but he hadn't messaged her yet. Karl looked around.

"Tash, have you met Karl? He's my boyfriend." Apparently Stella had forgotten that Tash had been the one to introduce them.

"Don't be silly," Karl objected sharply. "We ... er ... just live in the same villa. Where is Anna ... and the others?"

Stella pouted, trying to grab Karl's hand, but he pushed her away.

"Let's go and look for them," he said, taking Tash's arm. "Stella, stay here. Don't tag along."

The guys were talking at the bar while the ladies sat in a nearby gazebo in their luxurious dresses.

"Happy New Year!" Karl kissed Anna on the cheek. "Nice to see you."

The party was gaining momentum. Guests moved hectically around the villa to see who was present. There were pop stars dancing next to the pool, Hollywood actors brooding at the bar and models filming stories for Instagram. Zach was sharing his Christmas experiences when Tash noticed that the tall figure in a long white dress had temporarily disappeared from her sight.

"Have you seen Karl?" Stella tugged impatiently at the sleeve of Tash's lace jacket. "He left with you and never came back, and now I can't find him."

Tash didn't want to reveal her thoughts on Karl's whereabouts.

About ten minutes later, Tash spotted the white dress. Anna walked towards her, holding her hem with one hand and her gold shoes with the other. "I walked along the beach ... it's so windy there," Anna said with a blissful smile.

Karl showed up a few minutes later, wearing the same expression.

"Oh, Stella, what are you doing here?"

"You left me alone. Where have you been?"

Anna watched the skirmish that broke out between them with astonishment. Stella glanced at his moccasins – they were covered with sand. She looked to Anna's bare feet. She was about to say something, but after looking at Karl's smirk once again, she said nothing. Karl was jubilant. He had two stupid rich birds fighting for his attention, and he didn't care about either. He went to the bar basking in his exclusivity. Stella rushed after him.

"I don't get it." There was a confusion in Anna's eyes. "What the hell was that? What is *she* doing with Karl? I just had sex with him on the beach, and now I find out he's fucking that loser?"

Anna ran to find Nick. "Take me home, please. I'm tired!"

*****

The first day of the new year began with a stir at the villa. Tash was awakened by strange sounds coming from the side of the pool. Shouts were interrupted by a resounding yapping. Tash tried to cover her ear with a pillow and continue her sleep. However, a few minutes later she heard a plaintive whine coming from underneath her door. Still sleepy, she opened the door and a dripping little creature slipped between her legs, barked and rushed into the bathroom. Tash followed him. The puppy was so wet and ugly that she couldn't help but pity him. Tash took him in her arms.

"Oh, you smell like slop. Let's give you a proper bath."

She washed the puppy with shampoo and rinsed him with conditioner. Then she wrapped him in a large fluffy towel, leaving only his face exposed. The cleaned-up ginger face, with two round brown beads, looked much cuter than Tash had first thought.

When everyone got up, she introduced the new member of the villa. He had already dried off, eaten and realised that he shouldn't run too far from the breakfast table.

"Only you would wash a dog with your expensive salon products." Charlotte teased the puppy with a piece of sausage.

"He smells great, though. You have no idea how he smelled when we first met."

"Tash, the saviour of stray animals ... just like your Ben!" Anna laughed, trying to attract the attention of the puppy with cheese. As soon as Anna uttered the name, the puppy immediately rushed to her, forgetting completely about Charlotte's treat. "Oh my god, Ben." The dog's ears immediately perked up, and Anna rolled with laughter. "Now he has a name."

"Ben, Ben," Charlotte called, and the dog rushed towards her.

The housekeeper approached Anna. "The guests have arrived. Shall we serve for three more people?"

Zach came with a red gift bag in hands. He looked stern and focused as he approached Tash. "Can I steal you for a minute?"

When they entered her room, Zach said, "Two things. The first one is the pleasant one; this is for you." He handed her the present. "Sorry I didn't do it last night, but it was a bit awkward."

There was a box in the bag, tied with a ribbon in a bow. Inside there was a small diamond pendant in the shape of a heart.

"Wow! It's so beautiful." Tash turned the pendant in her hands. "But I can't accept it!"

"You can! I chose it myself and I won't take a no for an answer. Let me help you put it on." Once it was around Tash's neck, he added, "Now the second one is not so pleasant." Zach coughed. "Hmmm … I talked to Francesco last night. And today I called my friends to check his company. Francesco Ferrero doesn't exist. Rather, there is not and has never been any Francesco in the Ferrero family."

"What? But how is that possible?" Tash stared in disbelief.

"I wanted to ask you something … delicate." Zach sounded embarrassed. "We need confirmation. Could you ask the housekeeper where he keeps his documents?"

Tash thought for a minute.

"Let's go see for ourselves while everyone is having breakfast. There's no need to involve the housekeeper. I need to see it with my own eyes to believe it. He's my friend and my investor after all."

"You are my Mata Hari! Let's go. I'll ask Mark to distract him."

Tash stayed on lookout while Zach rummaged through Francesco's pockets. His passport was locked in the safe, but his wallet wasn't. Zach found it in his jacket from the night before.

"Here's a credit card in the name of Francesco Ferrero. Hmmm … and another in the same name." Zach was perplexed, but before returning the wallet to its place, he decided to check inside another slot.

His face broke into a satisfied smile. "Come here."

Tash approached him quickly. He handed her Francesco's driving licence, which read: "… issued to Luis Alvarez in the city of Cancun, Quintana Roo District." Zach took out his phone and snapped a photo.

Zach sent the photo of Francesco, or rather Luis, to New York. An hour later, he had the police report on Luis Alvarez in his hands. It said he had moved to New York from his native Cancun, where over the years he had managed to fill his pockets through bank fraud. He then bought off the Mexican authorities and became a good citizen by regularly paying taxes in both jurisdictions. The report also said that the tax authorities in both countries were initially confused because he didn't own any real estate but instead spent astronomical sums on leisure like renting planes, boats and villas, until they finally realised that he lived only on credit. Luis had spent all his savings and took out a bad loan in a Venezuelan bank through his old accomplices, a loan that no one would ever notice with the country's current mess.

When Tash told the Stowes the details, Anna couldn't stop laughing. Nick, on the other hand, was left astonished at people's desperation for social recognition. Wise Mrs. Stowe decided to hush up the case out of harm's way, in a family-like manner, gradually reducing communication with Francesco to zero. She was worried that had Nick announced that he knew the truth, Francesco could have blabbed about her infidelities with Karl.

It was also decided not to disappoint Charlotte in her delusion that she was already halfway to the top of European nobility. Tash reasoned there was no harm to Charlotte since Francesco was a simple swindler, not an evil mastermind, and the two of them actually made a perfect match.

Before his departure for New York, Zach persuaded Francesco to sell him his stake in Tash's business. They agreed on a favourable amount, shook hands and Zach became a twenty percent shareholder.

14. How to conquer new heights

St. Moritz

Two white swans swam gracefully past her, arching their long necks. Fuzzy yellow ducklings puffed funnily in the greyish water and distracted their mother, who was guarding breadcrumbs near the shore. Suddenly it looked like someone had splashed scarlet on the water and then added golden brushstrokes. In the blue space above the treetops, a fiery yellow ball was gently rising above Queen's Gate, bathing all in a warm glow.

So that's where Turner got his colours from! Tash was watching the sunrise from a bench in Kensington Gardens. She had started running early in the morning in an attempt to fully readjust to UK time after spending a month in New York. Tash glanced at her phone and smiled. The splash screen featured a photo of Benny, her adorable new bff, who was staying with Zach in New York to avoid a six-month island quarantine. His funny red face with his tongue sticking out barely fit on the wide screen.

Tash thought back to Lulu's call the day before. Her voice had sounded unusually perky. Lulu was receiving the experimental cancer treatments and they seemed to be working. At the hospital, she'd even met a guy, Thomas, who was undergoing the same course as her, and they'd been dating for a month now. She was full of energy and ready for new achievements. Things were definitely looking up. The beta version of their model platform was ready, and the tests went above and beyond. After buying Francesco's stake out, Zach's team was just waiting for the final tests to decide on further investments. But Lulu had called on a different matter.

"Miss Romanov, you're getting the cover. It's *Sport* and they only want you. It's a full spread with polo players in St. Moritz, at the end of the month. And they pay very good money. Shall I confirm you?"

Her heart clenched. St. Moritz – that's where the Viscontis lived. She wondered if they'd already announced the wedding.

*****

The car was waiting for them at Zurich airport. Karl announced he was going to Engadin for the weekend, so Anna decided to join Tash on her trip. Stella didn't bother her any more. Since Tash had become Stella's agent, her public image and her Instagram – indeed her whole life – had to be coordinated with the agency. The talent management branch was growing. A week ago, she was approached by a record company, dying to record a single with Stella. Tash knew about every movement of her ward and could swear that after Saint Barth, Stella hadn't crossed paths with Karl.

Three hours later, they were in the hotel room. Tash threw open the balcony door. The winter sun cast the snowy valley in warm light. White hospitality tents popped up like mushrooms on the frozen lake in preparation for the polo, which was starting the following day. The only Snow Polo World Cup attracted guests from all over to St. Moritz. Swiss bankers came here to entertain their clients, Arab sheikhs, to showcase their wealth, and car makers, to promote their products. It didn't matter whether it was advertising, status or just extravagant excitement, the maintenance of a polo team cost each owner an arm and a leg.

The film crew was waiting for Tash in the lobby. Today, it was just her alone. Tomorrow, the Deutsche Bank team would be joining her. While photographers tweaked the lights, she was killing time leafing through a local magazine on the hotel's outdoor terrace. A small photo from the social pages caught her eye. Sleek faces with toothy smiles looked at her from a black-and-white photo. Ben, dressed in a light-coloured pullover, hugged Flo in the Corviglia Club.

"Natasha." The photographer was ready for her. "Let's shoot your cover!"

Tash smiled at thought that they would always be relegated to the gossip section of the local magazine, while she would be shining on the international cover of *Sport*!

*****

The tray slid out of the waiter's hands and the pizza slices dropped. This was all Anna's fault for insisting that they make a splash. And they certainly did that! The waiter rushed to tidy up, peeling mozzarella off the wooden floor. What a crazy idea it was to dress like the sirens from *The Pink Panther*! Anna had convinced Tash to wear a flesh-coloured knitted jumpsuit, hugging all her curves, and woolly Mongolian Uggs, while Anna herself sported a short leather dress with high patent-leather boots. It would probably have been fine without the toppers, but Anna had insisted they each wear fox hats. That was overkill. The young waiter shook slightly at the sexy sight of them and instantly wobbled the tray.

"Karl should be here," said Anna, looking around and stepping over the waiter. "Maybe upstairs?"

While still on the stairs, they smelled the pungent scent of truffles and, stepping over the threshold of the room, saw its source. Tables with red-and-white chequered cloths were laden with platters of truffle pizza, the signature dish of Chesa Veglia. Karl walked over to greet the newcomers.

"Tash, you sit down next to Christian," he ordered, hugging Anna.

Tash obediently sat down next to an unkempt guy with auburn hair. Anna landed next to Karl. Tash noticed how that devilish glint lit up Anna's eyes once Karl's hand unceremoniously disappeared under her short skirt.

"Uh ... my name is Christian," the guy introduced himself feebly.

Tash smiled and looked around. The seat on her left was empty, so she had no choice but to look at her neighbour. A confused smile wandered across Christian's face, and his beautiful almond-shaped marsh-coloured eyes radiated sadness and humility.

"Do you live here?" Tash knew that he wouldn't remember her tomorrow, but she tried to speak clearly, helping him to understand the essence.

"Uh ... no, I live in Munich ... but yeah, I live here too ... I live everywhere. I live in Los Angeles. Yes, everywhere ... And also in London," Christian muttered to himself, curling his fingers and trying to remember all the places he had ever lived.

Karl looked away from Anna for a moment and said, "Christian, why don't you entertain us. There's a plate of fruit."

A wave of laughter rolled across the table and gazes turned to Christian. He looked around with a blank gaze before quickly jumping up. "What do you want me to do? I can do everything!"

"Yes, we know that you can," shouted a young man from the far end of the table. Karl whispered something in Anna's ear, which made her face grow longer. While Christian was figuring out what his friends wanted to see, Anna typed a message to Tash.

"He's mega rich, but he's a group jester. He once undressed and smeared his whole body with mango. Karl says everyone loves him." Anna winked at Tash.

Tash was watching Christian as he wandered around the hall, when she heard a man's voice coming from the doorway: "And here we are! Miss us?"

She didn't dare raise her eyes. Her heart was racing. She quickly asked Karl about the upcoming art auctions. Karl was flattered by Tash's unexpected interest in his dealings and promised to tell her about a promising artist he'd discovered after he'd said hello to the newcomers. She had to look up. For a split second, their gazes met, but he quickly looked away. Ben was wearing blue jeans and a jumper, very similar to the one he was wearing when they first met on Alberto Visconti's boat. She watched blankly as Flo dragged Ben to the empty seats next to her, and Ben treaded obediently.

"Hi, I'm Flo." She was sober this time. A short knit dress accentuated her boyish figure. She settled down next to Tash.

"Flo, you met Tash last New Year's."

It was clear from Flo's face that she hardly remembered the events of that night, but being a well-brought up person, she smiled easily. "Yes, of course, how are you? Long time …"

Tash smiled back.

Flo kept Tash talking all evening. Ben tried to break in but, met with their indifference, had to move on to Christian.

Ben stared at Tash. For the first time he observed her in a group of his own kind and, to his surprise, found that she wasn't that different from them; in fact, she even looked like one of them. She had always been beautiful, well-groomed and dressed in the latest fashion, but Ben used to feel that there was something that gave her away as an outsider. And then it hit him – it was her gaze. Where did that timid, over-the-moon excited look disappear to, the one that had looked up at him from under long eyelashes only a year ago? She had now acquired a look of indifference, the mandatory one in his circle. She looked so similar that she could have easily been mistaken for the rich jester's sister.

"Ben, don't you think Tash and Christian look alike?" Flo's words echoed his feelings.

216

No, she wasn't going to the club later. The thought of a swollen face on the cover of *Sport* magazine left her no choice.

"I'll walk you to the room," Anna suggested, but Ben seized the moment.

"I'll take her. I need to speak to the concierge."

Karl looked at him and marvelled, hoping to hear some acceptable excuse.

"I want to surprise Flo for Valentine's and need to ask the concierge to help me," he said quietly.

Ben put on his puffer jacket and helped Tash into her coat.

"See you at Dracula!" Ben shouted after them. He held the heavy wooden door for Tash to exit, and as the door closed, he pulled her in tight for a kiss.

"Are you out of your mind?" She pushed him away and walked towards the hotel.

"I don't care. I could hardly restrain myself all evening. I am dying from the desire to kiss you!" He overtook her and again tried to reach for her lips.

"I am sincerely sorry for you. How you suffered all those six months, dying from desire to call and explain your disgraceful escape from Ibiza." Her face twisted into a stinging grimace. "Or do your desires arise only when you see me?" Tash picked up the pace.

The snow crunched under her feet.

Ben treaded behind in silence. "Can I walk you to your room? I want to talk to you." The look in his eyes resembled her little Benny. This memory brought a sentimental smile to her face.

"Okay, but not for long."

From a beaten-down dog, Ben immediately turned into a happy puppy wagging his tail.

"Maybe we can sit at the bar?" Tash suggested, walking past the bar, but immediately snapped. "Of course not. You can't be seen with me in public because you have a girlfriend!"

217

Tash took off her sheepskin coat and opened the minibar in her room.

"Would you like a drink?"

He wouldn't take his eyes off her, but she didn't feel anxious or embarrassed.

"Vodka and soda." Ben settled into a deep chair with mahogany arms. "Do you want me to do it?"

"I can handle it! Open it, please." Tash handed him a bottle of water while she mixed his drink.

They passed each other their drinks at the same time, and Ben said thoughtfully, "You know, we would have a good life. We understand each other so well. Back in London, I noticed how smoothly everything was going—"

"Except for one minor fact. You had a girlfriend. And you still do, and the two of you seem to be getting along pretty well too!"

He dropped his eyes.

"Tash, listen. I already told you. It's not that simple. Flo and I have been together for a long time, and she's not a stranger to me or my family. Everyone around, including her, is waiting for my proposal. But I can't do it because I'm not sure that I want to spend the rest of my days with her. You know perfectly well how I feel about you. Please don't make the situation even more painful for me. It's really hard for me. I constantly think about you. In Ibiza, I ran away because I was afraid if I waited until you woke up, I would have given in. And that would be wrong—"

"You know, my dear, what was wrong was to start an affair when you were already in a relationship."

There was a silence in the room. Then he spoke, "All situations are different. And I … I didn't expect it to go that far."

"You didn't expect it would go that far?" Tash drew close to him. "You are a fucking spoiled brat playing with other people's lives! You are the one to blame! You're guilty to me for wanting to play and dump me, guilty to Flo for cheating on her and letting our relationship go that far, guilty to your parents, who hope that you'll marry her, and even now you're playing the victim. 'It was hard for me' … 'I didn't expect it would go that far' … Bullshit! You only care about yourself and your feelings. A man's decisions should be stronger than his conditions. If you want to save animals in Africa – save them, don't wander around the world with a rich chick and whine! I am very sorry for what happened in Ibiza; alcohol and drugs are to blame. Now the situation is aggravated by the fact that we have many mutual friends, and we'll probably have to constantly bump into each other. But I promise you, from this moment on, no intimate conversations or meetings between us will ever happen again. You're with Flo, and if you cheat on her, it sure as hell won't be with me. I'm going to live my life. Now you better hurry on your way so your real girlfriend doesn't suspect anything." Tash was livid as she walked to the door and opened it.

Shocked, Ben reluctantly got up from the chair and tried to hug her on his way out.

"Good luck!" She pushed him away and slammed the door in his face.

The alarm went off at exactly seven. Tash opened her eyes and looked at the bed next to her. It was empty. There were three messages on the phone. One from the photographer that the shoot was postponed till nine. One from Anna: "It's late, I don't want to wake you up, so I'll stay with Karl. Good luck with the shoot!" And the last one from Ben: "I love you."

"NO! You won't fool me again." She set the alarm for eight and immediately fell back asleep.

It was not the alarm clock that woke her but the slam of the front door. Anna's head with messy hair showed up from the hallway.

"Oh! You're not on set. Sorry. I didn't know you were in the room." Anna sat down on her bed and began to smooth her hair. The circles under the eyes were blackened by smudged mascara.

Tash leaned against the headboard. "Do you understand your risk?" she said. "You're playing with fire. Now everyone here knows you are sleeping with Karl. Oh, figure it out yourself. I have to go."

Anna lowered her gaze. "How did it go with Ben?"

While dressing, Tash filled her in on the events of the previous night. "I told him that he was a cheater and his behaviour is immoral and painful for all the parties involved."

Tash heard a gasp and turned to see Anna's face distorted with resentment.

"I'm sorry, Anna. I didn't mean it. Your behaviour is not immoral. I mean it is, but in a different way." Tash tried to calm her friend down. "You have a completely different situation because it's only painful for Nick and maybe not even for him, since he has no idea about it. There are different situations in life …" Tash surprised herself by repeating Ben's words.

The first match started at eleven, and the crew had to get ready before the break. At one o'clock in the afternoon, Tash, dressed in a Ralph Lauren suit and with a club in her hands, posed on the ice next to the pony. While they were shooting her, the players joined her for a few minutes to discuss tomorrow's disposition. An hour later, the second match began, and she was free until the next day.

After the shoot, she changed into a ski suit and rushed straight to the Corviglia Club, where Anna, Karl and the rest were having lunch. A light frost blushed her cheeks. The snow packed down by skiers was so hard that she almost glided over it in her moon boots. In a hurry, she had left her sunglasses in her room, and now she had to squint hard. The Corviglia Club was the ancestor of all membership clubs in the mountains and had maintained a strict tradition of admitting only a select few since the 1930s. Had a mere mortal wandered around, they would have never believed they were in one of the most exclusive clubs on the planet, as the members sitting on the benches in their colourful ski suits looked like ordinary humans, but in reality they were royals or the uber elite.

"Tash" – Karl waved his hand at her – "How did it go? Anna said you were shooting for *Sport* magazine?"

Karl called a waiter and asked him to bring another chair.

"Come with me, I'll introduce you to my parents." Flo grabbed Tash's arm and dragged her to the other end of the room.

Flo swayed from side to side. "Christian and I didn't sleep," she whispered. "Everyone went to bed, and we talked until everyone woke up. I took a shower and came straight here."

Flo led her to a large rectangular table. "Dad, this is Tash. She is a model, shooting here for the cover of *Sport* magazine. She's also Dory's friend."

It seemed to Tash that Flo was boasting to her father that she had friends with normal jobs and a lifestyle different from hers and Christian's.

A handsome grey-haired man in his late fifties got up and asked the waiter for two more chairs. Then he turned to Tash. "Alberto Visconti."

Tash held out her right hand to him, which he kissed.

"Tash … Tash … Short for Natasha? Like Natasha Rostova?"

The last time she'd heard that was from Ben. She glanced furtively at a nearby table. Ben's eyes were drilling right through her.

"Are you familiar with the works of Tolstoy?" she asked with a smile.

"I am not only familiar with his works, but a fan of all Russian literature."

The waiter brought chairs.

"Please have a seat, Tash. Let me introduce you to everyone."

His group was mostly made up of men, and the presence of the intriguing stranger sparked a keen interest. Alberto's friends were genuinely curious about her work, her hobbies, her values. She smiled at how only a few decades ago they wouldn't have let a person like her close, disdaining her with haughty looks as their children did today. Now, after being taken down a peg by life's roller coasters, older men didn't want to let a charming young woman go. After talking about art, politics and travel, Alberto said, "Please come tomorrow to our house. We're having a *piccolo* supper for friends and family. Tell Flo where I should send the car."

*****

The polaroids came out better than expected. In a couple of months, her face would be gracing the cover of *Sport* magazine. This was her first cover. How proud Mum and

Grandmother Hannah would have been now if they were alive. She had put her beauty into action, just like her grandmother always wanted. She'd managed to make it.

Once the tournament was over, she ran down to bask in the hammam after the long day in the freezing cold. Eucalyptus vapours gently enveloped her, and her tight muscles relaxed from the warmth of the hot marble. She lay down and closed her eyes to the gentle sounds of soothing music. There was a noise, and two men of about seventy, covered only with towels, sat down on a bench on either side of her. They opened their towels to ensure there was coverage between their wrinkled bodies and the hot stone. While they groaned and looked for a comfortable position in the thick steam, Tash caught a glimpse of their sweaty bollocks. Finally, one lay back, practically burying his bony thigh into her head. She pulled back to make room, but he moved closer. She put her feet to the floor and sat down. He followed her again.

"It's hot in here!" The man had his legs spread as he was speaking to Tash. "Aren't you hot in a swimsuit?"

"I don't think my swimsuit plays a big role in the heat exchange!"

"I'm sure it's synthetic. Your skin can't breathe. Let me see." He moved closer to look at the tag.

Tash jumped up and headed for the exit.

"Hey, Russian?" the old man shouted after her, "how much should I pay you to come back here and join me?"

An invitation to dinner from Senor Visconti awaited her in her room. Dress code: ski chic. Tash breathed a sigh of relief. She had an excuse to wear her new Missoni dress.

"Alberto wants to send a car. I don't get why he's paying me so much attention."

Anna looked through the polaroids from the shoot, sipping orange juice. After examining them carefully, she said, "When the cover comes out, they'll be sending planes."

At eight sharp the concierge called to let them know that Senor Visconti's car was waiting outside. Miss Romanov, in a striped yellow dress and mink vest, and Mrs. Stowe, in suede leggings and biscotti-coloured cashmere, went down the stairs of the hotel, and he personally escorted Senor Visconti's guests to the car.

The chalet was just a short drive away. The massive front door and wooden windows were decorated with pine branches with multicoloured lights woven into them. A girl in traditional Italian costume opened the door.

They made their way through a spacious vaulted hallway into a cosy living room with an open stone fireplace in the middle. The walls were decorated with wood panelling and antique stained-glass windows, and Persian carpets covered the stone floor.

"Natasha" – Alberto squeezed through the group of guests – "welcome! And you are Anna, my neighbour in Sardinia. Where is your wonderful husband Nick?" Alberto gave her a sly look.

"He stayed in London. Too much work," answered Anna quickly. "What a beautiful house."

Tight red trousers with a traditional Swiss vest over a shirt gave Alberto the appearance of a local old-timer.

He called the waiter.

"How did the shoot go? I've heard great. My friends said they saw a gorgeous girl with the Deutsche Bank team. From the description, I understood that it was you." Alberto smiled.

"Rumours about you are all over St. Moritz," Anna whispered in Tash's ear. "Local star!"

Tash looked around the room. The average age of the guests was above fifty. She recognised many – mostly from the media: Greek magnates who had staked out their presence a few generations ago, American businessmen hiding from justice in Europe, Italian aristocrats, German industrialists and Swiss bankers. They all were united by a love of high mountains and low taxes.

The guests were asked to proceed to the dining room. There was slight confusion while the invitees searched for their names on the cards.

Tash immediately found her spot. There was Mr. Engel-Jager to her left and Mr. Spencer to her right. Anna was seated between Christian and Ben. Tash said a special thank you to God that she wasn't sitting next to Ben. She looked around, trying to guess who her neighbours would be.

"You must be Natasha?" She heard a pleasant baritone with a posh English accent behind her. "It's a pleasure to meet you. I'm Alexander Spencer."

A tall, blue-eyed man sat down in the chair beside her. "I am incredibly lucky to be next to you at the table. I never expected that such a beautiful girl would be my interlocutor. Where are you staying?"

Her face flushed pink. Tash could not hide the pleasure of such an adorable dinner companion. "I am also extremely pleased to meet you. We are staying at the Kulm. And you?" She smiled sweetly.

"You have great taste. Kulm is my favourite hotel. Shall I give you carpaccio or bresaola?" Alexander was holding a platter with a selection of meats.

"Carpaccio, thank you." Tash looked to her left, but the chair was still empty. She assumed that Mr. Engel-Jager hadn't made it to dinner.

"We are staying in this chalet. Alberto and his family have been so kind to have us under their roof."

"You're lucky! Such a lovely chalet and such hospitable hosts."

The chalet was truly luxurious. Spacious and stylish. The dark wood and earthy colours were a nod to the nature surrounding them. For a moment Tash even thought she was dining in a pine forest, albeit an expensive pine forest with an Italian flair.

"Yes, my wife and I really appreciate it. There is my wife," Alexander said as he pointed to a skinny blonde in a beige jacket, who looked up and smiled. "And there is my son, Ben, at the end near Alberto."

Tash almost choked. "Ben is your son? I ... I didn't make the connection with Spencer." She couldn't hide her surprise.

"Yes, do you know him?"

She was at a momentary loss for what to say. "A little, yes. We first met very briefly in Moscow."

"Well, that explains it. Our Ben worked there for a while. He's such a fine young man. We always knew that something good would come of our son and that he would never let us down. After all, he is our only son."

There was pride in his voice. Obviously, by "something," Mr. Spencer meant Ben's ability to bring money to the family through marriage, which he and his skinny wife had squandered in pursuit of their own happiness. "We don't yet know where he'll settle once he marries because Flo divides her time between St. Moritz and Milan. Do you also know Flo?"

Tash so wanted to laugh. She was amused by the vaudeville in which she found herself. Just two days ago, Ben had confessed his love for her, and today she and his father were discussing Ben's plans after marrying Flo.

"Yes, I know her."

"We're very fond of the girl. And of her entire family. We are most fortunate with our relatives."

"Will you allow—" The words were accompanied by the rumble of a chair being pulled back beside her. Tash turned around and looked directly at the rude man from the steam room.

He looked much more impressive in his clothes than without. In a red club jacket, with a blue silk scarf peeking out of his pocket in the same colour as his trousers, he reminded her of a clown. The new guest swayed slightly, shifting from foot to foot. He'd probably had a glass or two before dinner.

"My god, who do I see? My mysterious Russian stranger?" He spoke to Tash. "Fate brings us together for the second time in a day, not without reason." He began to massage her shoulders. Tash leaned away from him and turned to Mr. Spencer.

Alexander raised his glass. "Thank you to our generous and most gracious hosts for gathering us all at this table!"

The guests raised their glasses, but before Tash had time to take a sip of wine, the obnoxious man grabbed her by the elbow.

"Didn't expect to see you here." He pulled his chair closer. "You have such a beautiful body. I'm ready to marry you. And I'm willing to pay whatever you want to see what's under those little pink panties you wore in the sauna today," he whispered in her ear, mixing words with sighs saturated with alcohol.

Tash quickly excused herself, grabbed her purse and ran from the table. She rushed towards the exit, and took a breath only when she reached the living room. She sat down on the empty sofa.

Soon she heard the sound of approaching footsteps.

"Natasha." Alberto sank down next to her. "Please do not pay attention to Lutz, he's off his trolley since his wife ran away with the tennis coach. He's an old friend of mine and a good man, but I fully share your feelings. His behaviour tonight is unacceptable. Let's go back. I'll find you a new place. Or we can sit here for a while and gossip." She felt care in his voice. "Tell me about yourself, I would like to know about your life."

And she told him everything. About her father, about the app, about Lulu and her fight against cancer.

"You know, you're a good girl. Send me some documents on your company. I am always open to new investments, especially in talented people like you. I know and respect Zach Cohen. He wouldn't invest in bad projects. And now, let's go back. We've been gone for too long and this can cause all sorts of speculation." He chuckled and stood up.

"I think I'll go. Thank you very much for your hospitality and support."

"Let's do a Madoff shot before you leave." Alberto took her to the bar. "Make us a couple of Madoffs."

Tash looked at him in surprise.

"You never had one?" Alberto laughed. "Worth a try! It's our signature cocktail. Remember Bernie Madoff?"

"The one who built a financial pyramid and then screwed everyone?" Yes, she remembered. His name was on the news when it was revealed that he'd made the biggest Ponzi scheme.

"Exactly. So, most of those whose money he lost are in a two kilometre radius. They are all close friends of mine. But after the whole Bernie story came to light, I became extra-sensitive to phoniness. And you, my dear, don't have it!"

Before leaving, she said goodbye to Mr. Spencer. "Alexander, it was a pleasure to meet you. I hope to see you again."

Mr. Spencer stood and kissed her on both cheeks.

"And I really hope so, child."

15.　In the light of day

Gstaad

The January calm after a stormy Christmas gave way to the February bustle with its piercing arctic winds. On Saturday, life was at full blast in Notting Hill. Passers-by were again hurrying on important matters, cars honked impatiently at leisurely drivers, and pigeons fought hungrily for crumbs left by café visitors. The rotor had started, and no cold could stop the work of the cogwheels of the mechanism. After hibernation, it unwound with renewed vigour.

Tash strode down Westbourne Grove, wrapped tightly in her warm sheepskin coat. Today Lulu had introduced her to Thomas, the spry fitness club owner. He had defeated stomach cancer and was now in remission. It looked like Lulu was seriously carried away with him. Tash knew there had to be a god for sending Lulu such a great guy. As an advocate of a healthy lifestyle, he convinced Lulu to quit smoking and to start living healthily. She blossomed. The treatment worked. Things were getting better.

Tash sighed when she saw the sign of Pharmacy café flashing in the distance. An empty fridge was waiting for her at home. She had to buy food. Now that work sucked up all her time, she simply had no time or energy left for cooking. The decision to go purely organic had flattened her wallet. After paying the rent, which, fortunately, was covered by the rent from her grandmother's house, less Daddy's allowance, a good chunk of the money she earned went to the specialty section. She knew that she couldn't buy her health, so she reasoned that she must earn it through healthy living. So she did. The astronomical bills for the gym and food paid off with an endless energy boost, toned body and velvety skin.

Tash was sipping cucumber juice and staring at the pedestrians through the window while waiting for her order to be ready. As usual on Saturdays, the eager healthy eaters queued up for organic salads.

"May I sit down?"

Tash turned her head. She saw a male figure in a blue double-breasted coat. Black curls fell onto high cheekbones that looked like they were chiselled from olive granite, illuminated by the bright sunlight. She hadn't seen Philip in over a year. Not since the New Year's encounter in his house.

She flushed with a rush of excruciating embarrassment. Memories of the fiasco, safely hidden in the depths of her subconscious, suddenly crawled out like worms after rain. Her story was as old as the world itself; in an attempt to get over the heartbreak from one guy, she ended up in bed with another guy, the first person she met, actually. And he hadn't even bothered to call her. She swallowed nervously, feverishly wondering which course of action she should take. Cold indifference? Attentive affection?

"Philip! What a surprise! Are you in London?" Thankfully her voice sounded easy, almost cool, not giving her true feelings away.

"Actually, I live here." Philip smiled. "This is one of those facts that you didn't manage to find out about me during our short encounter. So, can I sit down? There are no free tables."

She followed his facial expressions closely, trying to guess whether he was flirting with her or just playing it cool. She wondered if he had a girlfriend. "I'm waiting for my order, so you can stay here when they bring it. I'm leaving."

Tash smiled and took her coat from the chair, making room for him.

"Why don't we have a snack while you're waiting?"

Tash was confused. Over the past year, his image had repeatedly popped up in her mind as the image of an ideal man. Moreover, Anna had fuelled her with ideas that he was the one she deserved. In heart-to-heart chatter, his name was mentioned under the entry "an excellent candidate with whom there was a little embarrassment," but whose candidacy required further development. However, the candidate himself never once made himself present over this time, which in her eyes indicated his complete indifference.

"Philip, do you remember Newton's laws?"

He smiled. "Newton's laws?" He found the upcoming excursion into physics intriguing.

"Why do men, instead of calling, leave it to fate and try to portray it is a date!?"

"I look forward to an explanation of this phenomenon." His laughing brown eyes wandered over her face.

"Well," she continued, "this option doesn't work with me. If you wanted to see me, you would have made an effort. Newton's first law is the law of inertia. An object remains in the same state of motion or continues to move at a constant velocity unless a force acts on it." She clenched her hands into fists for greater clarity. "Until you make an effort, my movement will be inert." She continued to hold her fists. "But according to the second law, the resultant of all forces applied to an object, in this case I mean your potential efforts, is directly proportional to the acceleration of the body." She brought one fist closer to the other. "Of course, there is a question with direction of acceleration …" she sighed philosophically, "but it already depends on what efforts you have made." Her face softened, and she smiled. But her fists were still clenched.

Philip covered them with his large hands.

"Does such a brain and beauty combo exist in real life and not only in a Hollywood dream?" He seemed amazed that her arguments came from such a pretty plump mouth, not a professor's thin lips. "You have no idea how happy I am that I met you. I really wanted to see you. But I sincerely thought you weren't interested in me."

"If a guy doesn't call, he either doesn't want to call – or he died!" Tash wasn't giving up. "And you're very much alive."

"There are plenty of reasons why he doesn't." Philip's baritone sounded incredibly sexy. He released her fists, and she wanted him to immediately take them back. "A young man, as in my case, may think that the girl has no interest in him."

No interest? she thought. *I'm on the verge of orgasm from touching his hands.*

"Or he may just be shy. All situations are different. There is not only black and white." Philip moved so close to her that she felt his breath. "I couldn't imagine that a girl who likes a guy would run away without saying goodbye. It's illogical. And yet, you did run away … to Courchevel. And according to Newton's second law, all my efforts caused your acceleration in the direction away from me."

"Trust me …" Tash sighed, "my acceleration was caused by completely different forces applied at that moment."

"Nonetheless, I took your hint about casual encounters and scheduled dates. I suggest not to turn our casual meeting into a date and I will now leave you with your salads. But if you don't mind, tomorrow night we will have a real date, and I will have exclusive rights to your time. More exclusive even than your organic salads." Philip paused expectantly and then winked.

"Agreed!" Tash winked back and held out her hand to him. He held it in his warm palm and then raised it to his lips instead of shaking it.

"As you wish, my lady!"

*****

Tash turned the shower off and placed her foot on the thick beige rug. The home phone had been ringing for several minutes. She wrapped her wet hair in a towel and walked into the living room to answer it.

"Miss Romanov," the concierge sang in a strong Greek accent, "there is a delivery for you. When it's convenient for you, we'll bring it up."

"Thank you, Petros, you can come now."

A massive basket of red roses brought by Petros stood on the dark parquet near the window. Tash read the note once more: "I can't wait for our date."

Thoughts about the upcoming date didn't leave her head all day. Anna gave her detailed instructions: don't be a nervous schoolgirl, don't be a smart ass, don't talk about Ben, don't get drunk, and, most importantly, do not sleep with him again. He was the first man this year whose touch made her shiver, while also pushing Ben out of her mind. He was handsome, well-mannered and fabulously rich. What else did she want? It was just a pity that a whole year had passed before he reappeared in her life. Or was it necessary for some heavenly forces? She certainly felt ready for someone like Philip.

At eight o'clock, he called her from downstairs. Something deeply dormant in her was coming back to life.

"Where are you taking me?"

Philip, dressed in an incredibly elegant black suit of the finest wool, was holding her hand in the back seat of the car. "It's a surprise. How impatient you are."

The car turned off Kensington Church Street and drove towards Holland Park. A few minutes later, the driver slowed down. "We're here," he said politely. Philip walked around the car to help her get out.

"Where are we?" Tash looked around. The familiar contours of Upper Phillimore Gardens popped up in her mind. The house she had planned to live in with Ben just a year ago was around the corner.

"I live here." Philip pointed to the white stucco Victorian house. "I thought the best way to get to know a someone is to see his house. If you don't like it, I have a booking at Scott's."

But she did. The interior decor matched the Victorian spirit of the mansion. If his Swiss chalet was an example of top-notch high-tech, the London house was tastefully decorated in a classic style.

"I really, really like it. Are we here alone?"

"I released the staff for today. You see, we hardly know each other, but you've already been to both of my houses. Very few could boast the same. Do you want to have a tour?"

Tash was grateful that Philip, like a real gentleman, never mentioned their last meeting. He radiated with dangerous confidence, which intrigued her. Over the past year she had blamed him for callousness and indifference, but now she felt safe with him.

The tour of the house took a good half an hour. She didn't want to miss a single detail. She wanted to know everything about him – his tastes, his hobbies, his interests and his passions. Philip was a perfect guide. He had a story behind every object, its style, origin, weaving memories and funny comments. The Chinese vase behind protective glass turned out to be a five-pound copy of a Ming vase which his mother put on display to make fun of art "connoisseurs" who naturally took it for an original.

"What are your plans for the next few weeks?" Philip served the duck baked in advance by the housekeeper.

She was busy this week with work, but fortunately, she was going to Gstaad next weekend. Philip couldn't dream of a better scenario. He admired her independence, her passion for work and her kindness to Lulu.

"Interesting. I'm going there on Saturday. So please consider all your evenings busy. And perhaps your days too," he added with a wink.

*****

The cold wind chilled her to the marrow. Even a warm shawl over her sheepskin coat didn't help. The train was arriving and people gathered on the platform in anticipation.

"I hate you, Nick! Why did you suggest taking the train?"

Tash smiled at Nick. He was hugging an annoyed Anna, warming her up.

"So we can admire the views." Nick's romantic proposal sounded rather comical on this frosty morning. "You can't really see anything from the car!"

"I will soon freeze to death!" Anna hopped from one foot to the other. "Finally, it's here." She freed herself from the arms of her husband. "And who said that Swiss trains are always on time?"

In Montreux they boarded a local train with big panoramic windows. Nick was right – the view of snow-capped mountains really did look much better from a warm carriage. The train glided along a winding path, revealing dramatic landscapes of steep cliffs and narrow gorges.

"I will never stop admiring their tradition and style." Nick was glued to the window like a child. "I remember these train rides from my school years …" And he indulged in memories of long-gone years in Le Rosey.

The train driver announced a stop, "Rougemont," and teenagers with skis and wooden sledges barged into the carriage.

"Now I understand why we didn't take the car." Anna glanced at the kids and then back at her husband. "You're imagining you're still at school."

"Of course, darling. Can't wait for the alumni reunion. Haven't been here for the long weekend for a while." Nick turned back to the window to continue his reminiscing.

A driver with a sign saying "Nicholas" met them at the station. Plunging the suitcases into the trunk, he shook the snow off his boots and got into the car. "Es ist kalt," he said in German. "And it will be like this all week. Cold and a lot of snow."

He was right. The cobblestones on the miniature streets of the village were hidden under a snow-white carpet. The lanterns on the promenade were already lit up, even though it was still about an hour before dusk. The Palace Hotel remained on the right, and after a couple of sharp turns, the car stopped.

"How beautiful!" Tash jumped onto the wide leather sofa and wrapped herself in a blanket. "Let's just stay here and never go out! It's so cosy here!"

She put her feet down on the bearskin rug and looked at the fireplace made of grey stone. The traditional Swiss chalet with a mansard ceiling was decorated with dark brown wood.

With a happy smile on his face, Nick shook the bottle of whiskey he'd just got from the bar.

"We can easily stay here! We already have everything we need!"

"Shall we walk to the restaurant?" Anna was lying on the sofa opposite Tash with her legs on its back. "What time is Philip coming?"

"I thought you complained about the cold. We have climbed higher into the mountains." Nick poured himself a drink. "Let the guy show some chivalry."

"I'm still sick of your train." Anna was leafing through the German *Vogue*. "Okay, let's make Philip feel like a gentleman," she said mercifully. "For me, as long as it's anyone but Ben."

"I don't know about Philip yet, but Ben seems to be a wonderful guy. And the fact that he has a girlfriend makes him even more desirable in my eyes." Nick winked at Tash.

Nick's statement distracted Anna from her magazine.

"Nick, you don't know either of them. How can you judge? Drink your whiskey. Really, no one asked you."

"What are you reading there? You don't speak German, my darling." Nick loved annoying his wife sometimes.

"I look at the pictures, and the prices are the same in every language. Actually, the numbers are your concern." Anna approached her husband with the magazine open. "Look at this fur coat."

"When we leave the European Union your furs will become more expensive. Because of duties. I thought you were pro Brexit?"

"Shut up, Nick, you're in Switzerland. And the Swiss always stay away from politics. The only thing that matters here is money. Fork out!" She feigned anger and jokingly began to beat him with the magazine.

Tash took a shower and then spread out on the large bed, examining her rather sparse room. It was strange that the owners hadn't found the money for a fluffy white carpet to match the bedding. Perhaps they were building the house for themselves and then were forced by circumstances to rent it. She started fantasising who the owners could be. They were probably in their fifties, probably English. He was running a successful real estate business, and everything was going well until the financial crisis struck and his hard-earned money evaporated in the collapse of the Icelandic banks. Over the next few years, he got back on his feet, but another blow took him by surprise. Brexit. How could he – hmmm, Jonathan? John? – have guessed that the voice of the East Midlands workers would determine the fate of the entire country for the coming decades? Leveraged plots collapsed in value, and in order to pay off the interest, he and his wife – Victoria? Catherine? – had to part with their insanely expensive house on the now abandoned Bishop's Avenue and move to a small townhouse in Kensington. After that, Catherine – yes, John's wife was definitely a Catherine – insisted on renting out the chalet. The rent was enough to cover their international travels with friends, without whom she couldn't imagine their existence.

She rolled over, smiling, and switched her imagination off and the TV on.

Ringing laughter could be heard from Tash's bedroom. Anna, dressed for dinner, dropped in to check on her friend's readiness. Tash's bedroom differed from the chalet interior and reminded her of a cosy suite at the Plaza Athénée in Paris, from which it was most likely copied. The only difference was the massive bed of untreated wood, on which Tash lay, laughing at Dave Chappelle's jokes.

"Oh, how he trolls Trump voters. 'You're stupid! You are poor! He's fighting for me.'" Tash rolled with laughter.

"Don't you dare say that horrid name in front of me." Anna cut her off abruptly.

Anna's parents were long-time donors to the US Democratic Party. Anna had absorbed liberal ideas with her mother's milk. She abhorred Republican higher-than-mighty family values and considered their anti-abortion stance to be incredibly misogynistic. She felt sorry for her Republican girlfriends from university who were relegated to the role of mother to a whole brood of kids only to realise that their husbands didn't come close to the ones they had dreamed of at their Ivy League schools.

Her idol was known as the 'life of the party,' a close friend of her father's, the late Pamela Churchill Harriman. She'd lived her life on her own terms and just happened to have bed and wed some of the most famous and richest men on the planet. She was a diplomat, a socialite and a Democratic activist, who had played a major role in Bill Clinton's presidency.

Tash always wondered how Anna could have betrayed her idol by shelving her Princeton brains and her family's political connections to join the faceless aristocracy and poorly educated jet set.

"Okay, let's think about what I should wear." Tash sighed.

Nick pushed Tash outside to meet Philip, claiming that he couldn't find the keys. He then hid behind a curtain, waiting for the right moment so as not to break the sparkle hovering over the young couple.

"How mountain-sexy you are!" Philip gently touched her lips.

She laughed mischievously and gently pushed him away. "Let's save something for dessert."

Tash heard a door creak behind her, which signalled that Nick had realised their romance was being delayed.

*****

"How long ago did you graduate?" Nick had to raise his voice to shout down the hum in Rialto. Every year, Le Rosey grads, young and old, flocked to Gstaad for a long weekend in February to remember the good old days over an Aperol spritz.

"Almost eleven years," Philip replied.

"Gosh, I was *well* before your time, then." The age difference didn't bother Nick in the least. "I guess you and I didn't meet at school. But the main thing is we are both graduates." Nick laughed. "Hear, hear. Let's drink to that!"

"I'm afraid we'll have to drink to that all weekend," Philip said as he raised his glass.

In addition to enjoying their alcoholic drinks, Philip and Nick had a lot of mutual topics for conversation, so during dinner, the wine flowed along with the conversation. Meanwhile, Anna began yawning and glancing at her watch. Soon after that, she announced that she was tired. "Let's go home now and leave the youngsters to their fun. The mountain air has made me drowsy." Anna winked at Nick, and Tash blushed at her friend's not-so-subtle message to her husband that Philip had passed their test and Tash could take it from there.

Once Nick and Anna had left, Tash and Philip decided to visit the serpentarium, also known as the lobby of the Palace Hotel.

"You are so petite!" Philip took her sheepskin coat, admiring Tash's tiny waist.

As they entered the bar, her toned torso was admired by numerous guests. Some approached them to greet Philip, some waved, some called out his name. He was charming and proudly introduced his companion to everyone they passed on their way to the table. The head waiter, who remembered Philip as a mischievous boy, always found the best place for him even on the busiest evenings. Camilla was at the table.

Tash settled comfortably in the deep plaid chair and then heard a timid voice from behind.

"Tash, hello."

She turned around and saw Julia, who was unexpectedly honouring her with her attention. "I wonder where her snobby blue blood attitude went?" Tash chuckled to herself.

With Philip, she felt like a little girl who would be taken care of. The conversation revolved around her, and his friends showed genuine interest in the details of her glamorous life. Tash, like many others, could not resist the hidden flattery of rapt attention.

"So what magazines have you done covers for?" Craig, a handsome guy to her right, asked her about her modelling career. "You're the most beautiful girl here."

Tash enjoyed talking about her work. For a moment, she even reminded herself of Katya. Tash's popularity didn't escape the attention of Camilla, who was glued to her phone all evening, although she did cast a few conspiratorial glances at Tash.

"Shall we go down to the club?" Camilla asked the group.

Philip turned to Tash. "Should we go too?"

"Of course. By the way, I keep forgetting to ask you one question. It's been spinning in my head for a long time. When I first saw you at Stavros's charity event, you were bidding for a lot on Hugh Young's boat. Do you remember that? I was just curious why. Or is it that you're such a philanthropist?"

"No, of course not!" Philip put his lips together in a scornful grimace and shook his head. "My mum was on that committee and she asked me to raise the ante for Hugh's lot. I never would have given that much money to Syrian refugees, but everyone knew that your friend's boyfriend would pay any price, and the charity had to raise as much as possible."

Camilla paced hastily down the corridor, like a goose leading her goslings for a walk. They all followed obediently. Multicoloured lights filled the empty dance floor, gently dissipating into the darkness of the room. Philip was about to walk around the club, but Camilla, quickly grabbing him by the arm, drew him along. There were two figures on the steps. One was leaning his elbows on the railing and was telling the other some funny story, as they were laughing wildly. Next to them, there was a full table of women dressed to the nines, apparently determined to honour the Gringo Club with their presence after some smart dinner party. One of them was Flo. She waved gleefully to greet Tash, throwing Camilla into complete disarray.

Tash felt someone's eyes upon her. The glance caused a shiver in her body, and she felt how a slight chill tickled her bare belly. She looked up. Ben was standing several steps higher, but he looked somehow diminutive and unremarkable next to Philip.

"Please meet my friend, Tash," Philip introduced her.

"Uh … glad to see you, Natasha." Ben couldn't hide his surprise.

"Me too," she said, standing close to Philip.

"Where are you staying?" Ben kept his eye on Philip's hand as it gently stroked her waist.

"Not far from here, Chalet Laplana."

Ben breathed a sigh of relief. He wouldn't have been able to take the thought of her walking half-dressed around in Philip's chic chalet. She, however, felt captivating excitement. The sweetness of revenge was more intoxicating than any alcohol. She knew he was jealous. She saw his eyes fill with anger whenever Philip's fingers touched hers. She was relishing her position and didn't want to move away from Ben. She wanted him to fully experience what she felt. Once her bowl of retribution was filled to the brim, she decided to join the flamboyant beauties. Flo couldn't hide her excitement at the sight of Tash, her new friend who would soon be on the cover of *Sport* magazine.

"I've grown so tired of St. Moritz. Ben convinced me to move to Gstaad. At least there's some novelty here compared to our village."

Tash imagined how many people would be able to get tired and bored the way Flo did. She tried to remember the last time she enjoyed absolute idleness herself, but she couldn't. She wondered what Flo did all day, every day. She had so many opportunities and money was no object. She could fly helicopters, visit the South Pole, learn Swahili or, at worst, start some kind of business.

"Look." Flo removed a thin gold evil eye bracelet from her wrist. "I decided to go into jewellery. What do you think?"

Tash glanced at the bracelet, which was no different from the trinkets she'd find at a Turkish bazaar, and thought sadly that one more mediocre jeweller had emerged on the planet.

For some reason, the moment twigged a memory in Tash. One day, about twenty years ago, a little girl, Tanya, came to Tash's daddy's class in tears. Her mother had been fired from her job and her father was serving a prison sentence. They had run out of money and were hungry. Tanya couldn't help but devour the cakes that Tash's father bought for the kids daily. He reached into his pocket for money, but he only found coins. He glanced at Tash, but she shook her head. She couldn't sleep that night for guilty thoughts about Tanya. In the morning, she went to her daddy with a bundle of bills that her grandmother had given her before leaving.

"Daddy, please forgive me. I was saving up for a new bike," she said with tears in her eyes. "But I don't need it. Let's give it to Tanya."

Her dad stroked her hair, then took her head in his hands and said gently, "Take your money back, pumpkin. Now look me in the eye and promise that you will never lie again. You have to be honest. As your mother was. Most importantly, always be honest with yourself. Promise me!"

"I swear to you, Daddy, I will never lie again!"

They bought her a bicycle, but Tash didn't keep her promise. She turned the bracelet in her hands and replied, "What a cute little thing. It suits you very much!" And immediately felt embarrassed for her little lie.

"I'm actually thinking of making a full collection." Flo's eyes sparkled with enthusiasm. "Can you promote it on your Instagram?"

And she had to lie again. Tash, more than anyone, knew that Flo would have crushing success on her own Instagram page, and her boring creations would be bought in seconds by admirers who longed to feel closer to their idol.

Tash and Katya would occasionally go through some heiress's social media and be amazed by the adoring comments from desperate wannabes who hoped that their lives would be forever changed by heaping praise onto someone they would never meet: "You are divine"; "Your beauty blinds"; "No one compares to you." If they knew they could buy a piece of that world, even if it was a cheap trinket, they would snap it up in a heartbeat. Anything to feel close to the one they deemed so special.

At the same time, the excessive praise gave the poor heiress no choice but to sacredly believe in her "chosenness." Over time, that belief grew into the deepest conviction of her irresistibility. And by then, she, the divine Aphrodite, was already taking the services of her underprivileged fans for granted. She would bring them closer to dispel the unbearable boredom overwhelming her soul, only to throw them away as soon as her blues receded. The poor discarded leeches would be heartbroken for a couple of weeks, until they found another rich beautiful body to latch onto and their sucking up began anew.

The stream of her thoughts was disrupted by the high decibels of Camilla's voice,

"So, you and Philip are serious?" Her cow-like eyes were fixed on Philip, who was standing at a distance with Ben.

Tash smiled at the comparison of the two men. From afar, they quite looked similar: same age and similar physique. But as soon as Philip turned around, the differences were striking. How much courage was in this look! Sharp and shameless, his penetrating dark eyes under long black curls melted everything in his path. A haughty smile froze on his thin lips, like he alone had the right to decide his fate. His charisma and strength electrified the space around him. Ben, on the other hand, was imbued with boyish looks and charm. He tried to surreptitiously catch her eye, as if afraid of being publicly punished for his insolence. Although she remembered every detail of his face, it was only now, seeing him beside Philip, that she noticed his femininity.

"I hope so," Tash replied to Camilla.

*****

She was awakened by an insistent knock on the door.

"Can I come in?" Anna entered without waiting for an answer.

"Did something happen?"

Anna looked worried. "I vomited all morning. I passed out last night, as soon as we got home, and today I woke up with horrid nausea. My boobs are enormous." Anna pulled down the straps of the silk slip.

"Oh my god!" Tash woke up instantly. "That's amazing news! Have you taken a test yet?"

"No, I haven't, but I'm sure I'm pregnant. I've never felt so sick in my life."

241

"Did you tell Nick? He must be in heaven."

"That's the catch …" Anna lowered her voice in confusion, "I'm not exactly sure it's his." She paused, looking down.

"What? Oh my god, Anna! You're my smartest friend – how could you let this happen?" Tash almost shouted at Anna. "You didn't use protection with Karl?"

"We did … always. Except … once … on New Year's, on the beach. I'm sure I got pregnant then. Karl was like an obsession for me, a stupid, dangerous obsession. Well, there it is. I've been feeling nauseous for a couple of weeks now."

"What are you going to do?"

"I don't know," Anna sobbed. "I just realised that I really want a child. But only if it's from Nick. What if it's not?"

*****

Anna reasoned that in her current state, it would be much wiser for her to shop in the local boutiques than to possibly risk two lives on the dangerous slopes of Gstaad. So, Wispile slopes had to be mastered by Tash alone, without her faithful friend. Tash managed to jump into the overcrowded ski lift cabin and was watching the diminishing figures of skiers below, when someone tugged insistently at her sleeve. She turned around and saw the ruddy face of Stella, dressed in a snow-white jumpsuit.

Tash was pleased with her ward. Since Tash had taken her under her wing, Stella had been conquering the heights of the fashion world with double the tenacity inherent in someone still so young. Despite her average height, in just a couple of months, Stella had managed to become the media's darling. Her Instagram grew to two million followers, brands were showering her with their merchandise and fans were copying Stella Goldstein's styles. Her first single was due out in May, and everyone involved envisioned a brilliant future for her.

"I need to tell you something." Stella decided that greetings were overrated and immediately got down to business. "Just promise not to tell anyone."

Tash nodded vigorously.

The cabin was crawling up the snow-covered mountain.

"I'm seeing Karl," she whispered. "He asked me not to tell you, but you are my manager." Stella sighed. "You have a right to know, after all, because you introduced us. He is coming today," she continued, "and he wants to meet Mum. I'm so excited!"

To some extent, the news that Karl had bet on Vivien's connections and would finally leave Anna alone made her happy. Tash didn't worry about Stella. She knew that Vivien would put the poor guy under a magnifying glass. And if he planned to snatch something, he had little idea of who he was dealing with. There was only one cobra in that terrarium, and it wasn't Karl.

"Great news," Tash said. "I'm sure Vivien will immediately see how wonderful he is."

*****

"Happy Valentine's Day, Tash. Wake up," Anna said as she opened the door to her room. "There are flowers for you. Beautiful! Three bouquets."

But Tash was already awake. She stretched. Thin strings played in her upper abdomen, spreading joyful music throughout her body. In recent days, this music had played in her incessantly.

"Three? Who from?" She knew at least one was from Philip. They were together last night making final arrangements for tonight's gala dinner at his chalet, where Tash would be hosting the evening.

"Get up, sleepyhead." Anna sat down on her bed and pulled off the blanket. "Let's go and see who they're from."

Tash went down to the living room. Nick was browsing the morning press at a wooden table inlaid with mother-of-pearl. No matter where he was, he couldn't imagine his existence without the morning paper; iPhones and iPads were alien to him, so he had couriers deliver his newspapers to his door early in the morning.

There were four bouquets on the floor near the coffee table. The largest was a bouquet of white lilies interspersed with gypsophila. Tash was about to look at the card as Anna pulled it back. "Don't touch it – it's mine," she laughed. "Nick had an attack of gigantomania." She kissed him gently on the top of his head bent over the newspaper.

Not only was the size of the bouquet huge, but the smell of lilies overpowered all the others. Tash scanned the remaining arrangements. The basket of red roses was the exact copy of the one Philip had sent her before their first date.

"I think this one is from Philip." She took out the card and read, "Happy Valentine's, beautiful! Hope you won't run away from me this time."

The flashback of how he'd asked her to host the Valentine's dinner with him lit up her face.

The next arrangement was a heart made out of red roses. "That's kind of tacky." Tash was puzzled. Either by the sender's request or by pure chance, a gilded card with monograms stuck out of the heart. "With love, to the most beautiful girl in the world. Zach."

The last bouquet was pink chrysanthemums and blue alliums. It came in simple wrapping paper with a small piece of paper stapled to it. The joyful music gave way to a slight tingling sensation in her chest, and the smile left her lips.

Anna took the note from her. There was a hand-drawn heart. "It's from him, right?"

*****

"What a gorgeous dress!" Stella exclaimed rapturously upon seeing Tash at the entrance. Tash was radiating happiness, receiving hugs and kisses, and posing for pictures with the newly arriving guests. Around her neck gleamed a thin chain with a heart made of rubies, presented to her for Valentine's Day by the owner of the house.

Stella Goldstein was one of the first to arrive. In recent months, her fame had shone so strongly that wherever she showed up, people would run up to her to take selfies. Her stardom by no means stopped her from approaching each of Philip's guests and introducing herself with childish spontaneity. But when it came to the Stowes, who were chilling at the bar, Stella's tactic suddenly changed. She plunged into the world of Instagram stories, defiantly ignoring Anna, who stood right in her way, and rushed straight to Nick. Anna, still unwilling to share the latest news with her husband, pretended to be drinking champagne and stared blankly at the childish manoeuvre. Shortly before the reception, Tash couldn't restrain herself and secretly filled Anna in on Stella's revelations about her blossoming love life with Karl, who had continued to act as if nothing had changed in their relationship while corresponding with Anna.

244

The guests were still arriving, and Stella was making sure to meet everyone. She reconnected with Camilla, whom she hadn't seen since their lovely time together in Ibiza. Camilla's friend Florence, everyone called her Flo, turned out to be deadly sweet. Once Flo realised how popular Stella was, she removed her gold evil eye bracelet and put it on Stella's wrist. Flattered, the eager starlet instantly shared it with her million followers on Instagram, bragging that it was the new brand of her new best friend and jewellery designer Florence Visconti. When Stella tried to return the bracelet, Florence flatly refused to take it, saying it was a gift.

Stella studied Tash and thought she looked well with this new boyfriend of hers, a hot Latino guy who happened to be the owner of this luxurious chalet.

After finishing her boring hosting duties, Tash finally came to Stella. But she excused herself after five minutes, as she had to make some arrangements for the upcoming dinner. Stella looked at Philip and wondered how Tash, who wasn't that young any more, had managed to catch such a swaggy guy. Even though he made her yawn by naming all the places for sightseeing in Cartagena that she and Karl should visit, instead of telling her where to get the best powder, he was still cute. Stella scribbled everything in notes, and got distracted from the phone only for a minute to check where Tash was. Tash finished her duties and was already walking back, when suddenly Stella noticed that some handsome blond in a blue jacket grabbed Tash's arm. "Wow, this one is even hotter than the other! Is she like a magnet to them?" Stella thought as she watched the scene unfold. Tash tried to walk away, but the Adonis held on. Then he pulled her into him and tried to talk to her, but Tash only grinned in response. Stella looked around. It seemed that every single soul in the room was watching the show. Flo stood confused, staring at them, and Camilla whispered something in her ear.

Philip got up and walked quickly towards Tash. "Hello, Ben." Philip shook his hand and asked, "Tash, are you all right?" His every word permeated the reigning silence.

"Yes, of course. Everything is fine. Let's go to the guests."

Dinner was served in the black dining room. The long table for fifty people was decorated with compositions of red roses, Philip's favourite flowers.

Just before dinner, under the pretext of checking to see if everything was in order, Tash changed the cards, placing Flo and Ben at the far end of the table.

Karl arrived at the end of the dinner. He quickly greeted Anna and, pretending he was looking for an empty seat, slipped in next to Stella. Stella, who hadn't yet learned how to hide her feelings, threw herself on his neck with a joyful squeal. Annoyed, Karl kept glancing at Anna, fearing her reaction, but like a real snow queen, she totally ignored their presence.

After supper, everyone moved into the lounge. Karl was doing tequila shots one by one, and Stella was keeping up. After a while, her new friend Flo joined them.

"And here we are drinking tequila again, a new round, eh hey …" Stella filmed a story every time the glass hit the counter. "Happy Valentine's Day, bitches!"

The shots banged on the counter every five minutes, the rate at which tequila was consumed. The vibe had eased. Tash was chatting with Anna Stowe on the sofa. Ben, that was the name of the blond stallion according to Karl, kept to the other end of the room.

The DJ turned up the volume, and Philip was the first up to lead Tash to the dance floor. Stella admired how beautiful they looked together. Just like a prince with a princess! Stella turned her gaze to the second prince, the blond one. He was marching over towards the counter. On the way, he glanced furtively at the dancing couple, and then stopped in front of Flo.

"May I have this dance, my lady?" Ben held out his hand to Flo with a smile.

But she didn't budge. She just stood there holding a new shot of tequila and staring at him. Next thing Stella saw was tequila streaming down his confused face, and Flo began to smack him in the chest.

"Don't you dare deny it!" Flo yelled, bashing Ben. He covered himself as best he could, but Flo was relentless in her blows.

"What's happening? Flo, calm down." Karl tried to drag the angry woman away from Ben, but he wasn't able to. Stella tried to help him. Philip and Tash heard the screams and rushed over.

"Get this bitch out of here!" Flo screamed, pointing to Tash. "Right now! Immediately! Or I'll kill her!"

"Don't you dare threaten my girlfriend." Philip stood between Flo and Tash. "And if you've got a problem here, Flo, you can get out of my house."

Ben sat down, covering his face, now reddened from the blows and the embarrassment, with his hands. Tash stood shaking behind Philip's back as the guests crowded around them.

"Did you know your bitch is having an affair with Ben?" Flo flung her arms at Philip. "That they fucked this summer in Ibiza? Behind our backs! And this snake was at my house. I introduced her to my family while she was fucking my boyfriend." Flo's face contorted with pain.

"Tash, is this true?" Philip turned to her and asked calmly.

The crowd froze, waiting for her answer.

"No, it's not true." Ben finally uncovered his face and slowly got up off the floor. This time his gaze was unusually calm. "We really did *know* each other, and there really was some kind of *relationship* between us, but that is all water under the bridge. You have nothing to worry about, Philip. Come on, Flo," he took her by the elbow and led her towards the exit.

Realising that the show was over, the captive audience reluctantly began to disperse.

Philip turned to Tash. "Did he tell the truth?"

She swallowed nervously, feeling naked under his piercing gaze. "Philip, I would never have started dating you if there was someone else in my life." She took his hand and raised it to her lips. "It was because of Ben that I ran away a year ago. And we finally had closure last month. Honestly, I am absolutely free from any relationship and feelings."

Philip hugged her tightly. "I knew it. I'm sorry I doubted you for a second. Will you come with me to Paris to meet my mom?"

16. How much are you worth?

Paris

"You just asked, 'Who doesn't want to live in this house?'" Tash pointed to a grey, Haussmann house with a flat facade and running balconies encircling the upper floors. "But in fact, not everyone wants to."

After finishing their tea at the Café de Flore, Tash and Philip accompanied his mother along the Boulevard Saint-Germain.

"It seems that the more money one has, the easier their life is," Tash said to Violette. "But the paradox is that the more money one has, the more hassle."

She took a notebook and a pen from her bag. She held the notebook against a hewn stone wall they were passing and drew a circle. "This is one's high-net worth." She pointed to the circle. "Each one of them has a mini state. First, it's one's business." She drew a second circle. "They can employ thousands, tens or hundreds of thousands of people. Second, this is their environment." She drew a third circle. "Bankers, lawyers, concierges, secretaries, staff, coaches, boat and aircraft crews, all of them depend on that first person. Third, their family. Sometimes it's an extended family with many members." She added more circles. "Fourth, the entourage, which includes both friends and hangers-on. Fifth, houses, boats, planes, cars …" The whole page was soon covered with circles and arrows going from one circle to another. "All these circles represent commitments, therefore, worries, and the more circles a person has, the more they complicate their own life."

Philip looked at Tash then at his mother and smiled. He knew how surprisingly convincing his new girlfriend could be in her judgements.

"I agree with Warren Buffett," Tash continued, "who realised that happiness is not burdening oneself with excesses, but simply taking satisfaction in one's basic needs. That said, I'm by no means calling for Gandhi's asceticism." She laughed.

Violette glanced at Tash's sensible khaki dress, which was very appropriate for reasoning about asceticism, and coolly nodded her head.

"Buffett lives in a house he bought decades ago and drives to work in an old Cadillac." Tash tucked the notebook into her bag. "For him, a car is an everyday necessity, and his Cadillac fulfils this need."

"Shall we walk further?" Philip asked, holding the arm of his mother, who was wondering how long Tash's reasoning could last.

Tash adjusted her dress and quickened the pace. "Many things are simply not worth the asking price and are mainly bought by insecure people trying to prove to the whole world that they are worth something."

"Hmmm …" Philip thought. "I've loved racing cars since my childhood, and now I buy them. Do you think I have an insecurity?" He took Tash's other arm, trying to coordinate the women's pace.

"No, you are another matter. That is passion! Racing cars, art, whatever. When passion motivates you, you do it for yourself and not for others." Tash had to slow down so as not to get ahead.

"You know you are a genius?" Philip looked at her with tenderness. "You should write textbooks, not pose for magazines."

Violette was examining Tash and wondering what was hidden behind her alluring face and polarising rhetoric.

Violette looked like a quintessential French woman, effortlessly chic in her long ethnic dress and beige Chanel flats. Flowing hair parted down the middle added a rebellious spirit to her otherwise impeccable elegance. Having seen the heyday of Woodstock, Violette had never outgrown her love of bohemian clothing.

She was the daughter of a big French industrialist and had been spoiled by attention since childhood. But only New York showed her what real social life was. After Cornell, which introduced her to festival culture, she returned to the Big Apple to immediately vie for the title of style icon. A kaleidoscope of travels and a series of social events alternated with rehab. She was thirty-two when she met Andres Ribeiro Gonzalez. He was fifteen years older than her. The son of the ex-President of Ecuador, the well-groomed and well-educated Latin American ran the liquor empire created by his father. Violette was the only woman he was certain ever loved him for him, not for his wealth and power.

A year after the wedding, Violette broke down and almost died of an overdose. Straight after a rehab, she got pregnant with Philip. He became the meaning of her life, a substitution of her drug addiction. They had a deep connection, which only intensified after the death of Andres. Philip was the only significant person in her life.

Violette knew Sofia from birth. She was the daughter of her closest friend and both mothers had prayed that the children would like each other. Sofia was three years younger than Philip, and from early childhood they had been inseparable, like brother and sister. Their parents sent them to Le Rosey, and when, after graduation, Philip asked if she would wait for him while he studied at Harvard, she said yes. From that day on, they officially became a couple.

Three years later, Sofia moved to New York to study at the Parsons School of Design. Philip joined her in New York, where he headed one of the family companies. Three years passed with studies, work, parties and travel. She decided to stay in NYC after graduation to pursue a career in fashion, where she had acquired extensive connections over the years. Philip agreed.

For the next two years, she was "looking for a job," mainly in local clubs and restaurants. Philip repeatedly offered his help, but it eventually became obvious that the only thing Sofia had an interest in was endless parties. When one day he asked her directly if she was ever going to work, she threw a tantrum, saying that she wanted to live the way she liked, then slammed the door and left. A week later, Sofia fell in love with a DJ, and two weeks later, she moved in with him.

For a long time, Violette couldn't come to terms with the fact that her hopes were dashed and Sofia would never be her daughter-in-law. Philip, to her surprise, suffered the break-up with a very Buddha-like calmness. Six months later, he relocated to Geneva to focus on work. He left the family business in charge of the board and fully devoted himself to his own company, providing microloans at a high interest rate in the developing countries. He opened offices in Brazil, Mexico and his native Ecuador. However, Violette had bigger dreams for Philip. She envisioned him as a high-profile player in the world of politics. Perhaps as the president of Ecuador, or even France. With her connections, the path was clear. But until the time came, she nurtured his independence and success while gently steering him towards her goals. And like a silent spider, she waited patiently for him to screw up and get trapped in her web.

"Ma cherie" – Violette turned to Tash – "tomorrow we're going to lunch, and then you'll help me choose an outfit for the Met Gala. It's the perfect way for us to get to know each other better."

She played the role of a kind and understanding mother brilliantly, fully supporting the choice of her son.

The next morning, Philip left early, and Tash was finishing her tea on the terrace, enjoying the views of the rooftops of Saint-Germain when Violette returned from a walk with her dog.

"What lovely weather." Violette held a newspaper in her hand. "We wound our way through Le Jardin du Luxembourg and I bought the morning press. I suggest taking a leisurely stroll to the restaurant."

"With pleasure." Violette was standing against the sun and Tash had to squint from the bright light. "I don't understand why Parisians don't walk as much as Londoners. The city is magnificent."

"I agree, ma cherie, this is one of the few habits in which the British are ahead of the French." Like most French, Violette was an incorrigible snob and absolutely detested the Brits.

"I've got a shoot in the seventeenth this evening, and I'll definitely stroll down there." Tash had already planned a charming route to the right bank of the Seine.

"Walk? To the seventeenth?" Violette looked stunned. "Not only it is the banlieue, but you can easily get stabbed by an illegal immigrant. You left the European Union, and now you consider yourself entitled to all sorts of liberties? No, ma cherie, here we all follow the rules."

For Violette, Paris consisted of only six arrondissements, everything beyond was the "ghetto," filled with weapon-brandishing immigrants.

"Ma cherie, the driver will take you there."

*****

Ralph's in the Ralph Lauren Mansion was a favourite dining spot for Parisians who preferred Rive Gauche of the Seine to the right. Cosy Saint-Germain with its charming streets had the discreet charm of the bourgeoisie, so vividly poetised in Luis Bunuel's movie, that no one wanted to move to the pretentious right bank crowded with tourists.

"Have you seen what happens to cows before they end up in your burger? Those nine minutes will change your life forever." Violette, a staunch vegetarian for several decades, watched in horror as Tash was savouring a Ralph burger.

"I can imagine what that film is about," Tash said as she cut off a juicy piece of meat. "And I'm sincerely sorry for the poor animals, but I need animal protein in my diet, and I will never give it up." And as proof she took a big bite.

"Philip is the same; everyone is against me," Violette said as she sampled her salade verte.

"Oh, on the contrary … Philip worships you. He keeps you so well informed. All I hear is, 'I must call my mother' and 'I need my mother's opinion,' etc."

Violette smiled in relief that the girl wasn't trying to overthrow her from her throne. "Finish the meat and then let's go get our dresses."

The walk along Avenue Montaigne and Rue Saint-Honoré took no more than an hour. Whatever shop they entered, the assistants were waiting for them with a preselected assortment for Violette's discerning taste. Tash only had to nod or shake her head.

The last on the way was Chanel on Rue Cambon. The general manager, who was waiting for them at the entrance, signalled to the security guard to let them into the store, bypassing the line of Japanese tourists.

"Shopping reminds me of checking in for a flight lately. Same queues!" They followed an elegantly dressed middle-aged woman in a Chanel suit.

"Violette, when was the last time you queued at the boutique?" The woman turned, and Tash saw a sly smile on her face. "In fact, you even didn't have to come, we would have sent everything to your house."

"I wanted my friend to see the dresses," Violette lied.

Violette tried on four dresses. None suited her.

"I'll have to buy something in New York. Jacqueline" – she turned to the manager – "we'd like to look at bags, all shades of white and blue."

252

Jacqueline made a call, and a few minutes later the entire collection from snow-white to dark navy was presented in front of them.

"Which one do you like?" Violette looked at Tash probingly.

"It depends what you want." Tash picked up a sky-blue bag made of soft lambskin. "This one is so pretty."

"Jacqueline, we take this one and the white handbag, and I would also like a white standard wallet for a present."

"Evette, bring the ladies drinks while I pack everything."

Jacqueline returned with three bags.

"The wallet is our gift; we didn't include it in the bill."

"Thank you, Jacqueline. Next week, I'm expecting you at mine for poker." She kissed Jacqueline, and they left the store.

The Japanese tourists watched them go. Violette handed Tash one of the packages.

"This is a gift for you, for helping me with my dress shopping."

Tash was taken aback. "But you didn't buy anything. I can't accept such an expensive gift from you."

"You must have this bag. Philip asked me to buy one for you while we were out. It's really from him." Violette lied again.

She secretly called Philip as soon as they arrived home. "Tell Tash that it was you who asked me to buy her a bag," she whispered.

"Of course. Maman, I wonder why I didn't think of it myself. Thank you."

When Tash returned from the shoot, she found the living room roaring. Violette had invited a few friends over for ratatouille, her late mother's recipe. To Tash's surprise, they were all cool bohemian ladies without a touch of snobbery, who had ended up in Paris by pure fate. There was a Uruguayan artist, a Hollywood actress, the owner of the biggest German department store chain and Violette's long-time friend, Rosa, a famous Brazilian model from the seventies.

Each of them could have written a book about their lives. Tash was enjoying their company enormously, and they seemed equally interested in her. She proudly told Rosa about her and Lulu's modelling agency and showed the finished version of the MDL (short for "model") platform mobile app.

The app had come out much better than expected. A week ago, as soon as it was completed, Tash called Zach's team. They quickly tested it, spoke to the developers and reported back to Zach. He called a couple of days later. "Benny is bored and says hello to you. He misses you." Benny's furry face appeared on her phone screen.

Zach often video-called Tash, reporting Benny's achievements. The puppy was still quarantining in Soho. He migrated between Zach's apartment on Mercer Street and Charles's and Mark's apartments on Prince. Sometimes Carolina took the pooch away to Mark's country house in the Hamptons for the weekend. Benny was beginning to show signs of being a German shepherd–terrier mix.

"I miss him too." Tash sent an air kiss to the phone. "Benny, wait a little more and you'll be with me."

"Tash, I wanted to talk about your project." Zach sat Benny on the sofa and turned the camera to himself. "And I wanted to inform you about it personally. My guys reported back to me, and we decided to invest more money. After the lawyers get the papers ready, we'll go ahead."

"Oh, Zach!" Her heart was pounding wildly. "I have no words. It is like a fairy tale!"

"You've earned it and you totally deserve it!" Zach smiled. "You have a great project, and we're lucky that you came to us with it. We believe in you, and we know that you'll bring us a lot of money. But that's not all." Zach stroked the puppy on the head and said, "Benny has received all his necessary vaccinations, so now he can safely travel. And I can bring him over to you. We can fly to London later this week."

"But …" Tash hadn't yet come to her senses, while their conversation rushed in a different direction. "Zach, I'm in Paris," she said carefully, "and I'll be here for at least another week."

"Even better," Zach responded nonchalantly. "Then Benny and I will come to Paris." Zach smiled even more widely into the camera. "Benny?" he turned the camera to the pup, who was licking his tail with a contented look. "Benny says that he has never been to Europe and doesn't mind starting the Euro tour from the Eiffel Tower." Benny seemed oblivious, but Zach was very pleased. "Where are you staying?"

"I …" Tash hesitated. "At my boyfriend's mother's place." Only now did she realise that in conversations with Zach she had never mentioned Philip's name. Their romance had developed so rapidly that in the blink of an eye she'd ended up in Paris with Violette.

Zach looked somewhat confused. "That's what happens when I leave you alone for a couple of months," Zach spoke with obvious annoyance. "You didn't seem to have a boyfriend on Valentine's?"

"Ah, it all started pretty quickly." She felt remorse. After all, she really should have informed Zach earlier.

"Everything is fine. Don't worry, it doesn't change anything. We'll still come to Paris, and now, I'll meet your boyfriend. And I'm your investor, don't forget. I should know how my apprentice is doing. I will let you know about the date of our arrival."

From Zach's tone, Tash realised that there were much more complicated situations in his life.

Tash watched Philip. He was the only man in the room, but his laid-back posture and slightly flirtatious speech gave him away as a frequenter of female companionship. Women had lavished attention on him since his childhood, starting with Violette's all-consuming maternal love, ending with her countless girlfriends flirting with him. This attention made him a man who was empathetic, confident and not afraid of his emotions. The exact opposite to Ben! After the scene at the group dinner, Ben's and Flo's names never came up in their conversations.

Her thoughts were interrupted by a call from the concierge announcing a late arrival.

"I'll open it, Maman." Philip rose to let the guest in, and a minute later a familiar voice, with characteristic hoarseness, sounded from the hallway.

"Why doesn't the hostess meet me? I'm not welcome in this house any more?" Dory flew into the room like a whirlwind. Violette was already hurrying to her.

255

As the omniscient Vivien later told Tash, Dory and Violette had known each other for over forty years and were once the closest of friends. They met in the eighties, when they both shone on the glamorous scene of New York. A blonde and a brunette, Europeans, they got into the very den of the American elite. Despite her background, Violette instantly adopted the bright novice model into her circle. They had become almost inseparable. Dory whiled away the summer at Violette's house in the South of France, while Violette accompanied Dory to fashion weeks. However, as soon as Violette met her future husband, Dory was relegated to the background. Because of one small incident.

Violette and Andres had decided to join their pre-wedding parties at Violette's house in Saint-Tropez, and they brought all their friends together under one roof. Violette's hen night was long remembered as one of the longest, rampant and most boisterous in jet set history. Tabloids fought for the exclusive rights to cover the event, and paparazzi were spying at the gate, hoping to catch celebrities in the shot. But Violette had completely different memories. By the morning of the second day, exhausted from revelry, she lay down for a nap. She woke up in a couple of hours from the rumbling music, didn't find Andres and went looking for him. She wandered around the rooms for a long time. All were packed with guests, but Andres was nowhere to be found. Finally, she went down to the pool. There, on the sun lounger, she saw the half-conscious, sprawled body of her future partner. Her best friend Dory was kneeling in front of him and trying to bring his flabby cock back to life.

After this incident, which, until reminded, Andres couldn't even remember taking place, Dory was sent home to New York and was excluded from the circle of close friends. Violette, in contrast, received a huge ranch in Arizona as a wedding gift.

At Andres' funeral, Violette greeted Dory, but there was no question of returning to their former friendship. However, over the years, they were constantly crossing paths with each other on holidays, at social events and finally, at school where Gregory and Philip had both studied. Violette's heart had softened. Dory reminded her of her carefree youth, and Violette, as before, invited Dory to stay in her beautiful houses.

"Of course, we are waiting for you." Violette hugged Dory tightly. "Do you remember Tash? Apparently, you're to blame for this unexpected union."

Violette hadn't informed either about each other's presence at the dinner and was watching their reactions carefully.

"Honey!" Dory screamed out at Tash. "I'm so glad to see you!"

She grabbed Tash and didn't let her go.

"Violette," Dory said proudly, "did you know that I pulled her out of my two-timing son's dirty grip and took her straight to Philip."

Memories of Gregory gave Tash a nervous tic.

"I told her right away that Gregory wasn't good enough for her and invited her to Philip's." Dory rejoiced in her new role of matchmaker.

"Okay, Dory, calm down! Let her go now!" Violette grabbed Dory and led her into the room. She settled down next to Dory on her favourite Chinese sofa. "What do you think of her?"

"I think that Philip is very lucky, and my Gregory is a dunce who missed out."

Tash reminded Dory of herself in her youth: beautiful, intelligent and thrown into the ocean full of sharks.

"I think she has a great future ahead. She knows her own worth and doesn't play her beauty card. She's polite and patient. She even endured me."

Violette grinned. More than anyone else, she knew well what Dory was like.

"I give her an A." Dory summed up.

"You think she's not with him because of the money?" Violette still doubted Tash's motives for her son and, knowing that no one could see through a gold digger better than Dory, she needed her well-aimed look.

"No. I guarantee it," Dory whispered in her ear. "She's a romantic. She seeks love."

*****

Tash felt she was being watched. She couldn't get used to waking up in someone's arms. For several minutes, something soft as feather had tenderly tickled her breasts. She opened her eyes and tried to lift her head off the pillow, but Philip firmly returned it to its original position. She wanted to move, but his strong legs impeded her movements. He bent his knee and she felt a slight tingling sensation in her groin.

"I'm all wet," she moaned softly.

"I feel, baby." The feather moved lower, changing the rhythm from smooth to intermittent. "Good girl, do you like what I'm doing to you?"

She wanted to answer, but he covered her mouth with his hand, so she simply moaned with pleasure.

"Tell me, do you like it when you are caressed … or fucked?"

He turned her abruptly onto her stomach, twisted her arms behind her back and squeezed her wrists. A sharp pain shot through her body. She wanted to scream, but he kept clamping her mouth.

"So you like it better when you are fucked? Like this? Like a whore who spreads her legs in front of men for money?"

She struggled, but Philip didn't let go. "Whore!" He spat as he moved with wild frenzy. "So that's how they fucked you? How many were there?"

She didn't understand what was happening.

"Tell me, did they cum inside you? Or in your mouth?" Philip grabbed her hair and pulled her face to his cock. "Suck it! I want to cum on your face! As you should do with whores!"

He got off her and finished himself off, shooting a sticky ooze over her face. She curled up into a ball and closed her eyes. Everything inside burned from strong friction. Her throat was raw.

He got up and grabbed a magazine from the nightstand. "Enjoy your fame, whore! I hope it was worth it!" He threw it at her and closed the bathroom door behind him.

With trembling hands, Tash picked it up and began flipping through the pages with automatic movements, trying to find an explanation for what had just happened. Tears streamed down her face and dripped with semen onto the pages, spreading into ugly wavy blobs. Finally, on the penultimate page, in the gossip section, she saw a photo from a charity dinner. She and Philip were smiling happily, hugging each other around the waist. But what was under the photo made her shudder.

"Is this really happening?" The thought echoed in her mind.

They did their best! Three different photos of her were in one layout. At the top was her recent photo from St. Moritz with the polo team. And below, there were two photographs expertly arranged. In one of them from ten years ago, she was sitting on the sofa, her legs half-apart, holding a black cat in her hands. Tash's thoughts were spinning: "Where did this photograph come from?" But in the second one, smiling and completely naked, she was emerging from the sea. She had asked to get them deleted! That was the photo when she lost her bikini in the waves. Underneath the triptych the caption said: "Selling my pussy, it's expensive!"

What did he think? That she was sleeping with the photographers? With the entire polo team? And she only wants his money? She felt faint. And … Ben would see it … and Flo … and Violette … and her dad! She felt sick. The main thing now was Philip.

She got up and went to the bathroom. Her legs were jelly, her head was spinning, she was nauseous and her body covered with shivers. Philip was taking a shower.

"Philip!" She slid down the wall onto the marble floor. "It's rigged." She seemed to be frostbitten from his chilling stare.

"Really?" He turned to the wall. "Maman doesn't think so! We let you inside our house. She accepted you as a daughter, and you're just a run-of-the-mill gold-digging slut."

She heard a hoarse dull sound echo through the bathroom. It was her own yawp. For a second, she saw fear in his eyes. He looked at her like she was insane. But it immediately shifted to contempt. Her heart was pounding and her body shuddered in convulsions.

"All your stories about how decent you are – they're all lies! You are shameless and licentious! What did I actually expect? You slept with me an hour after we met. And you were fucking Ben, knowing that he had a girlfriend!" Philip turned the water off and, wet, stepped over her, reaching for a towel. He wrapped it around his thighs, cast a blank glance at her shrivelled body and left the bathroom.

The chill of the marble cut her to the bone. She had to pull herself together. Tash tried to take a deep breath, but it felt like a piece of lead was stuck in her throat. It took her painstaking effort to get up. When she came into the room, Philip was spreading the hair gel evenly over his dark curls in front of the mirror.

"You know, Philip," she said in a low voice, "if you really believe that's who I am, I guess I have nothing more to say."

"I trusted you when you said there was nothing between you and Ben." Philip continued styling his hair. "I took your side over one of my closest friends. It was a mistake. I bet you're still sleeping with him. I should have trusted Flo."

"Philip—" Tash began, but she immediately stopped and fell silent, catching his look of indifference. After a pause, she found the strength to continue. "How did you get this magazine?"

"Maman brought it in this morning. She and Dory went out for a coffee and bought the morning papers." Philip finished his hair and walked to the door. "These photographs are in all of today's newspapers."

And he left.

She had to get out by any means.

The light from the window was unbearable. Every passer-by there had already seen her naked. So had all her friends, enemies, clients and even Ben. "Thank god, Mum and Hannah are dead and can't see it." After a slight hesitation, she dared to take the phone from the nightstand. Tons of missed calls and messages. She stopped at a message from Zach. "Benny and I are at the Plaza Athénée. We are waiting for you!" He had attached a photo of Benny. She had completely forgotten that Zach was coming today.

She tried to focus on thoughts about Benny. She would see him soon and everything would be fine. Probably Zach already knew. How could she look in his eyes? She wanted to die. To literally fall asleep and never wake up. Maybe she needed to take some pills? Or jump on the first plane flying to a deserted island? Daddy. She couldn't leave Daddy. Or Lulu? Or Benny? What did psychologists advise you to do when the world was falling apart? Describe your feelings. There was only fucking emptiness inside.

One huge hole full of crap flowing inside endlessly. And this shit never ended. She had to get up and leave, because Philip would be back soon.

Tash dressed quickly and packed. She stopped for a minute at the door, behind which she would have to face Violette. She inhaled and, shaking her hair, left the room with her head held high. Violette and Dory were waiting in the living room.

"Good morning!" Tash was pointedly polite. The women nodded in return. Dory tried to say something, but Violette's sharp look stopped her.

"Well, we all know what happened," Tash said, trying to be as formal as possible. "These photos ... the entire collection, actually, was specifically made to slander me."

The women listened silently to her monologue.

"Philip didn't want to listen to me." Her voice broke. She cleared her throat and continued, "The photo with the polo players was taken for the cover of *Sport* magazine. The photo with a cat – it's from ten years ago, from my uni years. They must have taken it from a friend's Facebook page. The last one ..." She glanced at Dory, looking for support in her. "It was the purest and most ridiculous accident. We were doing a shoot for Mango in Saint Barth. There were three other models. It was a very windy day ..." Tash hesitated. "And when I was getting out of the water, my swimsuit untied in the waves and sank in the whirlpool. Everyone was teasing me, so I hammed it up for them. The photographers immediately promised to delete the photos, and I believed them. This is a set-up engineered to make me look like a money-grabbing tramp. I don't know who did it, but whoever it was, they knew what they were doing and the impact it would have on my life and on my character. It was done on purpose to frame me."

Violette's blank eyes didn't express any feelings. "Ma cherie, it's not up to me to decide. This is your business with Philip, and he makes his decisions himself." She looked up to Tash. "I can imagine very well how you feel now, but I also understand his feelings. The world that you've built for him collapsed. Time will tell who is right and who is wrong." She continued with tears in her eyes. "But now I see that he is very hurt and incredibly humiliated."

"I understand." Tash went to the front door. "I'll send for my things tonight. Thank you for everything."

And she closed the door behind her.

Tash looked at her phone; new messages were popping up every minute. She didn't have the courage to read them yet. She was worried about how she would get into the hotel since it seemed that everyone around had seen the latest issue of *Star* magazine. After passing the Pont des Invalides, the car drove onto Rue François Premier and turned onto Avenue Montaigne. The driver stopped right in front of the hotel and opened the door for her. She hesitated in front of the glass door, when a fat man in a striped suit nudged her, muttering, "Merde, quel limace ramolli." He looked at her and, not finding anything remarkable, continued his way. She looked around. People, as usual, were rushing about their business, not paying the slightest attention to those around them.

She walked through an oval foyer with a marble colonnade and hastily turned right into the bar.

"Look who's coming!" Zach turned Benny's reddish face in Tash's direction, pointing which side he should be expecting his owner from. Benny didn't move one bit to her approach. Instead, he strove to gnaw at a wooden chair leg.

"Benny!" The dog finally turned around after hearing his name. A stranger in a long black coat was walking towards him. "Benny!" She called again, leaning down towards him. A split second later, Benny, remembering the scent, started licking her face.

"Finally, reconciliation!" Zach, feeling involved in a family reunion, was filming everything on the phone to send it to Benny's fans in New York. Everyone there was worried about how Benny would handle the transatlantic flight.

Tash squeezed the puppy in her arms, not letting him escape for a second. Benny responded by licking her hands and wagging his tail happily. She was so glad to see Benny that for a minute she even forgot about the photos.

"Zach," Tash sat down, continuing to stroke the dog's head. "I don't know how I can thank you for looking after Benny all this time and bringing him to me." She kissed Benny on the nose. "Ask whatever you want!"

"Come on, it was a pleasure. But I don't know how I'm going to live without him. We are all going to miss him, especially Carolina. Now we have to visit you more often." Zach was nervously adjusting the cuffs of his immaculate white shirt. "So, where are you planning to live now? In London or with your boyfriend in Paris?" Zach seemed too nervous to look up.

Tash squeezed the wooden arms of the chair as she spoke. "I don't have a boyfriend any more."

He finally dared to look at her. Only now did he notice that her eyelids were swollen and her face was covered with pink spots. "Have you been crying?" Zach made an involuntary movement towards her, wanting to protect her, but stopped himself and pulled away. "What happened?"

"We broke up." Her eyes swelled with tears, and she wrapped herself tighter in her cashmere coat. "There's a magazine that came out this morning ... with my naked pictures in it. Someone took care to make it look as nasty as possible. Philip doesn't want to hear my side of it. He dumped me."

Zach was silent, digesting the information. "Did you explain that someone set you up?" He tried to imagine himself in this guy's place.

"No point. They made it look like—"

She reached into her bag for her phone. It was clear that by this hour the photographs were all over the Internet. She typed her name into a search engine, and the masterpiece popped up straight away as the very first result. Sobbing, she handed the phone to Zach. He silently studied the photographs and captions under them and a minute later summed up his expert conclusion. "In my opinion, it doesn't look that bad. The compilation is, of course, sketchy, but ... consider yourself lucky. You came out so pretty everywhere! Any guy who sees these pictures will want you even more. It looks like it went viral, which means now your popularity will only grow. Bad PR is still PR. Think of Kim Kardashian with her sex tape." Zach looked at the screen again. He clearly liked what he saw. "Trust me, it will only add points to you. If I were you, I would have immediately started promoting the app. Congratulations! You are a real celebrity now! Check your Instagram."

Zach handed the phone back to her. All this time she was trying to grasp the meaning of his words, but she only saw the scandalous photographs and Philip's indifferent face flashing in her head.

"Can you hear me?" Zach rubbed her sleeve. "Check Instagram."

263

Tash woke up and opened the app. Since the previous evening, the number of followers had increased by five hundred thousand.

"Five hundred thousand new followers?" Her head was spinning; she was gradually getting the meaning of Zach's words. Perhaps not everything was lost? And there was no reason to die over the photos.

"What did I tell you? Let's go celebrate!"

Benny fidgeted around her legs. Because of him, they had just been denied at Guy Savoie, and had to celebrate her unexpected stardom at a simpler place. The waiter uncorked champagne and poured a little into Zach's glass.

"Great." He looked at Tash. "We should drink to the health of your foes – they did an awesome job!"

Her phone chirped.

"Hmmm, it's an Italian number …"

*****

Philip came into the apartment and unbuttoned the top button of his shirt. The collar was squeezing his throat unbearably. He heard the sound of dice clinking against a wooden board coming from the living room.

"I'm doubling." Violette took the doubling cube from the board and placed it in front of Dory.

Dory narrowed her eyes, trying to assess her position. "Okay, your game." She decided to lose one point instead of the potential two. "Philip, do you want to play instead of me? I'm tired of losing to your mother." Dory got up from the chaise, giving way to him.

"No." Philip sat down on the windowsill. "I'm not in the mood."

"No wonder." Dory considered it was her duty to discuss the events that had taken place. "I think you jumped to conclusions too soon."

Violette shot her a furious look. For a second, Dory stopped short, but unlike the backgammon game, she was not going to lose this game. "Before leaving, Tash told us her version."

"I'm not interested," Philip interrupted her. "The fact remains. She's not who she said she was."

"Don't draw conclusions so quickly," Dory said gently as she sat down on the windowsill next to Philip so that Violette could no longer throw her angry glances. "Obviously, someone did it on purpose. I saw the pictures, and Tash's story sounds legit. She said the bikini was lost in strong waves and she asked the photographers to remove the photos. We've all been there!"

Philip looked at her sceptically.

"Do you know anyone who would want to harm her?" Dory asked.

Violette came closer to better hear what they were talking about.

"I can't think of anyone wanting to hurt her. Jealous, perhaps. It could be a rejected lover, the same photographer from Saint Barth or …"

"Or the woman whose toes she stepped on?" added Violette. Because of her love for her son, she was now determined to get to the truth.

"Do you know anyone she really annoyed? Maybe some jealous friend or rival? It smells like women's work." Violette gently pushed Dory off the windowsill and sat comfortably on the other side of Philip.

"The only person who openly hates her is Florence. Tash had an affair with Ben, and Flo had a huge fight with her when she found out."

"Of course." Dory clapped her hands. "That's her!" She was dancing, rejoicing in her discovery. "*Star* magazine belongs to Alberto, her father. What other newspapers published this?" She turned to Violette.

"*The Paparazzi.*"

Violette looked at Philippe, whose face alternated between despondency and amazement.

"It also belongs to Visconti." Dory picked up the phone. "I'll call him right now. He must apologise!"

"Alberto, tesoro," Dory's voice boomed into the phone. "Come stai?"

Philip turned away so no one could see his face. He felt nothing but shame. Shame that pervaded every cell of his body. He held on to the windowsill with his hands like it was a life raft, afraid to lose his balance and fall into the abyss of his own cowardice. He had lost her. She was gone forever. He looked at sunny Paris, biting his lips nervously. He wondered where she was now. He had to get her back by all means.

Violette was with him mentally. She felt guilty that she hadn't stopped Tash that morning, that she hadn't intervened and had yielded to the decision of her son, who'd behaved like a spoiled brat. Now she suffered, watching his torment.

*****

"Sei un idiota!" Alberto jumped up from the table in his office in Milan and kicked the brown leather armchair in fury. "How could you set me up like that?" he shouted into the phone. "Who gave you the right to sneak into my business?"

"But Papa, she fucked Ben behind my back," Flo babbled in her defence.

"Your Ben is an idiot that let her go because of you! If he was a real man, he would have dumped you long ago." Alberto ran amuck. "You are a mediocrity and a drug addict. Not only do you squander my money, but now you also set people up! It's all your mother's influence. All my life you did nothing but waste my money, but now you have to pay the price! You won't get a penny from me any more. Go and work!" He hung up, but then quickly hit redial.

"And tell Ben that I am releasing him from his promise to marry you. Who needs such a wife!"

He then asked the secretary to dial another number.

"Good afternoon. Senior Visconti would like to speak to you."

"Okay … I'm listening." There was surprise in the woman's voice.

"Natasha," Alberto's hoarse voice said. "How are you?"

266

"Good afternoon, Alberto." Tash winked at Zach, who was sitting across the table. "Are you calling me about my morning photos?"

"Yes, my dear." He cleared his throat. "Please, listen to what I tell you to the end. You might not be aware, but these photos were published in all my magazines and newspapers. And it was my daughter who made it happen. As I understand it, you had something with Ben, and she decided to take revenge in this way. She, without informing me, gave the task to my journalists to find dirt on you. They bought your pictures from photographers you had worked with, went through your friends' Facebook accounts and concocted this story, thinking that all this was being done on my orders. I take full responsibility for what happened. We will post an apology tomorrow in every publication. Florence went too far with her vendetta, so I will understand if you never forgive her. But ..." he paused briefly and cleared his throat, "... I remember what you told me about your company. Has Zach Cohen already invested money?"

She locked eyes with Zach and mouthed, "Oh my god!" She took off her jacket. Heat was spreading all over her body and her hands were sweating. She was reeling from everything she had just heard. She wanted to hurt Flo. To cause her physical pain. To push her into the abyss, strangle her or throw her to hungry sharks. At the same time, her left hemisphere forced her to calm down, to think about her brainchild, the MDL platform, which Alberto had just mentioned. And it was much more important than meaningless emotions.

"Yes, Alberto," Tash replied calmly. "Zach is sitting in front of me right now." She shrugged her shoulders in confusion and said, "Zach, this is Alberto Visconti."

"Fine," Alberto continued. "Please give him my best wishes and let him know that I am investing in your company exactly as much as he is, no matter the amount. Send me all the papers, and as soon as I receive them, the money will be transferred to your account."

Anger gave way to glee, resentment to hope. She didn't know what she wanted more: to be indignant or giddy. In a matter of hours, her life had changed. Her reputation was hopelessly damaged and her boyfriend had dumped her, but she had Benny, and Alberto had just promised to invest another million in her business.

The waiter poured the champagne into the glasses.

"Okay, Alberto," Tash said before taking a sip. "Thank you."

Alberto's Italian accent took on a fatherly concern. "You are a good girl, and you will succeed. I'm a good judge of people. And one more thing …" he paused "… I freed Ben from his commitment to marry Florence. I have no idea if that piece of information is of interest to you." And with that, he ended their conversation.

17. How to eat diamonds for breakfast and shine all day

London

Benny pitter-pattered playfully ahead, stopping by bushes now and then and carefully sniffing the grass around them. Tash tried to adjust her pace, but Benny either made her accelerate on areas with no bushes or slow down at the clusters of mysterious vegetation.

She was digesting all the things that had happened to her over the past week while walking home from Lulu's. Tash had rushed to her house straight from King's Cross Station to personally give her the news first-hand. Lulu's health had improved dramatically, for which Tash thanked both God and Lulu's boyfriend, Thomas. The couple had looked absolutely fascinated by the surprise twist.

"I almost died when I saw these photos!" Lulu took a baked turbot out of the oven and put it on the table. "I was calling you forever, but you never answered. Philip was looking for you everywhere."

"I know, I'm so sorry. There were just so many things happening at the same time."

Benny ran back and forth across the living room, barely keeping up with the ball that Thomas threw to him. Thomas glanced at Tash. "Are you cold? You're pulling your sleeves down."

The emerald dress set off Tash's white skin and made her auburn hair look almost coppery.

Lulu laid out the food on three plates while Tash was reporting on her crazy day. "Okay, okay. I've got everything about the investments. You and I are rich women now." Lulu cheered. "Clever me that I secured the consent of all our famous models."

Tash had never seen her happier. Lulu's latest transformation suited her enormously. So did her short pixie cut. As she liked to joke, chemotherapy had saved her tons of money on a hairdresser. She had lost a stone, but her novel healthy lifestyle and exercising under Thomas's strict guidance not only prevented sagging skin, it made her tighter and toned.

"With such funding, we can easily represent them all. Also, your talent management idea is just brilliant. After Stella's success, thirty more influencers signed with us." Lulu finished her serving duties and sat down. "So what about Philip? He didn't believe you?"

Tash hesitated for a second. Then she lifted the sleeve covering half of her left hand. A huge pink heart-shaped diamond was shining on her ring finger.

"Holy shit!" Lulu walked around the table to get closer to the glare. "Oh my! Just look at it!" Lulu was holding Tash's hand. "We need all the juicy details. How did it happen?"

"I haven't told anyone yet. Only Zach, Violette and Daddy know … and now you two." Tash was shimmering. "Well, it was the craziest day of my life—"

Her phone rang.

"Well, hello," she answered with a big smile. "I'm sitting with Lulu and Thomas and am about to update them about the sequence of events. … Yes, of course." Tash put the phone in the middle of the table. "Philip wants to tell you everything himself. Philip, you're on speaker."

"Hi, Lulu and Thomas," Philip's loud voice came out of the phone. "I behaved like a complete moron. Then I got scared that I would lose her forever. I knew that the only way to get her back was to beg for forgiveness and show her how honourable my intentions were. When I realised that the photos were Flo's scheme, it was like my world had turned upside down. I called Tash a million times, but she never picked up. I called all her friends; as you remember, I called you. Nobody knew where she was. Finally, I stalked her Instagram and saw Katya's story with Tash in Plaza Athénée playing with a dog."

"Yes." Tash stroked Benny's face. "Zach made a video and sent it to all Benny's fans back in New York."

Philip continued, "I rushed there, but on the way, I realised that she would never talk to me again. I called Maman and set to meet her at Place Vendôme. I was choosing a ring when Maman drove up. We bought the ring together and went straight to the

Plaza. While we were driving back and forth, Tash had already left the bar. We had to wait for her in the lobby until she and Zach returned from a late dinner."

Thomas looked confused. He was totally lost in the plot and didn't know who Zach was and why he was with Tash at the hotel.

"When she saw me in the foyer, she turned around to sneak away," Philip continued.

Tash laughed. "I thought that Philip ... I just didn't want to lose my high from Alberto and Benny."

"I ran after her. Poor Zach didn't know my intentions. He blocked my path and punched me in the chin. The guards swooped in from all over. The uproar forced Tash to come back. As soon as I saw her, I quickly took the ring out of the pocket and knelt down."

"Oh my god, I was so embarrassed." Tash's cheeks were burning with pleasure. "To get a proposal in the middle of the hotel lobby, surrounded by guards and a barking dog running in circles around us ..."

Lulu and Thomas both rolled with laughter, picturing the scene.

"Imagine," Philip continued, "I saw that one side of her hated me, but the other one was evaluating the ring." He laughed.

"He's lucky that Zach and I had started drinking champagne in the afternoon," Tash interrupted him. "Otherwise it wouldn't have gone that well."

"I don't know whether it was the champagne or something else, but she took my hand and pulled me aside. 'Don't you want to say something to me?' she asked me. And I said, 'I want to tell you so much, and I'm ready to repeat it every day of my life, that I love you and that I beg your forgiveness.' And then I flashed the ring again. After all, Tash is a natural-born businesswoman. She looked at the ring and said, 'Get back down on your knee and do it all over again.' But before I could, she took my hand and said, 'Okay.' Imagine, she said 'Okay' to my proposal!"

"It was definitely the champagne talking! I hated Philip and thought I would never see him again. But he was so sweet and sincere. Also, I'd been receiving emails and calls from magazines asking for interviews, and I thought how wonderful the engagement announcement could be for our business."

"That's true." Lulu hugged Thomas. "You are a big deal now, Miss Romanov. And if we announce the launch of our platform now, they'll fly to us like bees to a honey pot. Talking of pot …" Lulu reached out for her magic box.

"Well, I have a few more things to do today." Philip was still in Paris. "I'll leave you with that. *Bisous.*" And he hung up.

*****

Birds chirped in the bushes and flowers burst through the green grass in a rainbow of colours. Everywhere she looked, Tash saw signs of summer approaching. She walked through Hyde Park relishing an immense happiness that had suddenly engulfed her. She was young, beautiful, successful and engaged to one of the world's most eligible bachelors. What more could she ask for? The song in her head was interrupted by a ring.

"Natasha! What the hell? I haven't been able to get through for an eternity." Tash heard both irritation and curiosity in Katya's voice. "Where the fuck are you?"

"I'm in London. In the park with Benny."

"You were totally off the radar! What's up with the photos? Are you all right?" Katya had calmed down and was ready for the announcement.

When Tash finished her story, Katya sighed with relief. "Hallelujah! It's fabulous! Now you will eat diamonds for breakfast and shine all day! Stupid me – I was afraid that you had run away with Ben."

"Which Ben?" Tash pulled Benny by the leash. "I already have my Benny. Oh, yes, I completely forgot." She looked at her ring. "Now I also have Philip! Let Ben spend the rest of his days with his stupid Flo. Benjamin and Florence Spencer – sounds just lovely!" She couldn't stop looking at the ring.

"She's stupid for sure. I'm not that sure that she'll ever become Spencer, though." For some reason, Katya's uncertainty sounded certain enough.

"C'mon, they're engaged. And I'm engaged to Philip." Tash sat on a bench and let Benny off his leash.

"Oh! You haven't heard yet?" Katya paused dramatically. "Ben broke up with Flo. Charles told me yesterday."

Only a second ago, Tash had been the happiest person on earth and it seemed that nothing could tarnish her elation.

"Can I call you back?" Tash hung up and immediately messaged Philip.

"Please come back soon! I miss you very much."

*****

Philip returned and Tash moved in with him.

Her popularity was skyrocketing. Her Instagram grew to a million, magazines enquired about shoots and newspapers begged for interviews. Her face popped up in media every week. It was the best moment to launch MDL.

They planned to launch on the tenth of June. All the celebs from the guest list confirmed their attendance. Katya and Charles were back in Europe for the summer, and Tash couldn't think of anyone better than Katya to organise it. She, in turn, immediately persuaded Charles to hold it at his estate. He happily agreed, treating it as a major rehearsal for his father's birthday, which Katya was already planning for October. Thanks to Zach's and Alberto's generous investments, there was no cap.

*****

Black limousines queued up at the gothic-style wrought-iron gates. Two fat guards, looking like very important penguins, checked the names of the invitees against the lists.

The limos drove along a long cypress avenue past the stables and crossed a stone bridge spanning two picturesque ponds. The map on the invitations showed that after a roundabout, guests had to drive around the southern part of the exotic garden on the left to finally reach the car park. From there, they could either walk or wait for the buggies going between the car park and the main entrance.

A large black marquee was erected on the lawn by the front porch, where the hostesses greeted the guests. The dress code was black and white.

Tash was glowing. Her silk black dress was slightly tight at the hips, which had become curvier in recent months. Lulu was wearing black pants and a crisp white shirt.

Philip and Thomas chatted nearby at the bar, which was decorated to look like a chessboard. Guests strolled through chessboard squares, enjoying sunny summer weather and cool cocktails. When the lawn was full, the guests were asked to move to the marquee.

The interior inside was monochrome and minimalistic. Guests sat on black chairs at tables covered with white tablecloths set with black crockery. A strange black box hung over the stage.

The hostesses, together with their companions, close friends and investors, landed at the central table next to the stage.

Anna's pregnancy was already showing, and she was busy accepting congratulations. Carolina and Mark flew in from New York especially for the launch. Alberto discussed his joint investments with Zach.

Lulu was the first to climb onto the stage. "Ladies and gentlemen!" The audience responded with applause. "We are happy to present our brainchild, our platform, our model for everything, our MDL. And we are also launching our app today. In ten minutes, it will become available for iPhone and Android, so I ask everyone to take out their phones and download the app. We need high traffic," she joked. "But seriously, all this would be impossible without one wonderful person – Miss Natasha Romanov. Most of you know her simply as Tash." She smiled warmly at Tash, who sat at the table. "Please come and join me on stage!"

To the sound of applause, Tash walked embarrassedly to the stage.

"All of what we witness today is entirely her brilliant idea, with my tiny involvement," Lulu continued. "Most of you know, a year ago I was diagnosed with cancer. The person next to me helped me massively, she supported me and gave me faith." Lulu could hardly hold back her tears. "Despite the fact that I am still a co-founder of this venture, you should all know that in fact this beautiful and insanely talented girl is the brains behind MDL." Lulu turned to Tash, crimson from the attention, and hugged her.

The guests clapped, the music thundered and the suspended black box sank lower. Silver confetti shot out of it, and a black banner with huge silver letters MDL stretched in front of the audience, several of whom were filming the action for Instagram stories.

Tash grabbed the microphone. "I love you!" She kissed Lulu on the cheek. The she turned to the audience and added, "Thank you. And don't forget to download the application … now!"

Carolina raised her glass. "Today we all raise our glasses to the success of these wonderful women. Everything Lulu said is true. Tash is a wonderful person and we all love her very much."

Mark didn't take his eyes off Carolina as she continued her toast.

"Tash, you, like no one else, deserve everything you've achieved. Our life has changed so much, but we haven't changed at all. We went through a lot, but we've always stayed together. We are happy for our Tash today. For her project." She looked at Philip. "And for her engagement, which we never managed to celebrate."

Everyone nodded. Philip winked and then, smiling, replied, "Engagements are overrated, but weddings are not!" To chants of "kiss the bride," he sealed the moment with a kiss.

Indeed, how much their life had changed! Tash looked at her friends. Anna, in a white empire-style dress, looked like she had descended from the portrait of *Madame Récamier* by David. She embraced pregnancy like a modern-day Virgin Mary and got terrified when someone uttered the words "alcohol," "drugs" or "cheating." Carolina, freed from the shackles of her despot husband, adored her new status as a rich widow. Katya, who had finally applied her talents to something productive, continued to assert herself as forcefully and sexually as before, but now her mate met her on equal ground. Charles was still prone to unobtrusively tugging her ultra-short tight dress down every time she rose from the table. Watching them, Tash even imagined them all picking up their children from school in SUVs in a few years. Her thoughts were interrupted by a loud noise from behind her.

"Oh my goodness! Have I missed the main part with the confetti?" Stella's body fell heavily on Tash's shoulders. Totally ignoring the dress code, Stella had showed up in red sweatpants and a sparkly tank, as she was going to a rock concert afterward. Karl's messy head loomed behind her.

"Karl," she said, poking him in the chest with her phone. "It's all because of you! He made me stay at the boring Sotheby's auction! There were only old men and metrosexuals in glasses and tight pants. Look," she said, waving her hand around, "it's much more fun here."

Karl greeted Nick, who sat to the left of Tash.

"From the auction, you say. How is our beloved Rothko doing? Prices are up?" Nick asked.

Karl patted him amiably on the shoulder. "No Rothko today, but tomorrow there is one at Christie's with an estimate of thirty-five to forty-five million."

Nick broke into a smile. "Thirty-five million – wow!" He whistled. "Mine was seven times cheaper."

"Of course," Karl said. "You can get much more for it in a few years. Don't sell it just yet. Let the prices warm up. A couple of major exhibitions in famous museums and prices will skyrocket."

"Which prices are going to skyrocket?" Alberto turned quickly into the conversation on riches.

"On my *orange* Rothko." Nick's pride from the word "orange" came from the fact that several years earlier, it was the orange Rothko that sold for eighty-five million.

"I didn't know you loved abstract expressionists. I've got a decent collection." Alberto wanted to continue, but Anna quickly cut him off by inviting him to their house on his next visit.

Alberto turned to Carolina. "My dear, I have long wanted to ask for your forgiveness for my behaviour at the Grand Prix. Hugh did everything to convince us all of your greed, but Tash made me realise how wrong I was about you."

*****

The following day, thanks to Lulu's connections, MDL was in the headlines of every significant newspaper and magazine. Front pages reported about the success of the platform, with accompanying photo of Tash and Lulu, surrounded by models, holding a cheque for half a million pounds, which had been raised for lung cancer research and charity at the auction. All the top models signed up for MDL, and the app was downloaded over ten thousand times in just a week.

Tash was finally feeling it. The flow was unstoppable.

She opened the door. The day couldn't have gone better, as after five hours of negotiations, she had convinced the clients from Amazon to sign. Benny, happy to see his vanilla-smelling owner, rushed immediately to lick her from head to toe. In the hallway, she noticed Philip's briefcase.

"Baby, I'm home!" Tash kicked off her gold sandals and stepped into cosy slippers. She glanced into the living room, hoping to find Philip there.

The custom-made tweed sofa from Milan was empty. The TV was on, showing a programme about Princess Diana's life. Tash went up to the bedroom. She slipped on the polished steps on the way, making a mental note that it would be nice to cover the stairs with carpet. The mahogany parquet that lined the floors throughout the house was very ornate but had already caused lively Benny to fall several times.

The bedroom looked pristine from the morning cleaning, and only jeans casually thrown on the bed gave Philip's presence away. She heard the sound of running water coming from the bathroom. He should like her idea! She quickly dropped off her dress and walked to the door. She stood staring at his perfect bare ass. It looked like it was chiselled from stone. Her gaze slid sideways. Philip was holding onto the marble countertop with his big tense hand. His phone was propped on the counter in front of the mirror. Sighs and exclamations were coming from it and echoing across the bathroom "Harder, harder …" His lips were pursed in a satisfied grin. Suddenly Philip opened his eyes and noticed Tash's reflection in the mirror. He pulled his hand back to let go of his big erect cock.

Tash tried to hug him, but he pushed her away with irritation, grabbed his phone and walked away. "Can't I get any privacy in my own house?" he muttered and slammed the door.

Tash wrapped the robe around her and left the bathroom. Philip was watching the TV in the living room. Diana and Dodi were smiling on his yacht.

"Philip," she said softly as she sat beside him. "Do you want to explain to me what's going on? Why are you angry at me?"

"It's okay."

"No, it's not. I've got great news; we signed Amazon today. Imagine their advertising campaign. I wanted to go out and celebrate it with you over dinner."

Philip was staring at the screen. "Congratulations, but I ate already." He continued to look straight ahead. He reached for the remote, switched the channel and stretched out more comfortably. Benny nestled at his feet.

"Ah, okay." Tash jumped up from the sofa. "Umm, then I'll go alone."

She went up to the dressing room and, with some defiant triumph, chose the shortest dress she had – in red, his favourite colour. She moved emphatically slowly while descending the stairs, giving him the opportunity to see every curve of her toned body. He glanced at her furtively and clenched his fists. He wanted to grab her, carry her upstairs and tie her to the bed so that she could never leave him anywhere. The thought that she would now leave the house in this red – so sexy – outfit drove him crazy.

"Are you sure you don't want to come with me?"

Philip didn't budge.

"Benny, do you want to come with me?" Tash bent down and patted her thigh. The pup immediately jumped off the sofa and ran to the door, leaving Philip alone to sulk.

It was still light outside. A light summer breeze blew through her slender legs. Passers-by watched the tall auburn-haired woman in red walking an adorable ginger dog. The long days encouraged Londoners to happily while away their evenings in nature.

"Benny, we're going to the Belvedere," she reported to the dog.

Benny responded by wagging his tail. The Belvedere, located nearby in the park, had become her favourite spot. The evening chill emanated from the ground, and Tash realised that the short dress was a very rash decision. She had already heard the sounds of the opera coming from the summer stage. They were very close.

"Tash," someone called her quietly. She felt that the temperature outside had suddenly dropped, and she had an icy chill. She didn't turn around and quickened her pace. "Natasha," the voice sounded more confident.

She wanted to run away, hide, disappear, but Benny, hearing her name, ran to the voice, dragging her along. She had no choice but to follow the dog.

"Hi, Ben. Lovely weather."

"Yes, fantastic weather! How are you? And who is this little cutie?" Ben squatted down to stroke Benny's face. Benny got up on his hind legs and licked Ben's face.

"Benny, no!" Tash pulled on the leash.

"Benny?" For a second, he thought Tash was talking to him.

"Yes, his name is Benny ..." She understood that she had to explain the origin of the dog's name. "I found him on Saint Barth, but it was Anna who came up with his name." The story sounded incomplete and she was afraid to look at Ben, fearing that he would ask why Benny. But he didn't ask.

"Nice name." He laughed. "I guess you'll never forget me now." Ben was playing with Benny, letting him nip at his hands. "Where are you going?"

"To the Belvedere."

Benny didn't want to let Ben go, and he was trying to bite the cuffs on his jacket.

"Can I walk you there?" Ben caught her eye, trying to read the mood, but she averted her eyes.

"It's very close, we'll manage."

Tash tugged at the leash so abruptly that Benny had to plough the ground with all four paws. She almost ran away, fearing that Ben would follow them. But he didn't. He simply stood there watching her leave.

They put a bowl of water down for Benny and gave Tash the menu. She stared at the dishes listed, but her thoughts stubbornly returned to the meadow where she had just seen Ben. Did he notice her excitement? What did he think when she ran away from him like that? Maybe she should have invited him to dinner? She blushed at such a bold idea. She pictured him playing with Benny and she felt warm inside. She called Anna.

"Today Alberto dined with us," Anna reported while crunching an apple. "He admired the Rothko."

"Yes, he said he loved expressionists. He's so lovely. And so straightforward ..." Tash couldn't find the words to express her gratitude to Alberto, or to tell Anna about her recent encounter. "Umm, I just met Ben," she breathed out slowly.

And without waiting for questions, she told Anna the details.

"What are you going to do with all this?" There were edifying notes in Anna's voice.

"I'm not going to do anything," she answered. "I'll go home and make up with Philip. He loves me and wants to marry me. He's the man in my life."

When she and Benny got home, the man in her life was still in front of the TV. She stood beside him, pulled off her lace panties and shook them in front of his face. Their sex had changed over time, it had become rough, sometimes brutal. It was like Philip was punishing her for some offence. Tash obeyed, but deep inside she missed their former lovey-dovey.

"Next week we are going to see Maman in Saint-Tropez. And we have to set a wedding day," he said before going to bed.

*****

Tash sat on the edge of the pool, swinging her legs in the calm azure water, cooling off in the August heat. Only cicadas broke the silence. September was only a week away. She was looking forward to autumn and to her return to London. She missed the office, her friends and Lulu, and even her dad's visit, one of Violette's Machiavellian ideas, couldn't distract her from the blues.

Holidays changed Philip's mood; he was the same sweet Philip she first met. Perhaps it was sea air, but he strove to make love to her at every opportunity. And he didn't let her out of his arms after love making. Violette was kind and helpful. She gave her Andres's former office and asked the staff not to bother her over trifles.

Every morning, after walking Benny, Tash escaped into the office and closed the door. She was glued to her computer and sometimes sat like that all day until her evening walk with the dog. She had an ideal groom, a sympathetic mother-in-law and a luxurious house full of caring staff. She even entrusted Benny to one of the assistants if she was too busy for a walk. When Daddy came over for the weekend, Tash devoted her time to him and the house was filled with happiness. They took long walks along the beach while Violette and Philip received guests at home, or they rode bikes to the neighbouring villages when Violette went shopping in town. At the end of his stay, Daddy presented Violette with a small painting of the Bay of Saint-Tropez, which he did in the style of Van Gogh. Violette decided it would look best in the kitchen and hung it over the stove. After Daddy's departure, Tash again locked herself in her office. She was obsessing with work, disregarding time zones and rigorously checking on everyone: developers, agents, models and even clients.

The afternoon silence was broken by a call from London. "Hi, Thomas," Tash pulled her legs out of the water.

"Tash … Lulu is dying."

She thought she had misheard. "What do you mean? Is this a joke?"

"No." He sounded serious. "All this time she was fooling us, but in fact …" He hesitated. "The cancer's almost everywhere … it metastasised," he cried.

"What? No, she's cured, in remission. You're mixing things up—"

"She confessed to me today, when we walked past the hospice." His voice broke. "Some girl there greeted her … it turns out Lulu goes there once a week."

"I'm coming back. Today. Calm down. We'll figure something out!"

Thomas silently opened the door. It was quiet in the apartment. Lulu lay on the sofa, staring at the ceiling.

"Why all this hysteria?" Lulu slowly turned to look at Tash. "This is my life, and I'll do whatever I want with—"

Tash didn't let her finish. "Yes, it's your life, but you hurt people around you, misleading them. You should have told us the truth. Maybe we would have done some things differently." Tash sat down next to her and hugged her.

"For instance?" Lulu asked. "You wouldn't have built MDL? Or you, Thomas, you wouldn't be with me if you knew I was dying?"

"Don't you dare say that. I just would have prepared myself … somehow …" Thomas hesitated.

"Prepared for what? My death?" Lulu sat up. "Yes, you have to learn how to pronounce this word: death, death, death. I'm already used to it." She smiled. "All this time I was going to a hospice once a week. I signed up as a volunteer and worked there three hours a week with people like me. And no matter what you did, you couldn't give

281

me what I got there. Your mindset changes …" She grabbed Tash's hand. "If you want to understand me, let's go together tomorrow."

"Okay." Tash nodded, swallowing tears.

She woke up to birds chirping outside. The last days of August had brought unprecedented heat to London. She fought with the air conditioner at midnight, adjusting it either warmer or colder, but ended up opening the window to let the night air cool the room. Philip had stayed in Saint-Tropez with his mother, and Tash wasn't used to sleeping alone.

She tossed and turned, remembering her last conversation with Lulu. She had looked so calm and peaceful. She tried to imagine what she would do if she were in Lulu's place, but the puzzle didn't fit together. Only by the morning, desperate, did she give in to slumber; she slept in short and restless bursts.

She took a shower and went down to the dining room. In just a few years, children would be yelling at this very table, demanding her to smear a bun with jam before school. Philip talked a lot about children. She looked at the empty table and couldn't catch the strange feeling that flashed through her at this thought.

Lulu was waiting for her on Exmoor Street. To Tash's surprise, the hospice didn't resemble a hospital at all; it looked rather like an art centre. The drawings on the walls reminded her of Daddy's art groups. She walked on the yellow and orange parquet remembering how he'd taught her that orange and blue were complementary colours. The furniture around was blue. They reinforced each other, but when mixed, they made a boring grey. Orange was the colour of the sun and joy, and blue symbolised the sky and eternity. She looked at the patients passing by and wondered if they knew the true meaning of these colours. She wanted to cry, but she controlled herself.

Lulu took her upstairs to say hello to eight-year-old Christina. Tash knew what death was from her youth because Mum had died overnight. Her heart had suddenly stopped beating, like it decided that it had worked long and hard enough. But Tash had no idea what the anticipation of death was like. When you knew exactly how long you had left. She was staring into the smiling eyes of a little girl in the final stage of leukaemia. Her eyes were full of life and happiness. Tash felt unbearably ashamed. Ashamed for being healthy. For being successful … for being loved … for being alive. She quietly got up from her chair and walked quickly out of the room.

She ran down the hallway, choking back tears. Only when she got down the stairs did she stop to catch her breath. Inhale … exhale … inhale … exhale … People were moving towards her, but she was still too ashamed to look up. She caught a couple of lines from the conversation of people walking nearby. They were discussing finance. Tash darted past them and hurried towards the exit.

"Tash!"

She kept walking.

"Tash!" Someone touched her shoulder. She stopped and turned.

"You can't run away from me all the time. Alistair, I'll catch up with you," Ben shouted back to a stout middle-aged man, who stood beside a tall red-haired woman. "I need a few minutes."

Ben came closer to kiss her on the cheek. "Can I?" he asked and then took her by the shoulders and pulled her closer. She was too weak to resist. The few minutes with Christina had changed her mind more than years of her life. Everything she was worried about in her life instantly became so insignificant. All her past grievances looked like mere trifles. The spectrum of her emotions bubbled over as she ran her trembling hand over Ben's stomach. He hugged her tightly, trying to find her lips with his.

"This is the worst place to kiss," she whispered just before kissing him.

Tash opened her eyes when someone coughed behind her, tactfully trying to get Ben's attention.

"Ben, I apologise, but I have to go and I really need your signature first," Alistair said.

"Sorry, I have to finish something; it's important. Have you changed your number?"

"No." She was still recovering from the kiss.

"I'll call you," Ben said before he left.

Tash returned to the room. Christina was listening to Lulu reading *Alice in Wonderland*. Tash settled down beside her.

"Thank you for bringing me," she whispered in Lulu's ear. "This day has given me more than my whole life."

They walked to Lulu's flat along Ladbroke Grove.

"Until you face it yourself, you see everything with rose-coloured glasses. But sometimes," Lulu paused, "it's much better to live with that rosy view. Let's sit down." It had become difficult for her to walk for long, due to a severe shortness of breath.

"I'm glad I took them off today." Tash looked into the distance. "I met Ben there. Do you remember? My Ben. He was with a man named Alistair. They were discussing finance."

Lulu was rolling a joint. Tash threw a judgemental look, but laughed immediately. "It's okay."

"Finally, you understand me." Tash was soon covered with a marijuana cloud. "At least I can enjoy my last days. So what about Ben? What does he look like?" Lulu took a drag. "You want?"

"He is handsome." Tash nodded. She inhaled and her lungs filled with hot smoke. She laughed as she exhaled. "Tall, blue eyes, dirty-blond curly hair—"

"I saw him." Lulu's eyelids grew heavy. "Alistair is fundraising. Your Ben has been giving money to this hospice for several years now and has been working with Alistair on a project to open a hospice in Botswana. There has been a very high death rate there due to AIDS."

Lulu laughed. And Tash joined her. The two close friends hugged one another on that bench, shared a joint and laughed. A few passing Notting Hill residents didn't look impressed, but others winked in solidarity as they walked by smelling the pot. They knew that sometimes even the high death rate in Botswana could make people laugh.

*****

Tash thought she knew everything about Ben, but it turned out she knew very little. He had been quietly supporting the hospice for years without ever mentioning it. Back in

Moscow, he said that he dreamed of returning to Africa, but she hadn't taken his words seriously.

She went upstairs to the bathroom and turned on the water in the tub. All day she'd tried to load herself with work, but there were only two thoughts in her head: death and Ben. She undressed and sat down to check her mail before the bath was full.

A message popped up on the screen: "Hello, neighbour."

"Hello."

"You're alone?"

"Yes."

"Did you eat?"

"Yes."

"Come over for dessert" and an ice cream emoji.

"5 minutes."

She knew that what she was about to do now was called cheating. The exact thing she'd warned Anna against, and of which she repeatedly accused Ben. She knew how dessert would end, but she couldn't stop herself. The only way to get rid of temptation was a complete yield. She turned off the water, put on a silk shirt-dress and ran headlong downstairs.

Five minutes later, she rang his doorbell. The door opened immediately. Then everything happened so quickly that when she looked around, they were lying in the hallway on the parquet floor, their belongings scattered all over.

"How dare you?" Tash began with a laugh.

"How dare you for coming here in an unbuttoned translucent robe without underwear?" He picked up her dress from the floor.

"Robe? I'll have you know it's a Diana von Füstenberg!" Tash choked with indignation.

"Tell this Diana that such a dress should be included in the investigation materials as an absolute provocation!"

How she missed his sense of humour!

"A provocation for what?" She narrowed her eyes and rose slowly.

"Provocation for seduction. I propose to conduct an investigative experiment." Ben put the dress on her. "Let's see if this is a provocation." He buttoned the buttons one by one. When he'd finished his work, he walked away to look from afar.

"I can see your nipples." He came closer. "And I see how everything inside you contracts. Now, in the name of an experiment, it is necessary to test my statement."

He knelt down in front of her and pulled up what some call a dress.

"Oh, yes. It was clearly a provocation!"

That night she stayed with Ben. When she opened her eyes in the morning and didn't find him nearby, she shuddered, remembering his escape from Ibiza. Déjà vu. She then smiled at her ridiculous fears. He wouldn't run away from his own house. She looked around the room. After all, in this very room almost two years earlier, she had spent one of the best days of her life. She suddenly remembered the face of little Christina and thought, "I am happy today. And this is what is important."

Tash went downstairs. She heard dishes clinking, and it smelled of something cosy and tasty. Ben stood by the stove, preparing an omelette.

"Mermaid, you're awake."

Tash kissed him on the forehead.

"Well, set the table quickly; it's almost ready." He pointed to the small kitchen table.

He finished with the omelette, she set the table and they sat down to breakfast.

"Enjoy your meal!" Ben said with a smile. "I love you!"

"Enjoy your meal!" she answered with an even bigger smile. "Me too!"

After breakfast, she returned home. He didn't ask anything; she didn't say anything. She walked through her plush living room and sat down at the huge dining table. Only then did that strange feeling, which she had not been able to grasp yesterday, finally take shape. She was able to put herself in Lulu's shoes. If she had a month left, she would have chosen breakfast with Ben at his small kitchen table without hesitation.

18. The fine line between vice and virtue

London

Tash opened the door with her key. She heard Olivia Colman's voice as Queen Elizabeth coming from the bedroom. Lulu had been spending her time bingeing *The Crown* lately.

Lulu's condition had worsened, and the doctors gave her no more than a month. Tash visited her almost daily. For Tash, it had been a reason to sneak out of the house since Philip had returned to London.

"Ah, Miss Romanov. How is it outside?" Lulu was lying on the large bed, wrapped in a thick duvet. "How are our models doing?" She wanted to sit up and lean against the pillows, but she changed her mind.

"All is just amazing on the work side. Our models love us, and our clients do too. We have so many deals, we're expanding."

Tash wasn't lying. The agency was growing by leaps and bounds. There wasn't enough time to hire new managers.

"We took three more on board today. There is no capacity to cope. This is exactly what I wanted to discuss with you." Tash took some business cards from her bag. "I had a meeting with these guys from LA. They are niche but super-cool, working with the best influencers. They want to merge with us."

She handed Lulu a stack of colourful business cards.

"They have about forty accounts – all high profile. I thought it would make sense to separate our talent management part from the modelling part. Into a new entity. What do you think?"

Lulu smiled at her protégé. Tash was asking for her opinion, but it was clear from her confident voice that she had already made a decision.

"Give me my box, please." Lulu pointed to her marijuana treasury. Tash obediently handed her the carved wooden box. Lulu took out the grass and rolling paper. "I think my opinion doesn't really matter." She added some tobacco. "You have to learn to make decisions on your own. You know better than me what to do. And in this, I trust you completely." Lulu lit the joint. "You're not even thirty and you already have a successful business and a handsome fiancé who adores you. You definitely know how to make the right choices." She eagerly inhaled the smoke into her failing lungs.

Tash listened intently. "Well, that's the problem …" She straightened the sleeve of her white shirt, which she had put on especially for the meeting. "Lately I'm not so sure of my decisions any more."

And she told Lulu about the night she'd spent with Ben.

"I'm really confused," Tash murmured plaintively. "After all, Philip is good and—"

"—And fabulously rich," Lulu added, clearing her throat.

"Yes, he's fabulously rich," Tash repeated obediently.

Lulu got out of bed to open the window. Tash was already feeling high from the marijuana-soaked air.

"But Ben is different. I don't know what it is if not—"

"—If not love?" Lulu finished for her. "Miss Romanov" – Lulu, in a crumpled floral-print nightgown, padded in her bare feet across the room and sat down next to Tash on the loveseat – "I'm not sure if I'm the right person to give advice, especially in love affairs." She pointed to her nightgown and added, "I always chose love and look at me. I've lived alone all my life, and in a month, I'll be gone. There won't be anyone left behind: no children, no husband, no heirs. Have I made the right choices in my life? Only God knows!"

Tash's phone wouldn't stop chirping during Lulu's monologue. When she finally looked at it, it was lighting up with messages from Anna and Stella.

"Oh my god!" Tash managed to read only half of them, but what she learned didn't look promising. "Do you remember the Rothko that Nick bought?" Tash glared at the screen. "Alberto told the experts about it, and they are sure that it's a fake!" She continued reading. "Anna called Karl and told him to pay the money back."

Lulu whistled. "Drama, drama."

"Lulu, I'm sorry, but I have to run. I'll call you later." Tash kissed Lulu and left.

After she'd closed the door tightly behind her, she dialled Anna.

"That asshole!" Anna was breathing heavily. "I can't believe he was capable of doing that. How right you were!"

"Anna, calm down. You shouldn't get worked up. Think about the baby. Is Nick with you?"

"No. Imagine, he's on his way to New York now. Flew there this morning for a couple of days."

"I'll be right over."

Fifteen minutes later, Philip's black Mercedes drove her to Eaton Square. Anna sat at the oval dining table staring at the bright orange spot above the sofa. Despite Anna's dramatic pose, she looked like a bored housewife with a huge belly sticking out from a Ralph Lauren denim dress.

"Nick wanted it so much," she said with rage. "How could I be such an idiot?"

Tash hugged her shoulders.

"Do you know what Karl told me when I called?" She couldn't tear her eyes away from the multi-million-pound fake. "He said that if he was me he wouldn't tell Nick because it might end up causing him stress about the child's paternity."

It was worse than Tash could have imagined.

"Your favourite influencer also messaged me," Anna continued indignantly. "She said that I should have thought before unreasonably accusing her boyfriend of a crime. She said I'm doing it out of jealousy because Karl is with her, not with me! Is Stella out of her fucking mind?" Anna's face was red. "That social climber! They're both blackmailing me!" She rose heavily from the chair. "Let's move to the balcony! It's stuffy in here, and I can't look at this ghastly painting any more!"

Tash helped her up.

"What shall I do now?" Anna looked piteously at Tash. "Please don't tell me that you warned me. I know you were right." Anna walked like a duck to the deck chair and flopped down clumsily on it.

289

Tash tried to calm her down. "Let's start with the Rothko," she began reasoning calmly. "Sooner or later, Nick will find out. Even if we manage to convince Alberto not to tell him anything, if he ever decides to sell it, you can't really hide its authenticity. And there's bound to be another expert who'll discover it's a fake. So Nick has to know. Sorted. Secondly, your affair with Karl. That's a bit more complicated." She lowered her voice. "They can't meet. If that happens, Karl won't miss a chance to squeeze something out."

"I just don't understand why," Anna whispered in confusion. As she reached the end of her pregnancy, her thoughts were getting muddled.

"To protect himself! Karl will either tell Nick that you've made it up to take revenge on him because you're jealous that he is with Stella, well, the same nonsense Stella said, or …" Tash paused, but decided to finish, "… he can say that you did it together, that you were an accomplice in tricking Nick out of his millions, to ensure that Nick won't report him."

Anna groaned. "Is that really possible?"

"Hardly." Tash already regretted that she'd expressed all her suspicions. "Hardly," she repeated. "Don't worry, please. Think about the baby."

"Yes, my head is exploding from these thoughts!" Anna burst into tears. "What if the baby is from Karl? I'm so tired … fuck Karl … and fuck Stella …" She got up slowly and wandered into the living room. She took the phone from the table and dialled Karl's number. A few seconds later, Stella's squeaky voice answered.

"You can't take that he's chosen me?" squealed Stella. "Stay away from my boyfriend!"

"I can't listen to this," Anna whispered and handed the phone to Tash.

"Do you think I didn't get that you were fucking him on the beach on New Year's Eve under your husband's nose? When you both came back knee-deep in sand! Remember?" Stella obviously still thought she was talking to Anna. "I can count. January, February, March, April, May, June, July, August, September! You will soon give birth! I don't think Nick wants to know whose child it really is."

"Stella," Tash interrupted her harshly. She'd had enough of listening to the stream of threats. "This is Tash."

"Oh. Hi, Tash, how are you?" Stella chirped.

"Stella, I strongly suggest that you do not involve yourself further in this story. Let its participants figure it out," Tash said coldly and restrainedly. "As your manager, who is looking out for the success of your career, I strongly encourage you to withdraw and not associate yourself with anyone suspected of a crime. This could be very detrimental to your popularity and contracts. Nobody wants to hire a criminal's girlfriend."

"What about Jeremy Meeks?" Stella tried to argue.

"Stella," Tash's voice went from cold to icy, "if you want to ride a wave, sign a contract with L'Oréal, get a million new followers, you will go home to your mum right now." Tash knew that Stella's craving for success was well above any love, and a potential growth in followers could easily buy her silence.

"All right, Tash," Stella answered docilely. She was quick. Tash mentally praised her for her correct behaviour. She hung up and turned around and saw Anna curled up in a ball on the sofa, right under Rothko.

"Are you sick?" She rushed to Anna.

"Yes. Please call Dr. Reeds."

Dr. Reeds asked Tash to bring Anna to him at once. Tash accompanied her to his office, while she herself remained in the waiting room. She was talking to Philip when Dr. Reeds came out and said that Anna should stay in the hospital under supervision. He asked her to collect Anna's things and bring them to the hospital. When Tash returned, Anna was in intensive care and she was asked to come back the following morning.

*****

The phone was ringing off the hook. She looked at her watch – six in the morning. Who would be calling so early? She realised it must be something urgent, so she reached for the phone.

"Tash," she heard a happy voice. "It's a girl!" Anna sobbed with happiness.

"Already? So fast?" Tash couldn't believe that while she was sleeping Anna had managed to give birth to a whole person.

"Yes! I was so scared last night … and I was shredded a little, but I'm officially the happiest person in the world."

"Wow! Congratulations! I'm coming now!" She wanted to hang up but suddenly realised that she hadn't asked the most important question: "Who does she look like?" She held her breath.

"She's Nick's!"

Tash sighed with relief.

She spent the next few days going between the office, Lulu's and the hospital. The baby girl was Nick's clone. He caught the first flight home from New York and was overjoyed at the birth of his daughter. Anna took advantage of his joy and told him the truth about the painting. Nick took the news surprisingly calmly, leaving all communication with Karl to a criminal lawyer. Anna never found out what exactly was told to Karl, but by the time she returned from the hospital, the painting was gone, the money was refunded, and Karl had disappeared.

Stella followed Tash's advice and returned to New York under Vivien's wing, breaking off all contact with Karl.

*****

October brought autumn coolness to town. The daylight was waning each day, and the nights were pierced by wintery gusts. Through the car window, Tash watched how quickly people were filling the streets of Soho as evening approached.

"Andrew, what's the temperature outside?" she asked the driver.

He looked at the dashboard. "Eleven degrees, ma'am."

Tash opened the window and leaned back in the seat. A light breeze blew through her thin blouse. After passing endless traffic in Covent Garden, they finally reached Piccadilly. Philip was waiting for her at the restaurant. The previous month, they'd barely found time to go out together. Tash often stayed in the office for eighteen hours; Philip was constantly travelling. In recent months, he had opened four new offices. The popularity of microloans in developing countries was growing exponentially, inversely proportional to their impoverishment.

"You know, you're robbing the poor," she said as she mixed steak tartare with an egg. She then straightened the stripe in her pant leg, which was caught under the leg of the wooden chair in the Colbert brasserie.

"I help people in difficult situations by lending them money."

She looked up at him. Philip, with a glass of Chassagne Montrachet and a dozen oysters in front of him, didn't remind her of Robin Hood.

"At a predatory interest rate." She sounded irritated.

"It's called capitalism! Since when did you become a socialist? You do business the exact same way." Philip set his glass on the table and winked at her.

She felt everything inside her boiling. The heat was rising up from her solar plexus. How could he compare her business with his? Her cheeks flushed with rage. "Unlike you, I don't take advantage of people! I only create conditions for customers to meet with contractors—"

"For a percentage," Philip quipped and rolled his eyes.

"Yes, but my percentage is lower than that of other agencies. And your interest is much higher than the banks."

She was wound up. Recently, she'd noticed that capital gain was becoming the driving force of Philip's life.

"Tash, we live in a capitalist world. Everyone receives something depending what they contribute to society. I invested a lot – I got a lot."

"What about the disadvantaged and the sick?"

"They need to be maintained for social balance, but not for long." Philip swallowed an oyster. "Their problems and early deaths are not at all bad for society. In general, they are not required for the progress."

"Are you sure?" Her voice trembled. "What about Stephen Hawking?"

"Okay. Those who bring something to society, let them live. But weakness is God's mistake. Only healthy and strong people should remain in order to create a genetically ideal generation and produce a profitable product."

Tash looked at him with disbelief. She couldn't speak.

"I didn't come up with it," Philip continued calmly. "Look how nature itself works. Epidemics clean the world of the old, the weak and the sick, clean the planet of garbage! Maman said that intelligence reported another deadly virus raging in China. Let's see who it takes this time …"

"Are you serious?" Tash couldn't believe he'd said that. "So you think that the elderly and the sick are rubbish? If I suddenly got sick, was no longer healthy and beautiful, you wouldn't want to be with me? You wouldn't want to have children with me?"

"Do not talk rubbish." He took a sip of wine. "I want to have children with you. When, by the way, will we finally deal with this issue? It looks like Anna and Nick are happy in their new status. Let's visit them after dinner. They live around the corner."

Tash hadn't seen them for weeks. With the birth of her daughter, Anna was fully immersed in her family and had found her new "I" in it. Nick met them at the door. As always, he was dressed to the nines and happy to see them. He ushered them into the living room.

"Elizabeth just fell asleep," Anna said with a tenderness that Tash had never heard from her before. "Thanks for stopping by."

Tash looked at the wall above the sofa. A small painting in white and pink fit the interior much more harmoniously than the infamous Rothko.

Nick caught Tash's eye. "It's all thanks to Alberto." Nick poured wine into glasses. "He helped me find this miracle." Nick smiled modestly. "When we found out about the Rothko, my lawyer contacted Karl's parents. They were keen to cover the cost of the painting, plus my mental suffering. So I had enough for the de Kooning."

"And it suits the ambience," Anna added.

Philip went up closer to the picture to study it better.

Tash walked over to Anna and asked casually, "Any news about Karl?"

"You won't believe it …" Anna said. "Remember Charlotte?"

Tash had lost contact with her after Zach's discovery of Francesco's scam.

"Charles and Katya visited us a couple of days ago to see Elizabeth. They said they saw her with Karl in Ibiza last week. Charlotte has changed beyond recognition; she's

294

become a blonde bimbo with huge boobs. She deleted her old social media so no one will see how she looked before." Anna laughed. "Apparently she spent the whole summer with Francesco, got to know everyone and then left him after finding out he wasn't the one he claimed to be."

"She doesn't know yet that she's bet on the wrong horse again," Tash chuckled. "Poor little not rich Charlotte."

"Everyone gets what they deserve." Words of wisdom came from Nick's chair. "So, fate has intervened and deemed them worthy of each other!"

"That's for sure." Tash and Anna looked at each other. "I'll go and check on my little angel."

"I always knew she would make a wonderful mother." Nick stood and leaned in to Tash, whispering in her ear, "Even when she fucked Karl." Tash nearly dropped her glass. "Don't tell Anna that I know."

Tash said nothing and only nodded in shock.

She was silent on the way home. Nick's words had moved her deeply. It was less than a year ago that Anna was ready to sacrifice everything, including his love, because of her lust for Karl. He let her enjoy the affair enough to get burned, but instead of humiliating her and making her crawl to him, he generously forgave her. And he made the right bet. Anna learned her lesson and drew conclusions for life. Nick was wise! Tash wondered what Philip would say if he found out about her night with Ben. She suddenly wanted him to know, to understand what was happening in her soul. Her thoughts were interrupted by a phone call.

"She died," Thomas's voice was quiet. "Just now."

"At home?" Tash asked. For some reason, she was also calm; there were no tears.

"No, we spent the whole day in the hospice. She was so funny and happy. I even told her over lunch that she looked great, and she replied, 'Finally, I became one of the ladies who lunch. Why should I look bad?'"

Tash laughed. "We'll be right there."

*****

The funeral was quiet and humble, as Lulu had wanted. Vivien couldn't miss the opening of a museum in Doha and instead sent her London driver with an incredible floral arrangement. After the funeral, Tash and Thomas went to the lawyer's office to go over her will. Everything had been settled before her death. Lulu had taken care of her finances in advance. In the absence of close relatives, she bequeathed her apartment and money to lung cancer charities, and her shares in their business were completely transferred to Tash. A small house on the Costa del Sol, inherited from her mother, went to Thomas on the condition that he would set up a farm to produce healthy products.

"Miss Romanov," the lawyer said in conclusion. "Miss Lourdes Lucetta left you this letter. And she asked me to hand it over to you personally."

Tash took an envelope made of heavy brown paper from him.

Once in the car, she sent a message: "I need to see you."

The answer came quickly: "Come over, I'm home."

The front door was open. The sound of rock and roll thundered from the kitchen. She followed the smell of basil with sandalwood. Ben, in jeans, was cooking something at the stove.

"Hello."

"Hi." Ben turned to her for a second and immediately returned to the stove. "Have you had dinner?"

"No."

"Then set the table. Today, we'll be having spaghetti with tomatoes and basil." Ben sang along to the music, performing dance steps.

"Ben, I wanted to talk to you." Tash came closer.

"Okay." He turned off the burner. "Can we talk over dinner? Or will this conversation contraindicate digestion?"

Tash laughed. Together they set the table and sat down to eat.

"Ben," Tash began. "What do you think about us?"

He looked at her in surprise, weighing the seriousness of the question.

"You mean 'us' as a couple or as friends or as individuals?"

"I mean us as a couple." Tash was twirling the pasta on her fork, her eyes focused on the process.

"Mermaid, you know perfectly well what I think. I've told you many times, and nothing has changed. I believe that we are made for each other, but due to circumstances, first from my side and now from yours, we are not together. I think these circumstances will be overcome and eventually we will be together. It's only a matter of time." So simply and frankly, he explained to her the essence of the problem.

"So you will wait for me?"

"Sure! This is what I am doing now. I will wait until you realise what I did long ago."

"Even if I marry Philip?" She was tempted to confuse him.

Ben laughed. "You will not marry Philip."

His confidence angered her. "Why not?"

"Because you love me!" Ben got up, walked over to her and, wrapping her hair around his arm, pressed her face to his bare belly. "And only me!"

She kicked back, but he held on.

"Why do you think so?" she boomed dully.

"I just know!" He leaned over to kiss her. Instead of kissing him back, Tash freed herself and slapped him.

"Who gave you the right to think so? You made it all up!" She grabbed her bag and ran away, not looking back.

*****

A reception for the sixty-fifth birthday of Marquess Montague was scheduled for the twenty-eighth of October. Five hundred guests were flown to the Montague estate for the celebration. Naturally, they came from all over the world.

Anna, Nick and Elizabeth left for their country house a few days before the date. The rest were supposed to join them for the weekend.

Philip was glad to be away from the bustle of the big city and endless silent days alone with his bride-to-be. He felt that she was eluding him. Every day she drifted further and further away, moving to another universe. He was pissed off by her success, by her mind, and even by Benny, who loved her more than him. And most of all, her agency angered him. Those endless meetings with the clients! It was another facet of her life in which he had no place. "As soon as you have a baby," Violette's words rang in his ears, "she will forget her career in a minute and sit at home to nurse your little one."

When Nick, out of politeness, suggested hunting in Haye, he grabbed the excuse like a magic wand to avoid another strange day with Tash. They left for a pheasant shoot early in the morning.

Tash and Anna went for a long walk around the estate. It was dripping with rain and their rubber boots sank in the mud.

"How do they shoot in the rain?" Anna was pushing the stroller covered with polyethylene. "I hope the weather improves tomorrow or else how will we get out of the car without getting our hems soaked?"

"Look at Benny."

Wet as a chicken, Benny was frolicking in the wide-open spaces, rejoicing in the bad weather, which gave him so many new joys.

"I hope everyone gets here without a delay. Faina didn't invite her new girlfriend. Apparently she's some famous Swedish model. She says she's not ready to introduce her to her friends yet."

Carolina, Mark and Faina were due to land at Luton in an hour.

"So what did you want to tell me about Lulu?" Anna looked into the stroller to check if everything was okay with her daughter. "It's unbelievable how one has no relatives! This is so rare! You are very lucky. Lulu made you a rich woman."

"Stop it, Anna," Tash interrupted her with annoyance. "You know perfectly well how I treated her. I wanted to tell you something else. She and I talked about happiness … not long before her death."

"And?" Anna stopped and looked inquiringly at Tash.

"So I wondered if I live a happy life?"

"Are you saying that you are unhappy?"

"Well, I'm not sure that what I do and how I live brings me satisfaction. You see, when you look at the faces of terminally ill people, you realise that money is the last thing that worries them. And I'm not the only one who thinks so. I met Ben there."

"Are you serious?" It wasn't entirely clear what struck Anna more – Tash's dissatisfaction with life or meeting Ben in the hospice.

"Absolutely serious." Tash nodded.

Anna peered into her confident face. "Did you sleep with him?"

"Yes."

"What about your declaration that you would never cheat on anyone?"

"You were right. Situations really are different."

"And what are you going to do?"

Tash would give a lot to know the answer!

The guests of Meadow Hill were chatting by the fireplace and sipping cabernet when Nick and Philip returned from the shoot. The cook was waiting for Anna's command to serve the food.

"We shot the hell out of the pheasants!" Nick, with the face of a professional hunter, walked through the living room into the kitchen. "Is the supper ready?"

"Yes, Mr. Stowe," the cook replied. "We can roast the birds tomorrow."

"Tomorrow we are dining at Marquess Montague's. Leave them for the day after that." Nick returned to the guests. "Well, what gossip will you please me with?"

The men discussed their shoot, while the women discussed their outfits for the big event the following day.

"I'll show you the dress I snagged in Beverly Hills." Faina was searching for the picture of a black Alexandre Vauthier dress in her phone. "By the way, I completely forgot to tell you! I bumped into Sasha at the Chateau Marmont. Well, I never expected to see him in LA."

Tash glanced quickly at Anna. Her eyes lit up. They were both dying from curiosity.

"There was a Veuve Clicquot tournament in LA, and he said he had bought a polo team."

Tash almost giggled. Katya's groundwork had not been in vain. Sasha had made his way into high society with a maple club.

"But Sasha's social success isn't the only news from La La Land. It turns out that he divorced his wife in the end to free his heart, and you will never believe who he's with now. Our old friend Ella. She quit directing and went into blogging. Thanks to Sasha's investments, there are already more than a million subscribers on her YouTube channel."

Carolina didn't get who Ella was and why Tash and Anna were rolling with laughter.

"Do you know which channel?" Through the laughter, Anna tried to help Faina with the search.

They found the channel. Ella, in her signature bright-blue Chanel suit, sat on a tall, pseudo-Gothic chair. In broken English, she was teaching subscribers the manners of high society, family values and an aristocratic lifestyle, which she says she's known since childhood. On an "aristocratic" protruding finger was the very same emerald ring that Sasha had presented to Katya last New Year. Talk about recycling!

"Nick was right," said Anna. "Everyone gets exactly what they deserve."

*****

The forecast was accurate. Tash parted the curtains in the east bedroom that Anna had assigned them and smiled at the sun. After a quick shower, she hurried to take Benny out for a walk. As soon as she let him off the leash, he began to scamper in circles, following the sunbeams on the neatly trimmed lawn.

At six in the evening, on that very lawn, the ladies were posing for each other in their gowns. Tash was examining the photo that Carolina had just taken, and Philip was examining Tash, trying to figure out what had been going on between them in recent months. The red velvet of her dress gave off a touch of royal pomp against the grey stone wall of the Stowe estate. Her hair was pulled off to one side in a dramatically sexy wave.

"Aren't you tired of taking pictures?" Philip hastened the girls gloomily, after waiting a suitable amount of time to make sure the ladies had taken multiple shots in front of the camera. Mark and Nick were waiting for them in the cars.

They were at the Montagues in less than twenty minutes. At the entrance to St. Mark's Square, reconstructed especially for the celebration, guests were offered a choice of Venetian masks, hats, turbans and a whole host of exquisite handmade accessories. Katya greeted the guests in the sky-coloured dress of Marquise de Pompadour, trimmed with white lace, and in an exotic hat with white feathers. For Tash, Philip chose a velvet hat with a red feather and an incredibly wide brim, making sure no one could come within a metre of her. On him, Tash put a multicoloured turban, with a giant blue stone in the middle and pearl beads hanging down the sides.

The King and Lady of Hearts – the Marquess and Marchioness Montague – and the Pope, Charles, received guests at the front door. Tash wanted to find some acquaintances, but all her attempts were unsuccessful. Recognising the guests in carnival masks and period attire wasn't an easy task. At least she had arrived with her closest friends and knew their outfits.

She smelled sweet vanilla when they were moving up the steps. They passed through tall carved doors and found themselves in a huge hall with columns and balustrades. The sculptures were also wearing gilded masks. Twisted bronze lamps with peacock feathers protruding from them illuminated the red carpet leading to the main hall. Exotic birds locked in openwork forged cages echoed in the hall, and gondoliers in multicoloured gondolas sailed along the channels created on both sides of the path, singing Venetian songs.

Tash admired the antique mirrors in their massive baroque frames hanging on the tapestry-draped walls. They reflected the ceiling, painted with magnificent Rubenesque bodies, which, it seemed, were about to step into the festive crowd. Long, endless tables were decorated with tall bronze candelabras. The guests gradually took their places.

"Look, what a fan I have!" Tash wanted to show off to Faina, but she was disappointed that such fans had been supplied for each of the invited ladies. Tash laughed. "Tell me about your new girlfriend."

She missed Faina and wanted to leave behind the awkwardness that had arisen between them in Courchevel. They hadn't seen each other for almost two years. After that awkward frankness, Faina had distanced herself. Tash had heard from Katya that in the tough choice between a pistil and a stamen, she'd chosen the feminine pistil. And fortunately, she was much more successful with her chosen path.

"Nothing major to report so far. You'd better tell me about Philip. He seems so relaxed."

They chatted, like in the old days, and when Tash finished, Faina said, "I would never have guessed he was straight."

Tash almost choked. "You thought he was gay? Are you mad? Just look at him," she said, laughing. "He is easily the most masculine man I've ever met."

Faina just smiled and shrugged her shoulders.

The guests took off their masks for dinner, and Tash studied Philip's manly profile again. A chiselled Hispanic profile with high cheekbones, a strong pointed chin and a very confident look made her think that Faina didn't know men at all.

Katya came for a minute to gossip with Tash. "Marquess Montague is delighted with the feast! Charles said that I managed to breathe life into centuries-old walls and give the party a touch of glamour." And then Marquise de Pompadour disappeared into the crowd in search of her Pope.

Music played in the neighbouring room, and guests, putting their masks on again, slowly moved there to dance. In the middle of the hall whose walls were decorated with *trompe l'oeil* "windows," lay a red oval carpet with gold ornaments. Bulky velvet armchairs and exquisite couches covered with brocade lined the walls. Carolina sat down on one upholstered in burgundy damask.

"I'm tired of dancing," she sighed and grabbed a crystal champagne glass from the tray of a passing waiter, clad in golden livery. "Do you recognise anyone here?" She turned to Tash and Faina, who'd just landed next to her.

"Katya asked everyone not to take their masks off before the birthday boy's speech! Otherwise, she says, the degree of carnival reality will drop."

Tash fought the urge to rip off her stupid mask, as her skin was really starting to itch.

302

"Reality is reality, but my reality will be acne if I don't take it off, at least for a while. Perhaps I'll do it in the loo."

Her place next to Carolina was immediately taken by a petite woman in a black velvet dress with a pearl necklace.

As she expected, the skin under her mask was reddened and slightly swollen. Enough of the masquerade! After powdering and spreading the feather on her hat, she went out into the corridor. She walked in the twilight. A path was slightly illuminated, as if by moonlight. She suddenly heard the sound of approaching footsteps. Tash looked around and sighed on seeing the familiar turban with its blue stone. "Philip, don't scare me like that."

He grabbed her hand and pulled her towards him. The immense brim of her hat brushed against his turban, and it flew off his head, revealing blond curls.

"Ben?"

Ben pulled her closer. She felt the warmth of his breath on her lips.

At the other end of the moonlit path, another owner of a turban with a blue stone came to a halt. His fists were clenched, his eyes bloodshot, but he turned around and returned to the ballroom with a smile. Finally, everything fell into place in his head.

In the meantime, the woman in the velvet dress who had settled next to Carolina attacked her. "You're a mean, ungrateful girl! When are you finally going to take revenge for my boy?"

Carolina recognised Lady Young's high-pitched voice at once. "Good evening, Lucinda. I don't understand what are you talking about."

"Did you bring Mark Greenberg here on purpose? To annoy me?"

"Lucinda, Mark and I are seeing each other, and it's none of your business."

Carolina wanted to get up, but Lady Young's dry, wrinkled hand stopped her. "You're wrong, dear. This is very much my business too. Less than a year after Hugh's death, you are already dating his enemies." Her stunted hand shook convulsively.

"Enemies that he made himself out of his own greed."

"Are you kidding me? Greed?" She burst into a rattling laugh. "Greed has to learn from your date. He framed my son and almost put him behind bars. Thank god the judges were smart enough to see it."

"What are you talking about?"

"About the fact that Mark screwed him with a Libyan contract, that's what I'm talking about!"

19. How to see diamonds in the sky

London

"Do you believe her?"

The world so skilfully woven by Mark's lies collapsed for her instantly.

"I have no reason not to trust her. She's never lied to me. And she promised to send me some old court files as soon as she gets home." Carolina looked calm, but the corners of her mouth dropped.

"Do you love him?" Tash stroked her hand.

"Love him?" Carolina grinned. "Didn't we leave this concept behind in the nineteenth century? Hugh taught me a great lesson, and now, I'm afraid, I can only love myself." She looked at Tash. "Well, and you. Don't tell anyone yet, okay?"

"Okay, just don't tell anyone that Ben wanted to kiss me." Her cheeks flushed pink.

This time Carolina's face reflected the whole gamut of her emotions, and her eyes sparkled with excitement. "You're crazy! Now what?"

"Nothing. I didn't let him do it."

The weather was unseasonably warm, and breakfast was served on the terrace.

"What a magical evening it was," Tash said dreamily.

For a moment, anger flashed in Philip's eyes, but, pulling himself together, he added, "It's unbelievable how Katya managed to hide her talent all this time." He took a small sip of coffee. "I ought to ask her to help us with the New Year." Smiling, he looked around. "You are all, of course, invited. There are enough rooms for everyone."

Tash was confused. The invitation to Gstaad sounded like a done deal, even though this was the first she had heard of it.

"I was thinking of going to Africa for a safari," she tried to argue.

"My dear," – he kissed her tenderly on the forehead – "we can go on a safari in December, but let's celebrate the New Year together."

His words sounded quite reasonable.

"Great idea! Carolina now has her own house there," Mark said.

Tash watched him wipe his glasses with a serviette. How could she not have noticed the falseness in his oily voice before? Lady Young had sent scanned documents to Carolina that morning. He really had tried to put Hugh behind bars. While Mark was showering, Carolina ordered all of her belongings to be taken from his penthouse and sent to London. Once everything was done, she would inform him of their break-up.

Unlike the majority of coffee lovers present at the table, Nick started his morning with a glass of white.

"We're in! I'll get a plane. Only now we have to choose who we are staying with." He took a sip and, rotating the glass by the stem, stated, "Life is about choices."

*****

November days passed quickly. MDL was gaining momentum. Despite the fact that they expanded only six months ago, the office in Covent Garden could no longer accommodate everyone. And every carnation there reminded Tash of Lulu. Her new assistant, Davina, who had just graduated from Imperial College and had a youthful zeal for every assignment, found a fantastic space in Shoreditch. Since then, Tash had been spending her days in the hippie East and was returning to the conservative West End only late in the evenings. After the masquerade party, Philip had become unusually affectionate. He bombarded her with gifts, arranged surprise dinners and indulged her every whim.

With the arrival of December, life spun in the pre-Christmas bustle. Tash had to respond to multiple party invitations, but now she sometimes had no one to go with. Philip was on endless business trips. Anna spent her days fussing with Elizabeth, who each day resembled Nick more and more, and by evening she had no stamina for social life. This was the same Anna who just a year ago wouldn't miss a fashion week! Katya finally moved into the Montague estate and, under Charles's mother's guidance, learned the basics of horse breeding and hunting. The same country life that used to made her pretty nose wrinkle now completely captivated her. She proved to be an excellent hostess, and the Marquess proudly introduced her beautiful future daughter-in-law to the neighbours. After breaking up with Mark, Carolina hadn't returned to New York but had decided to settle in their old chalet in Gstaad and invited Lady Young to join her. After all, the poor old woman had not a soul left in this world.

Violette's call caught Tash at Harrods. She was wandering the floors looking for Christmas gifts.

"Ma cherie, I'm in town and would like to see you. Will you join me at George in an hour?"

Tash was looking at David Hockney posters when the December frost burst into the restaurant from the door opened by Violette and chilled her with winter cold.

"I'm very glad to see you, ma cherie."

After exchanging the formalities required by etiquette, she moved on to the main purpose of her visit.

"Natasha." Tash cringed under her emotionless tone. "You must understand that I'm not young any more, and it's time for me to think about heirs." Her dry hand, covered in brown age spots, rested on Tash's wrist. "I saw the lawyer the other day to discuss my financial affairs." Violette spoke in an insinuating voice. "I hope you and Philip will get married very soon and have a baby." She did not take her eyes off Tash's face. "Philip doesn't own anything, so when you get married, you'll have nothing to count on. But I want my grandson's mother to never care about money. You are a businesswoman, and I want to make you a commercial offer. My son loves you, and I'm sure you will be a wonderful wife to him, and you will have beautiful and healthy children. I decided …" Violette paused for effect, "… that for the birth of my first grandchild, you will receive one million pounds, and each subsequent healthy child will bring you an additional million."

Violette released her wrist and went back to her dish. Smoked salmon was waiting for her.

Tash was at a loss for words.

307

"You don't need to answer now; the documents are drawn up." She gave an encouraging smile to the future mother of her grandchildren. "All you need to do for the deal to take effect is to give birth to a healthy child."

Tash quickly looked down at her salad. Smooth little pale cauliflower florets peeped out from under grated Parmesan like babies' heads. The work of art was topped with slightly toasted grated almonds. The chef had done a great job, laying the inflorescences in an even circle. And only one tiny piece was knocked out of the general picture of perfection, violating the creation with a flaw of the form.

"And if the child is not healthy?" Tash asked, not taking her eyes off the greens.

Violette was silent.

Tash repeated, "And if it is not healthy?"

Her eyes flashed like lightning, and for a moment Violette felt that Tash was ready to slash into her with her claws.

"If it's not healthy, there will be no money." Violette calmly chewed her salmon. "The weak breed the weak. They can't reproduce. The best we can do for them is let them die."

*****

"Of course, have his child. What is there to even think about?" Katya's sonorous voice was persuasive over the phone. "He is your fiancé, and you love him, don't you?"

"Katya, you don't understand! They want to buy me as a copy machine!"

The wind whistled in her ears, blowing away everything on its way. They were right with the forecast. Here it was, the promised storm. She pulled her coat tighter and turned off South Audley Street towards the park.

"To buy a child for a million, considering that his father is your husband, seems like a win." Katya genuinely didn't understand Tash's indignation. "You give birth, and for all your suffering and efforts, a certain amount of money is transferred to you. What's wrong with that?"

"She started by saying that it was a commercial offer. And I have to give birth to a healthy child. They believe that everything in the world is for sale. Do you know what

308

he said to me once?" She tried to recall Philip's exact words. "That only healthy and strong people should remain in the world to create a genetically ideal generation and produce a product, and everyone else is rubbish."

"So what? Tash, you analyse everything too deeply, who said what, who thought what. Take it easy. They will give you a million for something you'll do anyway. I say take it. As for a healthy baby," Katya touchingly softened her next statement, "I also want a healthy and strong child, and if I was to find out that something was wrong with my unborn child, I would have an abortion. Absolutely. Charles and I even discussed this recently. There are so many children being born, who previously had no chance of surviving, because of IVF, freezing and all that. All these children with defects who shouldn't have—"

Tash didn't let her finish. "How can you say that?" She was shaking. "They all have the right to live!"

"But this is against nature. The fittest survive. Look what is happening in China right now. This new virus ... it's like God is doing some house cleaning."

Tash hung up.

*****

An icy, gusty wind whipped the flags over Park Lane and tore the hats from passers-by. She had to find some peace by any means. "Exmoor Street, please," she told the driver. Fifteen minutes later, the taxi pulled up outside a grey brick house. She went up to the ward to see little Christina, but a large black woman in a green headscarf was in her bed. Confused, Tash went out into the corridor. Imperfect and unhealthy people, "people with defects" as Katya just called them, who were living out their last days, walked towards her. A thin old man in a striped robe winked at her, and she smiled back. Finally, she reached the room where Ben had been in such a hurry the last time.

"Good afternoon," she said to the stout man who had interrupted their kiss. "You're Alistair, right? I'm Tash, a friend of Ben Spencer and Lulu ... um ... Lourdes. I would like to make a donation."

"Yes, I remember you. Please have a seat." He gestured to the opposite chair. "You just have to fill out these forms. You can do it at home and come back tomorrow."

She walked home. Suddenly, the utmost clarity came to her head. She only had to ask him one question!

Seeing his owner, Benny wagged his tail. Hiding, he waited until she took off her shoes, and as soon as she bent down to him, he hurried to lick her neck. Tash scratched his ear. This was an unconditional love. It didn't matter to him whether she was young or healthy or beautiful.

Philip turned his head away from the computer. "How was lunch with Maman?"

"Fine."

"Where were you then?" He got up to kiss her. "Maman said you finished a couple of hours ago," he said gently.

"Philip," she said once she came close to him, "your mother offered me money for the birth of our child."

He silently waited for what she had to say.

"After lunch, I stopped by the hospice where Lulu died."

He nodded in understanding.

"I want to make a donation." She took the papers out of her bag. "A decent donation. You see, this is important to me. I want you to donate money for this hospice too. I'll leave the papers for you, so you can fill them out yourself, as much as you think is appropriate." She got up. "Nick chartered a plane for us all tomorrow at eleven in the morning, and we still need to pack before leaving. I want to get up early and stop by the hospice before we leave so they've got the money by Christmas."

She set the alarm for seven. In the morning, she looked out the window. Gloomy December clouds hung low over the city. After her shower, she went downstairs. Benny dozed in the kitchen, resting his muzzle on his outstretched front paws and waiting for breakfast and a walk. He jumped up to caress her. She kissed him on the nose.

"Benny, wait."

She took the papers from the table. The papers were filled with neat, almost calligraphic, handwriting. Name: Philip Eduardo Ribeiro Gonzalez Junior; amount: one thousand pounds. A lump rose up her throat. They were ready to give a million pounds for one healthy child, but for a million sick children, they would only offer a thousand.

Tash filled out the rest, drank some tea, took Benny out for a walk, and rushed to the hospice. Alistair was waiting for her in his office.

"I filled it out; could you check it all, please." She handed him the papers.

"Yes, everything seems to be in order," Alistair confirmed, examining the document. "Thank you very much for your extraordinary generosity, Miss Romanov and …" – he glanced at the papers again – "Mr. Ribeiro Gonzalez too."

She had been sitting on the bed, staring for several minutes at the pale grey dot on the wall.

"Have you packed everything?" Philip appeared in the doorway with a stack of cashmere jumpers.

She turned her head slowly. "Philip, I'm not going anywhere."

He stopped, but then, laughing, he continued packing. "Stop joking, let's get ready. Quickly now."

He folded his jumpers into his suitcase and reached out to take his watch from the nightstand, when he noticed something pink – a pink heart. Tash's ring. He took it and twisted it slowly between his fingers.

"I don't understand." Philip sank down on the bed.

"Please forgive me, but you and I are just so different." Her voice was quiet, but firm. "We wouldn't last a year. It's all an illusion."

"Don't say that," he interrupted her. "I love you."

"No, you don't. You only love yourself. And you don't want to lose me, just as a little boy doesn't want to lose a toy that he hasn't played with enough."

"That's not true!"

"You and I, we live like strangers, even our sex … is kind of predictable. There's no emotion."

"Why do you care that much about sex? Marriage is not about sex and not about love! You and I, we're the perfect match. Young, beautiful and successful, and we will have perfect children. And with my mother's connections, I will have a brilliant political career. I might even become President. Don't you want to be the First Lady? Together we will reach unprecedented heights! Such a power couple, people will envy us. Doesn't it sound like a perfect future?"

"Don't you understand that you just confirmed my words? I don't want to be part of a perfect couple. I don't want to be a perfect breeder. I want love with all its imperfections! I want to help imperfect people and give them hope. It makes me stronger. It makes me happy. And you didn't understand anything I said."

"Tell me, is this because of him? Because of Ben?"

"What does Ben have to do with it?"

"I saw you kissing at Marquess Montague's party."

Tash swallowed hard.

"Are you leaving me for him?"

"No, Philip. It's not about Ben at all."

She wanted to hug him to make him understand, but he dodged her. He jumped to his feet and threw her onto the bed roughly. With one hand he held her wrists, and with the other he pulled at her jeans. The damned jeans didn't budge, but he pulled them down with all his might. She groaned in pain.

"Lie down, bitch, do not twitch!" He unbuttoned the fly on his pants. "You want unpredictable? You want emotion? You'll never forget this fuck!"

She felt nothing but monotonous shocks accompanied by loud curses.

"You are such a pathetic fool to give up a million pounds. Run to your loser Ben and let him fuck you in poverty and create poor bastards!" He squeezed her neck. "In the meantime, let's make one for me. Nice and healthy." The frequency of the tremors increased, and then she heard a stifled wheeze. "Get it, bitch, get it." She felt the tremors gradually subside, but he still didn't let her free.

"To tell you the truth, you're not even my type." He finally got up. "You're too girly, too weak. I like someone masculine and strong, someone like me. With you, it was all just to keep face. There is no political future for a gay man. I'll need a woman on my arm to get elected, and Maman decided that you fit our goals. A girl next door, an immigrant. An exemplary family. But you had to have Ben. He'll use you and throw you out and return to Flo. With her dowry. Now get out!" He stood with his fly open in the middle of the bedroom. "And take your dog with you! Two outbred mongrels!"

Without a word, Tash got out of bed, pulled on her jeans and silently left the room. Benny was waiting for her at the door.

"Benny, let's go for a walk!"

She walked down the stairs and Benny slid awkwardly in front of her. "I never did put carpet on the steps!"

Benny wagged his tail excitedly in anticipation of a long walk. She wrapped herself in the first coat she came across, grabbed her bag and slammed the door behind. Chilly December rain drummed on the sidewalk. They walked along the deserted grey streets towards the park. Benny walked dignifiedly beside her, realising that now wasn't the right time to play. The bare trees lurched in the wind. Tash raised her head. Dark clouds covered the sky. She wanted terribly to get there, beyond the clouds. She lay down on the bench and Benny settled next to her. She hugged him to keep warm, kissing his ginger face. Two mongrels in the freezing cold. Tash smiled.

"But there's one thing, Philip, you're wrong about. We can handle it! And our strength is not in eliminating the weak, but in helping the weak! Humanity has evolved for thousands of years not to live according to animal laws."

Tash opened her purse and took out a folded brown envelope that she hadn't dared to open since Lulu's death.

My dear Miss Romanov,

I know the letter sounds a little melodramatic, but in recent days, I have thought a lot about our last conversation.

I won't waste ink on agency manuals. I'm sure you can handle this much better than me. But I wanted to share with you one observation that I only realised in the last couple of weeks. Throughout my life I was too afraid, too shy, too hesitant and too cowardly. Now, being one step away from my deathbed, I realise what a dumb fool I was! After all, the main thing in life is happiness! You should go where you want, fight for what you want and be with whoever you want. This is your life, and you only live once (believe me, I know it like no one else). In the face of death, you don't remember how you were rejected, not chosen or betrayed. You remember how you were loved, how you enjoyed and how you shone with happiness. You asked me which path you should choose. So, my answer is: choose the path that will make you happy! People who will make you happy! The work that will make you happy! When waking up every morning, ask yourself if today was the last day of your life, would you still live the way you are? Nothing else matters!

Your Lulu

Tash and Benny huddled together in the middle of the park. A rare passer-by looked at them askance, wondering what they were doing on the bench on such a rainy day. The brisk wind drove the lazy clouds, and they reluctantly floated away to the east. One cloud lingered briefly over the park, and then, moving, revealed a thin strip of blue sky. And only for a moment, a powerful sunbeam pierced this tiny island with its bright light. Tash looked up. She knew that there, above the gloomy clouds, the boundless blue shined, the sun dazzled and great universal love ruled.

She felt they were all watching her from the heavens. Lulu, her mother and her grandmother. And suddenly her father's words came to her mind: "You have to be honest with yourself. Promise me!" She smiled and nodded.

Tash took her phone out of her bag and sent a message: "Daddy, I kept my promise!"

www.ingramcontent.com/pod-product-compliance
Lightning Source LLC
Chambersburg PA
CBHW070537120726
47909CB00007B/2164